MAGIC TREE HOUSE®

THE KNIGHT AT DAWN

MARY POPE OSBORNE'S

MAGIC TREE HOUSE®

THE KNIGHT AT DAWN

THE GRAPHIC NOVEL

ADAPTED BY
JENNY LAIRD

WITH ART BY
KELLY & NICHOLE MATTHEWS

A STEPPING STONE BOOK™
RANDOM HOUSE 🏠 NEW YORK

Text copyright © 2021 by Mary Pope Osborne
Art copyright © 2021 by Kelly Matthews & Nichole Matthews
Text adapted by Jenny Laird

All rights reserved. Published in the United States by Random House Children's Books, a division
of Penguin Random House LLC, New York. Adapted from *The Knight at Dawn*, published by
Random House Children's Books, a division of Penguin Random House LLC, New York, in 1992.

Random House and the colophon are registered trademarks and A Stepping Stone Book
and the colophon are trademarks of Penguin Random House LLC. RH Graphic with
the book design is a trademark of Penguin Random House LLC. Magic Tree House
is a registered trademark of Mary Pope Osborne; used under license.

Visit us on the Web!
rhcbooks.com
MagicTreeHouse.com

Educators and librarians, for a variety of teaching tools, visit us at RHTeachersLibrarians.com

Library of Congress Cataloging-in-Publication Data
Names: Laird, Jenny, adapter. I Matthews, Kelly (Comic book artist), artist. I
Matthews, Nichole, artist. I Osborne, Mary Pope, author.
Title: The knight at dawn, the graphic novel / adapted by Jenny Laird; with art by Kelly & Nichole Matthews.
Description: First graphic novel edition. I New York: Random House Children's Books, [2021] I Series: Mary Pope Osborne's
Magic tree house I Summary: "Retells, in graphic novel form, the tale of eight-year-old Jack and his younger sister,
Annie, who are whisked back in the magic tree house to the time of knights and castles" —Provided by publisher.
Identifiers: LCCN 2021009066 (print) I LCCN 2021009067 (ebook) I
ISBN 978-0-593-17472-2 (hardcover) I ISBN 978-0-593-17475-3 (trade paperback) I
ISBN 978-0-593-17473-9 (library binding) I ISBN 978-0-593-17474-6 (ebook)
Subjects: LCSH: Graphic novels. I CYAC: Graphic novels. I Time travel—Fiction. I
Knights and knighthood—Fiction. I Middle Ages—Fiction. I Tree houses—Fiction. I Magic—Fiction.
Classification: LCC PZ7.7.L28 Kn 2021 (print) I LCC PZ7.7.L28 (ebook) I DDC 741.5/973—dc23

The artists used Clip Studio Paint to create the illustrations for this book.
The text of this book is set in 13-point Cartoonist Hand Regular.

MANUFACTURED IN CHINA
10 9 8 7 6 5 4 3
First Graphic Novel Edition

This book has been officially leveled by using the F&P Text Level Gradient™ Leveling System.

For Gail Hochman
—M.P.O.

For Randy, a royal, steady keeper of the light
—J.L.

For Jan Morgan
—K.M. & N.M.

CHAPTER ONE
The Dark Woods

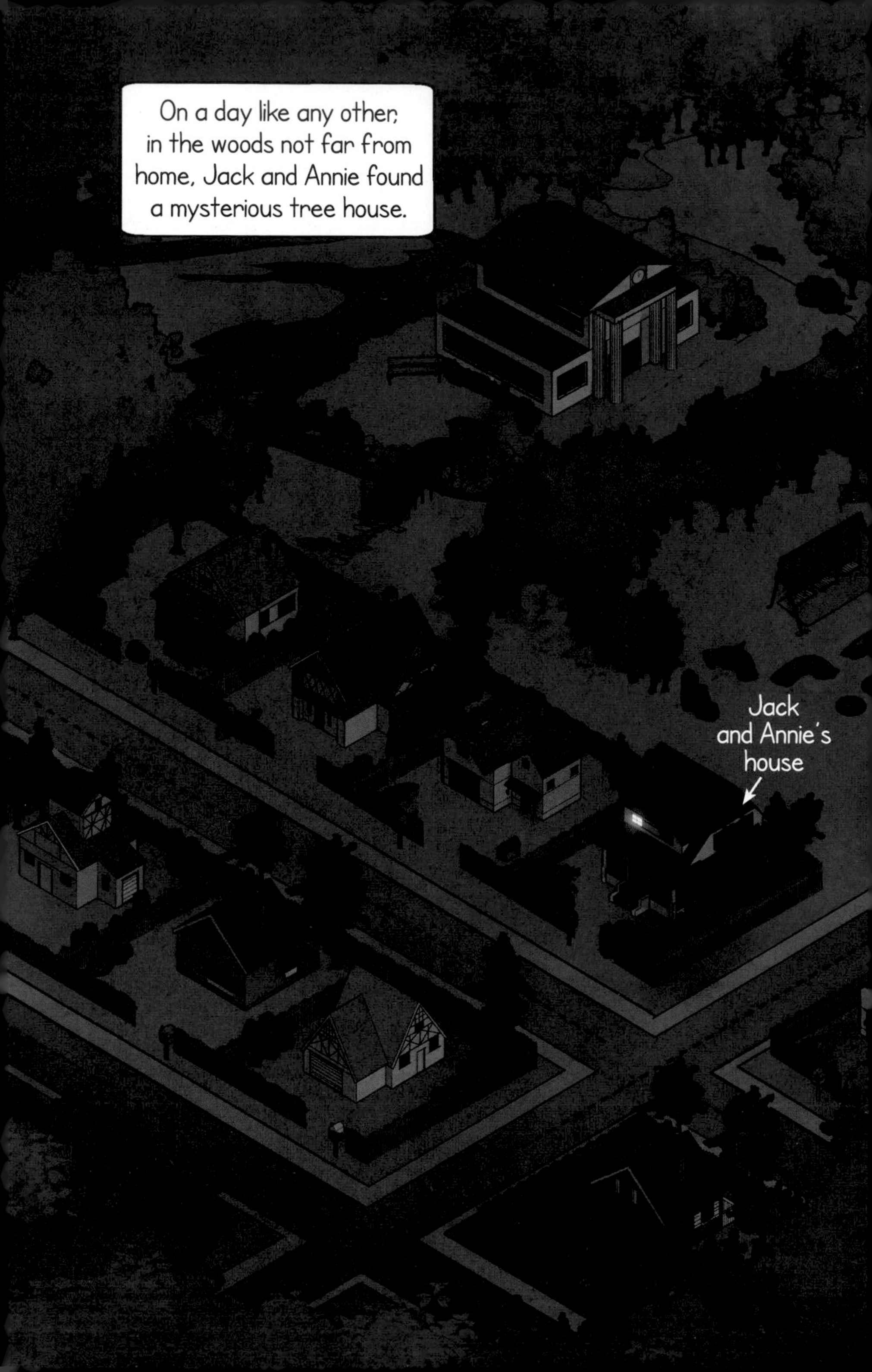
On a day like any other, in the woods not far from home, Jack and Annie found a mysterious tree house.
Jack and Annie's house

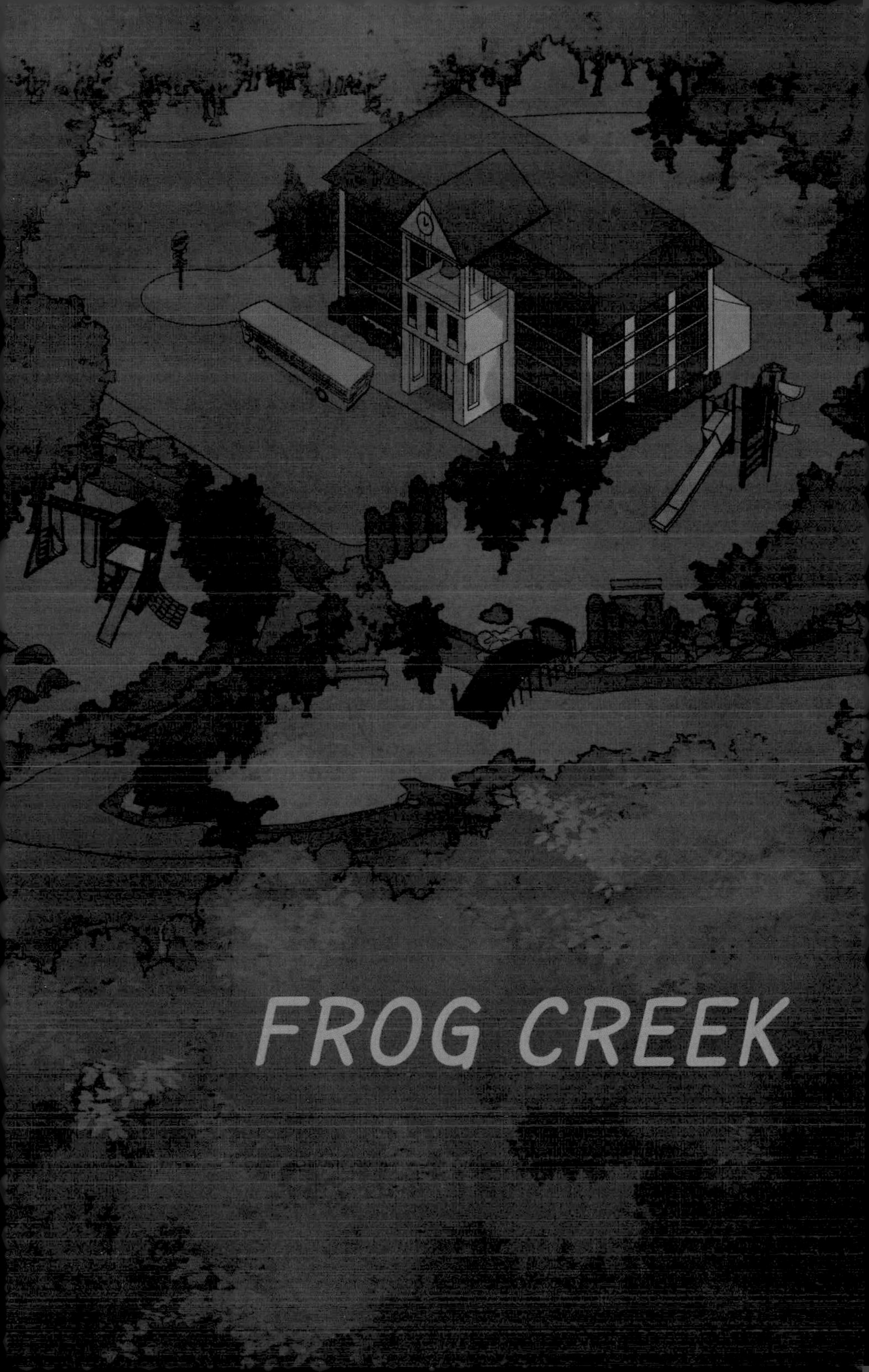
FROG CREEK

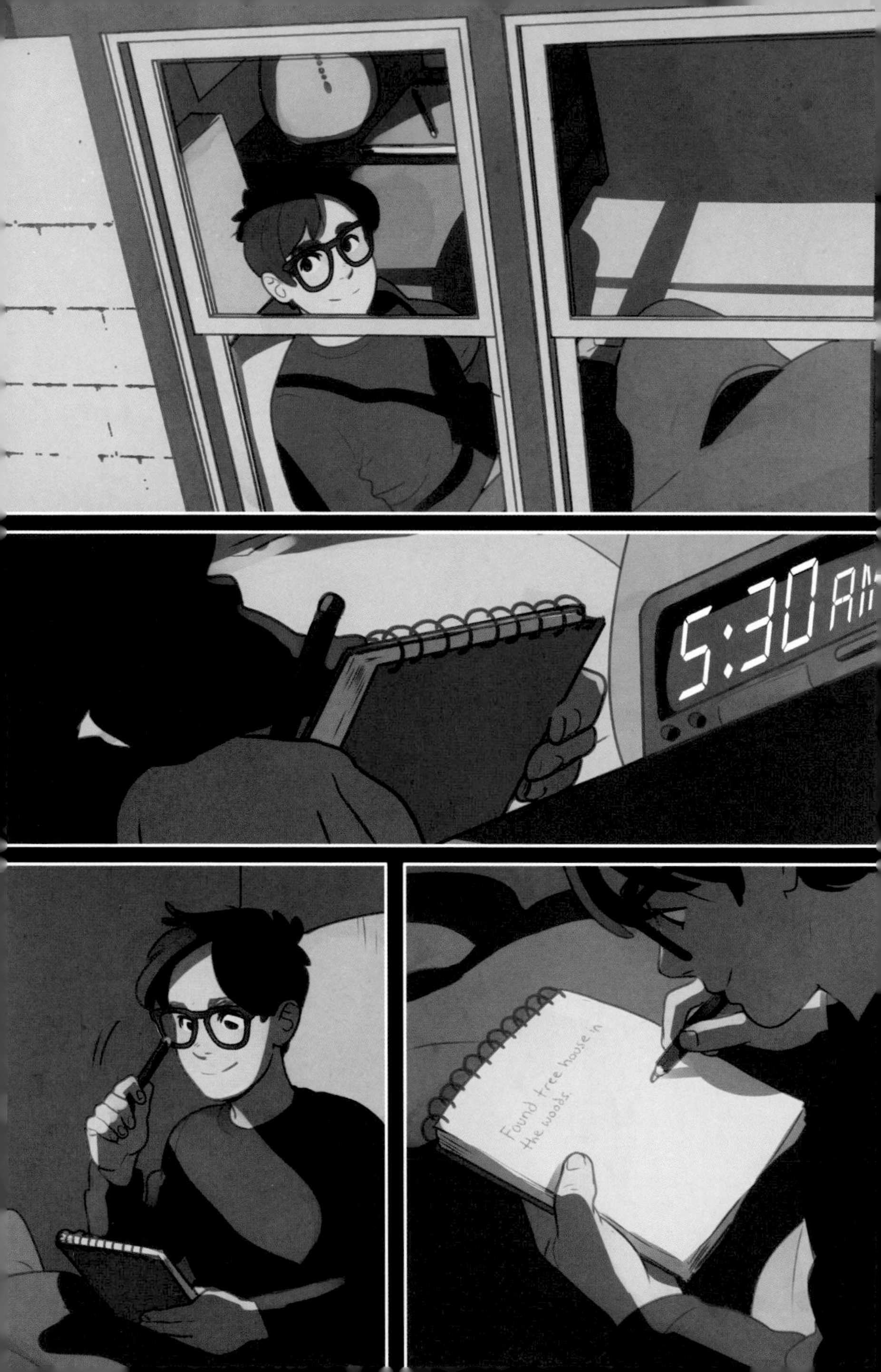
5:30 AM
Found tree house in the woods.

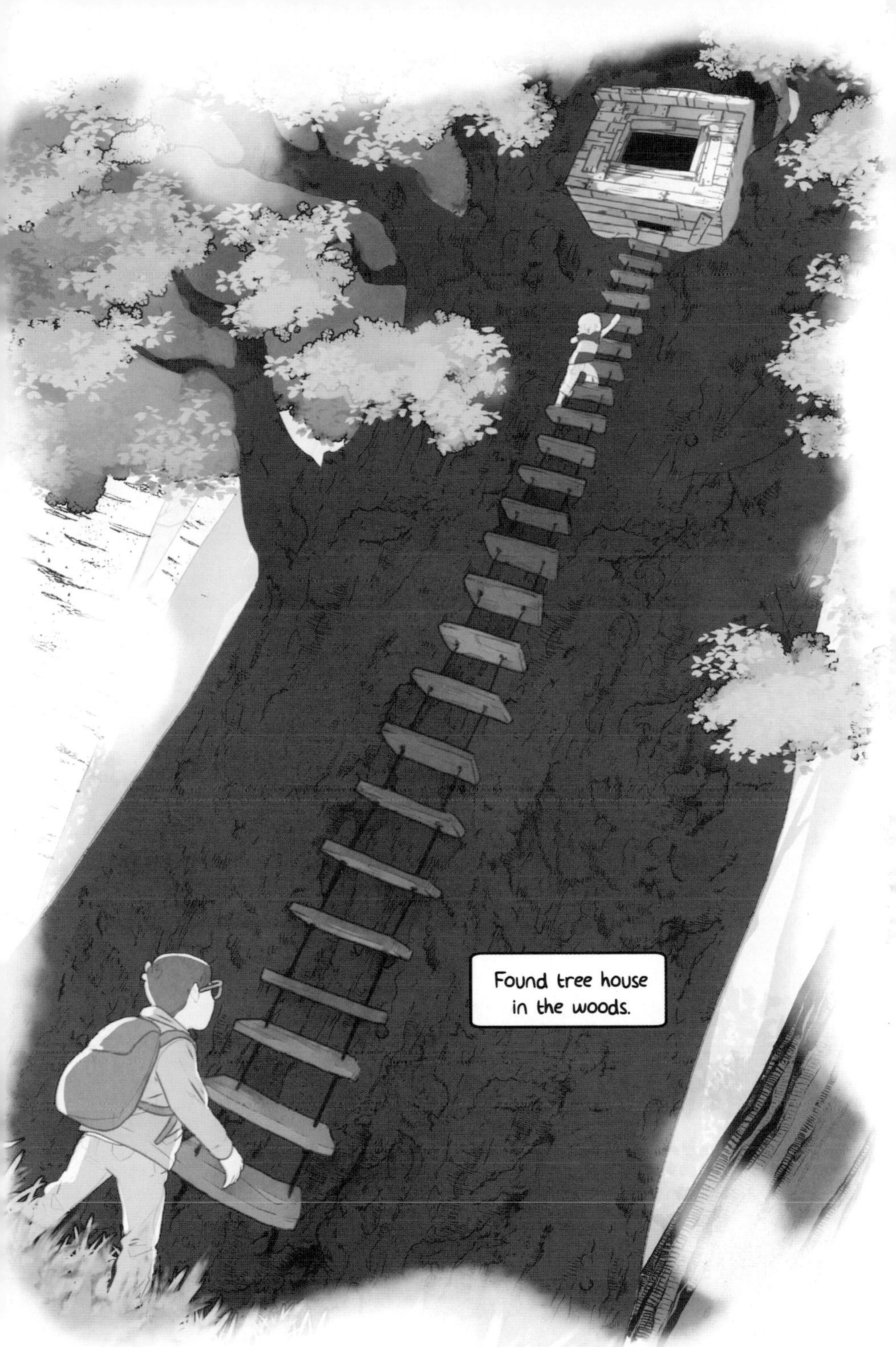
Found tree house
in the woods.

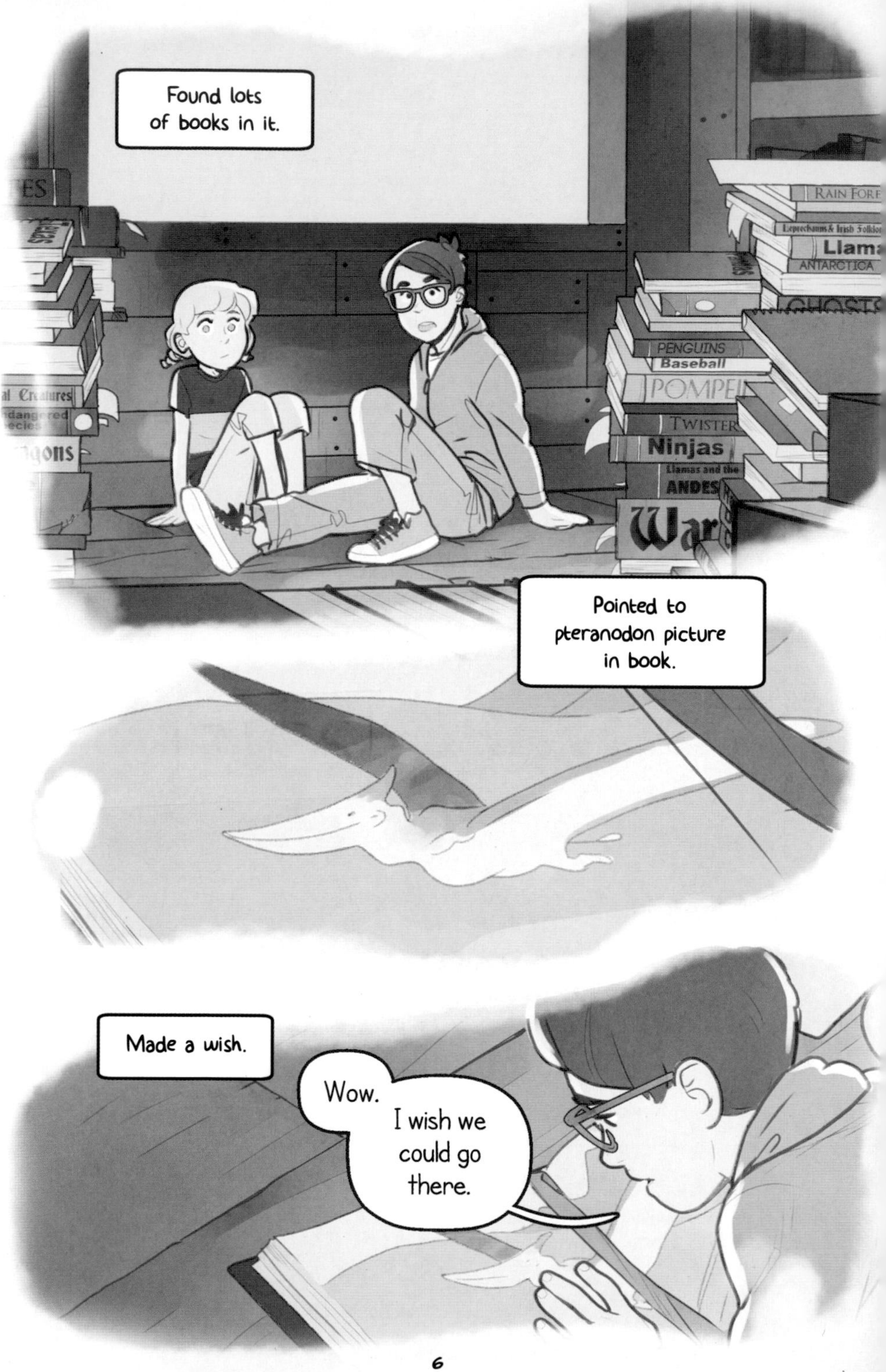
Found lots of books in it.
ANTARCTICA
PENGUINS
Baseball
TWISTER
Ninjas
Llamas and the ANDES
Pointed to pteranodon picture in book.
Made a wish.
Wow. I wish we could go there.

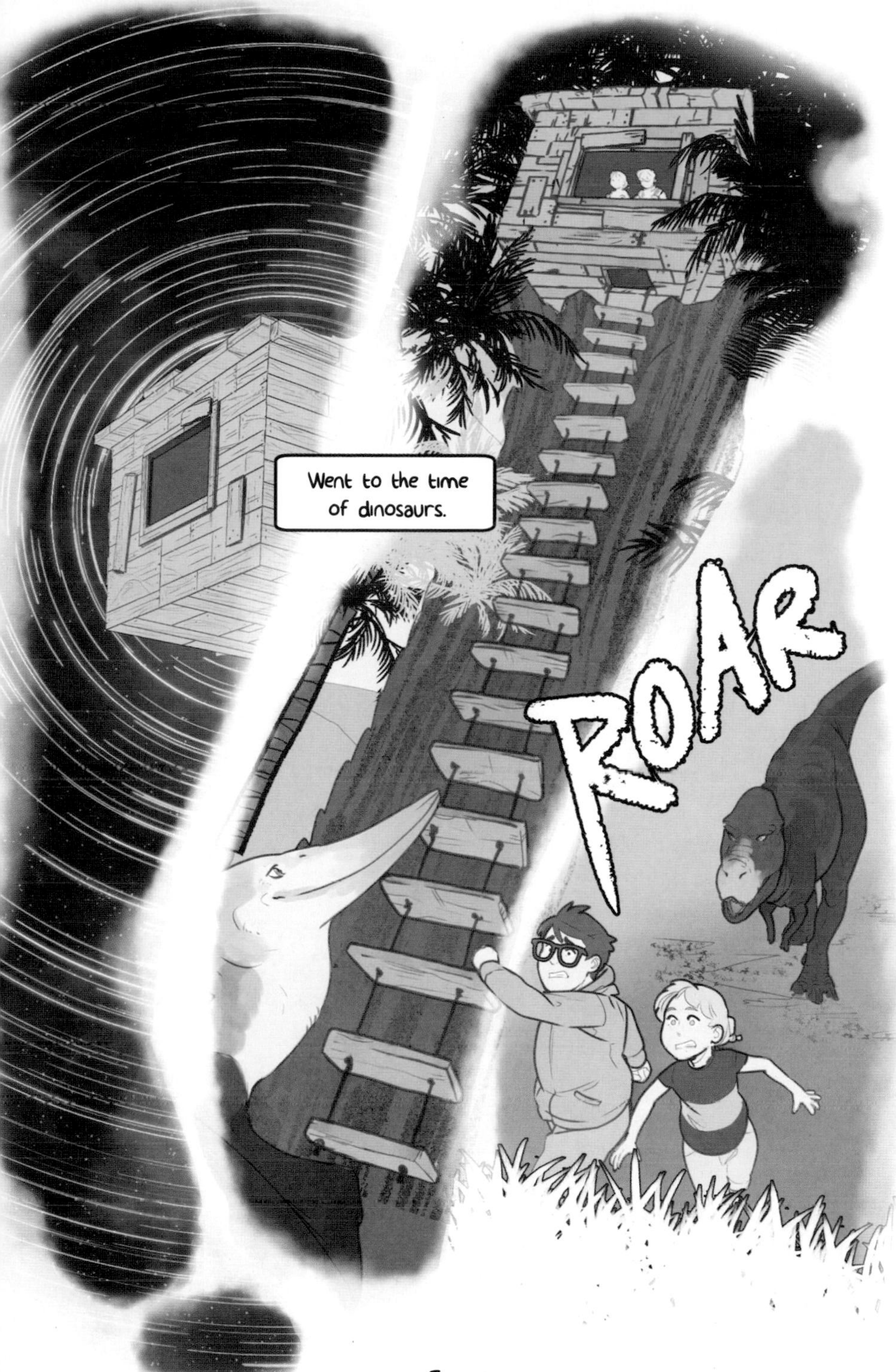
Went to the time of dinosaurs.
ROAR

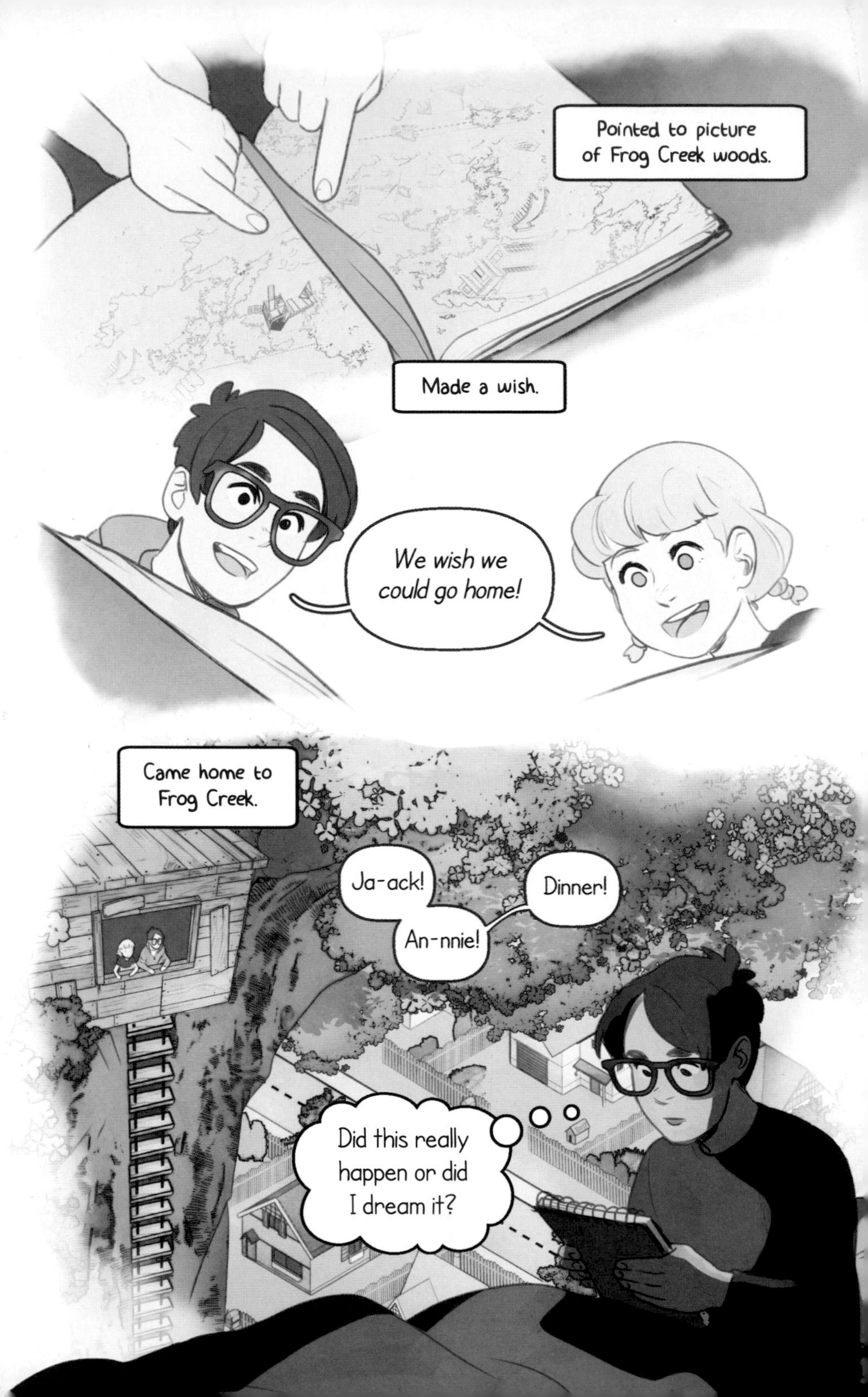
Pointed to picture of Frog Creek woods.
Made a wish.
We wish we could go home!
Came home to Frog Creek.
Ja-ack!
An-nnie!
Dinner!
Did this really happen or did I dream it?

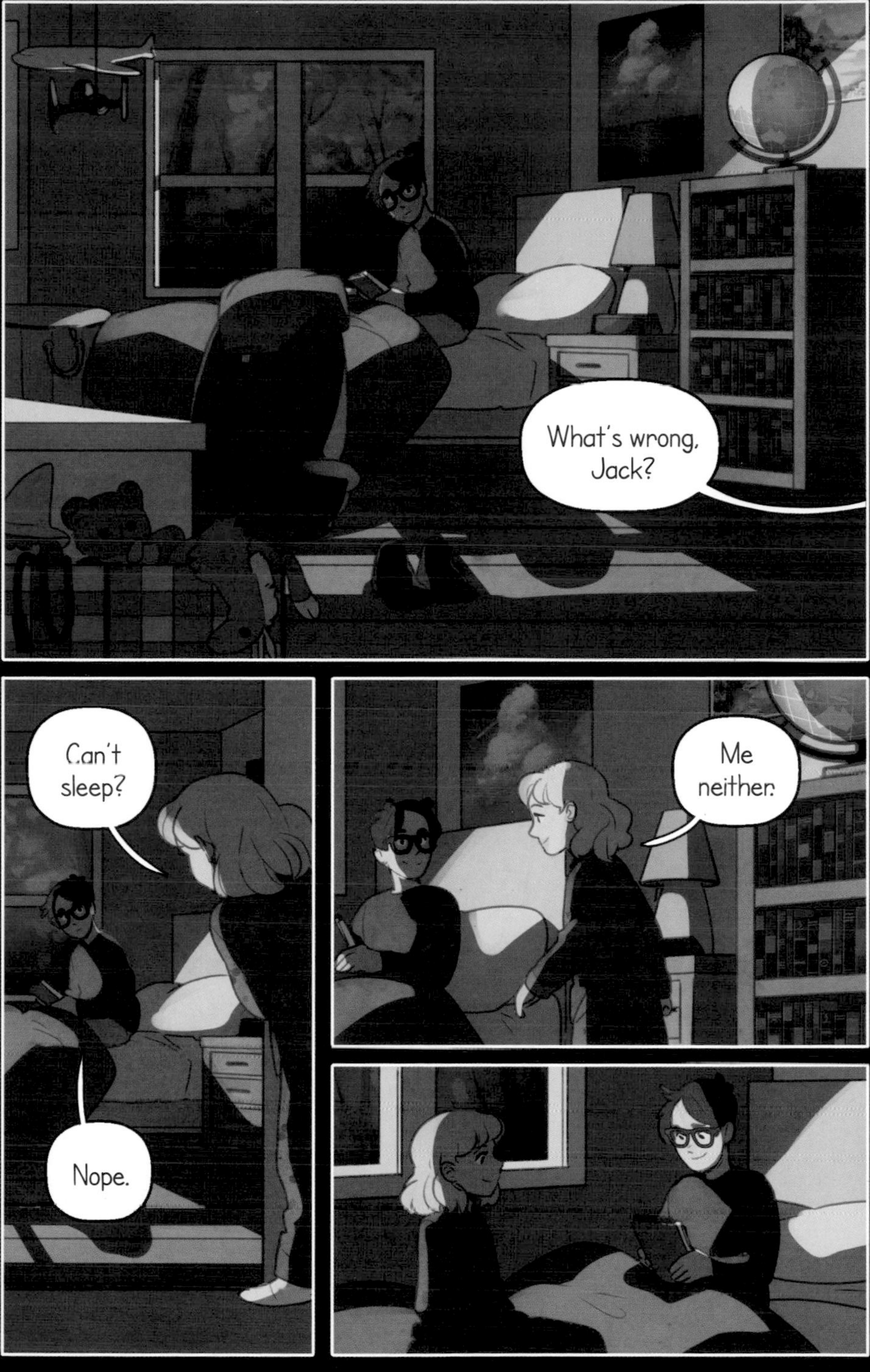
What's wrong, Jack?
Can't sleep?
Nope.
Me neither.

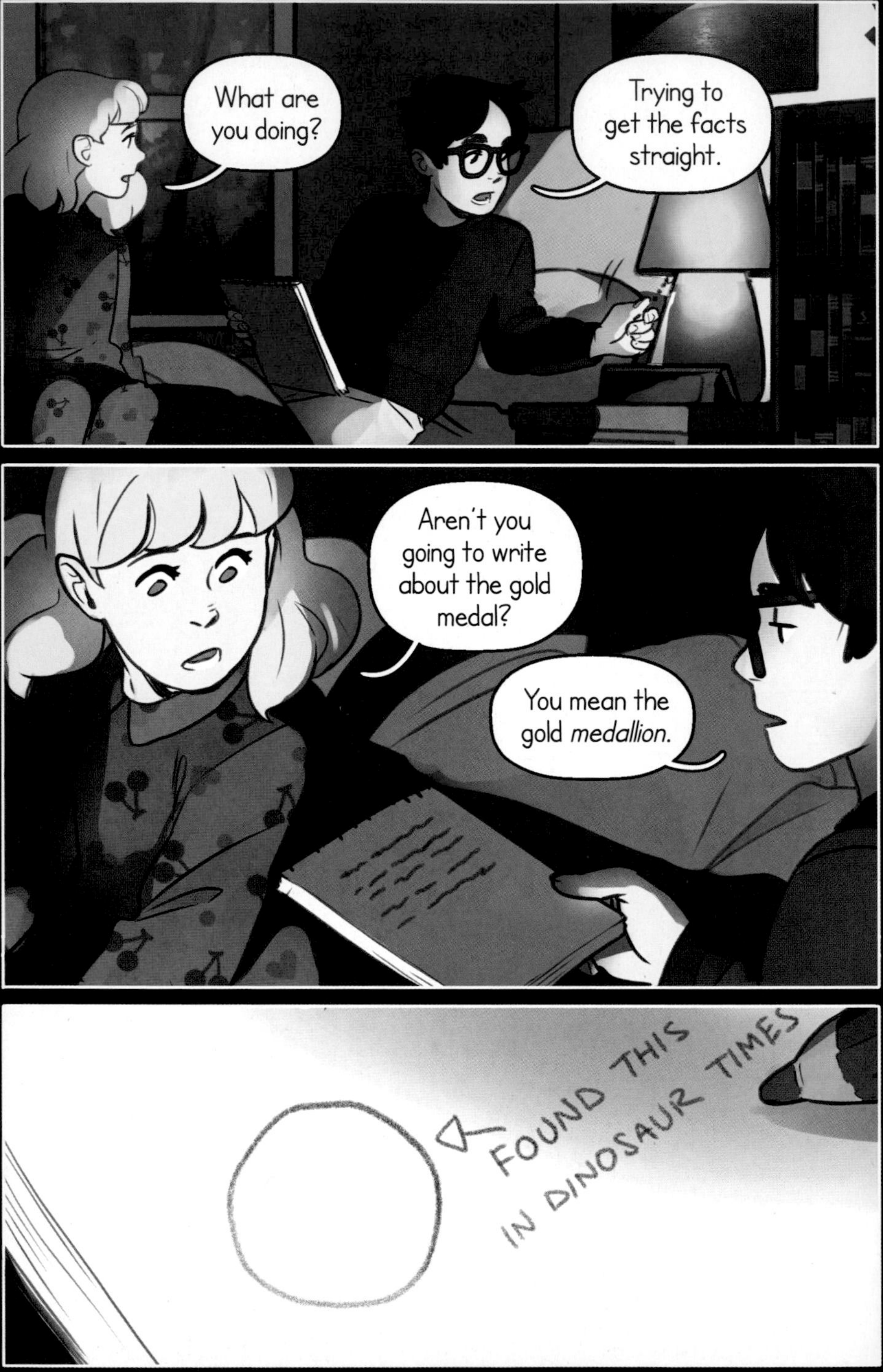
What are you doing?
Trying to get the facts straight.
Aren't you going to write about the gold medal?
You mean the gold *medallion*.
FOUND THIS IN DINOSAUR TIMES

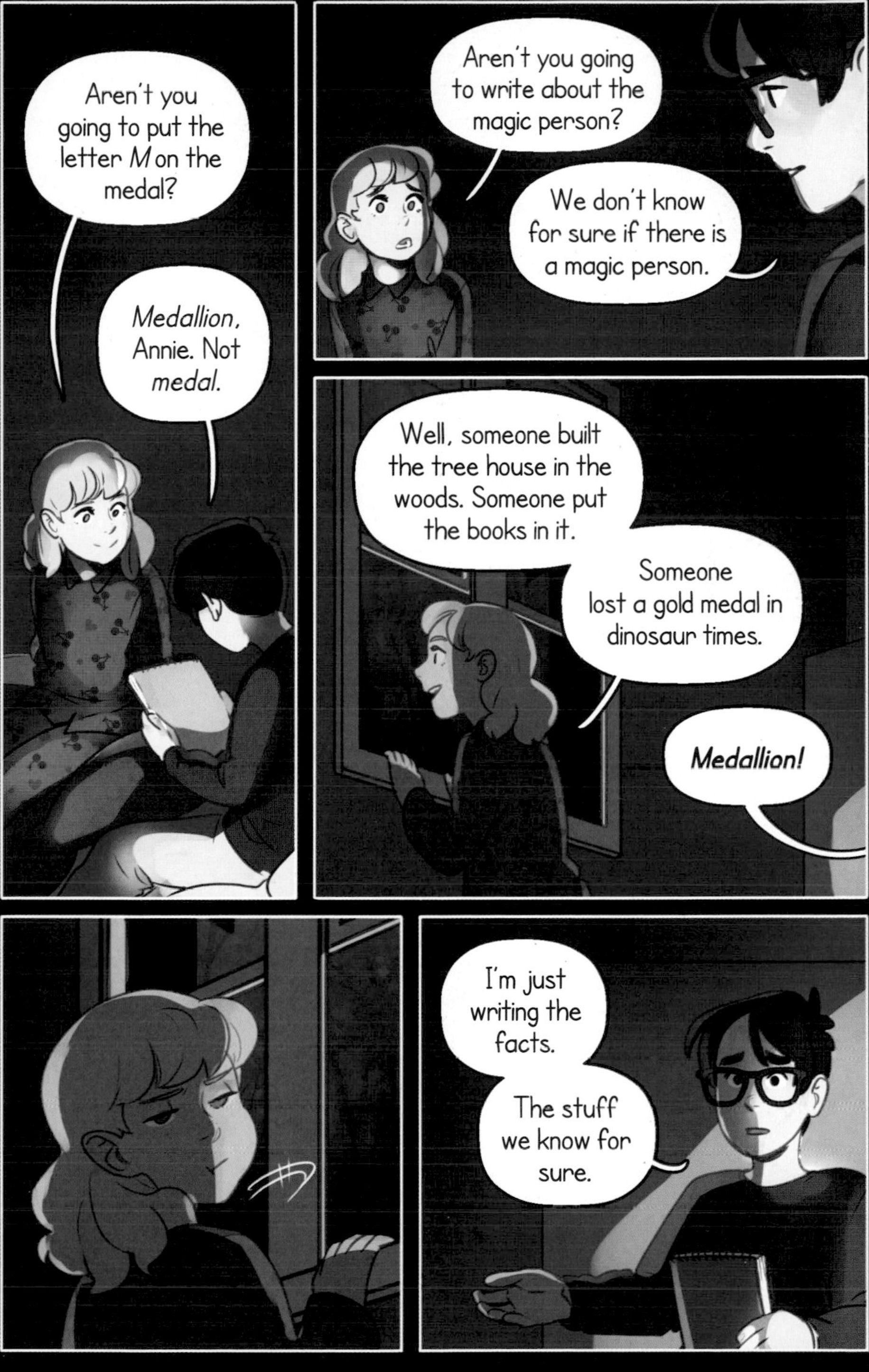
Aren't you going to put the letter *M* on the medal?
Medallion, Annie. Not *medal*.
Aren't you going to write about the magic person?
We don't know for sure if there is a magic person.
Well, someone built the tree house in the woods. Someone put the books in it.
Someone lost a gold medal in dinosaur times.
Medallion!
I'm just writing the facts.
The stuff we know for sure.

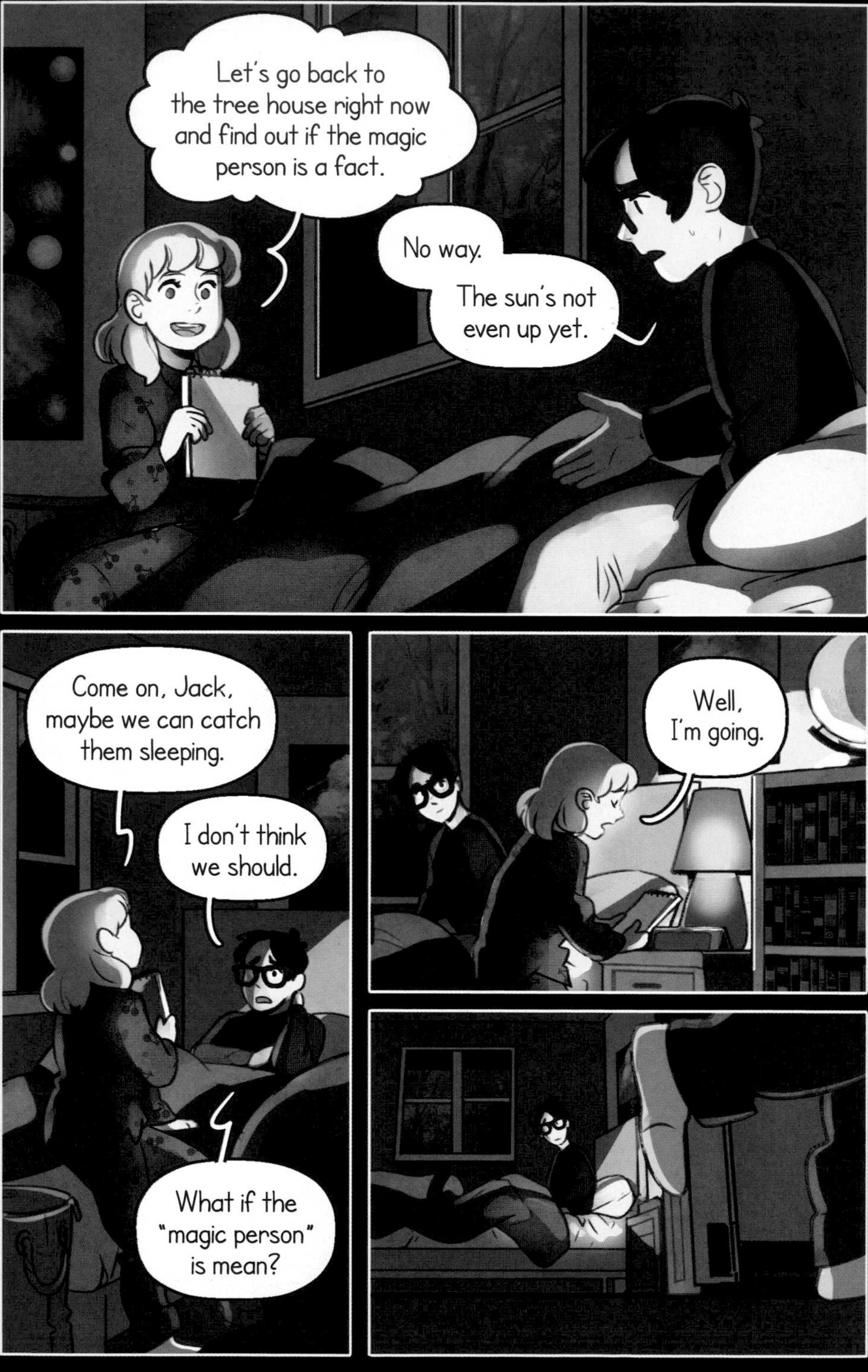

Let's go back to the tree house right now and find out if the magic person is a fact.
No way.
The sun's not even up yet.
Come on, Jack, maybe we can catch them sleeping.
I don't think we should.
What if the "magic person" is mean?
Well, I'm going.

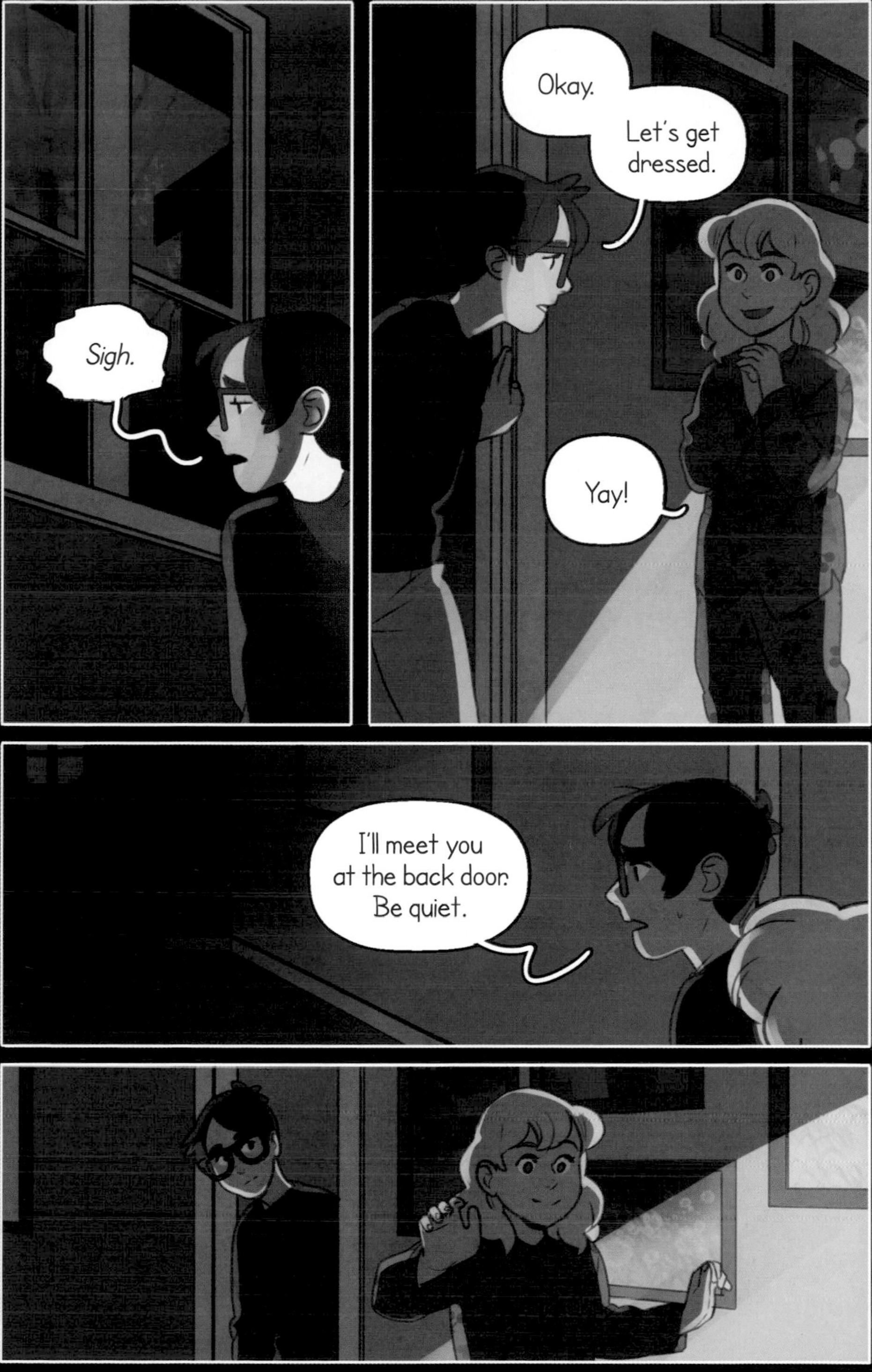
Sigh.
Okay.
Let's get dressed.
Yay!
I'll meet you at the back door. Be quiet.

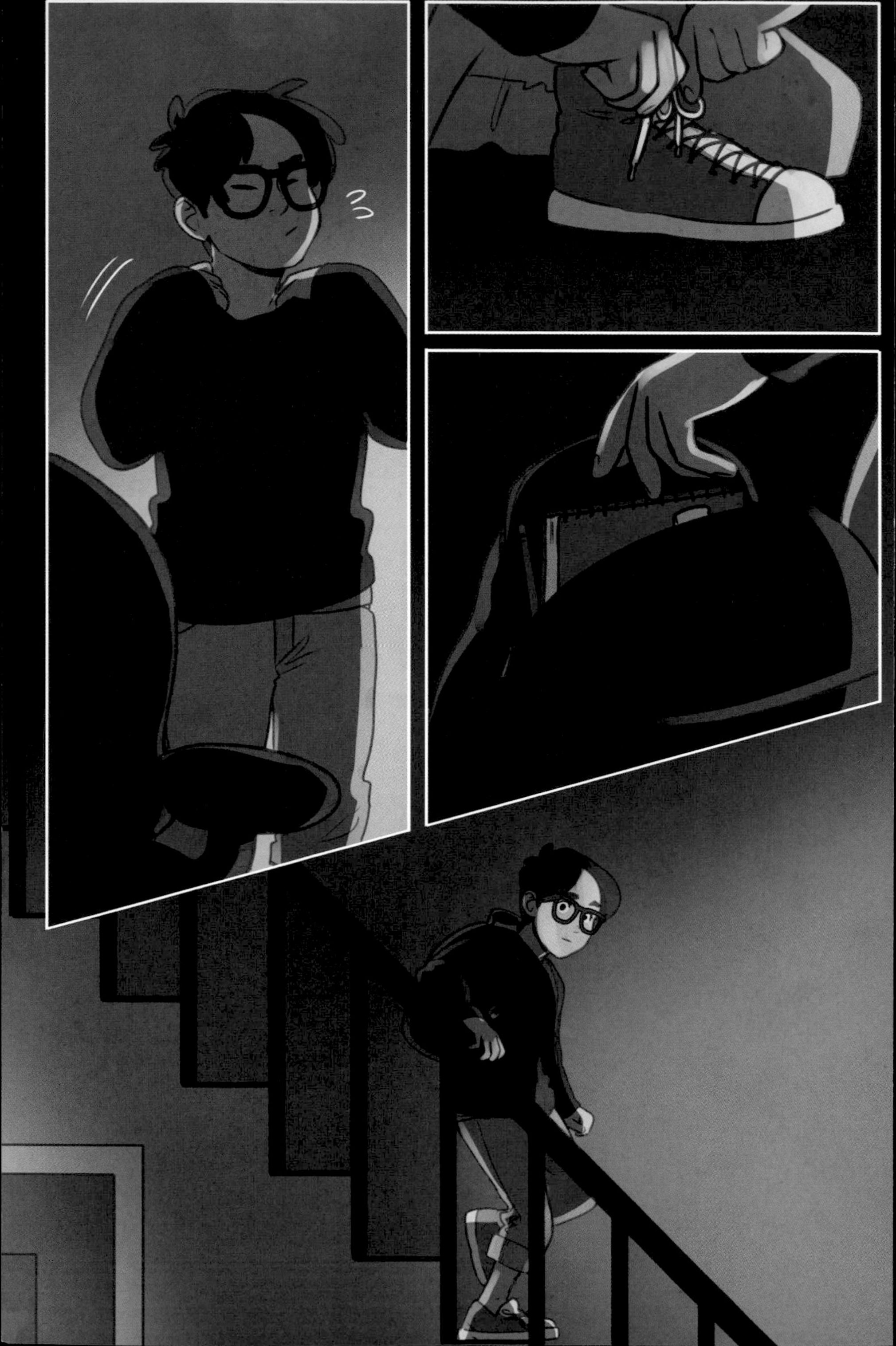

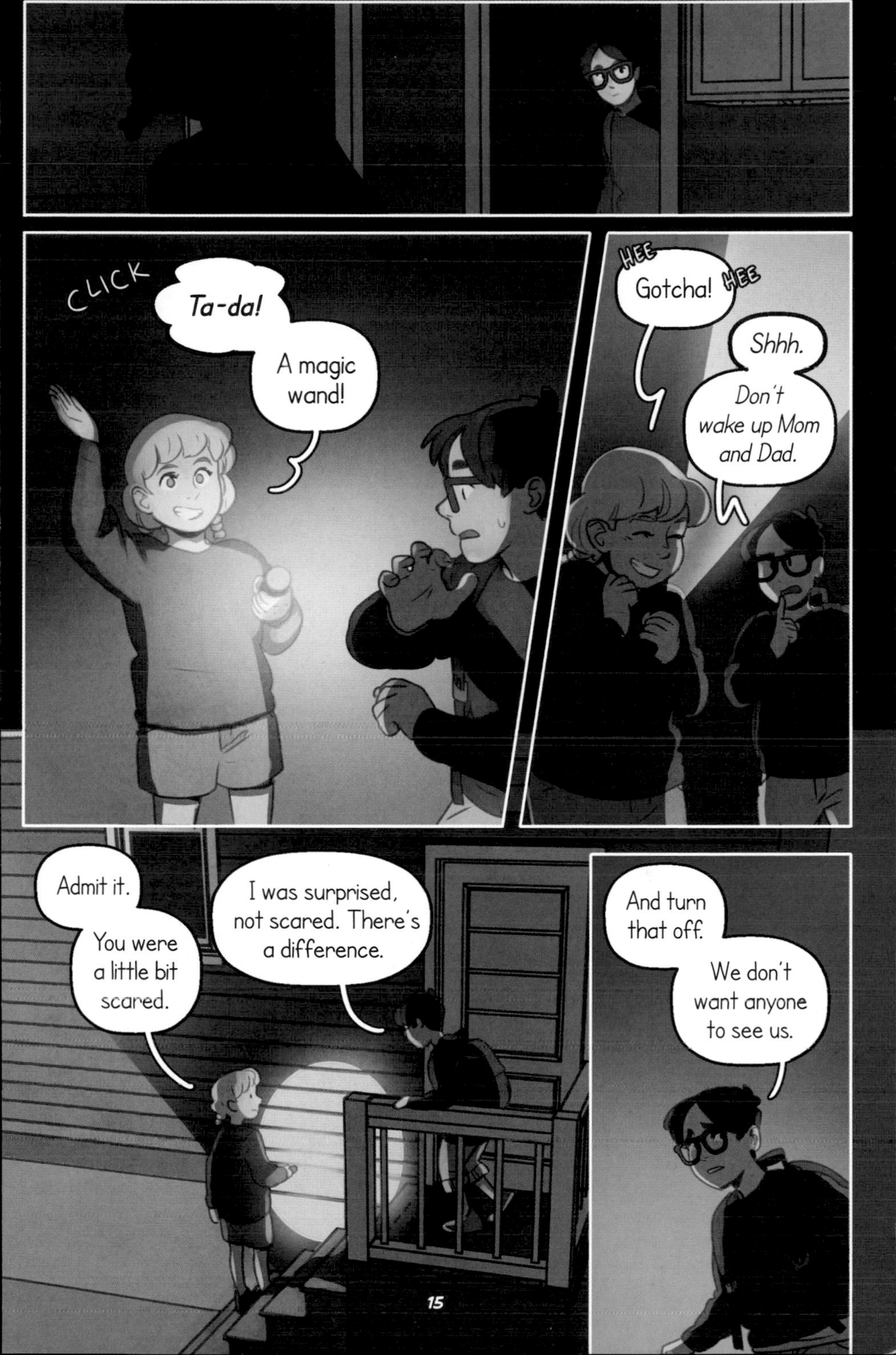
CLICK
Ta-da!
A magic wand!
HEE
Gotcha!
HEE
Shhh.
Don't wake up Mom and Dad.
Admit it.
You were a little bit scared.
I was surprised, not scared. There's a difference.
And turn that off.
We don't want anyone to see us.

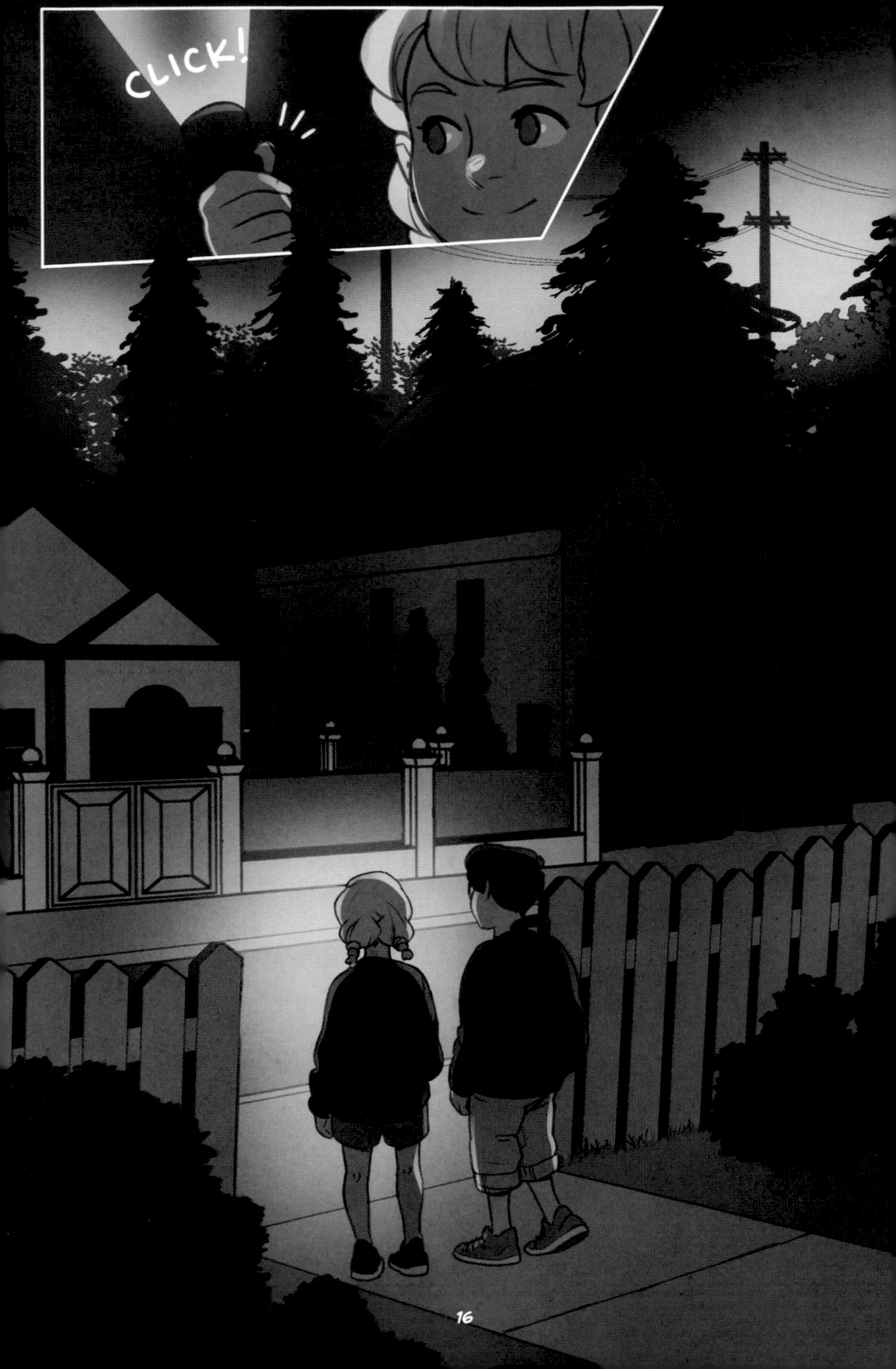
CLICK!

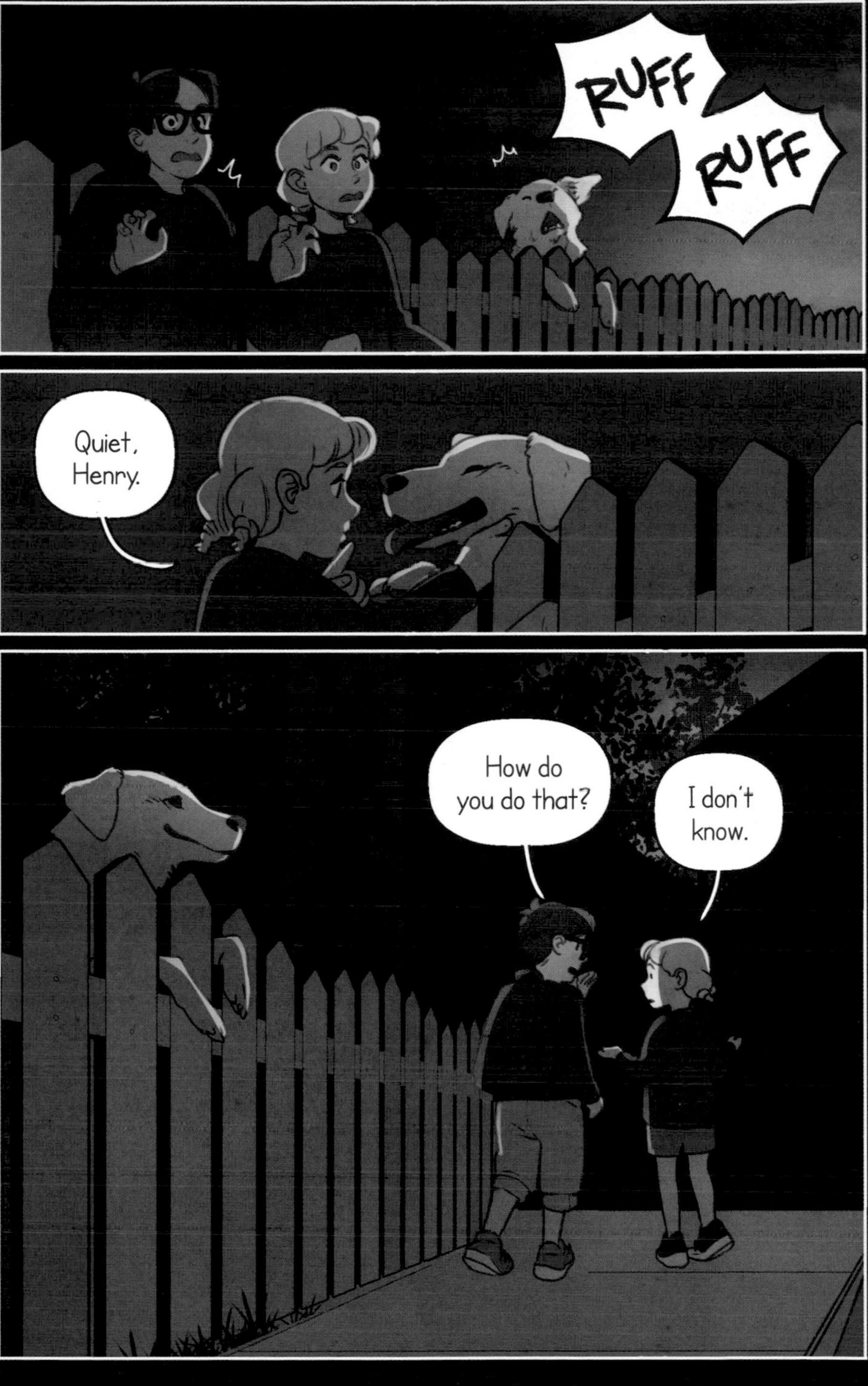
RUFF
RUFF
Quiet, Henry.
How do you do that?
I don't know.

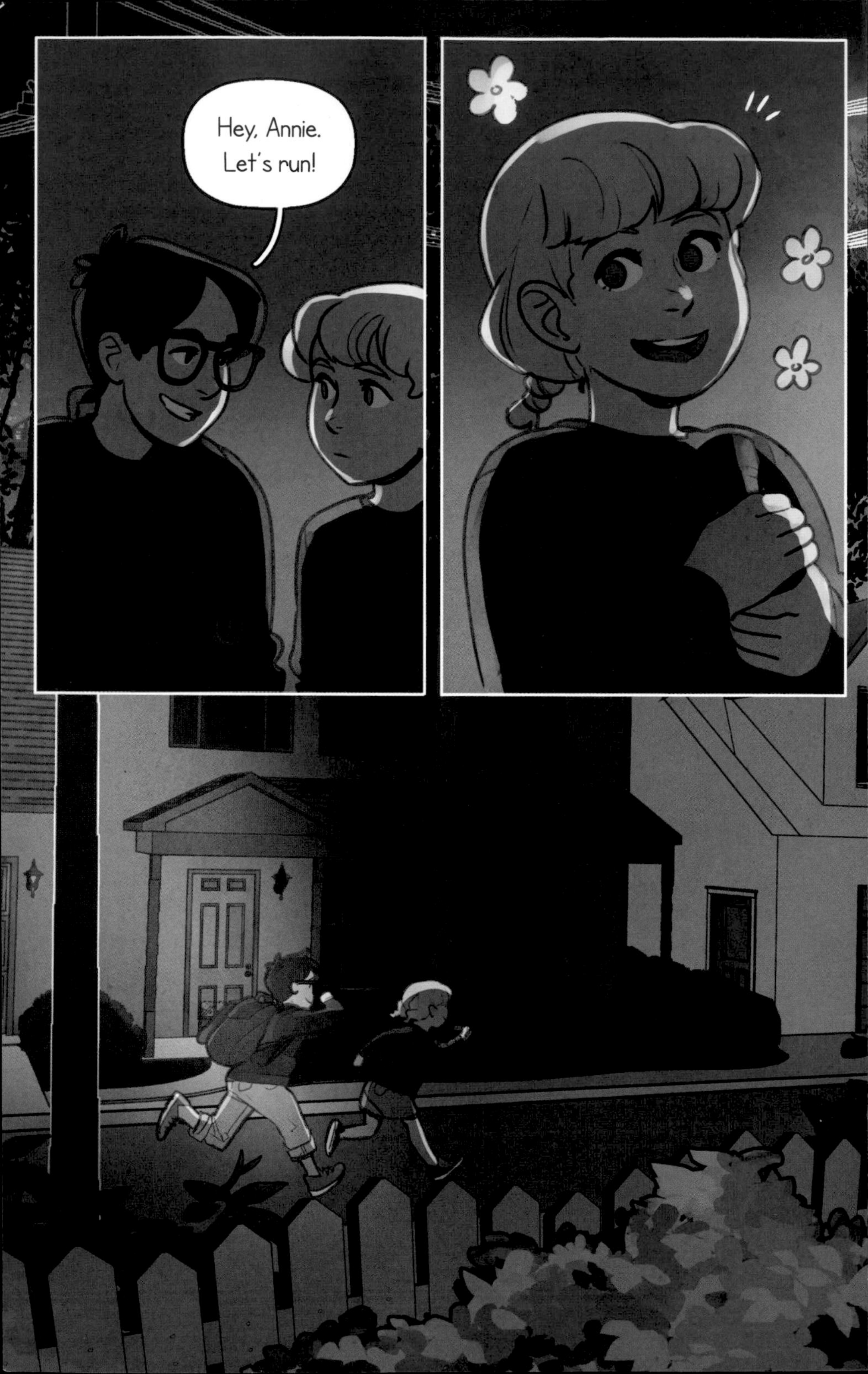
Hey, Annie. Let's run!

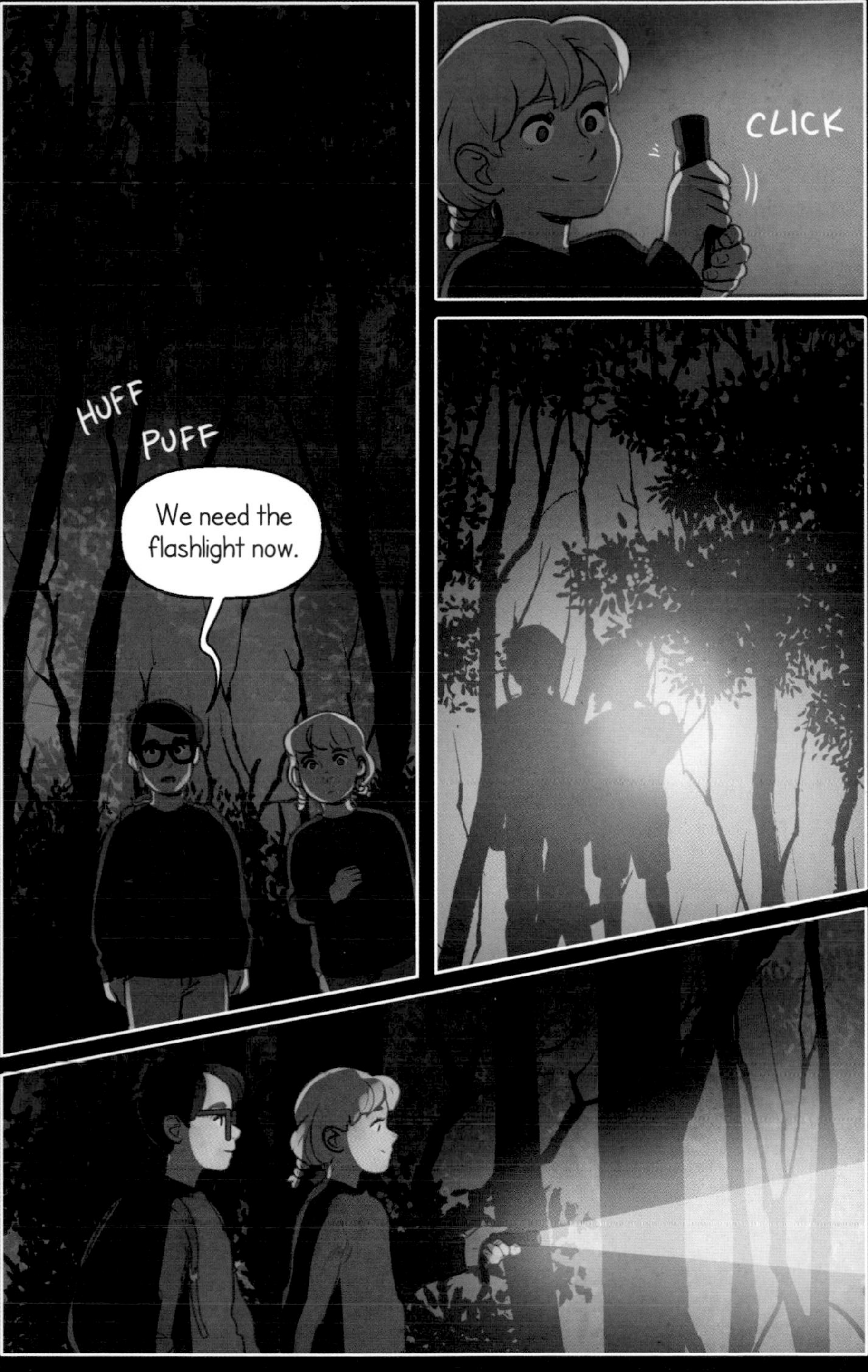

CLICK
HUFF
PUFF
We need the flashlight now.

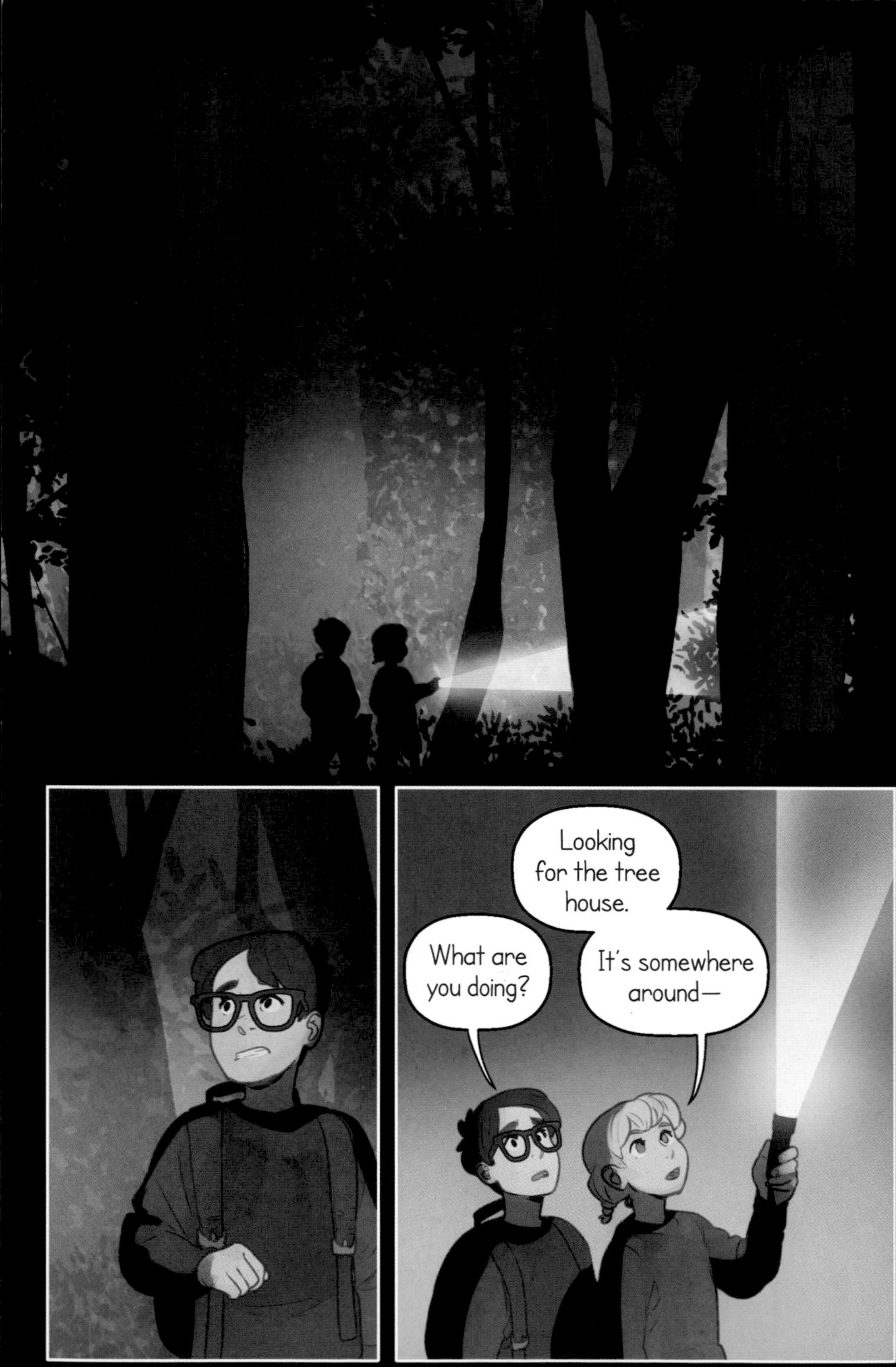

What are you doing?
Looking for the tree house.
It's somewhere around—

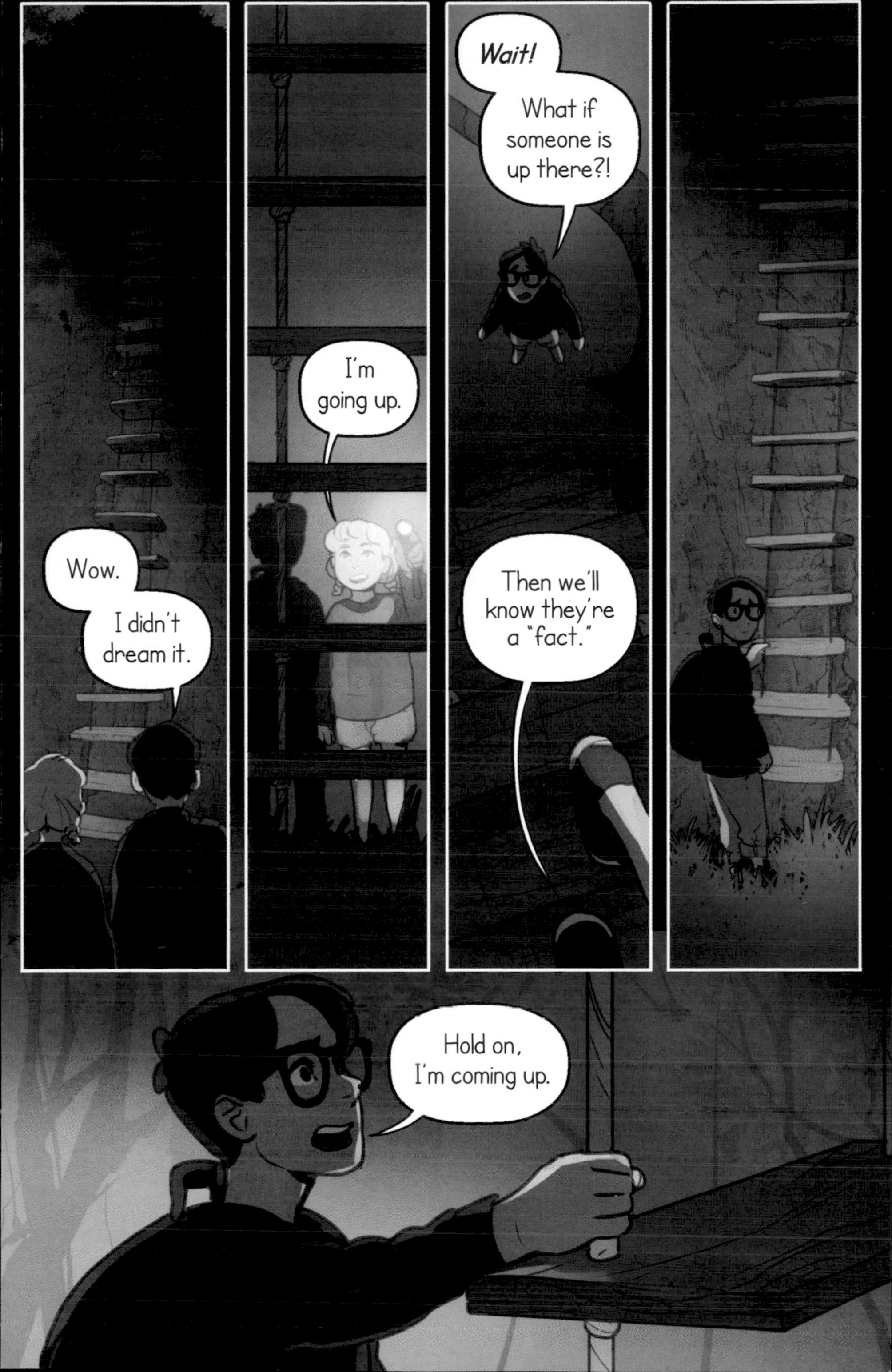
Wow.
I didn't dream it.
I'm going up.
Wait!
What if someone is up there?!
Then we'll know they're a "fact."
Hold on, I'm coming up.

CHAPTER TWO
Leaving Again

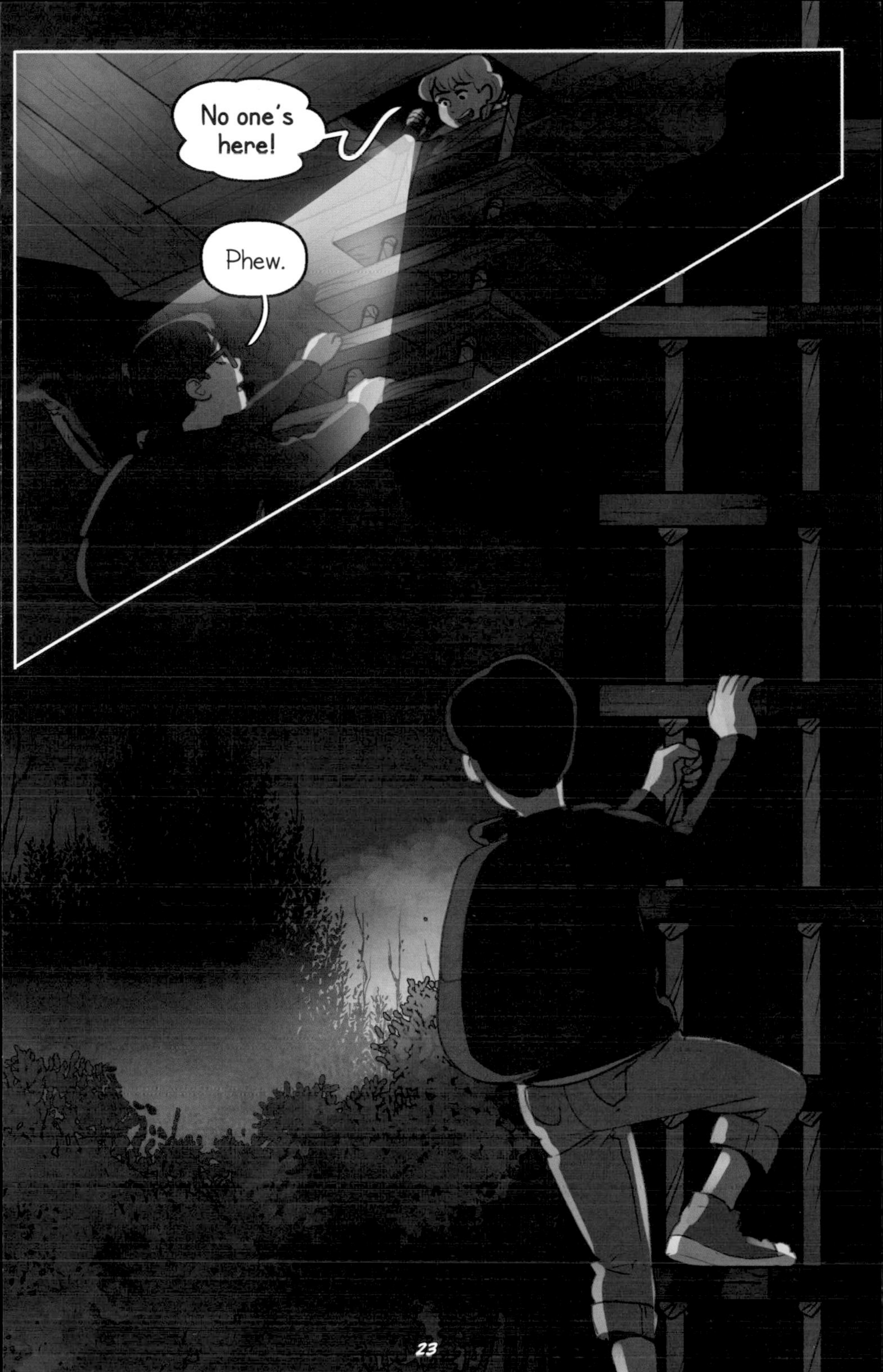
No one's here!
Phew.

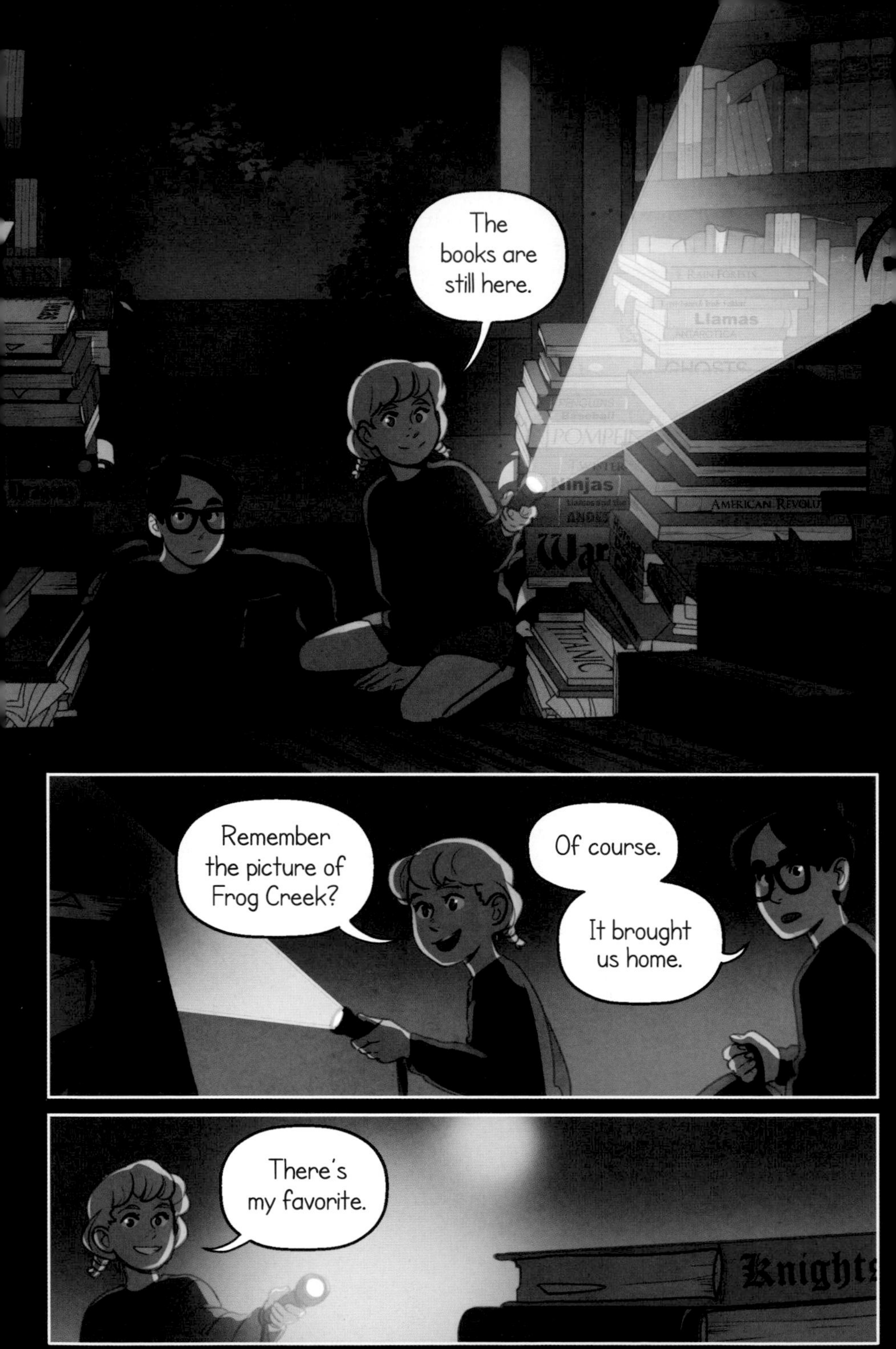
The books are still here.
Remember the picture of Frog Creek?
Of course.
It brought us home.
There's my favorite.

Annie, close that book.

I know what you're thinking.

Hey, there's some kind of writing on this.

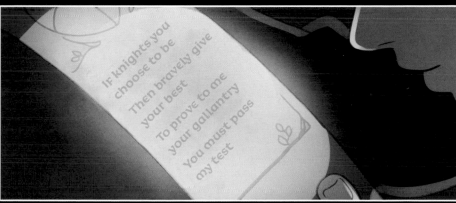

If knights you
choose to be
Then bravely give
your best
To prove to me
your gallantry
You must pass
my test

"You must pass my test" . . . ?

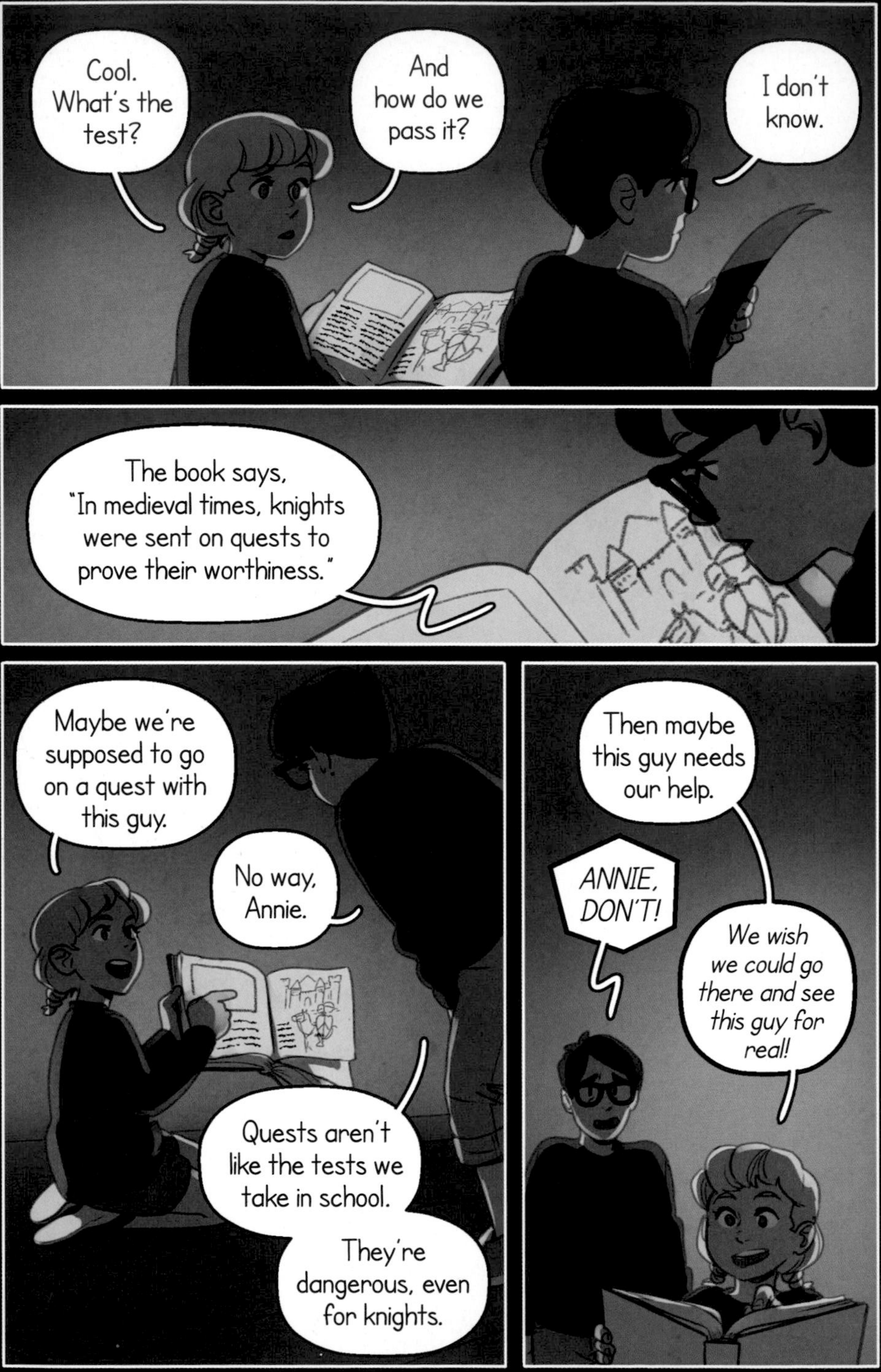
Cool. What's the test?
And how do we pass it?
I don't know.
The book says, "In medieval times, knights were sent on quests to prove their worthiness."
Maybe we're supposed to go on a quest with this guy.
No way, Annie.
Quests aren't like the tests we take in school.
They're dangerous, even for knights.
Then maybe this guy needs our help.
ANNIE, DON'T!
We wish we could go there and see this guy for real!

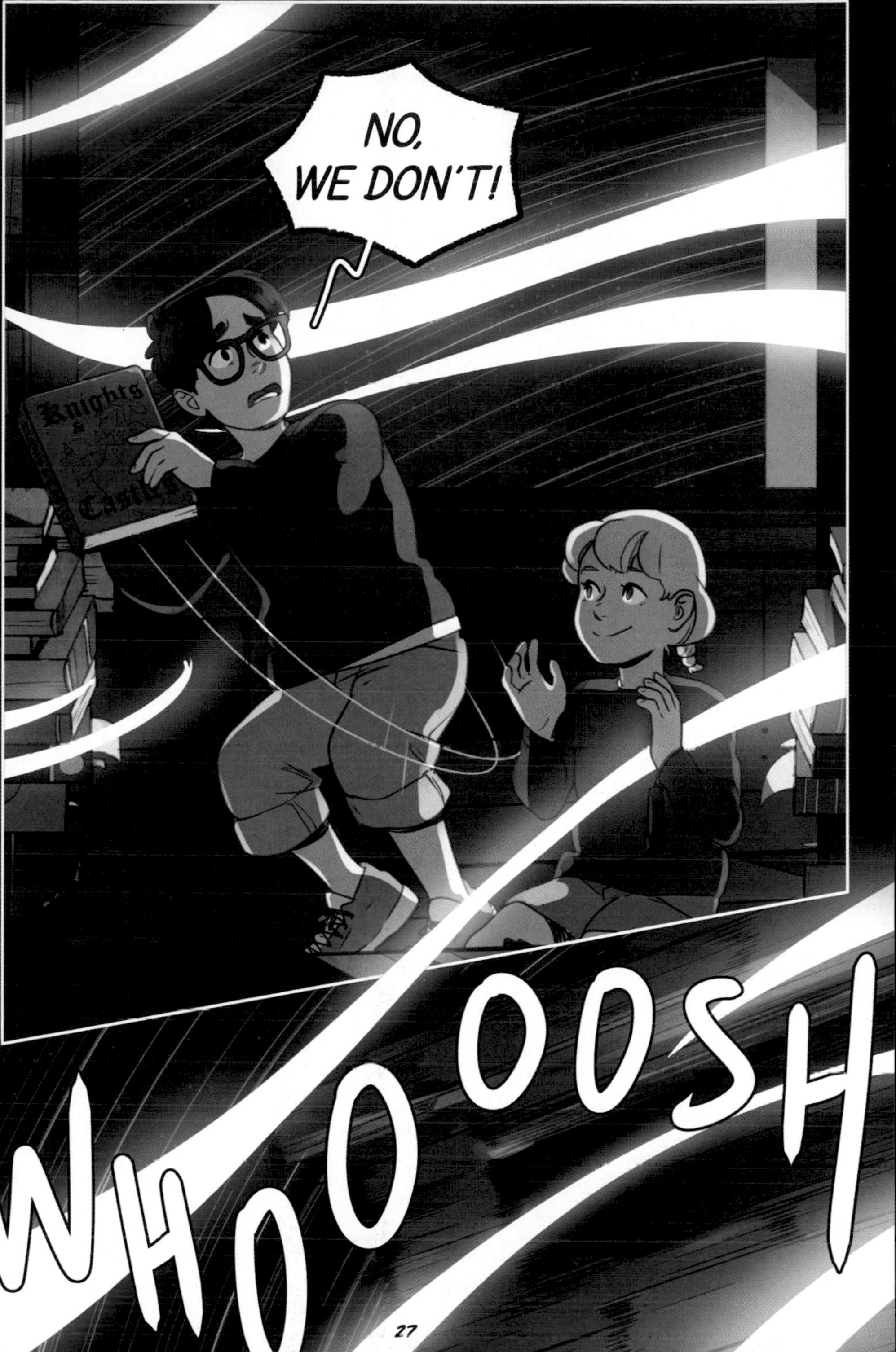
NO, WE DON'T!
Knights & Castles
WHOOOOSH

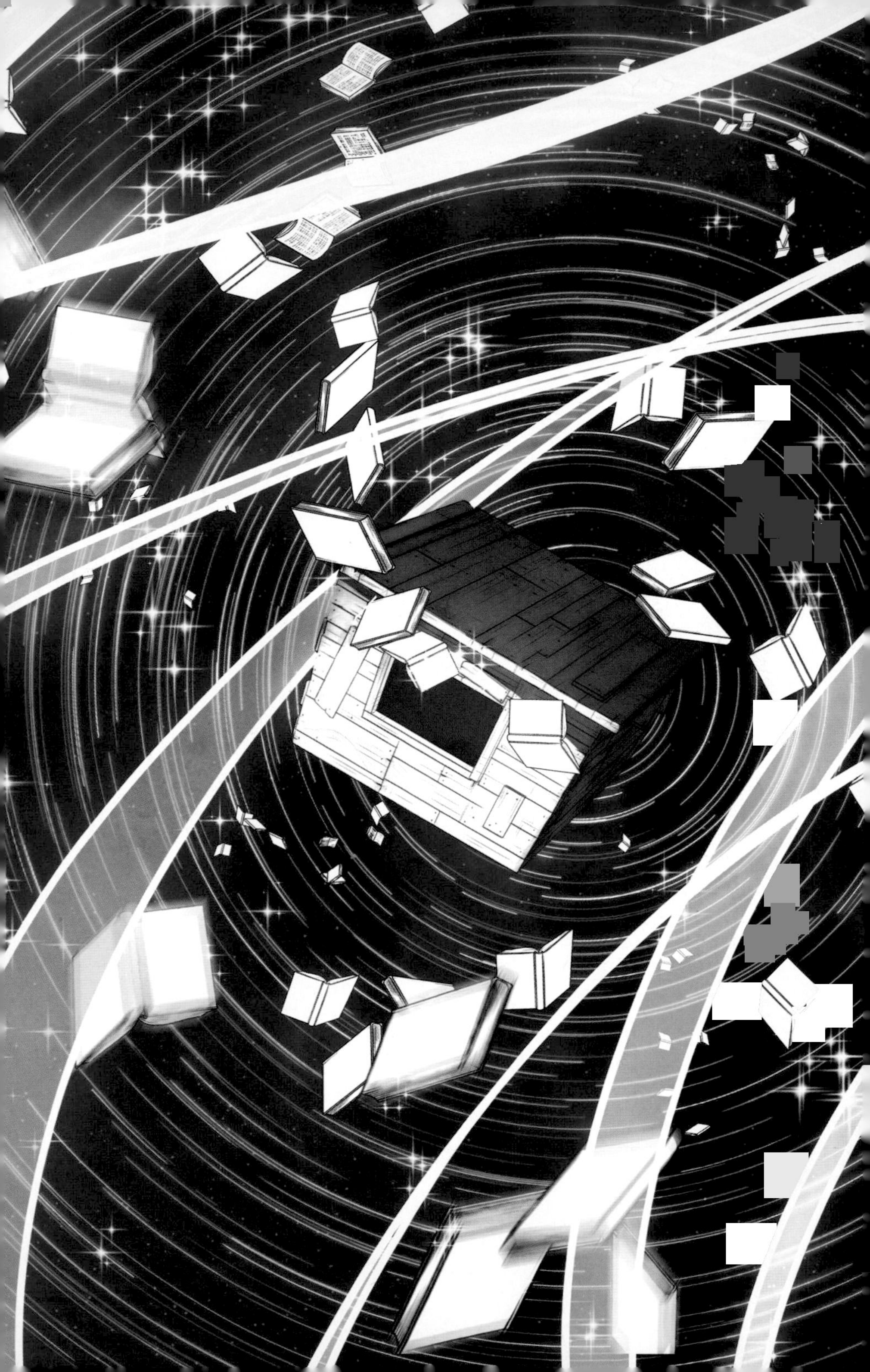

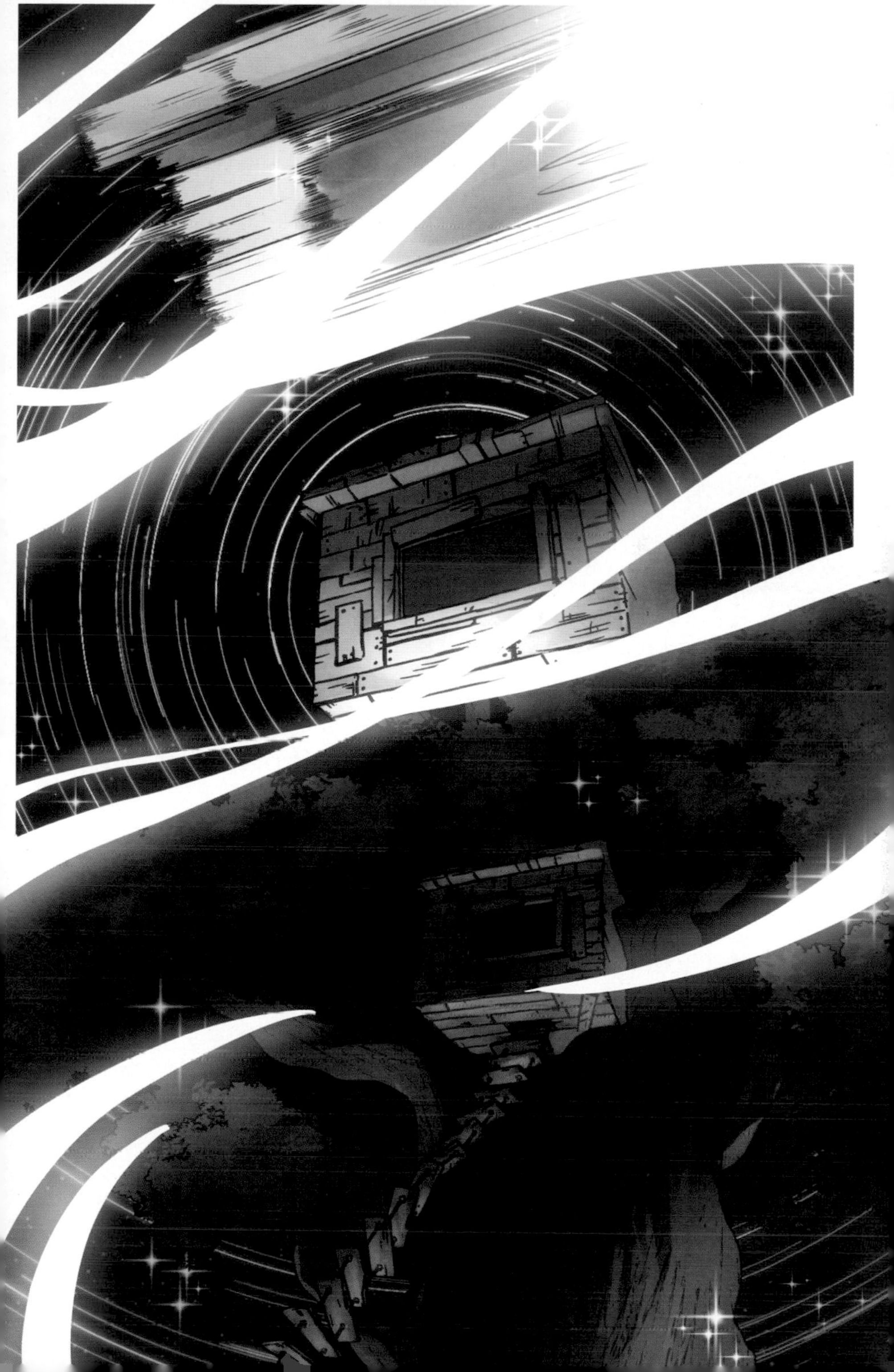

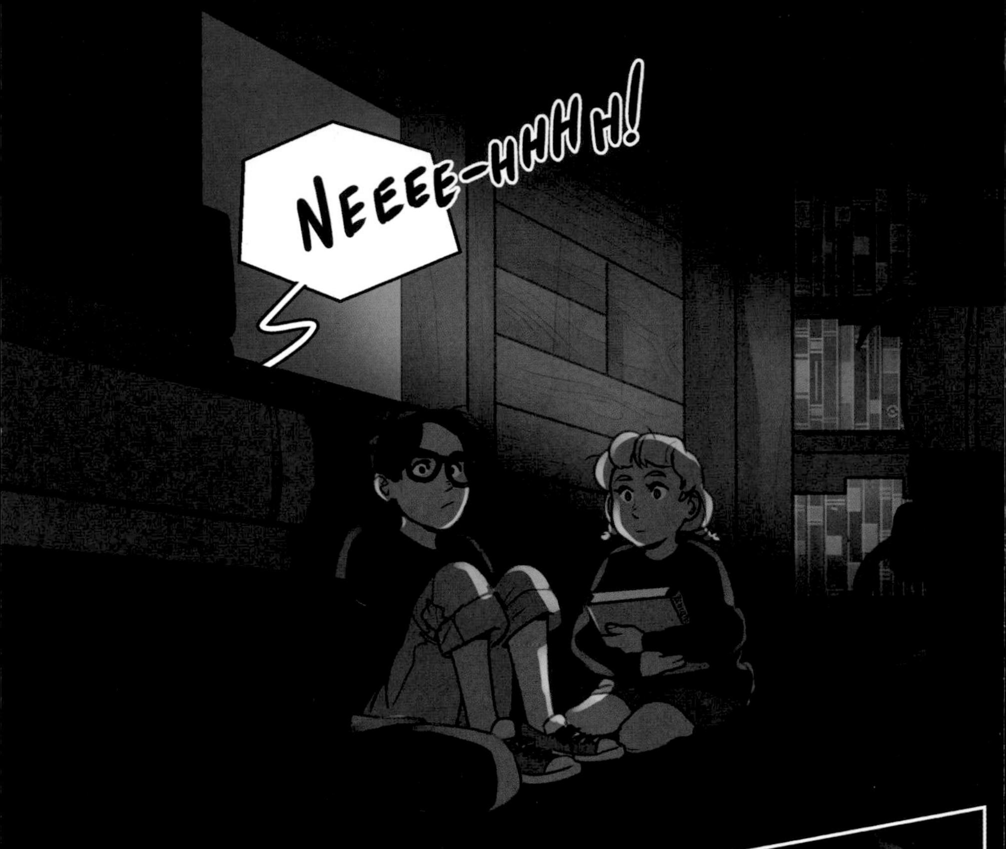
NEEEE-HHHH H!

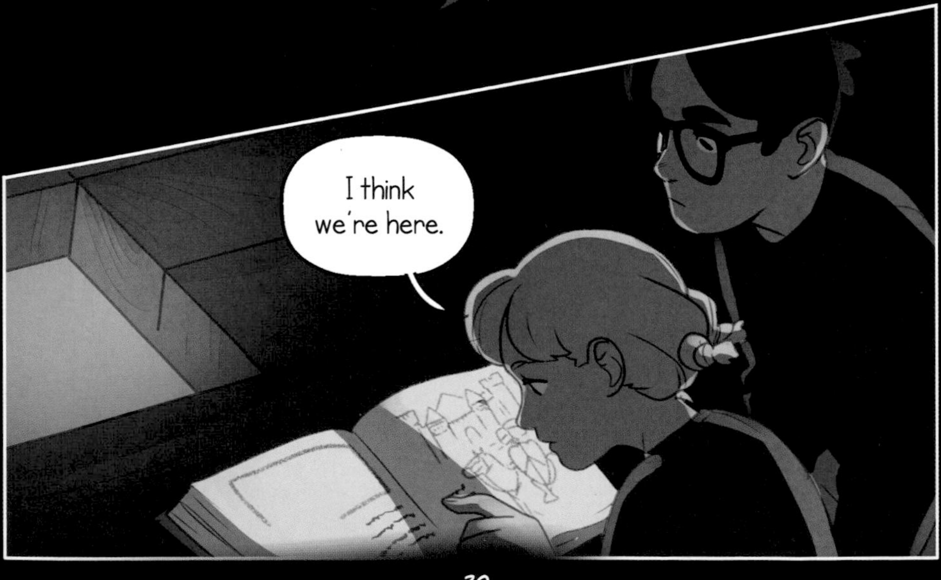
I think
we're here.

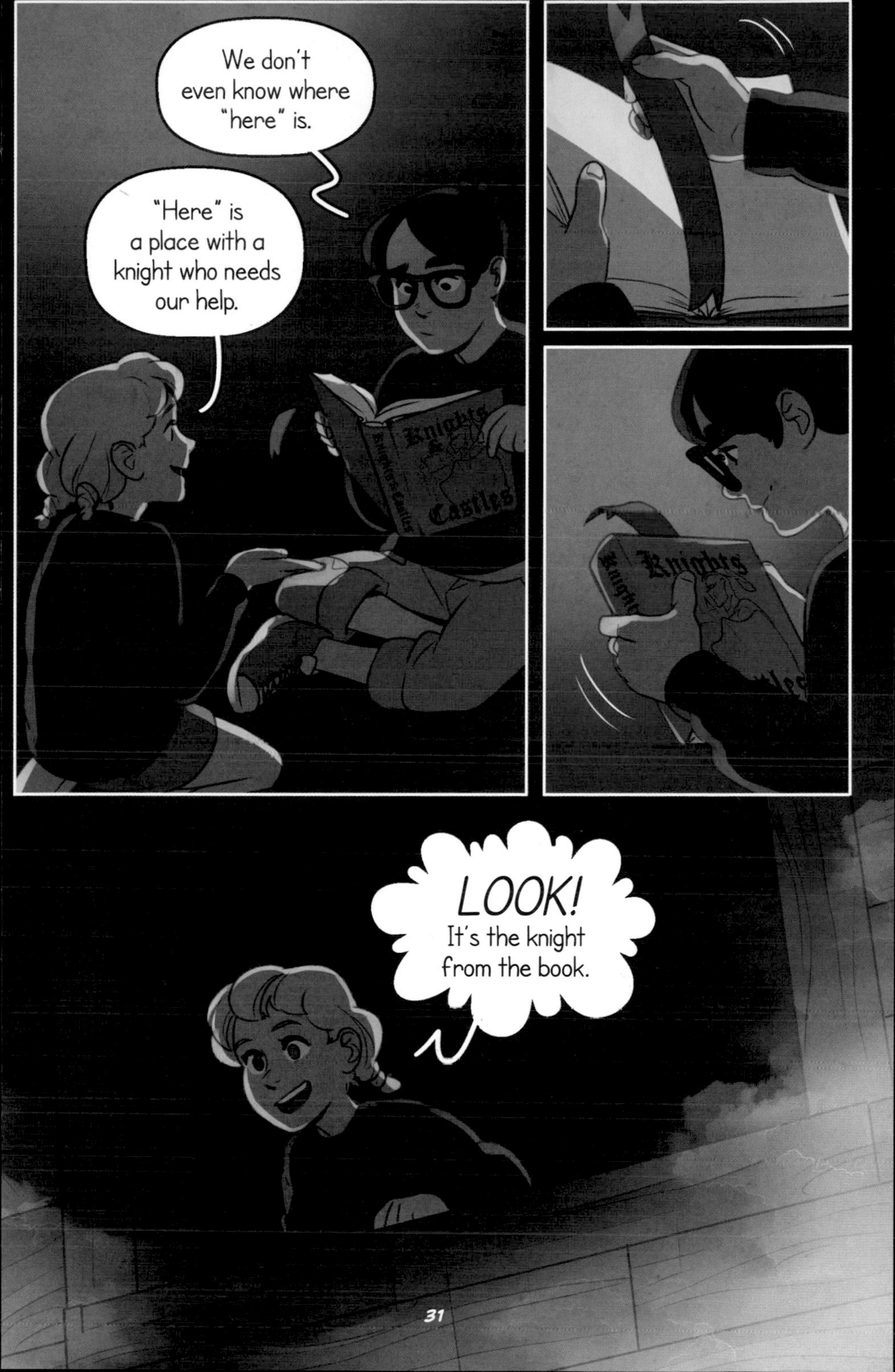
We don't even know where "here" is.
"Here" is a place with a knight who needs our help.
LOOK! It's the knight from the book.

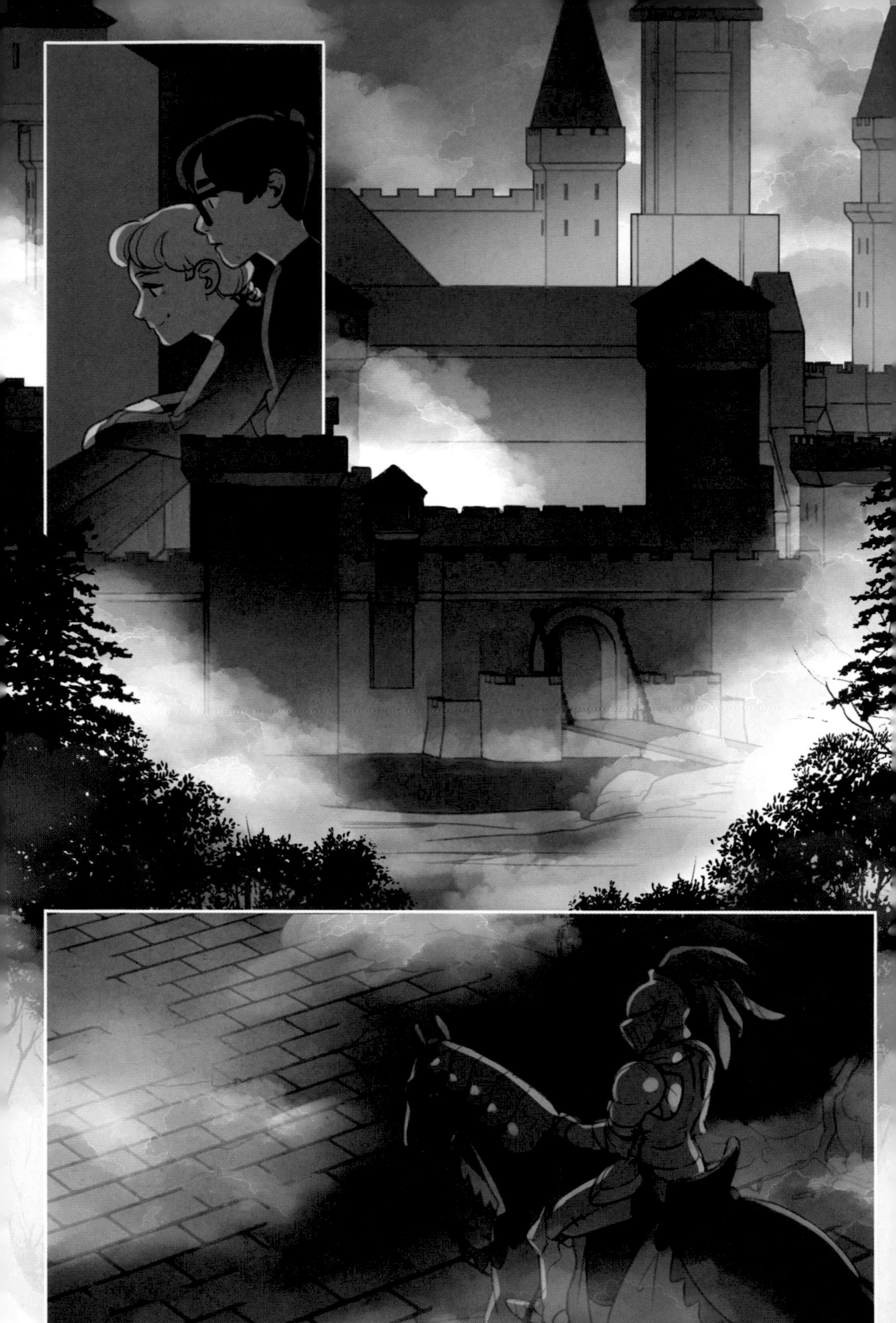

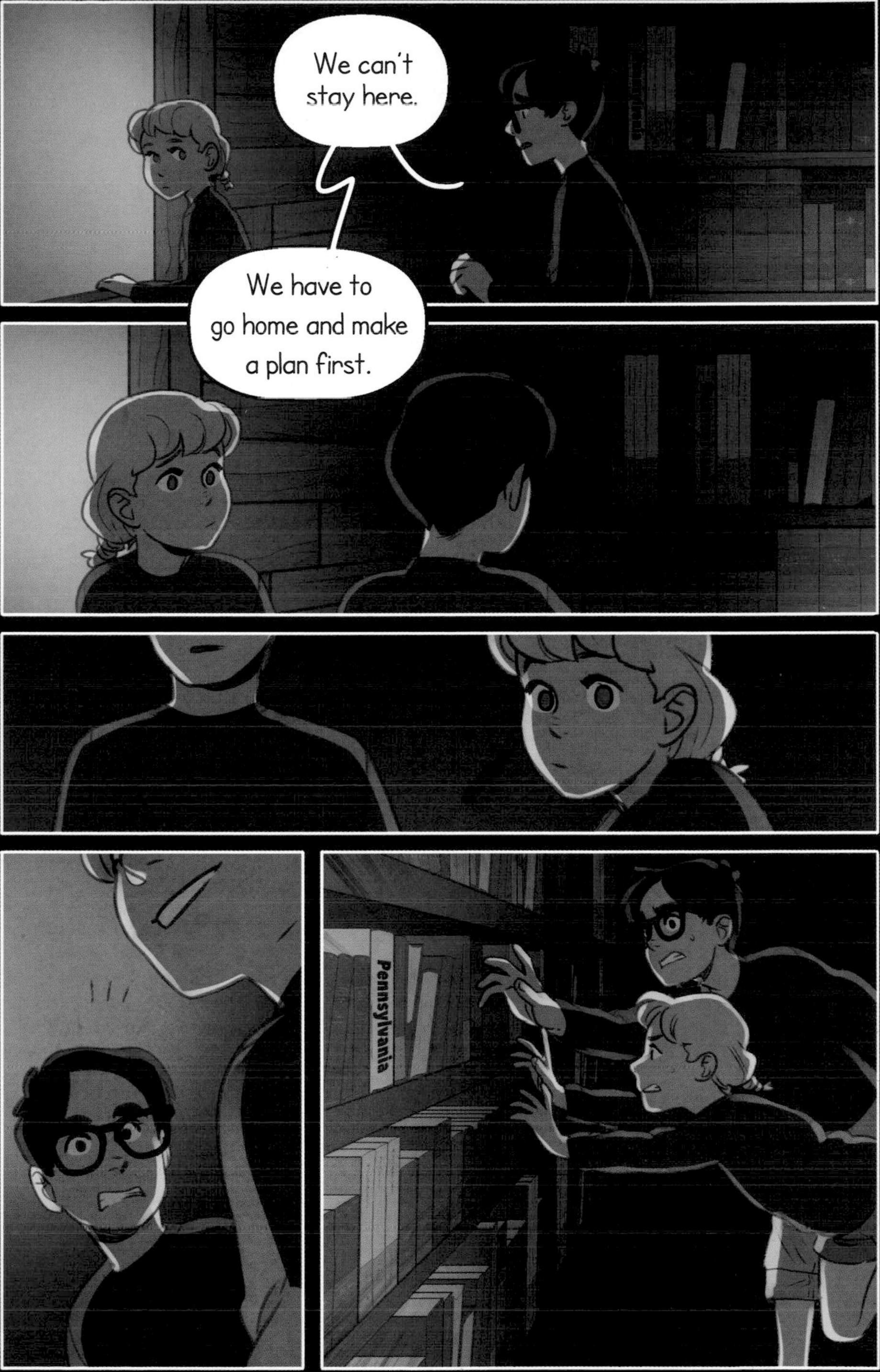
We can't stay here.
We have to go home and make a plan first.
Pennsylvania

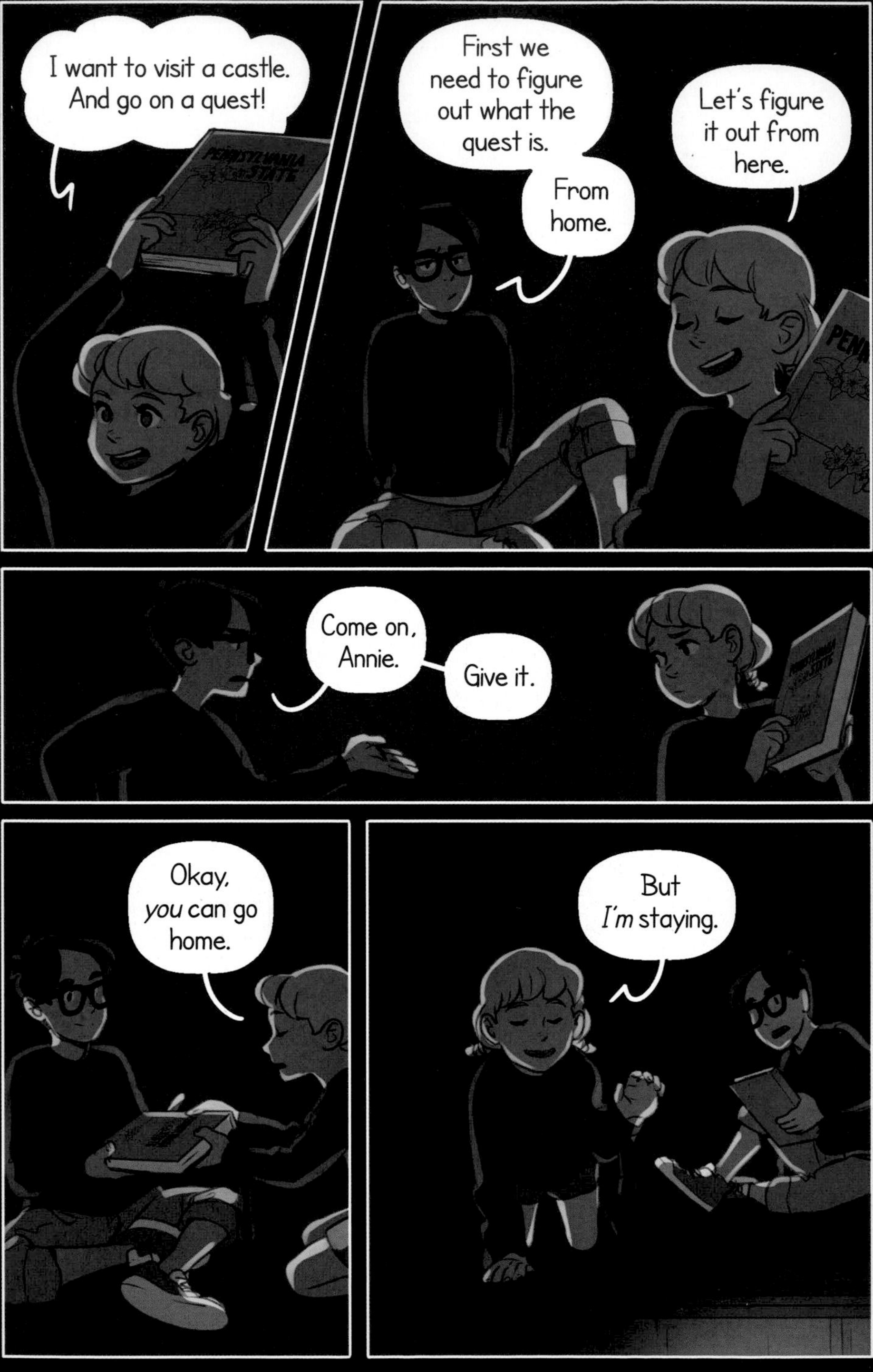
I want to visit a castle. And go on a quest!
First we need to figure out what the quest is.
From home.
Let's figure it out from here.
Come on, Annie.
Give it.
Okay, *you* can go home.
But *I'm* staying.

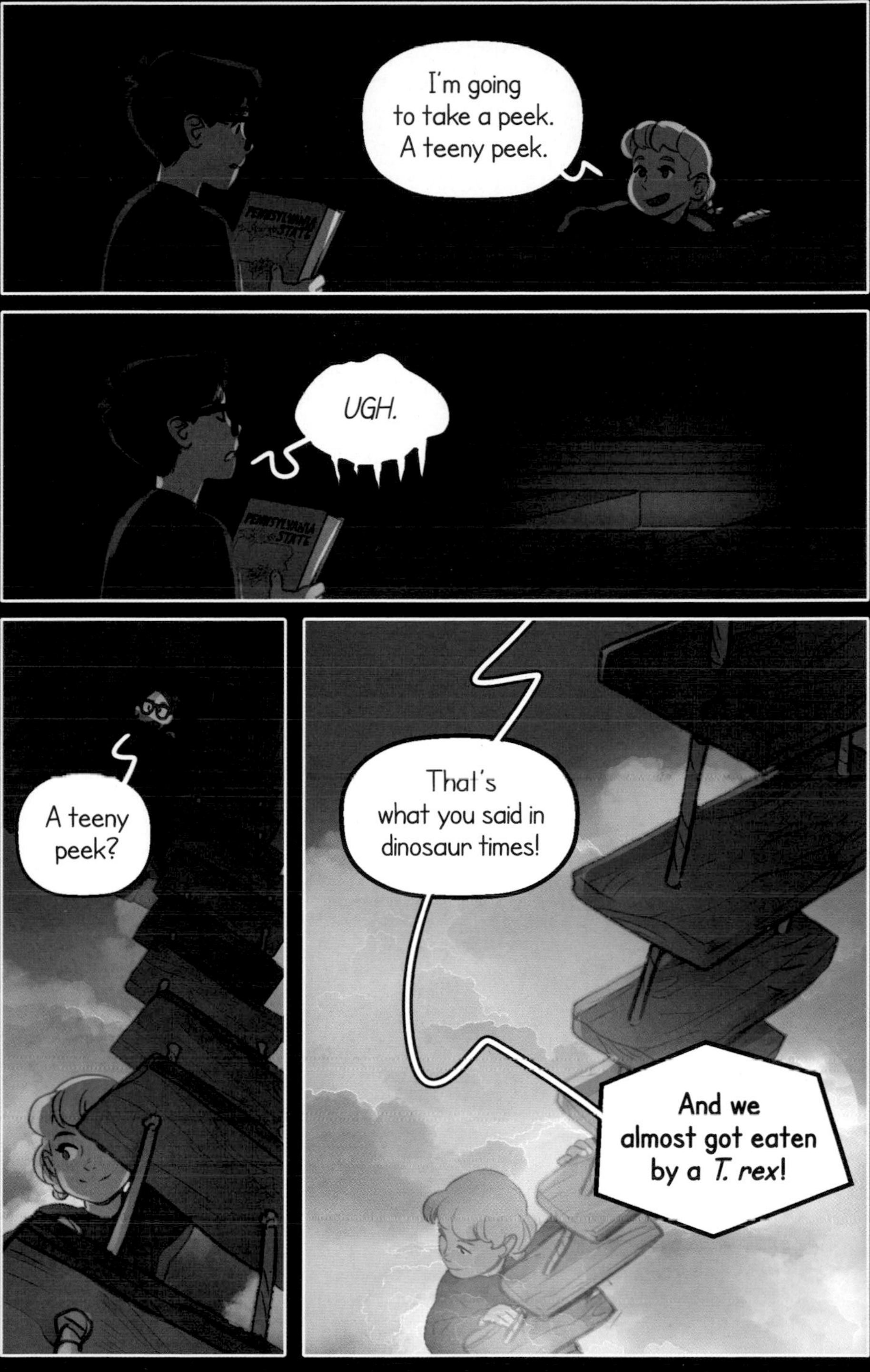
I'm going to take a peek. A teeny peek.
UGH.
A teeny peek?
That's what you said in dinosaur times!
And we almost got eaten by a *T. rex*!

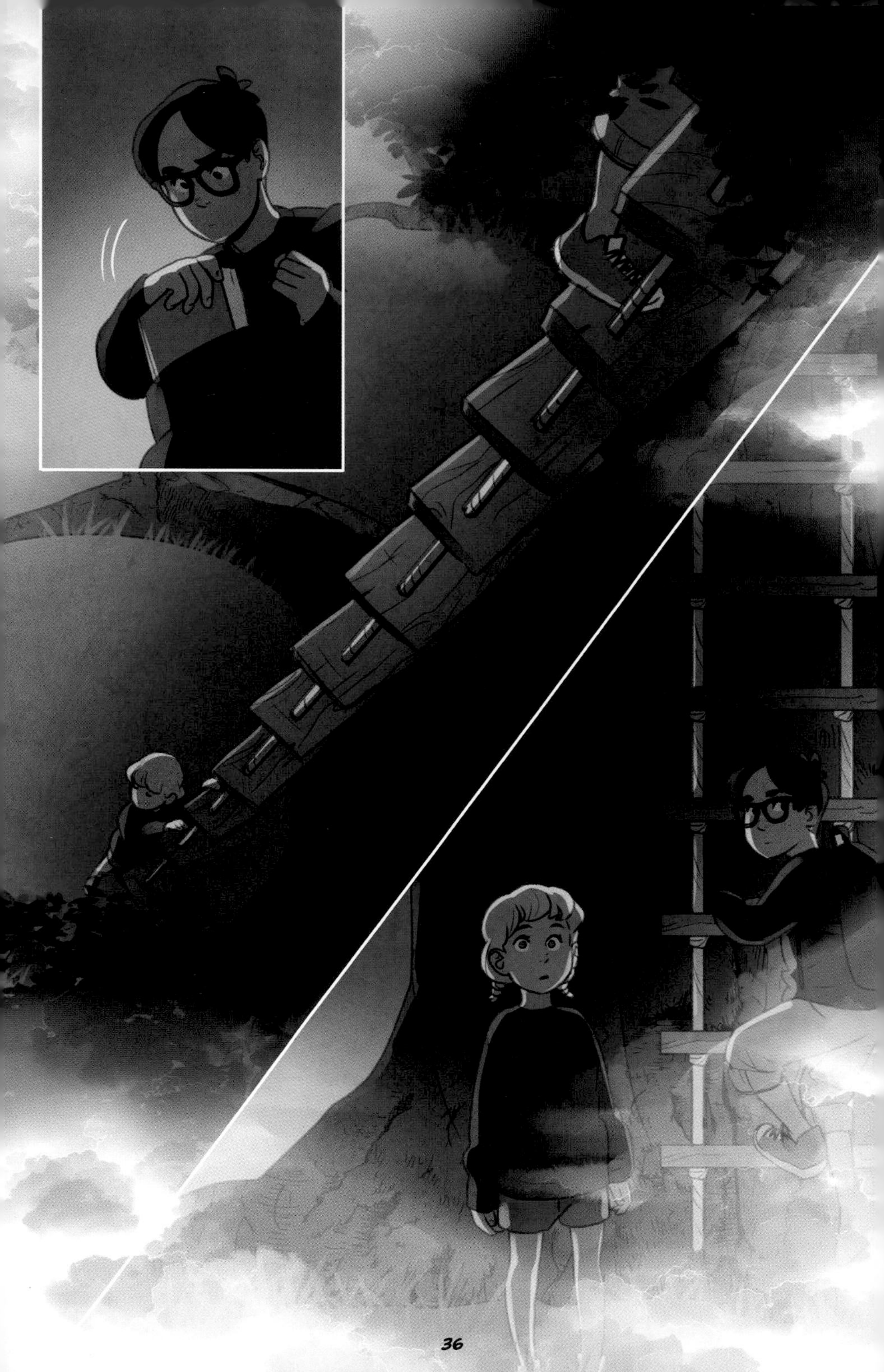

CHAPTER THREE
Across the Bridge

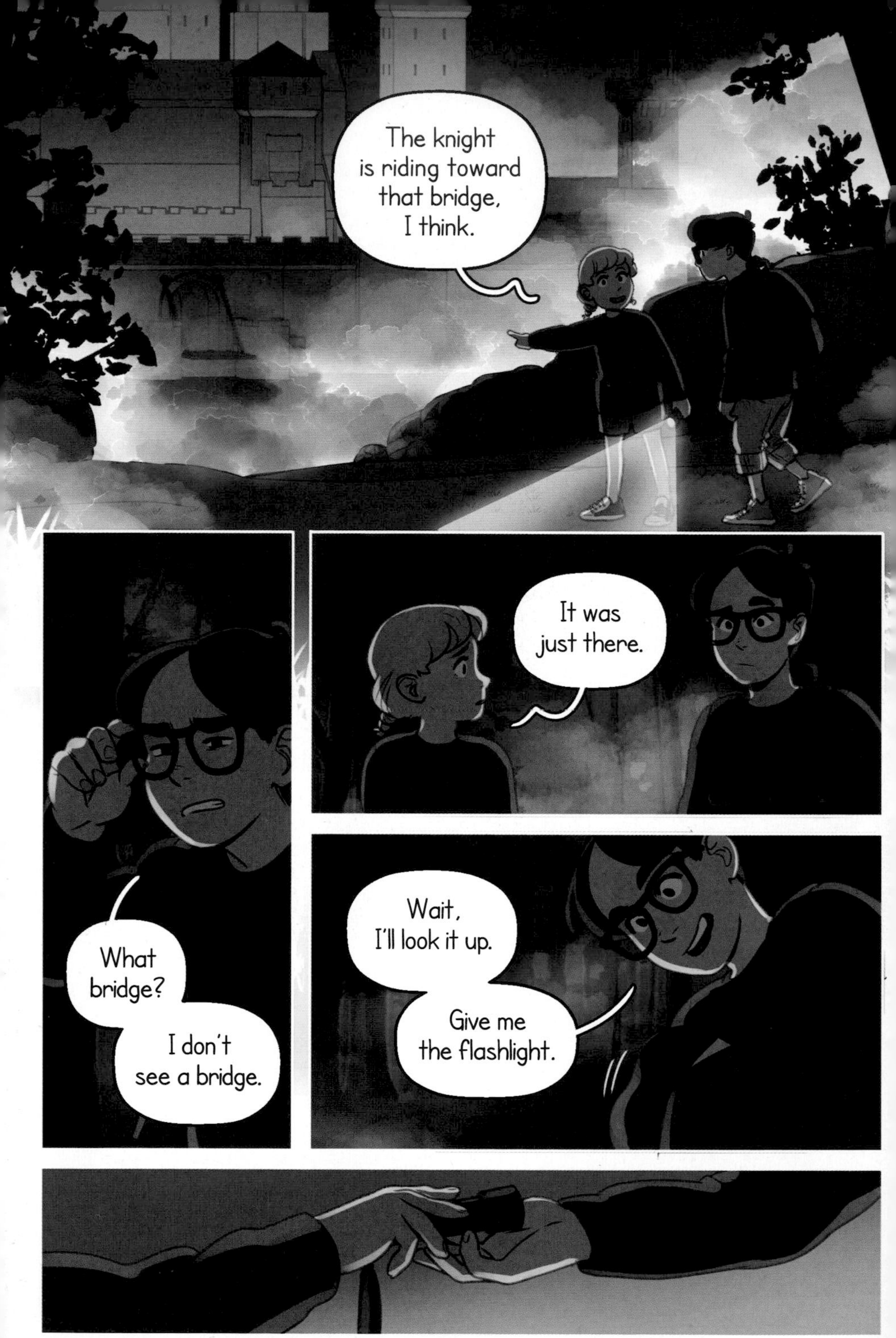
The knight is riding toward that bridge, I think.
What bridge?
I don't see a bridge.
It was just there.
Wait, I'll look it up.
Give me the flashlight.

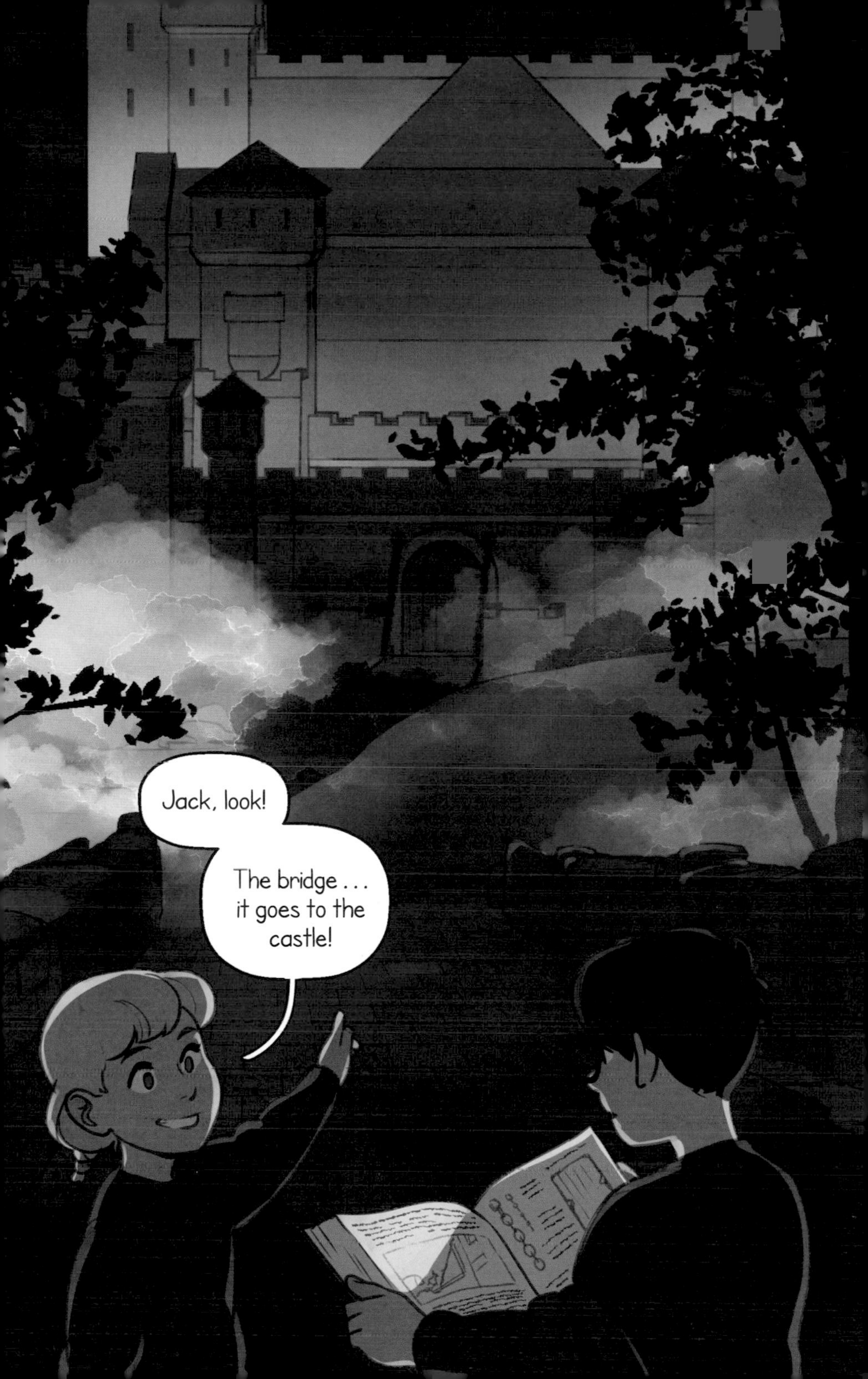
Jack, look!
The bridge . . . it goes to the castle!

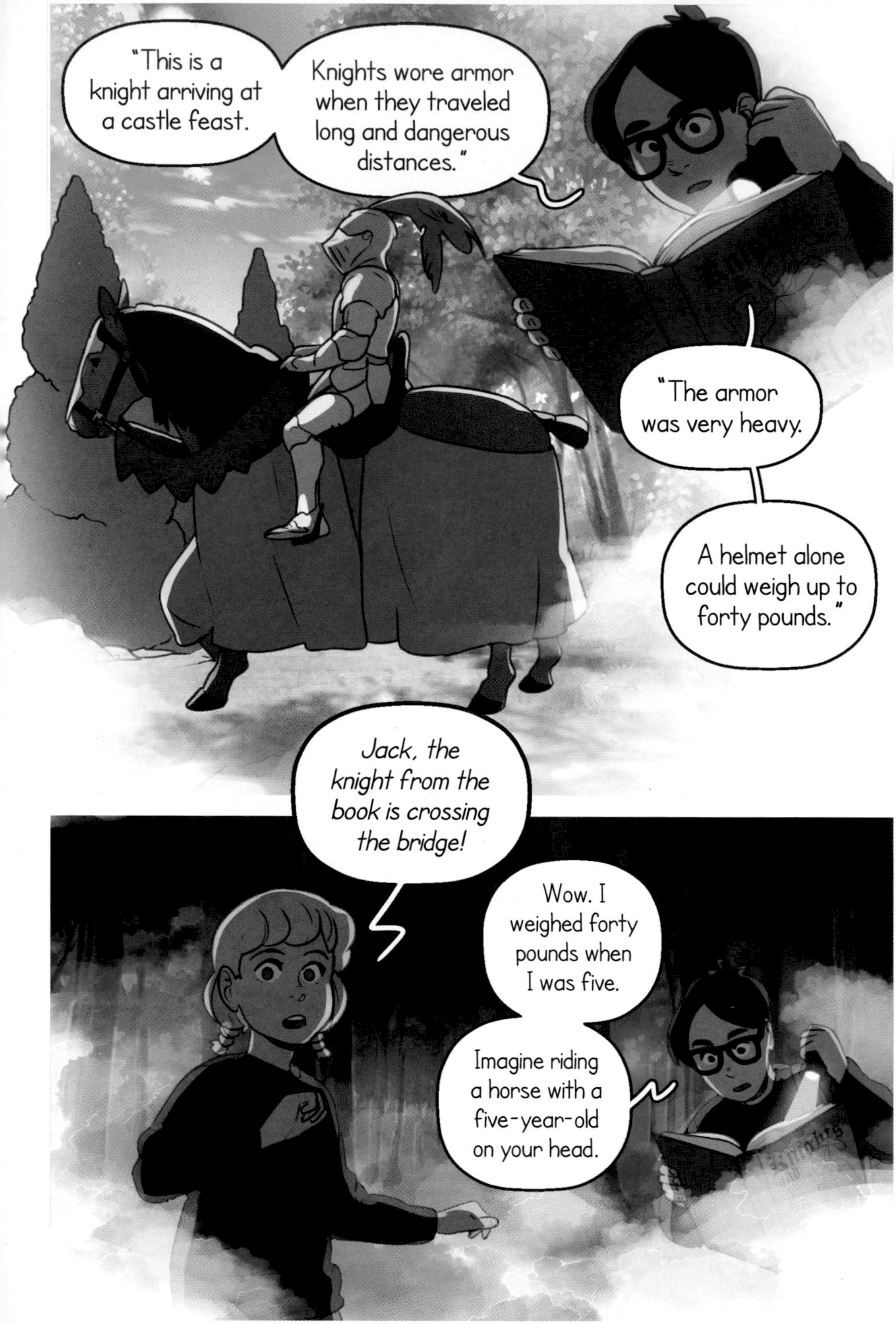
"This is a knight arriving at a castle feast.
Knights wore armor when they traveled long and dangerous distances."
"The armor was very heavy.
A helmet alone could weigh up to forty pounds."
Jack, the knight from the book is crossing the bridge!
Wow. I weighed forty pounds when I was five.
Imagine riding a horse with a five-year-old on your head.

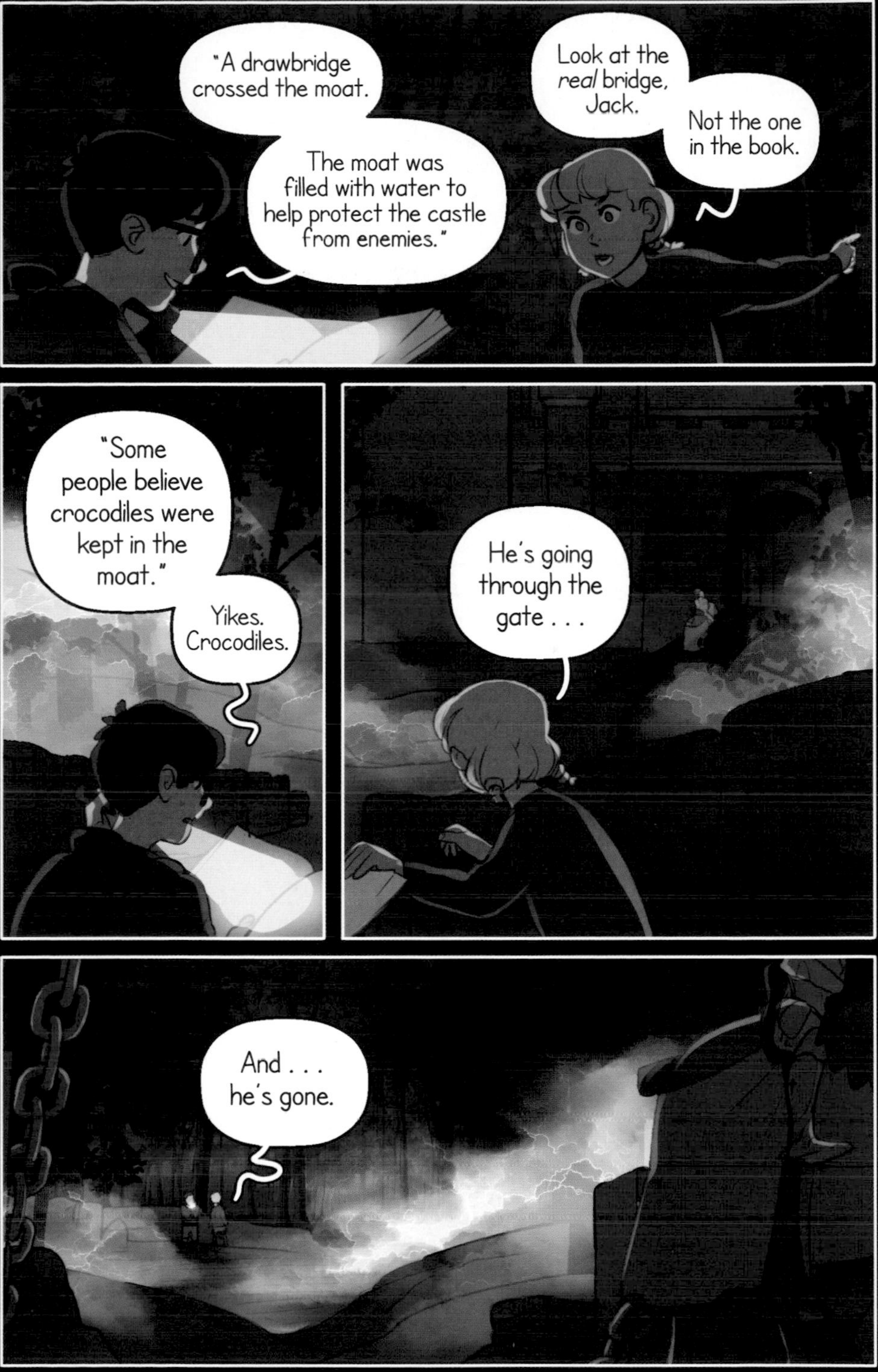
"A drawbridge crossed the moat.
The moat was filled with water to help protect the castle from enemies."
Look at the *real* bridge, Jack.
Not the one in the book.
"Some people believe crocodiles were kept in the moat."
Yikes. Crocodiles.
He's going through the gate . . .
And . . . he's gone.

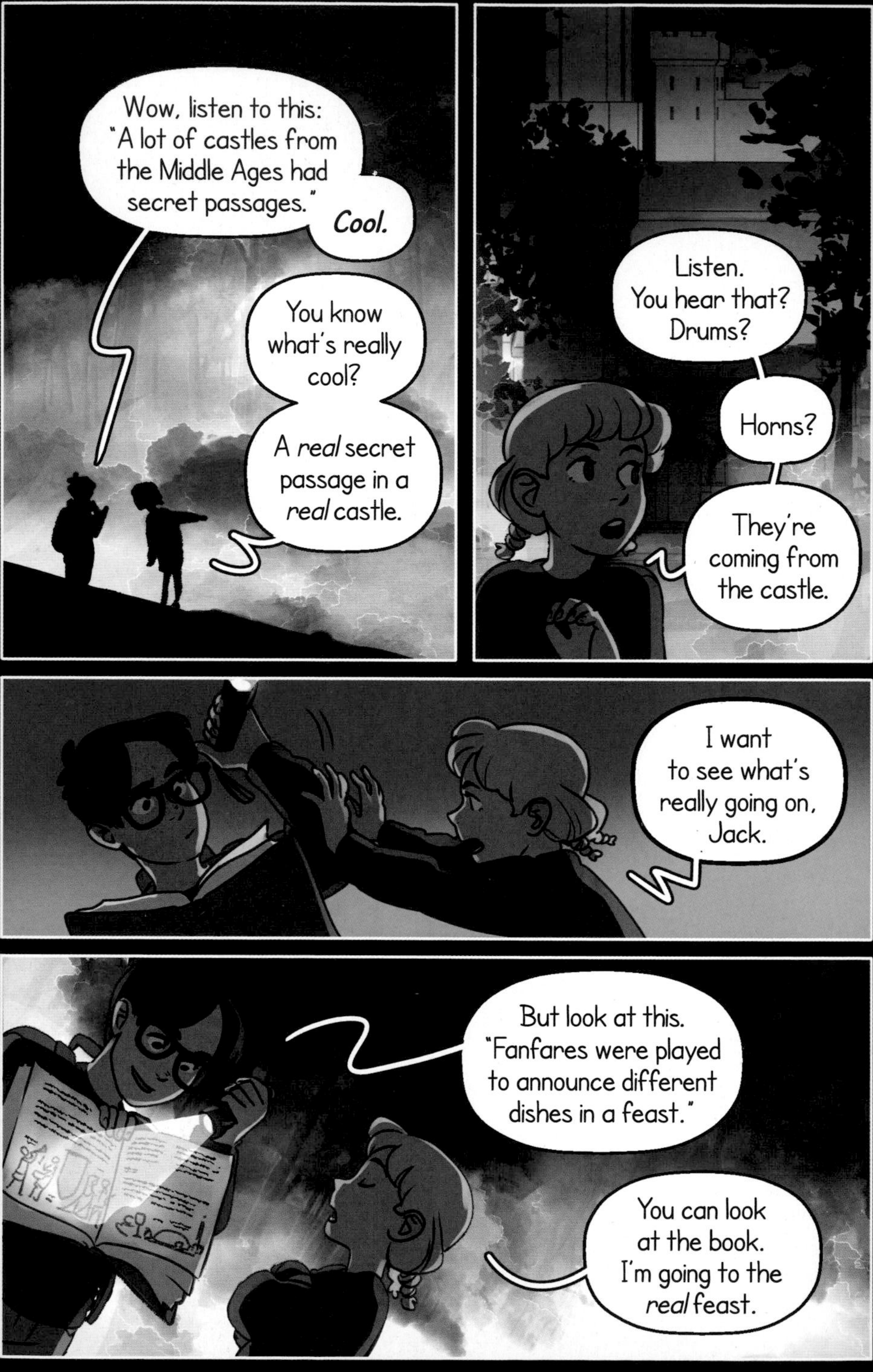
Wow, listen to this: "A lot of castles from the Middle Ages had secret passages."
Cool.
You know what's really cool?
A *real* secret passage in a *real* castle.
Listen. You hear that? Drums?
Horns?
They're coming from the castle.
I want to see what's really going on, Jack.
But look at this. "Fanfares were played to announce different dishes in a feast."
You can look at the book. I'm going to the *real* feast.

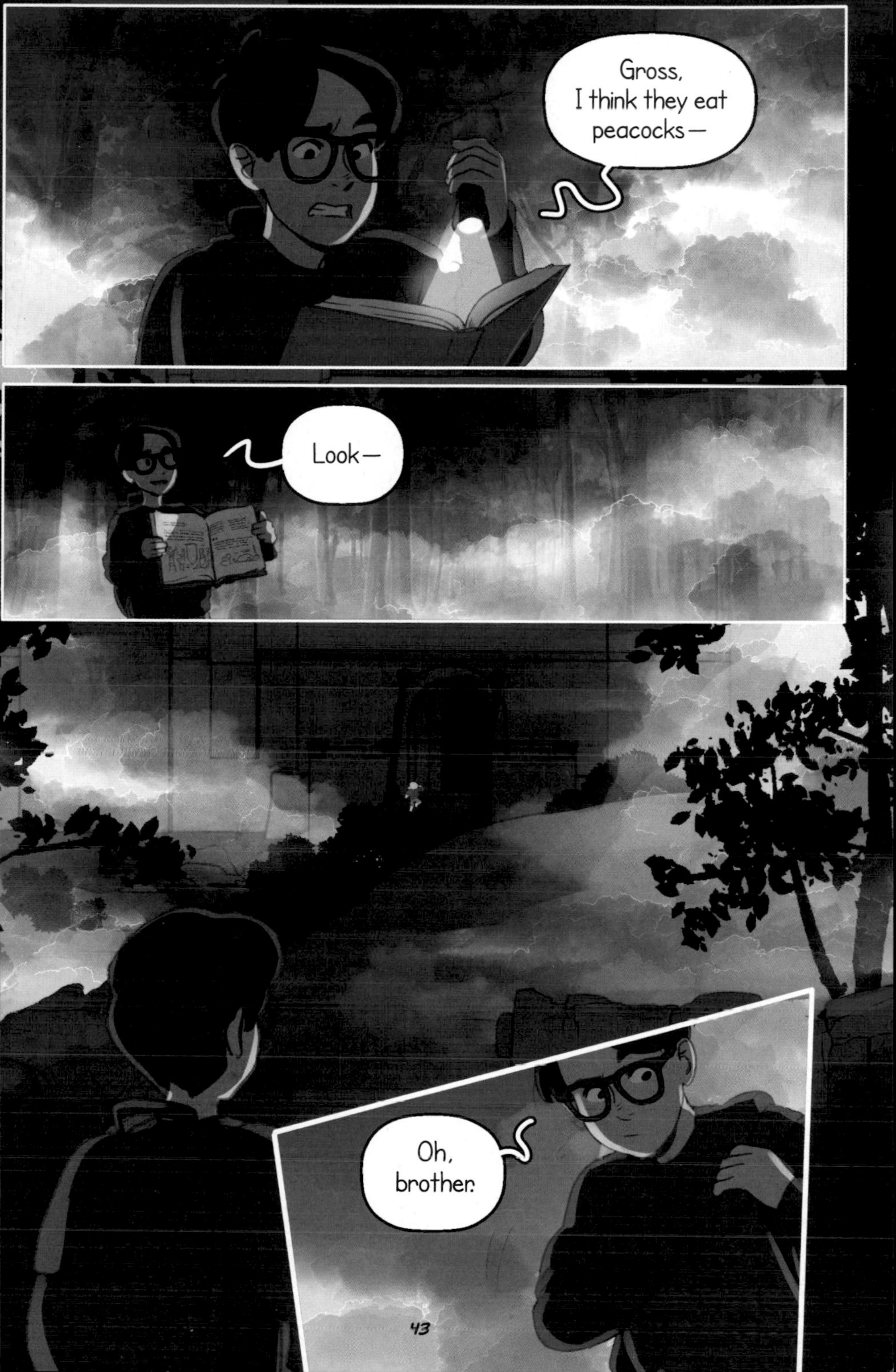
Gross,
I think they eat
peacocks—
Look—
Oh,
brother.

CHAPTER FOUR
Into the Castle

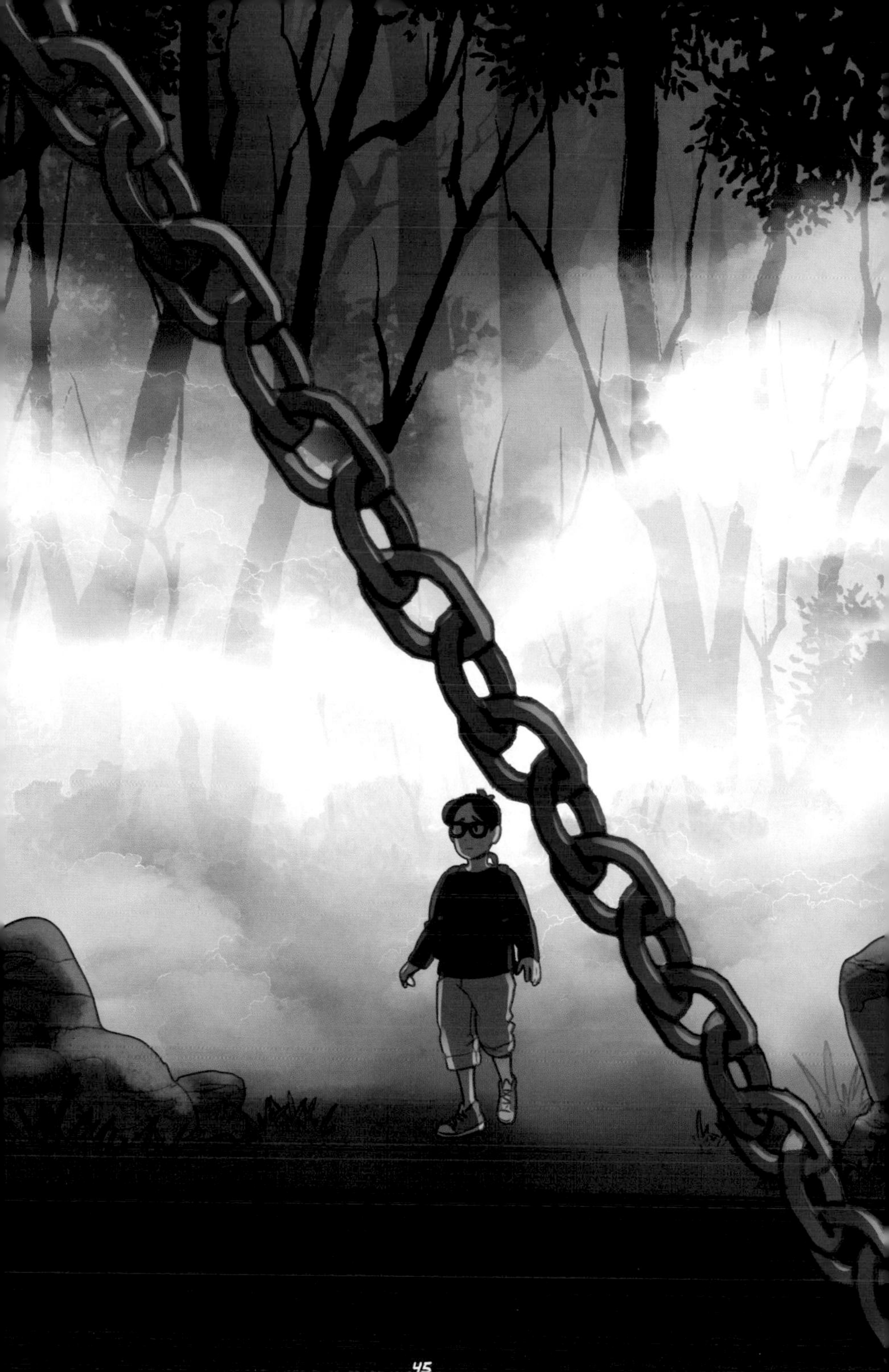

CREAK!

HALT!

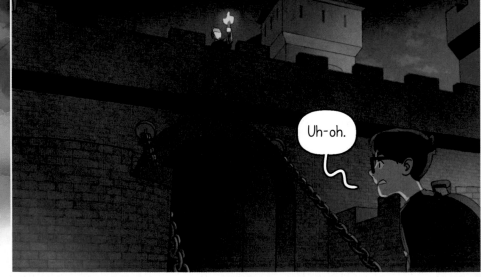

Uh-oh.

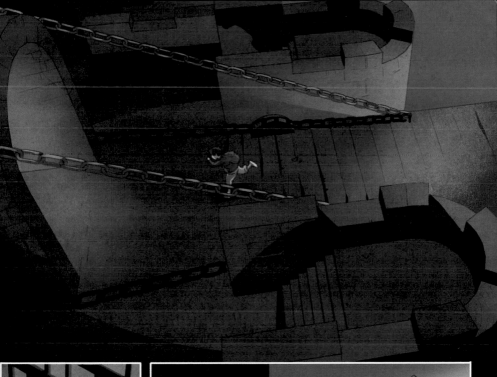

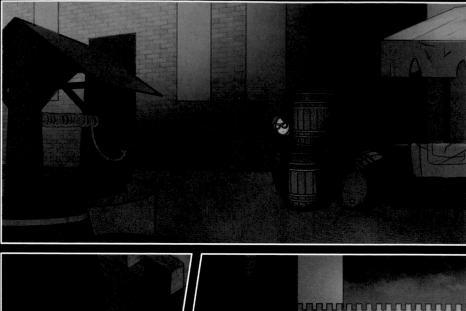

Pssssst!

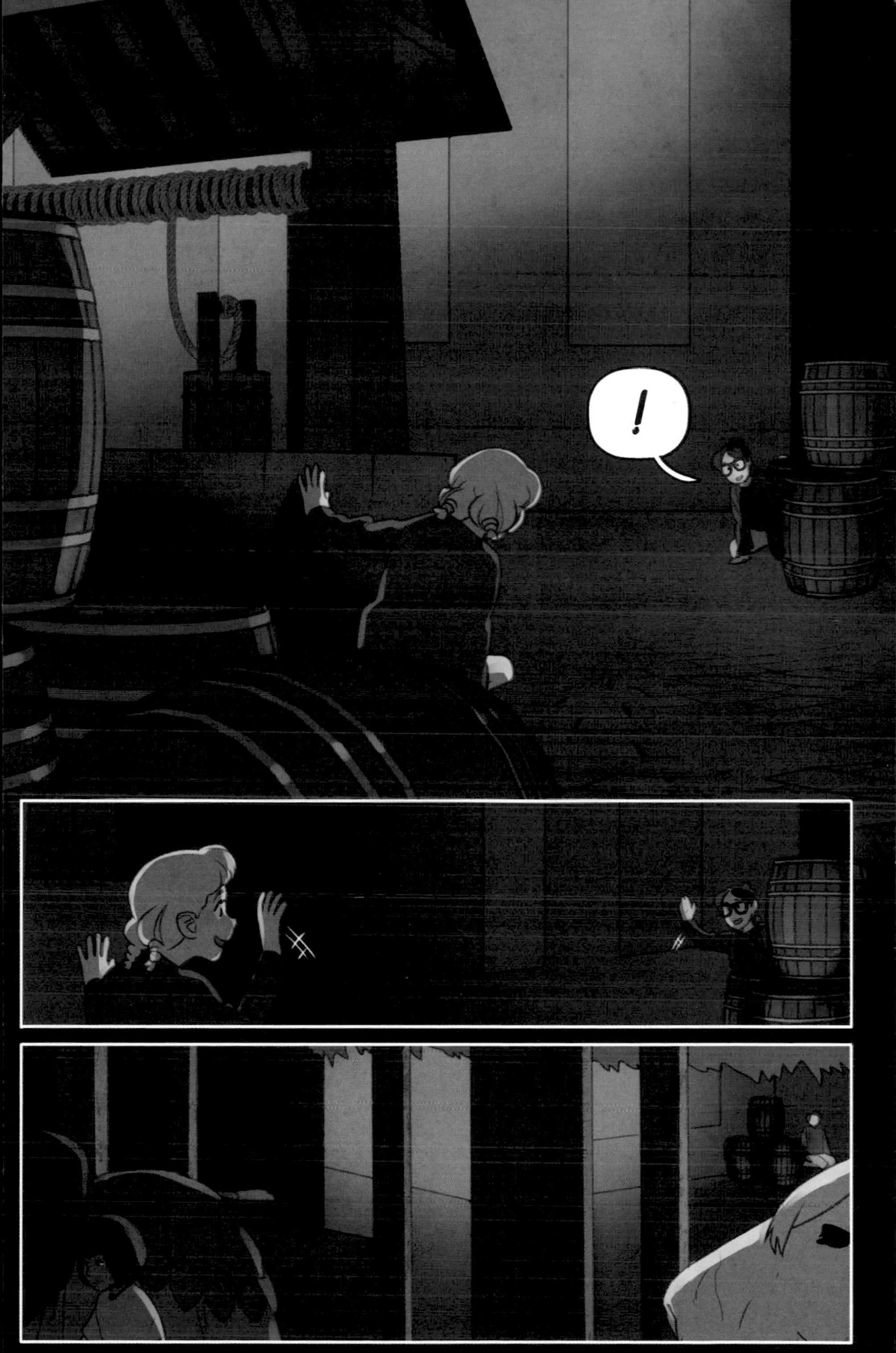
!

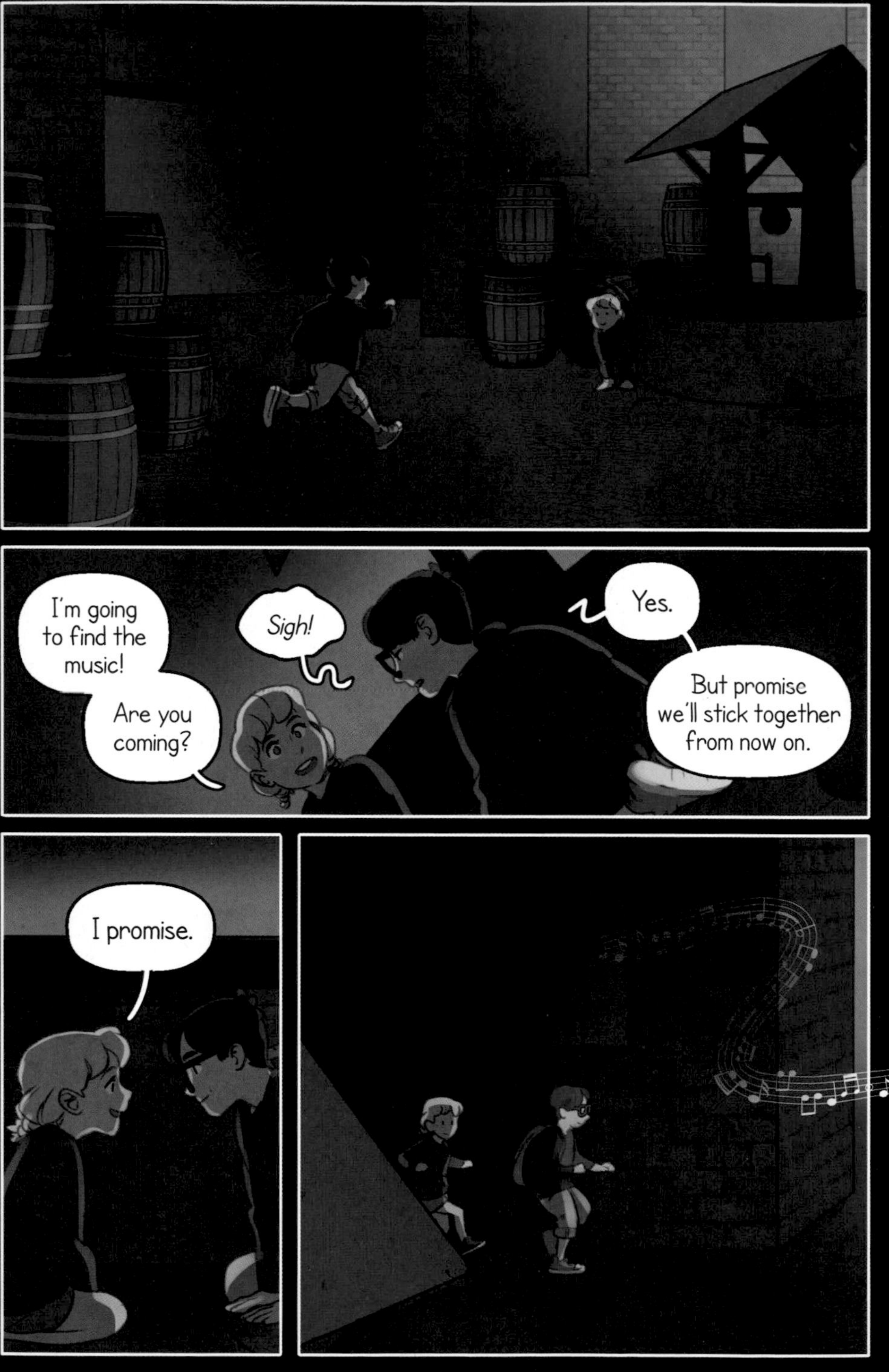
I'm going to find the music!
Are you coming?
Sigh!
Yes.
But promise we'll stick together from now on.
I promise.

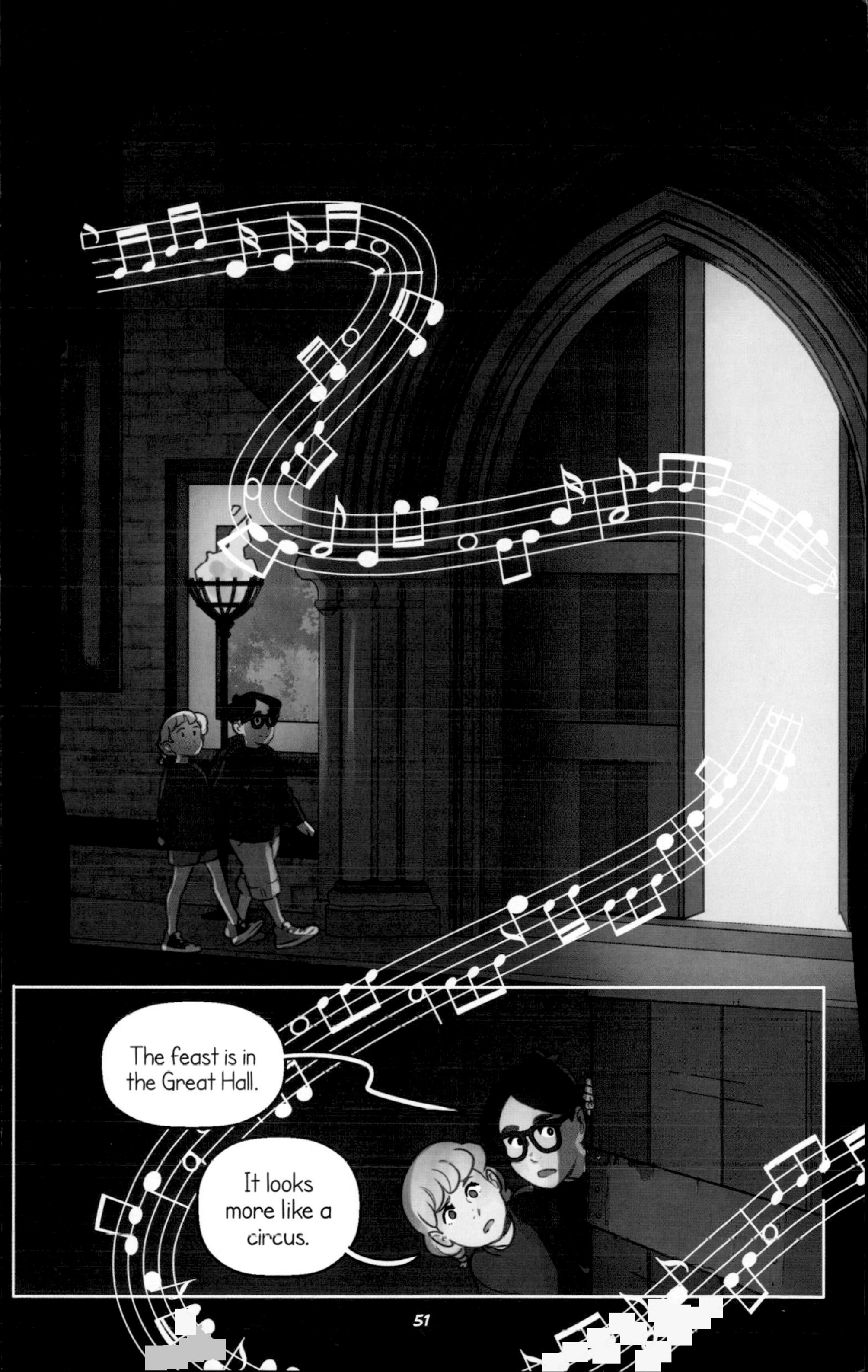
The feast is in the Great Hall.
It looks more like a circus.

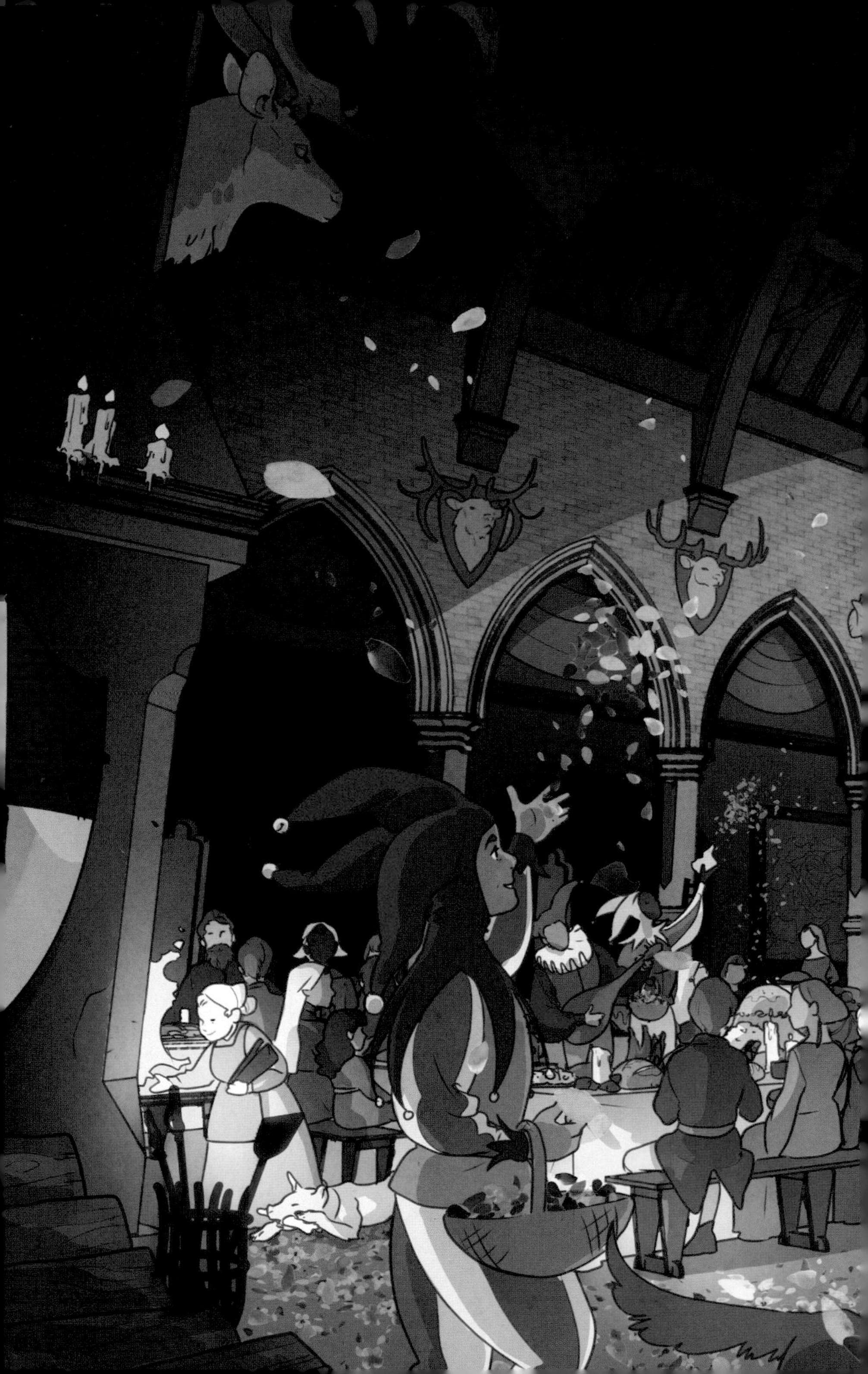

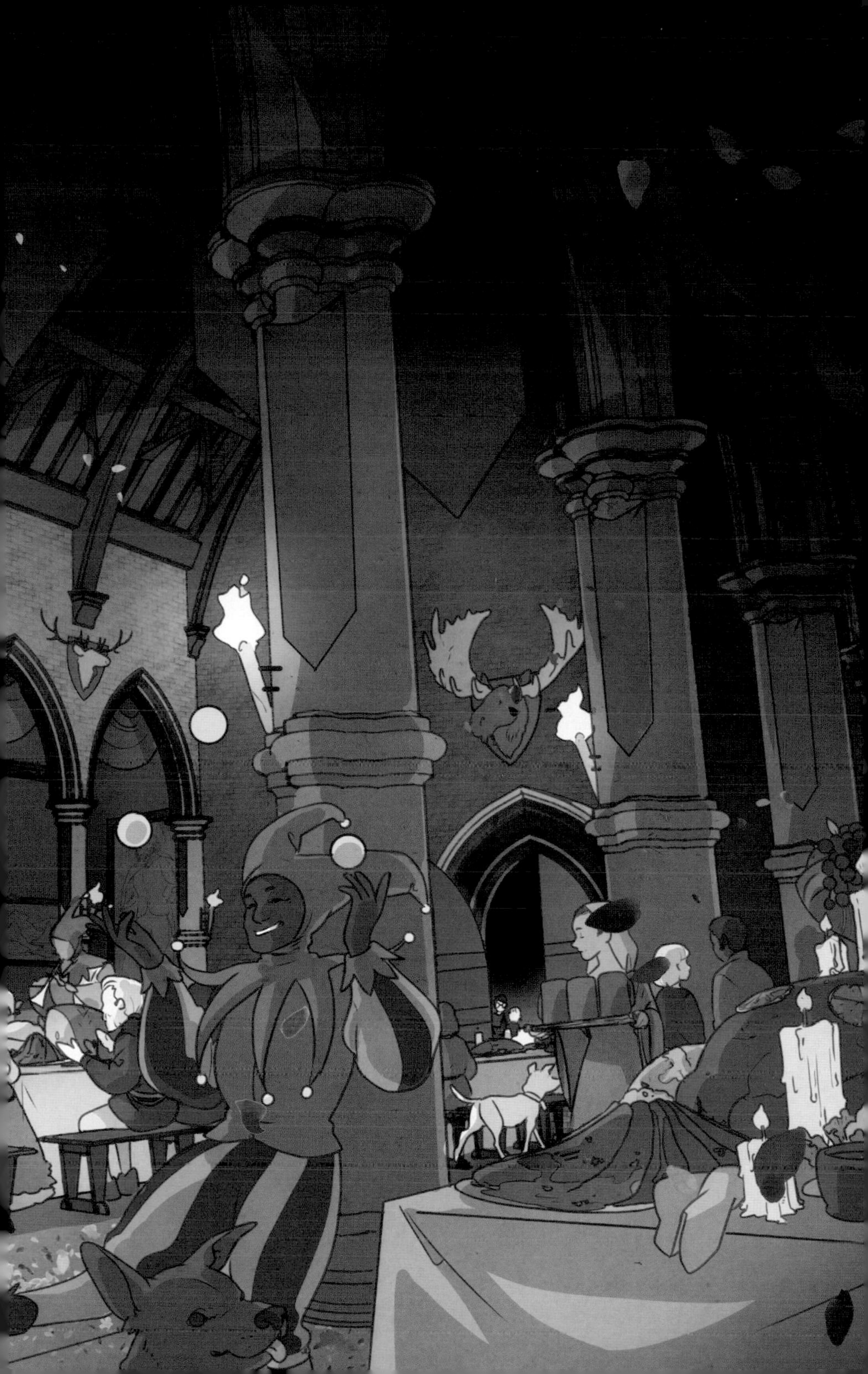

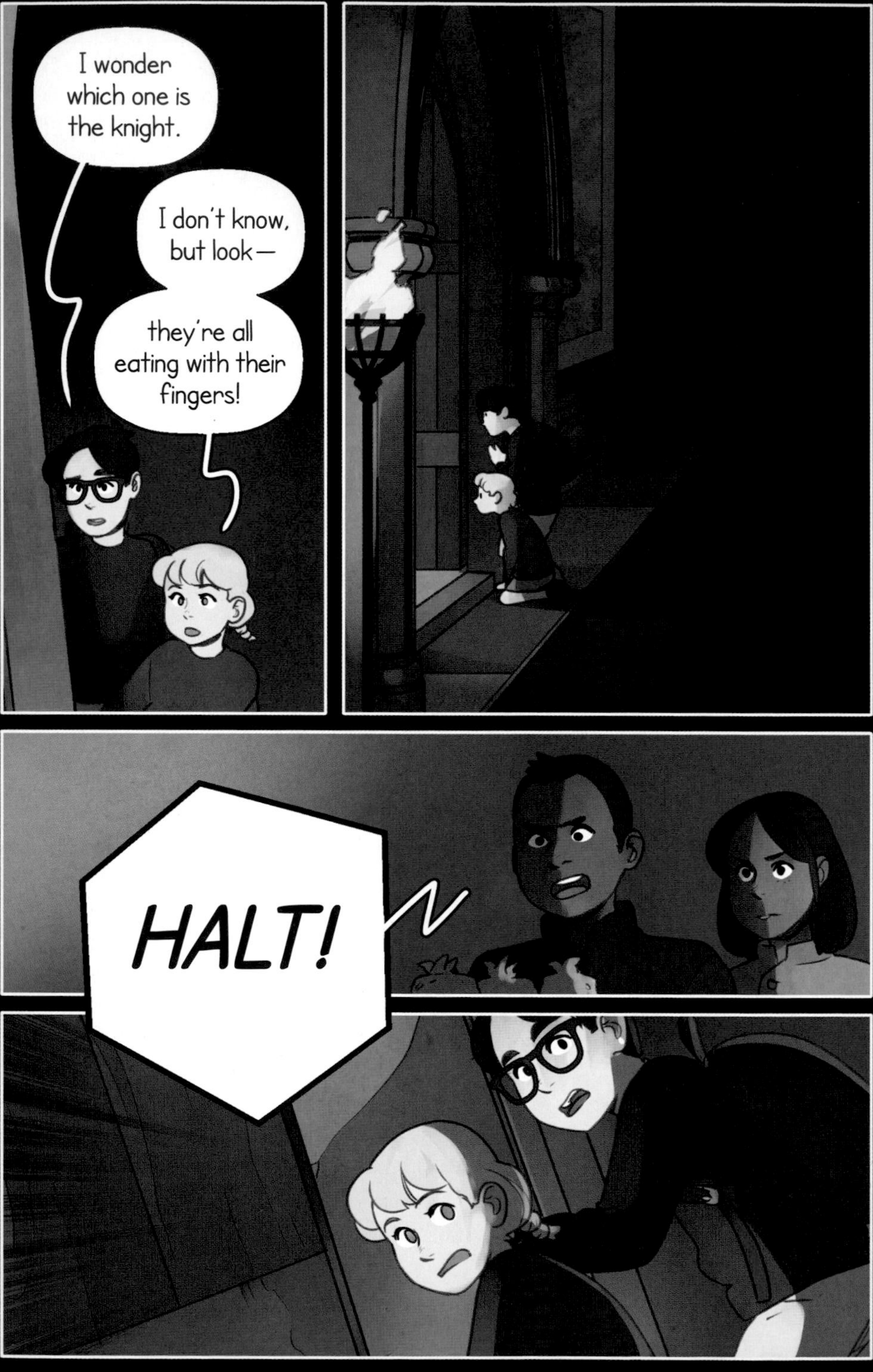
I wonder which one is the knight.
I don't know, but look—
they're all eating with their fingers!
HALT!

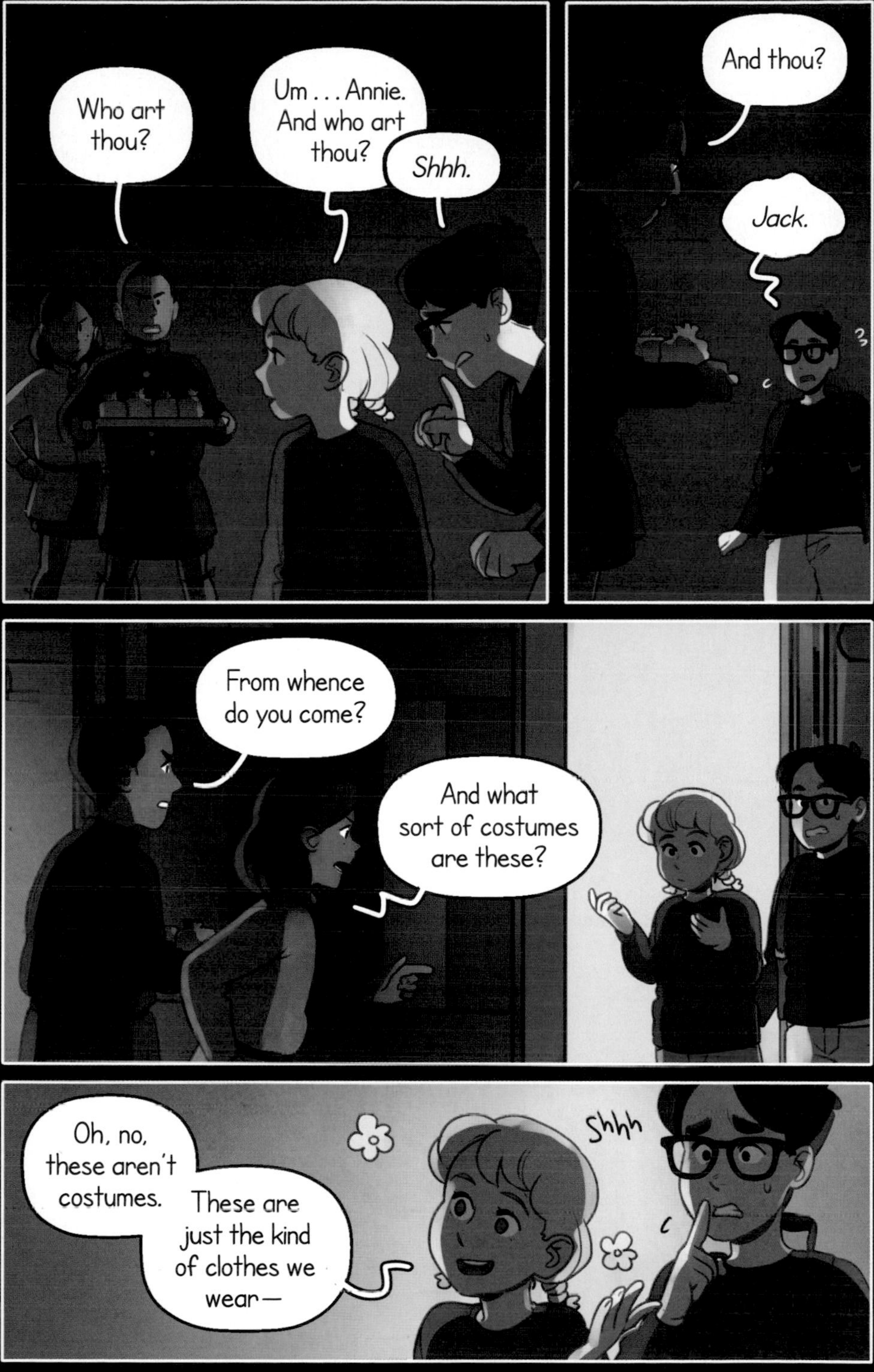
Who art thou?
Um . . . Annie. And who art thou?
Shhh.
And thou?
Jack.
From whence do you come?
And what sort of costumes are these?
Oh, no, these aren't costumes.
These are just the kind of clothes we wear—
Shhh

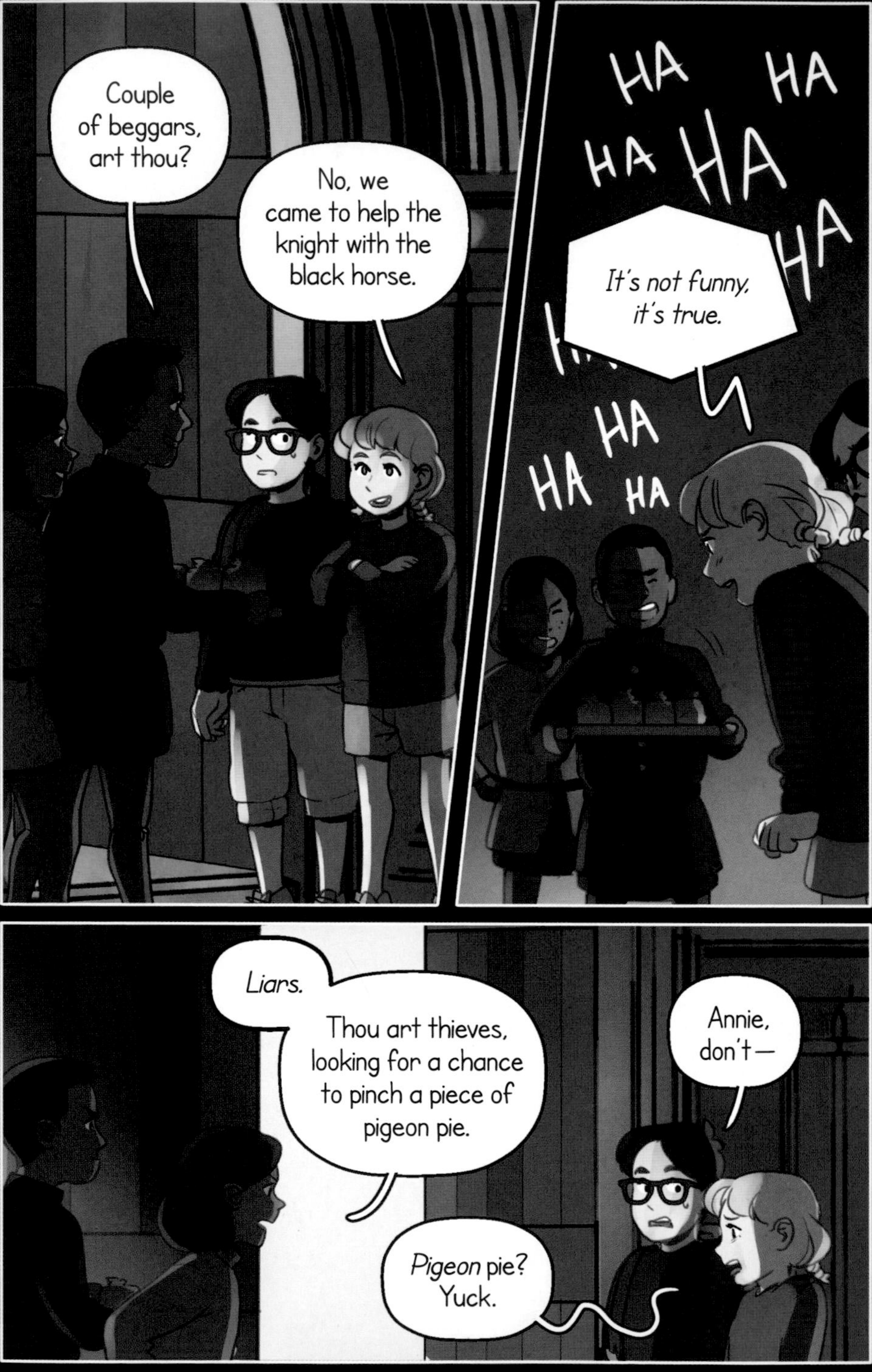
Couple of beggars, art thou?
No, we came to help the knight with the black horse.
HA HA HA HA HA HA HA HA HA
It's not funny, it's true.
Liars.
Thou art thieves, looking for a chance to pinch a piece of pigeon pie.
Annie, don't—
Pigeon pie? Yuck.

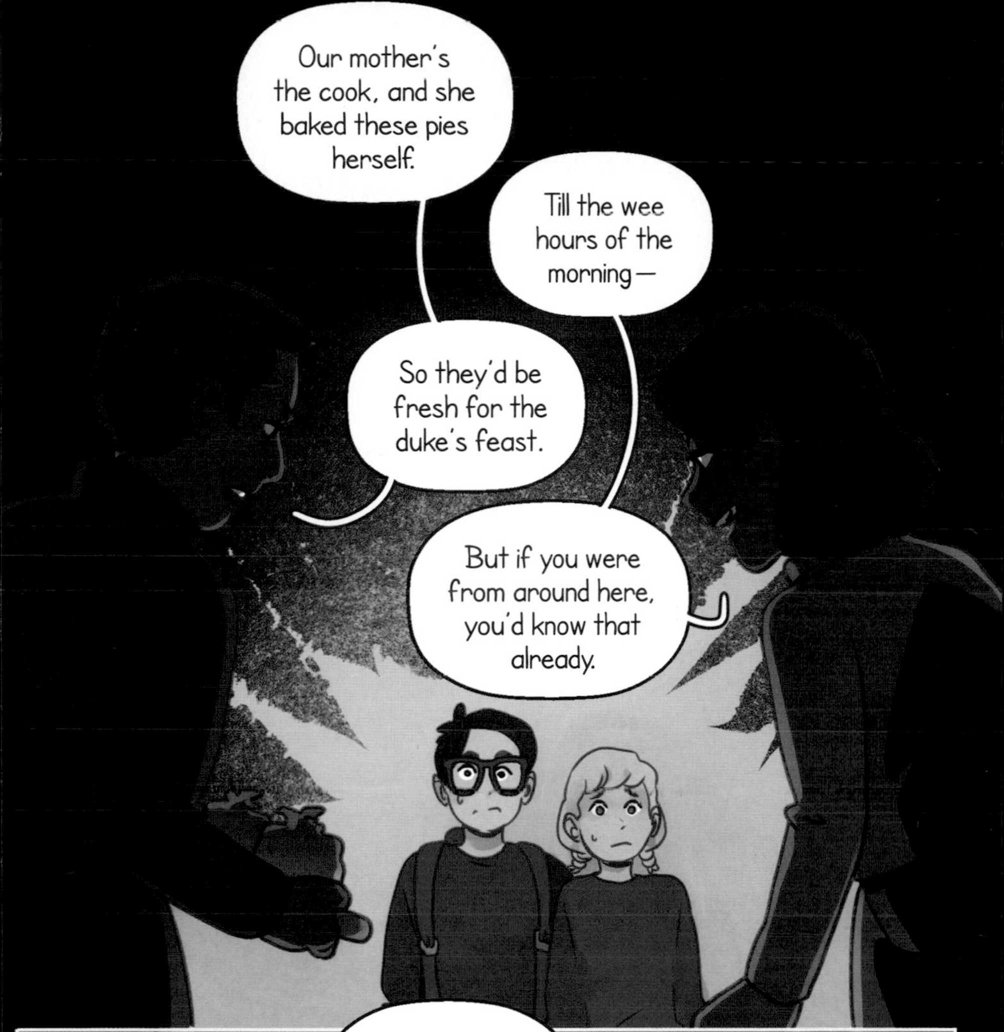

Our mother's the cook, and she baked these pies herself.
Till the wee hours of the morning—
So they'd be fresh for the duke's feast.
But if you were from around here, you'd know that already.

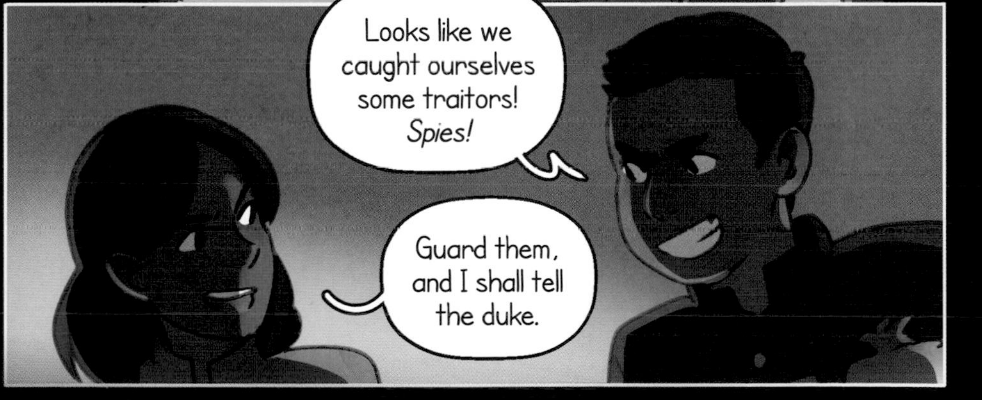

Looks like we caught ourselves some traitors! *Spies!*
Guard them, and I shall tell the duke.

No, take these and I shall go.
SHOVE
Do not!
No, I run the fastest—
PUSH!
CRASH!

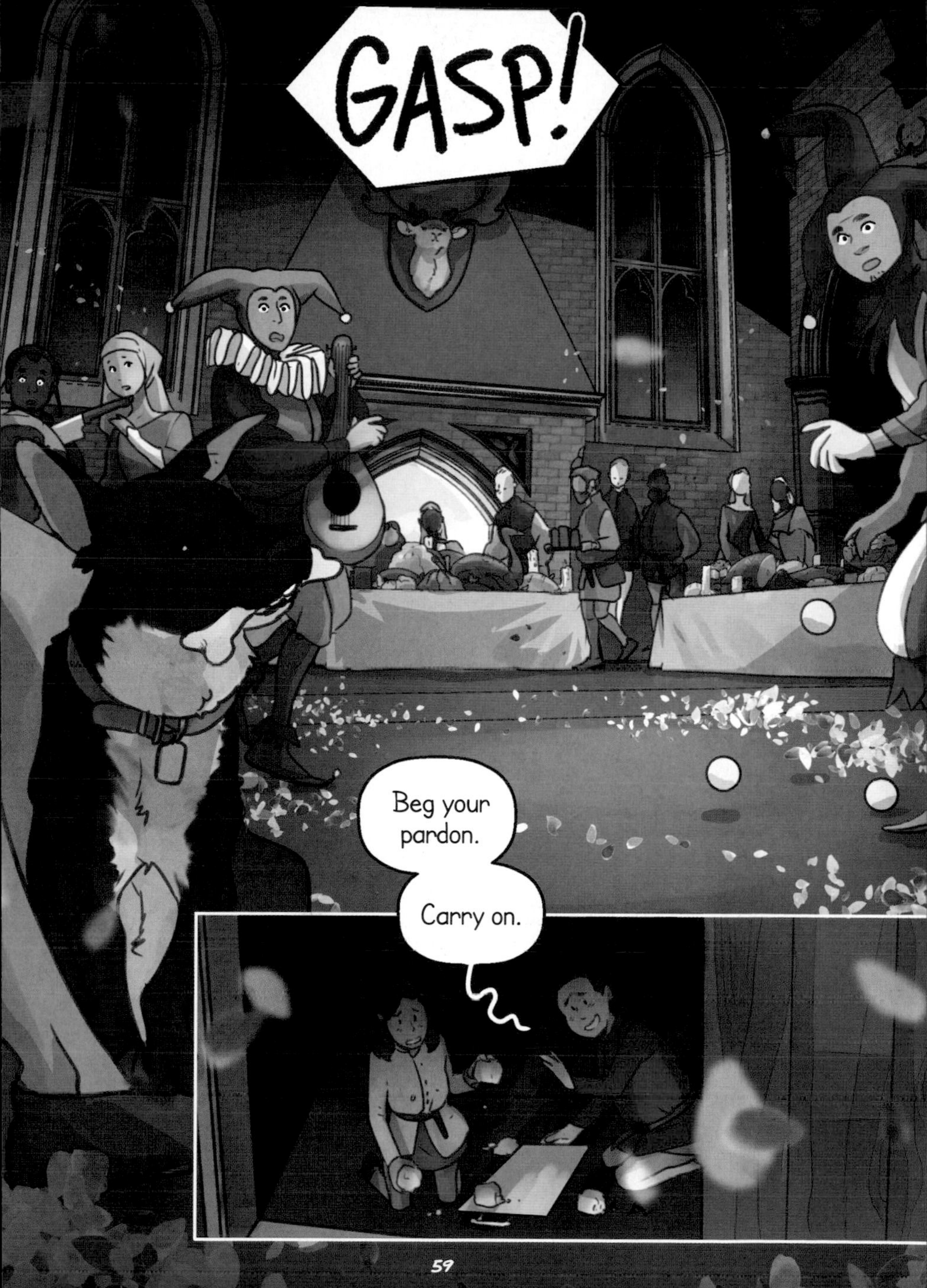
GASP!
Beg your pardon.
Carry on.

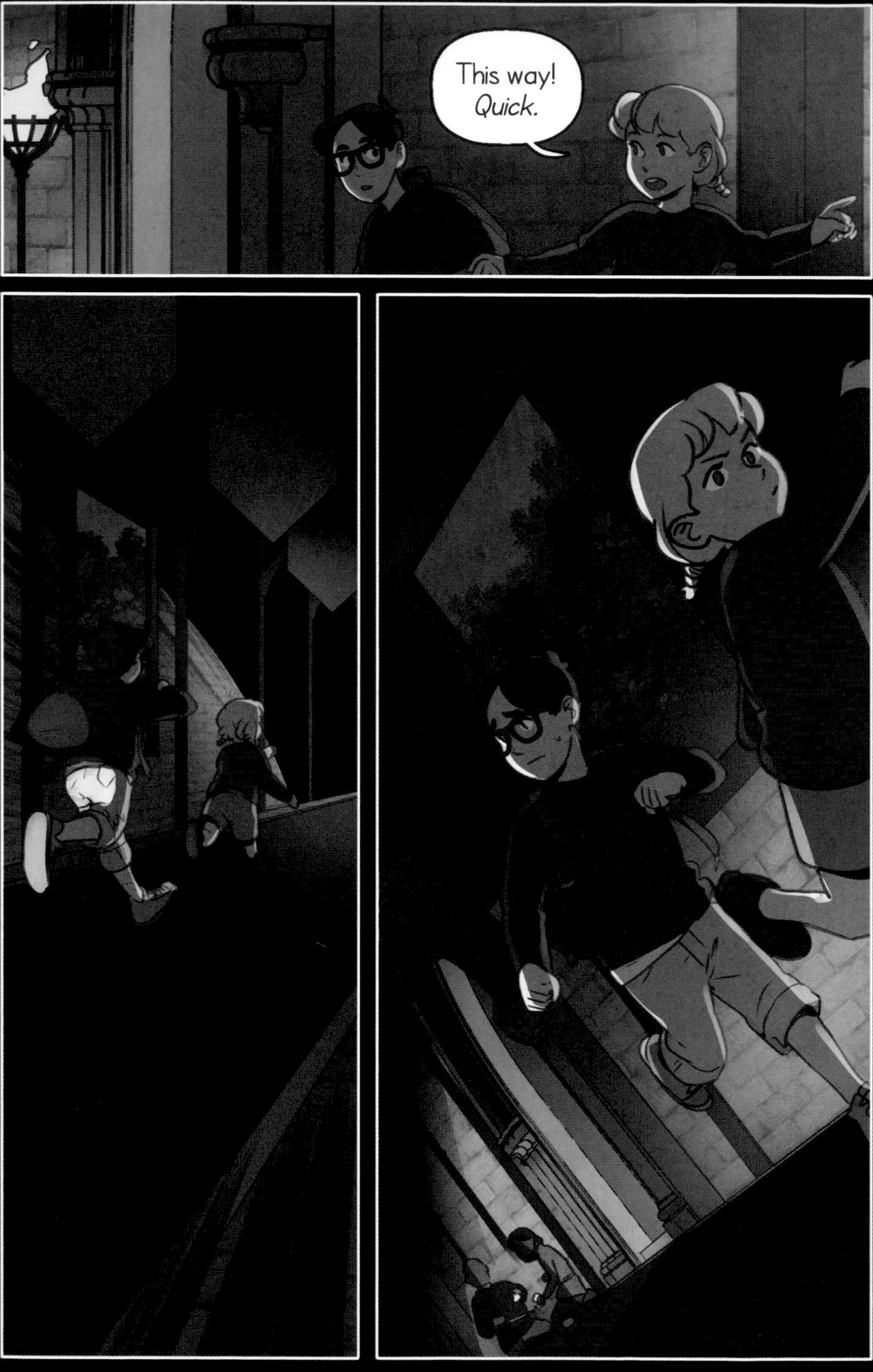
This way! Quick.

CHAPTER FIVE
Trapped

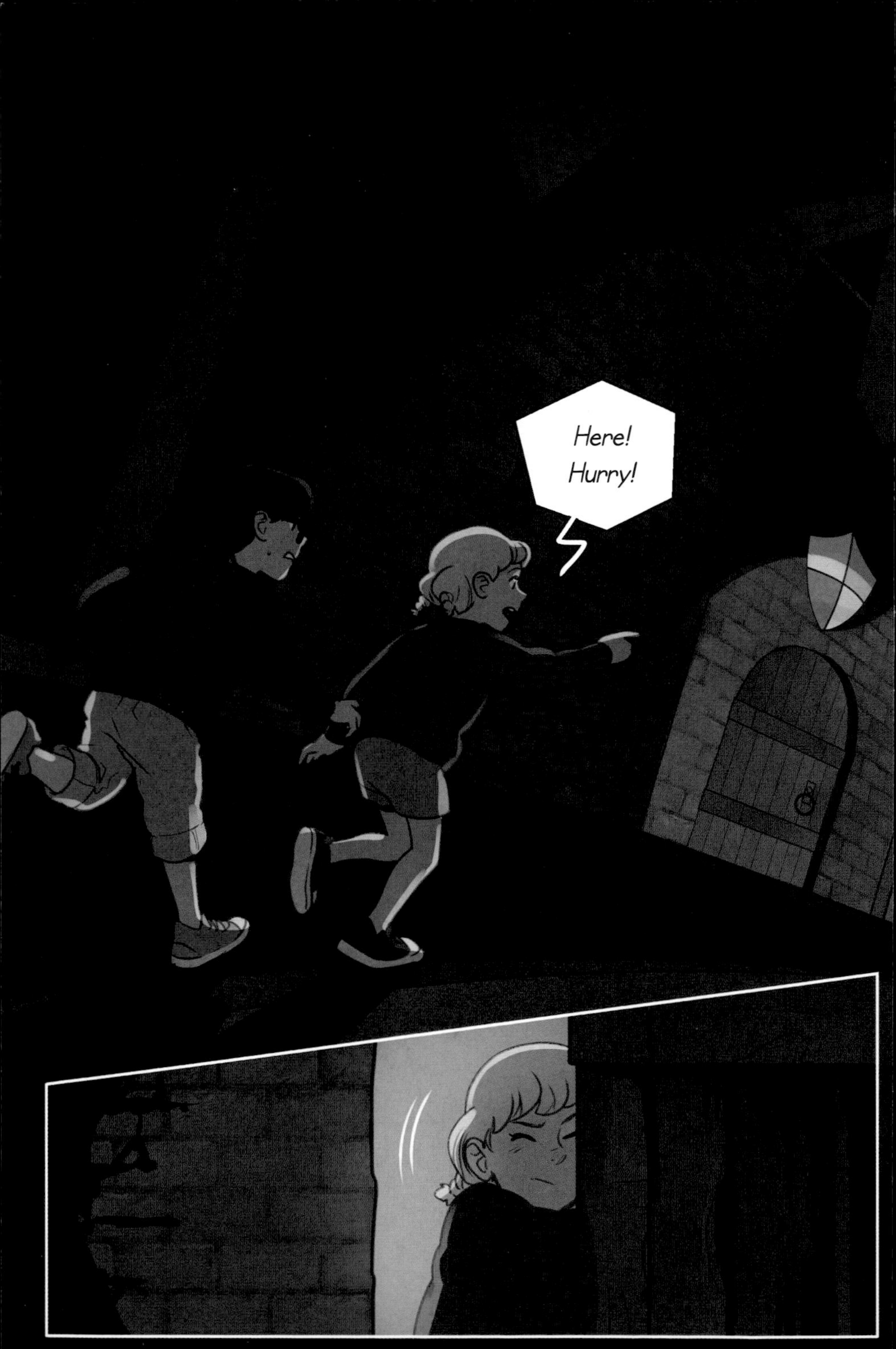
Here!
Hurry!

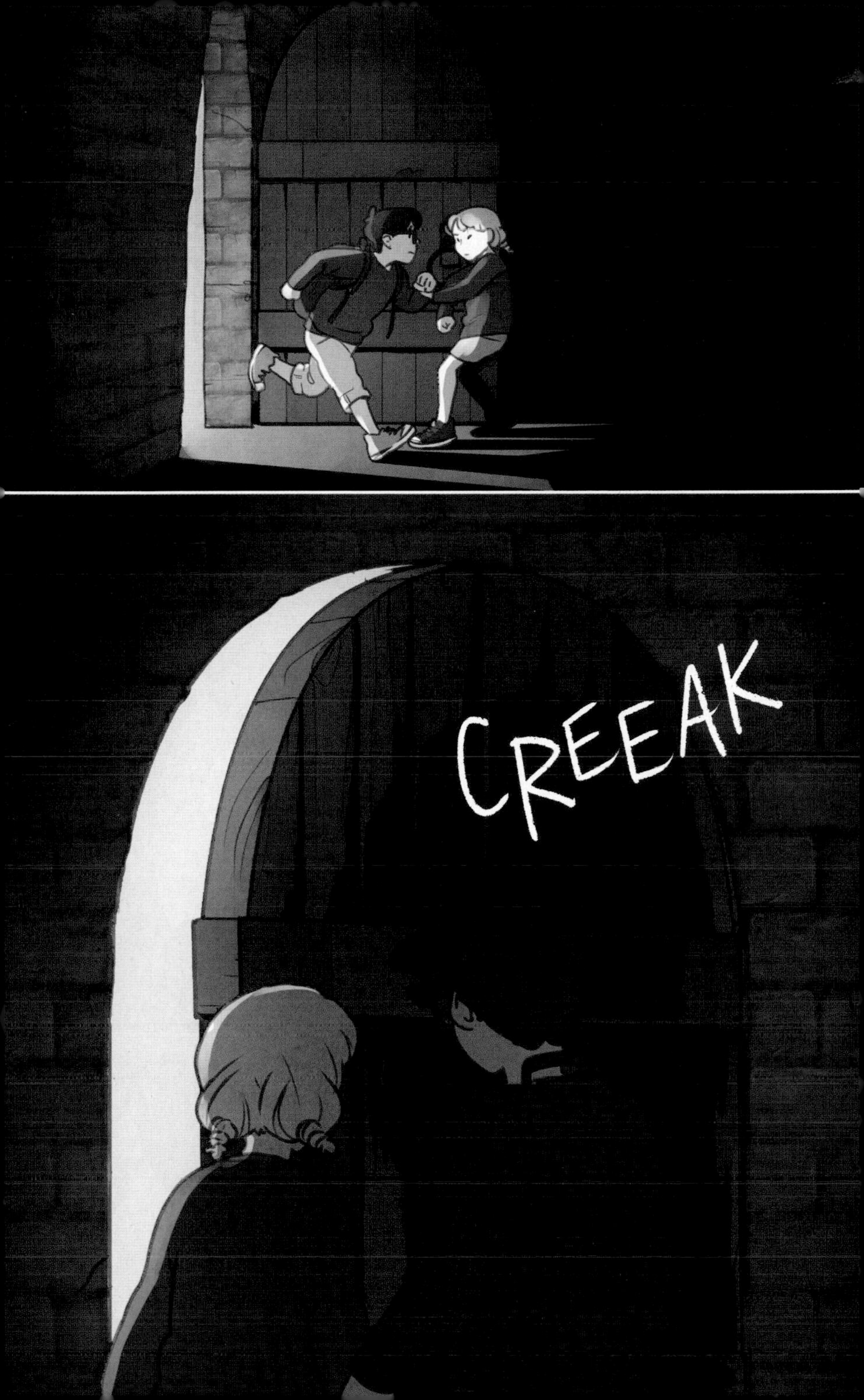
CREEAK

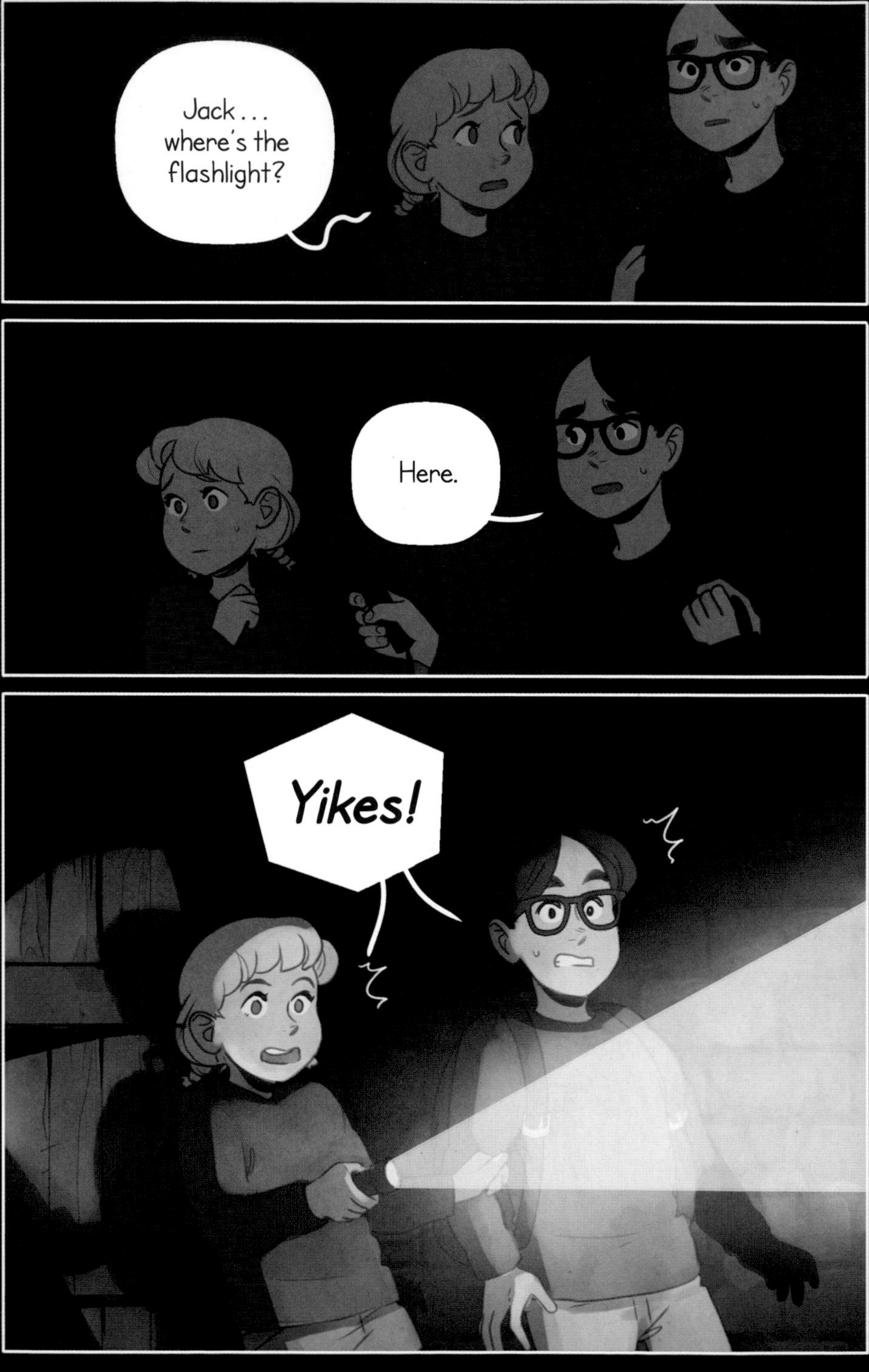

Jack . . . where's the flashlight?
Here.
Yikes!

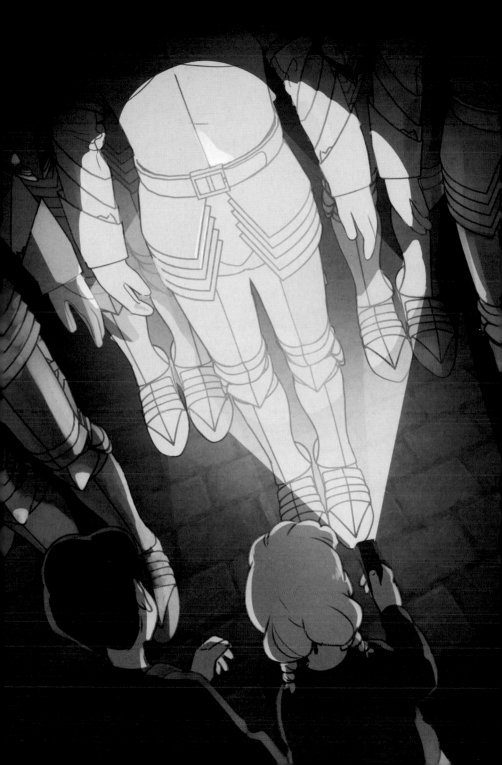

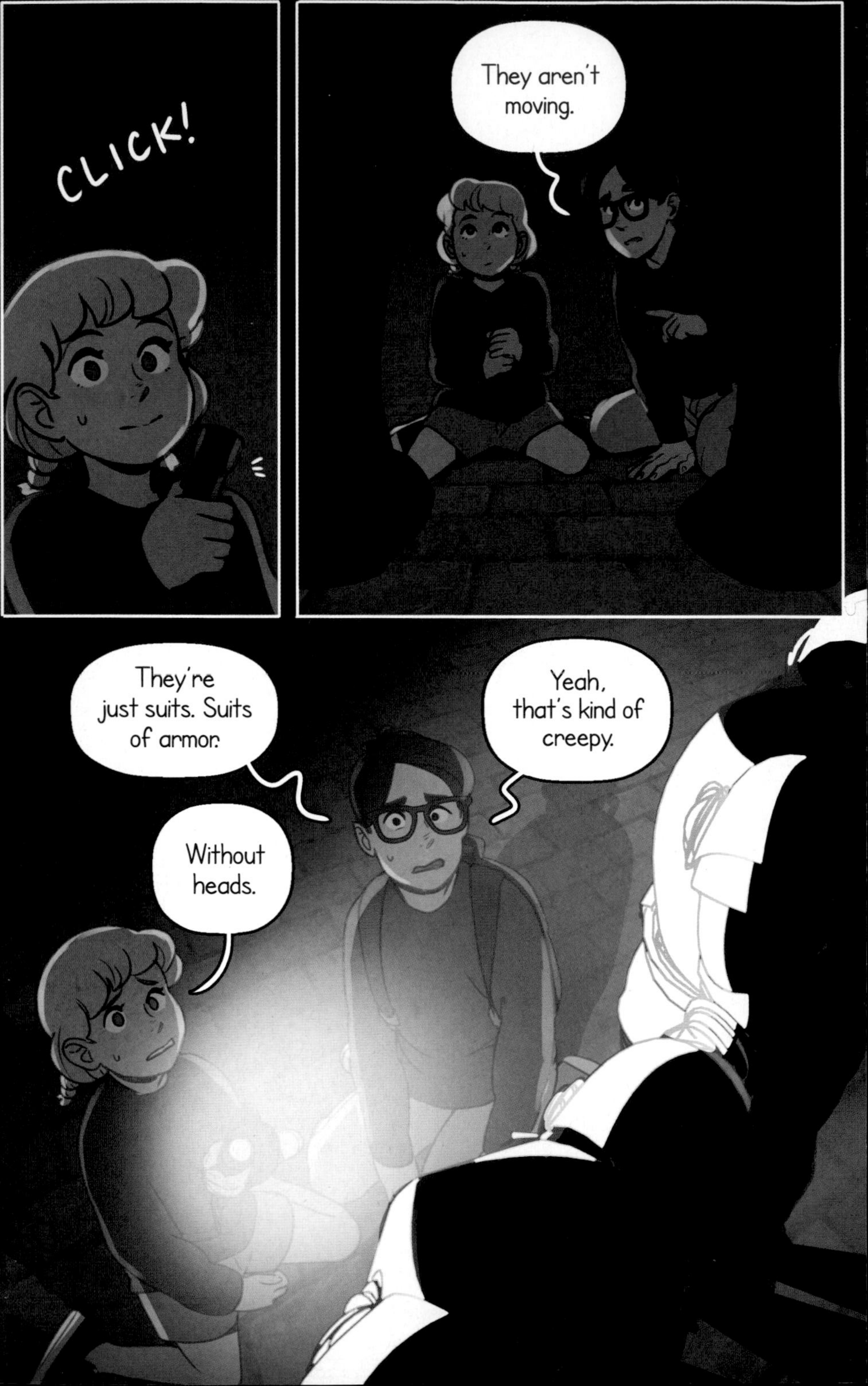
CLICK!
They aren't moving.
They're just suits. Suits of armor.
Yeah, that's kind of creepy.
Without heads.

Let me have the flashlight so I can look in the book.

Well?

It's called the armory. It's where armor and weapons are stored.

SHFF

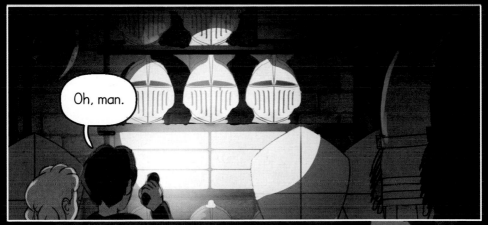

Oh, man.

THUD

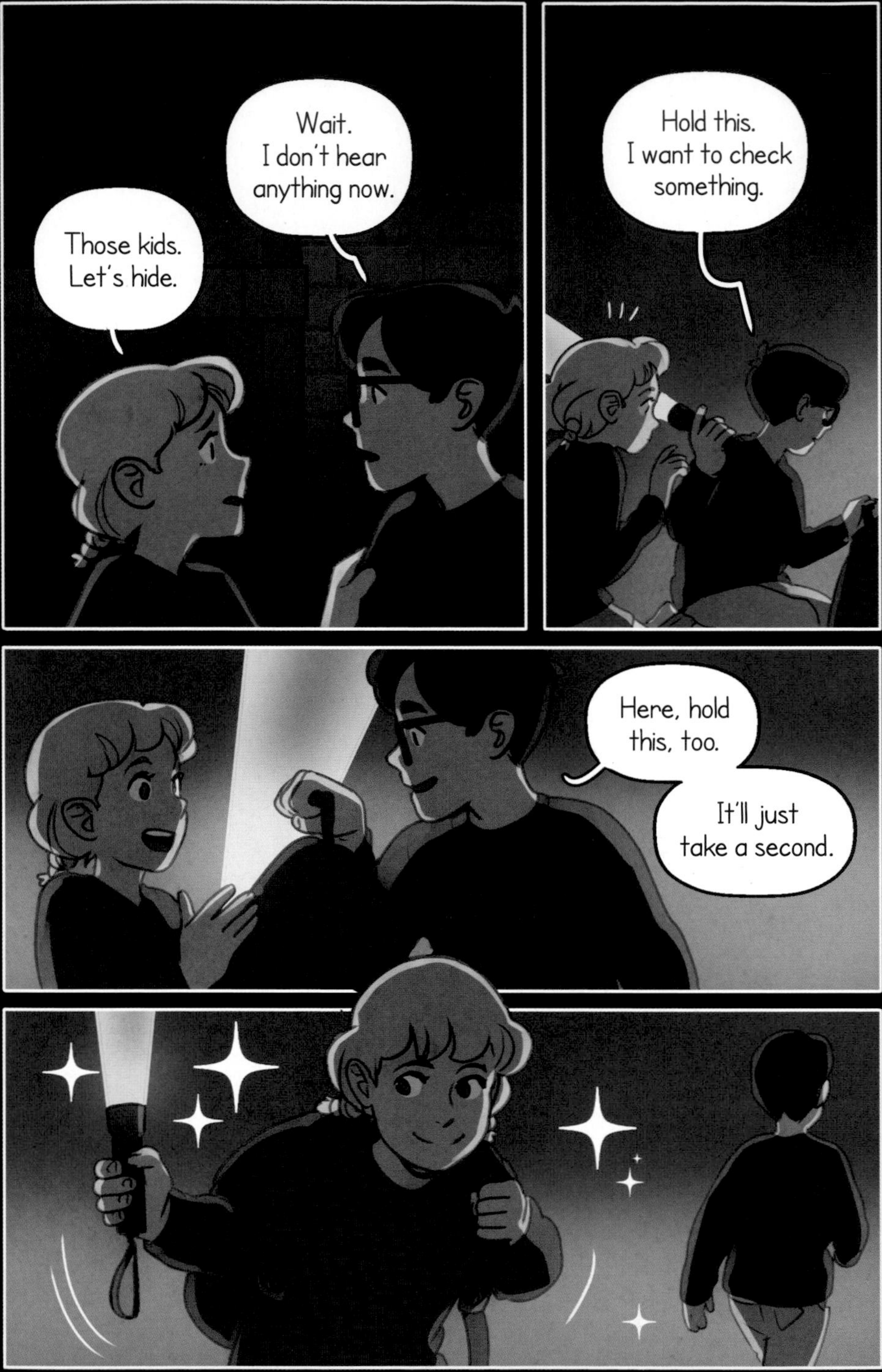
Those kids. Let's hide.
Wait. I don't hear anything now.
Hold this. I want to check something.
Here, hold this, too.
It'll just take a second.

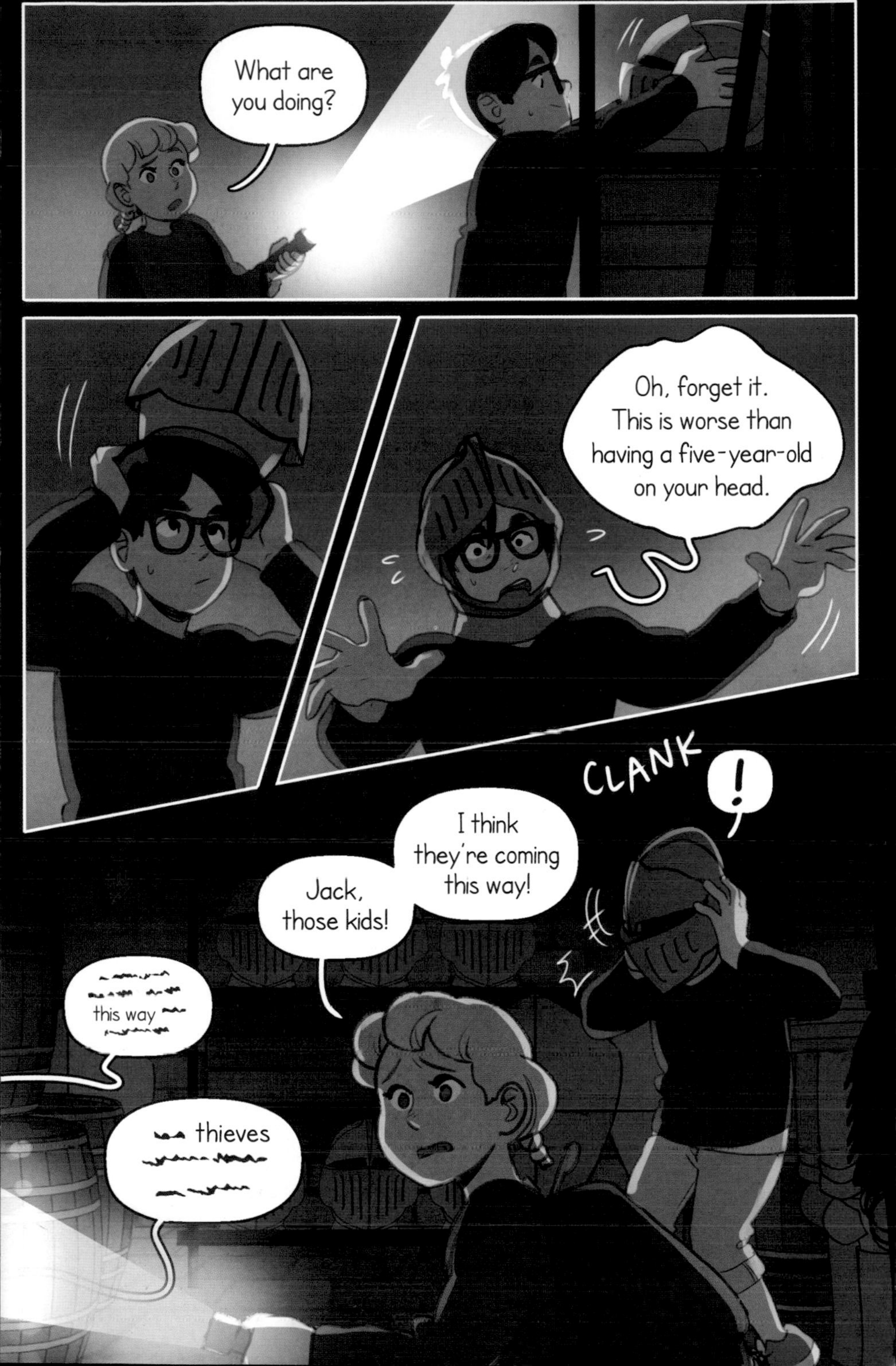

What are you doing?
Oh, forget it. This is worse than having a five-year-old on your head.
CLANK
!
Jack, those kids!
I think they're coming this way!
this way
thieves

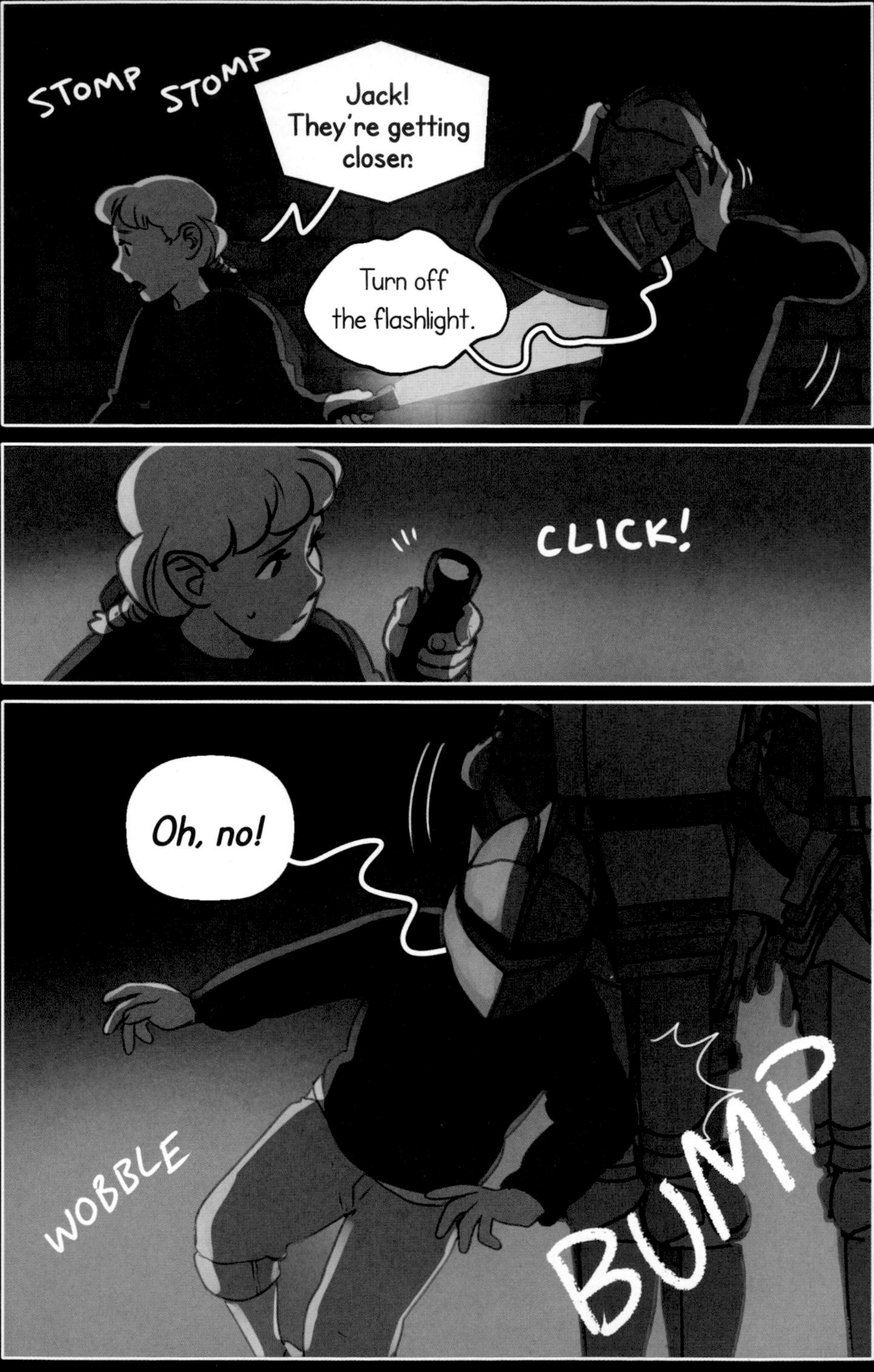
STOMP STOMP
Jack! They're getting closer.
Turn off the flashlight.
CLICK!
Oh, no!
WOBBLE
BUMP

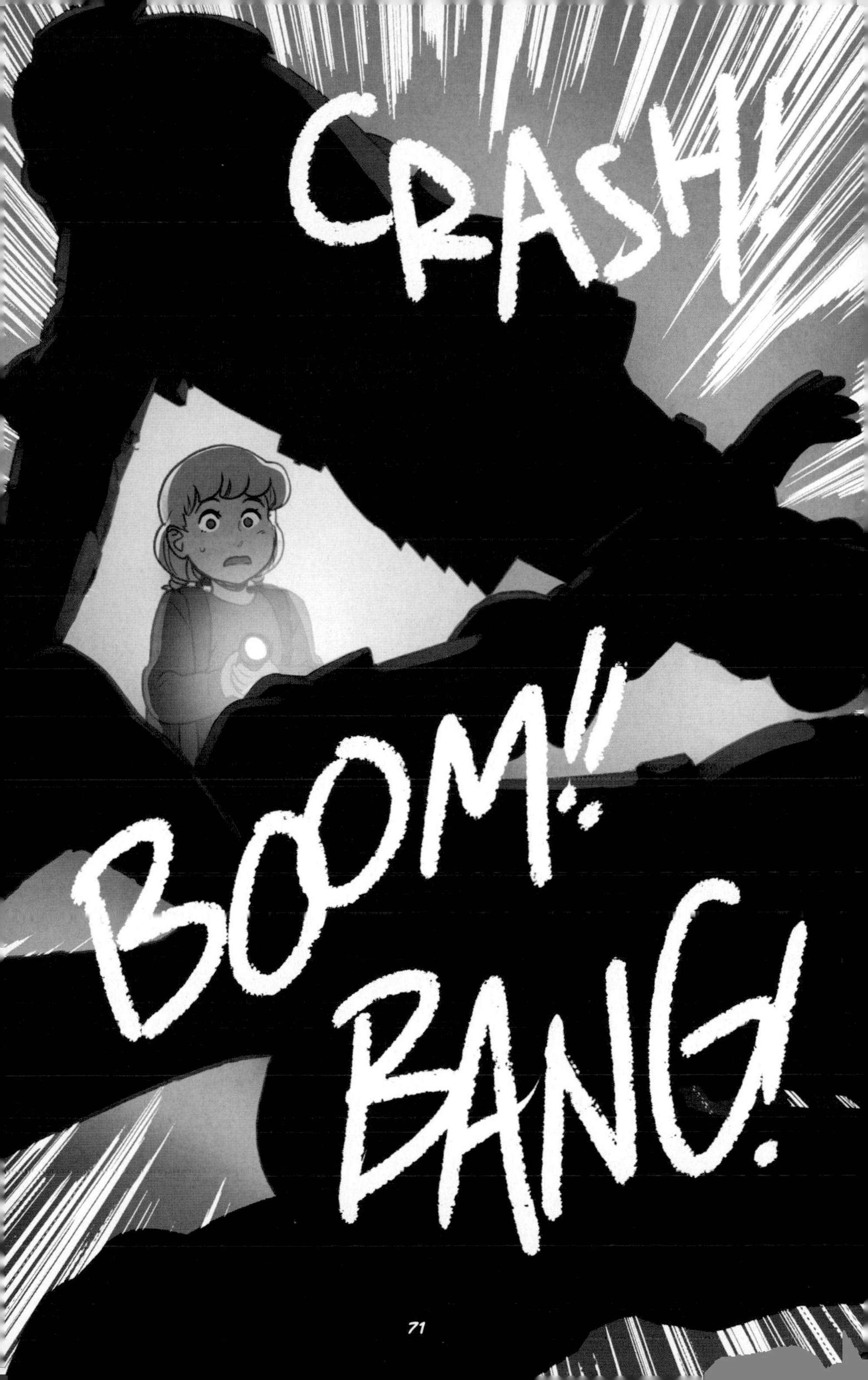
CRASH!
BOOM!
BANG!

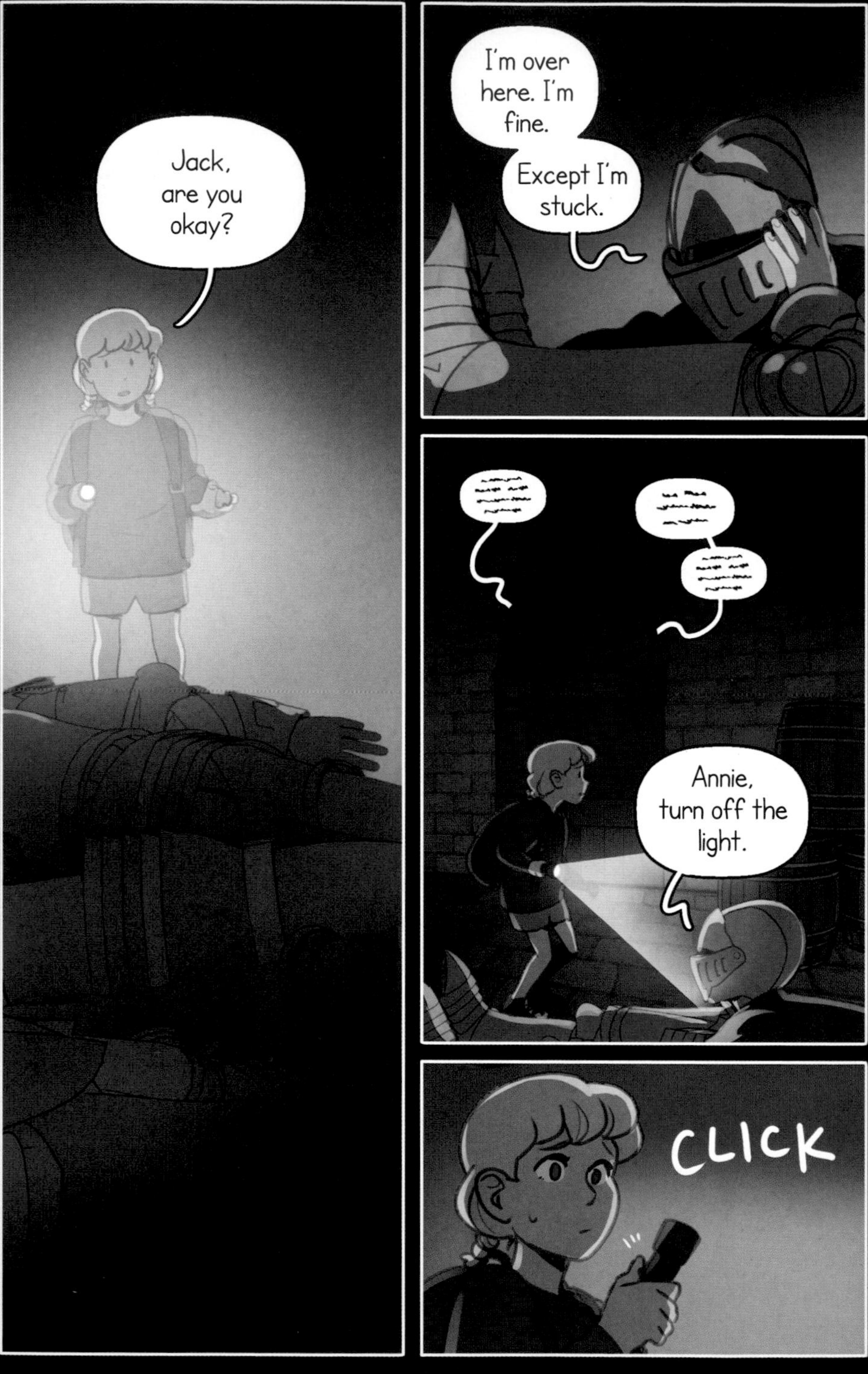
Jack, are you okay?
I'm over here. I'm fine.
Except I'm stuck.
Annie, turn off the light.
CLICK

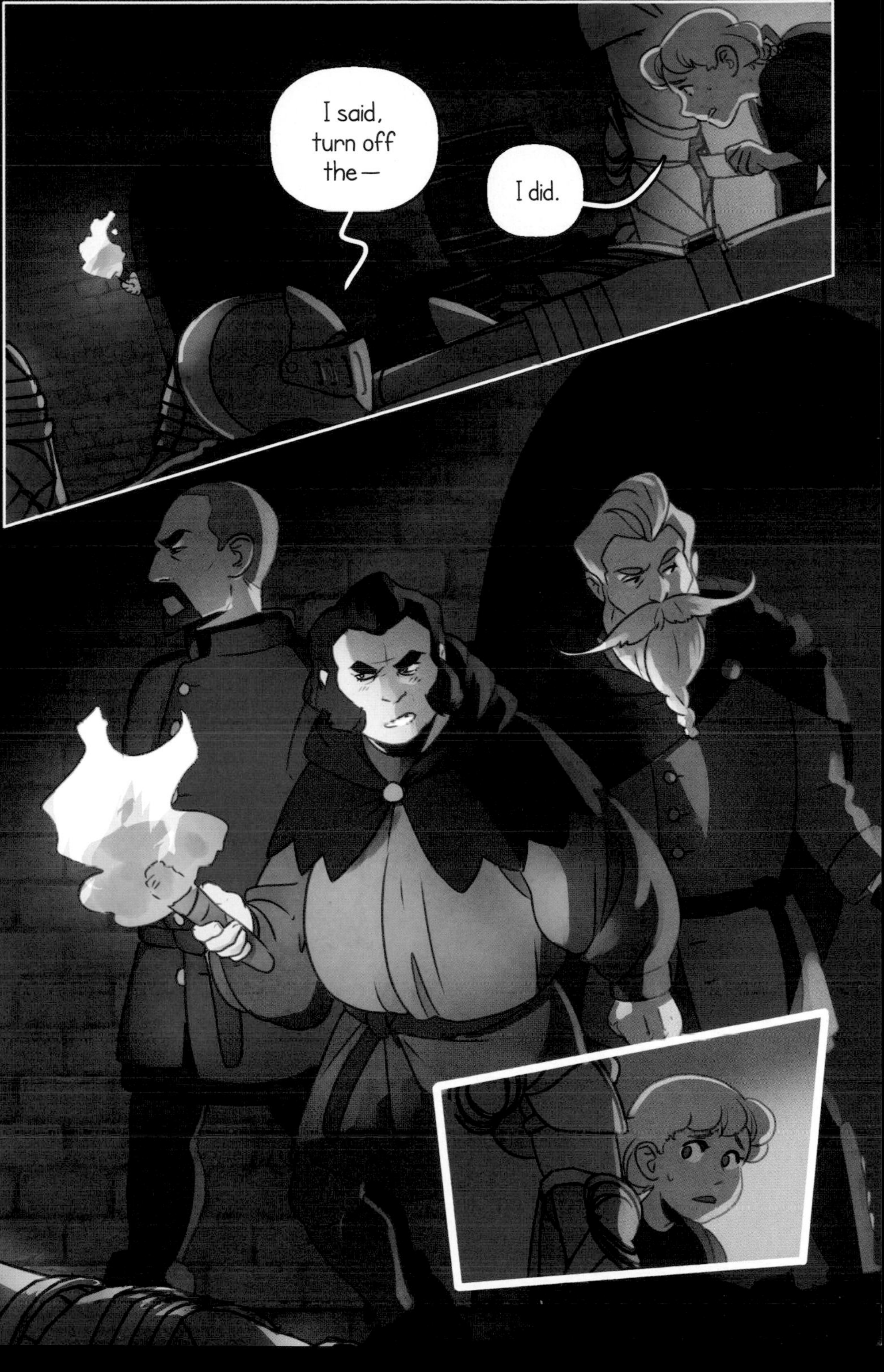
I said, turn off the—
I did.

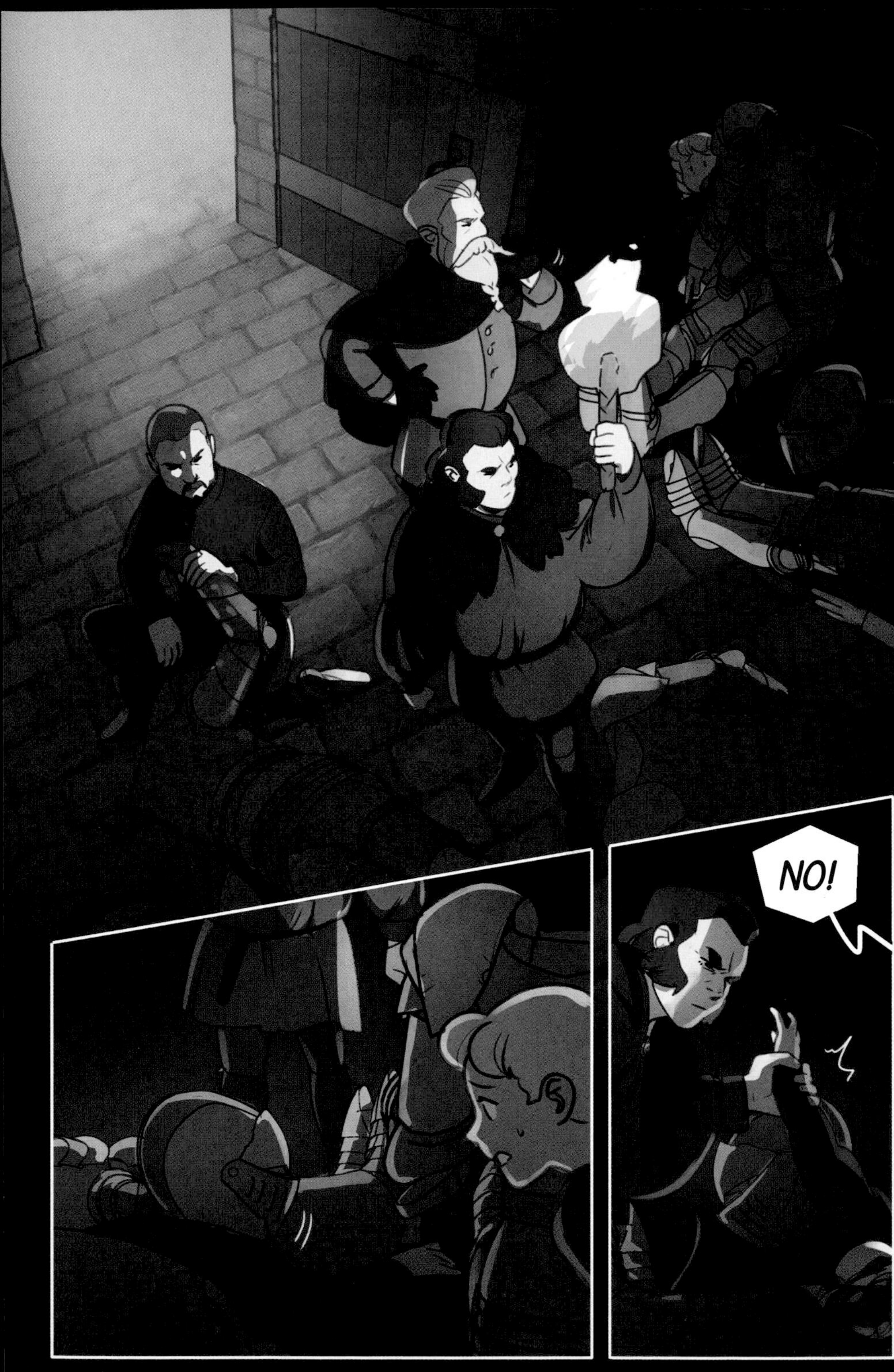
NO!

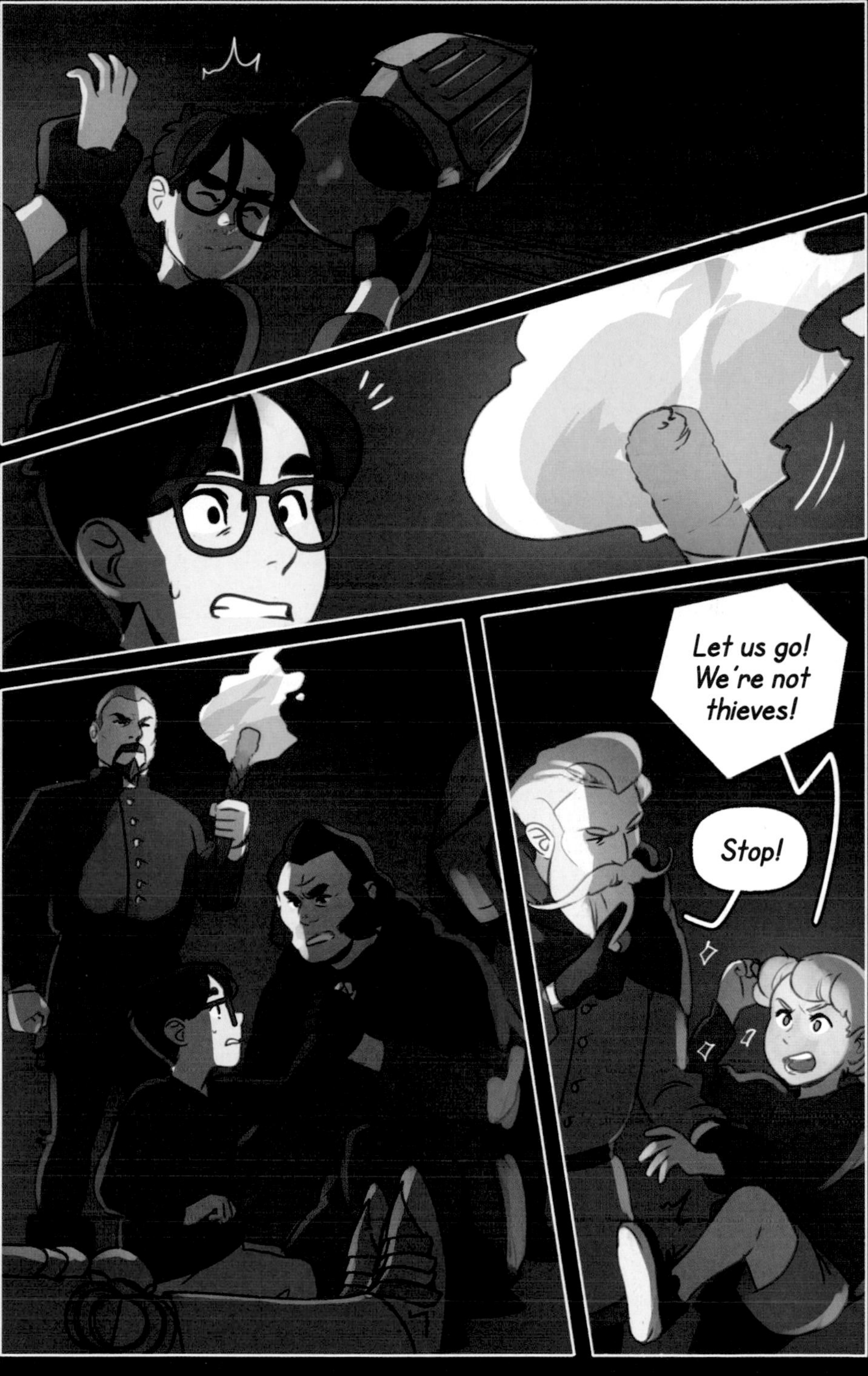
Let us go! We're not thieves!
Stop!

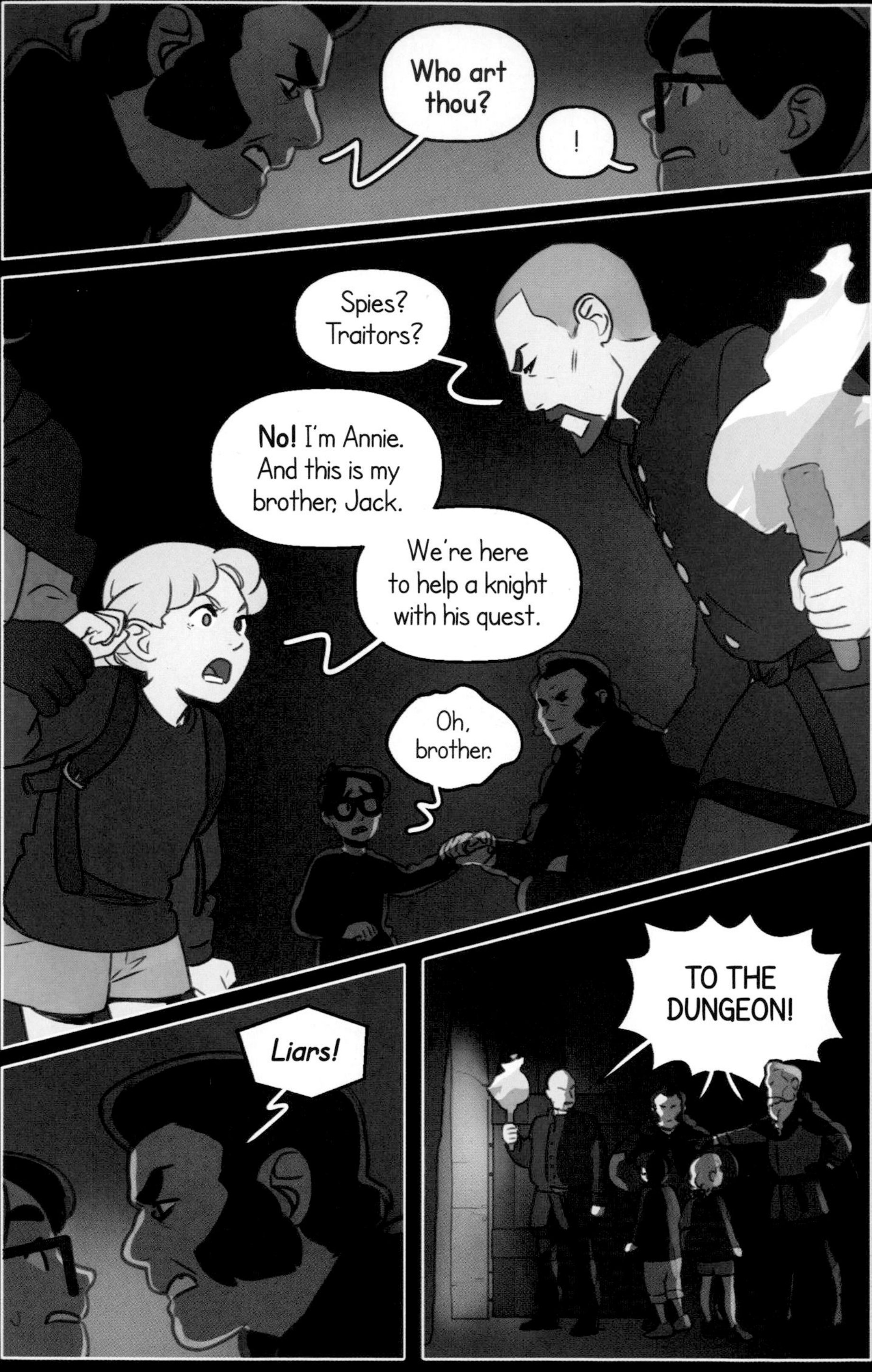
Who art thou?
!
Spies? Traitors?
No! I'm Annie. And this is my brother, Jack.
We're here to help a knight with his quest.
Oh, brother.
Liars!
TO THE DUNGEON!

CHAPTER SIX
The Dungeon

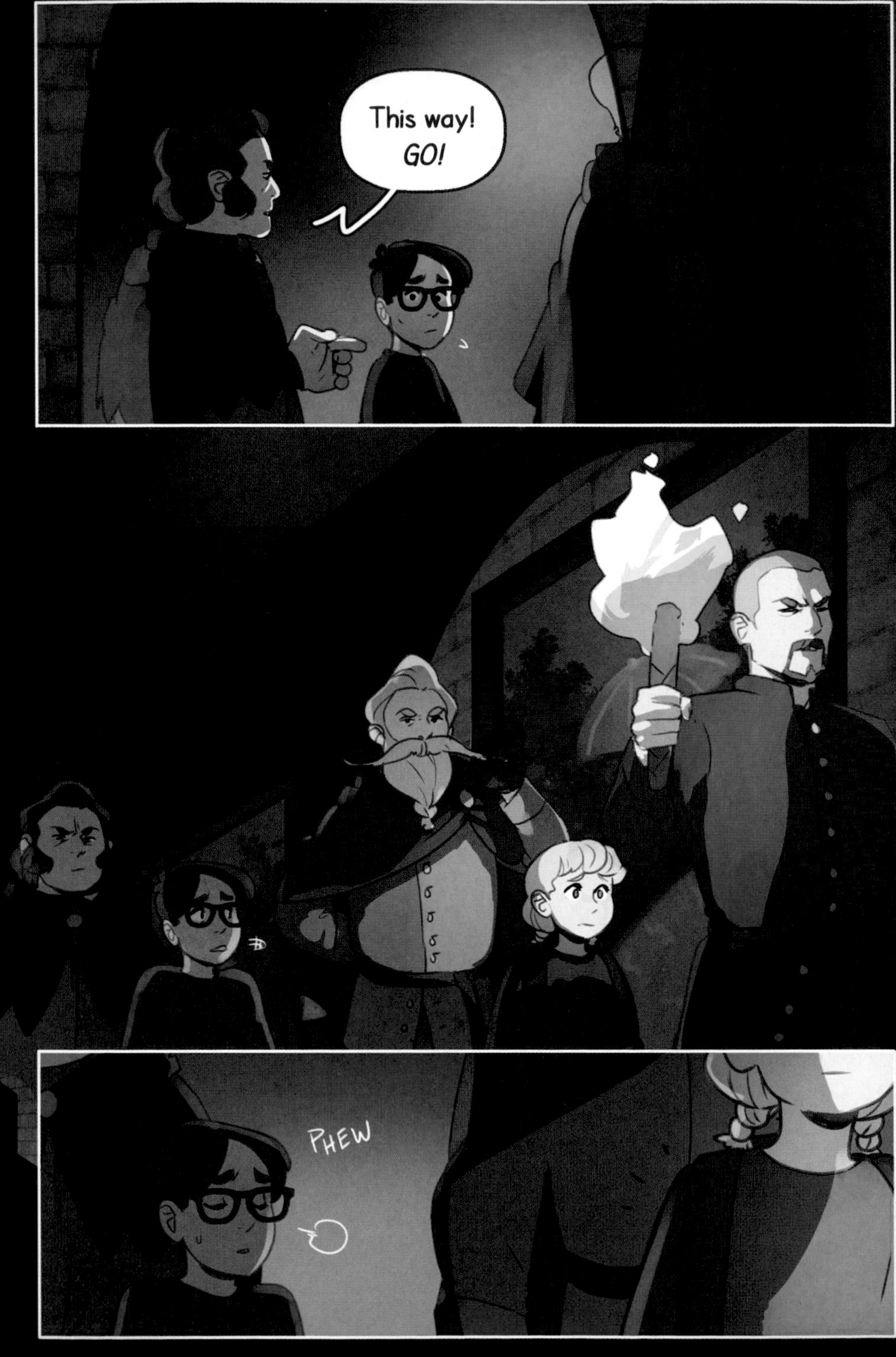
This way!
GO!
PHEW

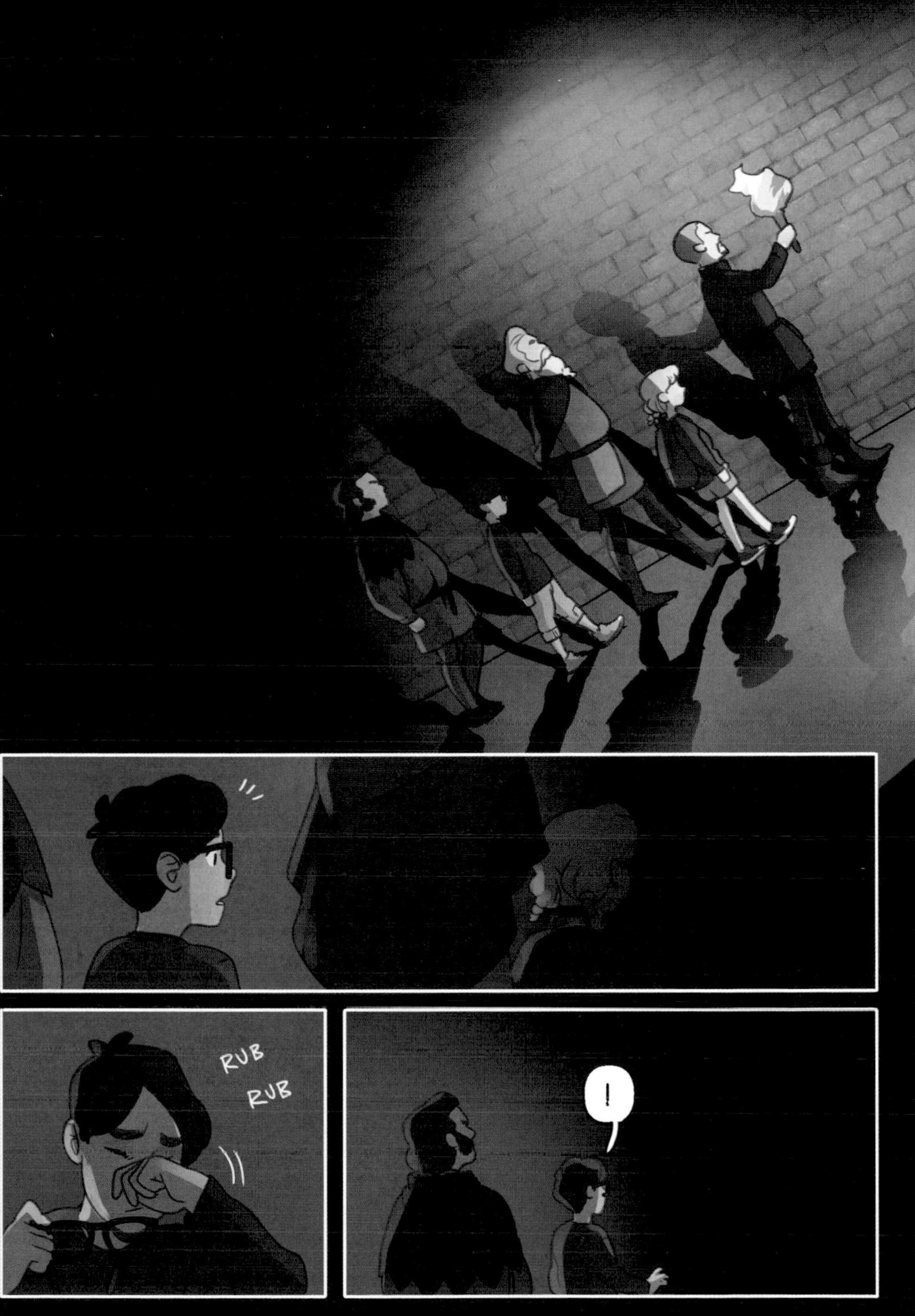
RUB
RUB
!

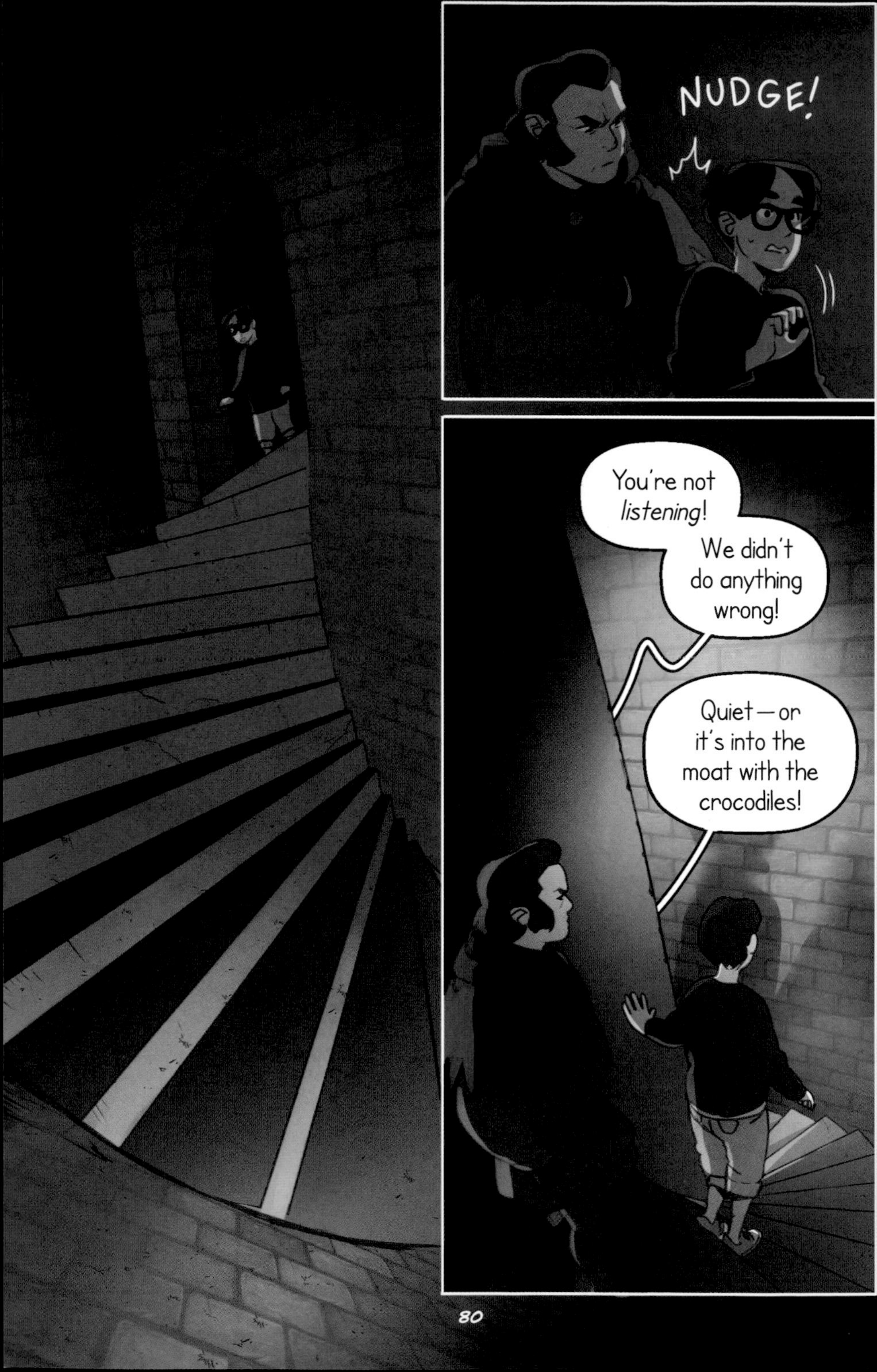
NUDGE!
You're not *listening*!
We didn't do anything wrong!
Quiet—or it's into the moat with the crocodiles!

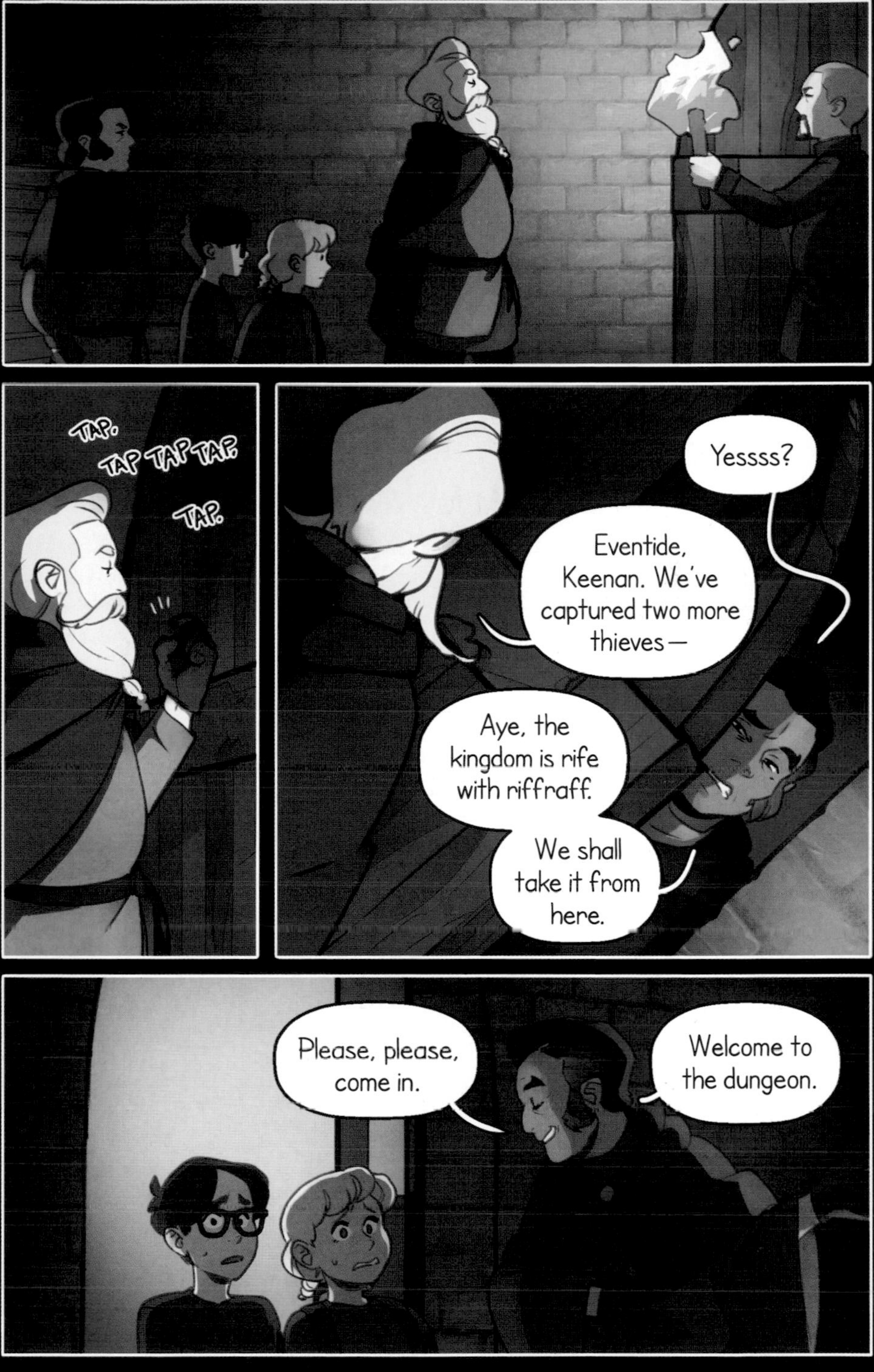
TAP.
TAP TAP TAP.
TAP.
Yessss?
Eventide, Keenan. We've captured two more thieves—
Aye, the kingdom is rife with riffraff.
We shall take it from here.
Please, please, come in.
Welcome to the dungeon.

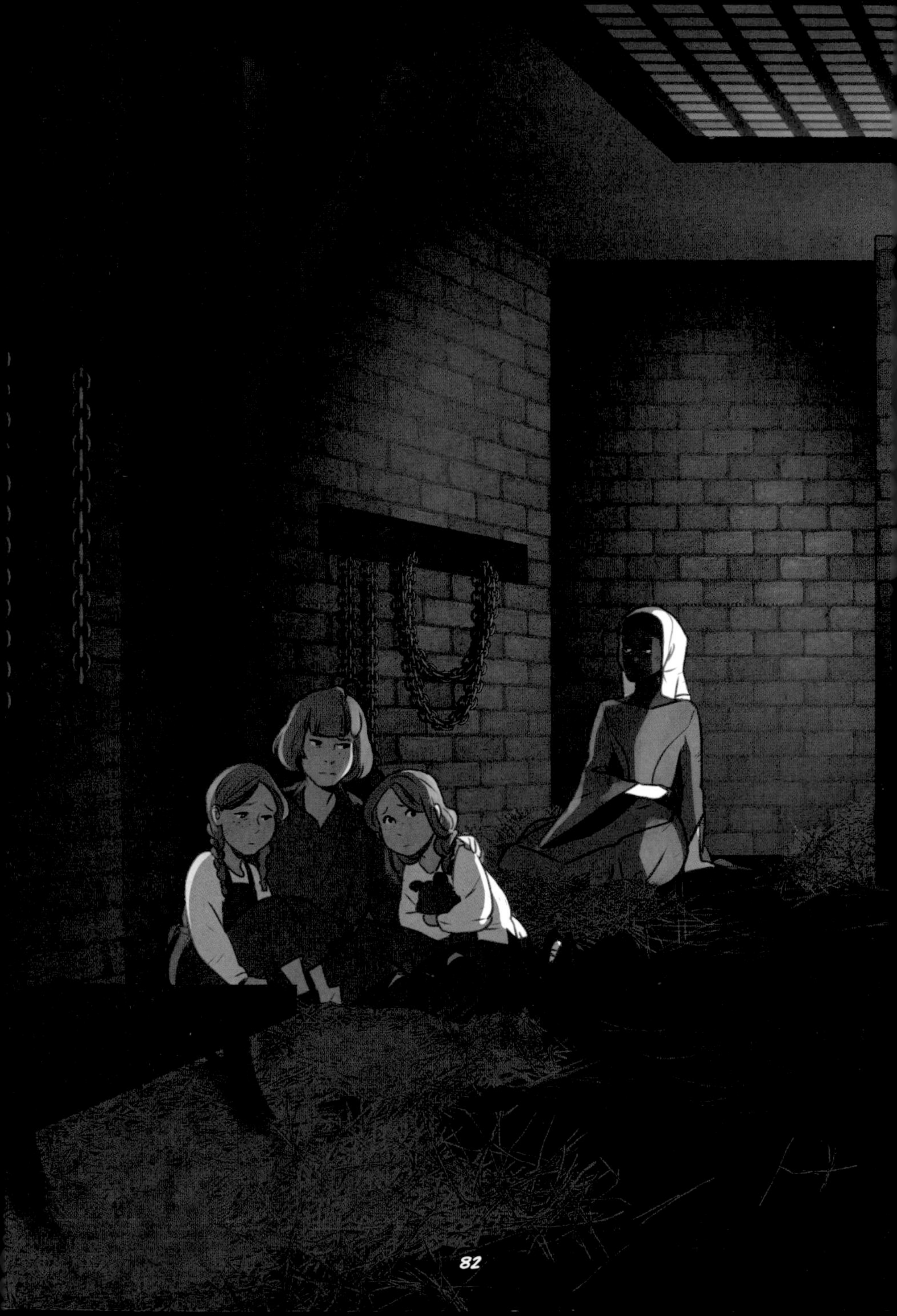

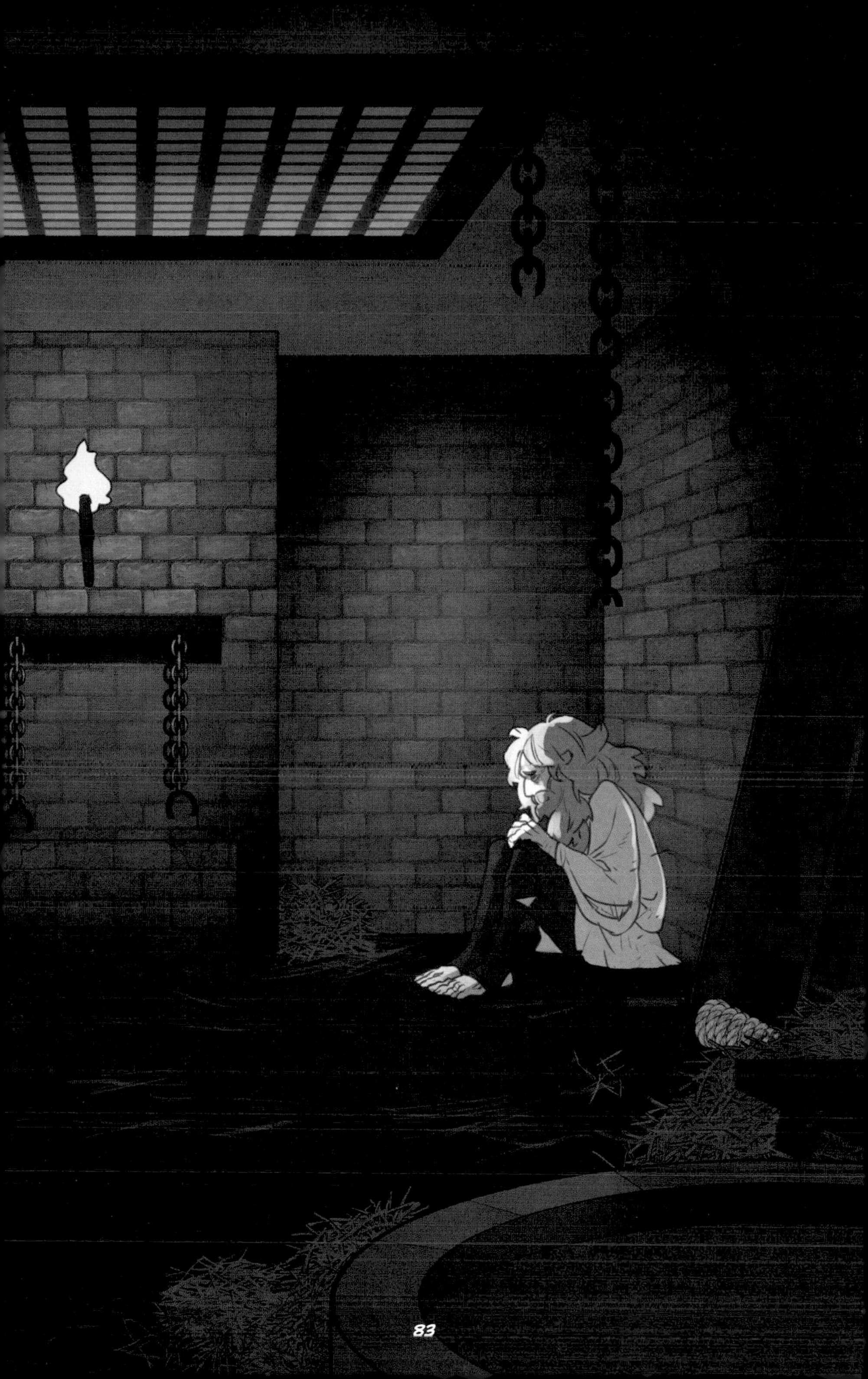

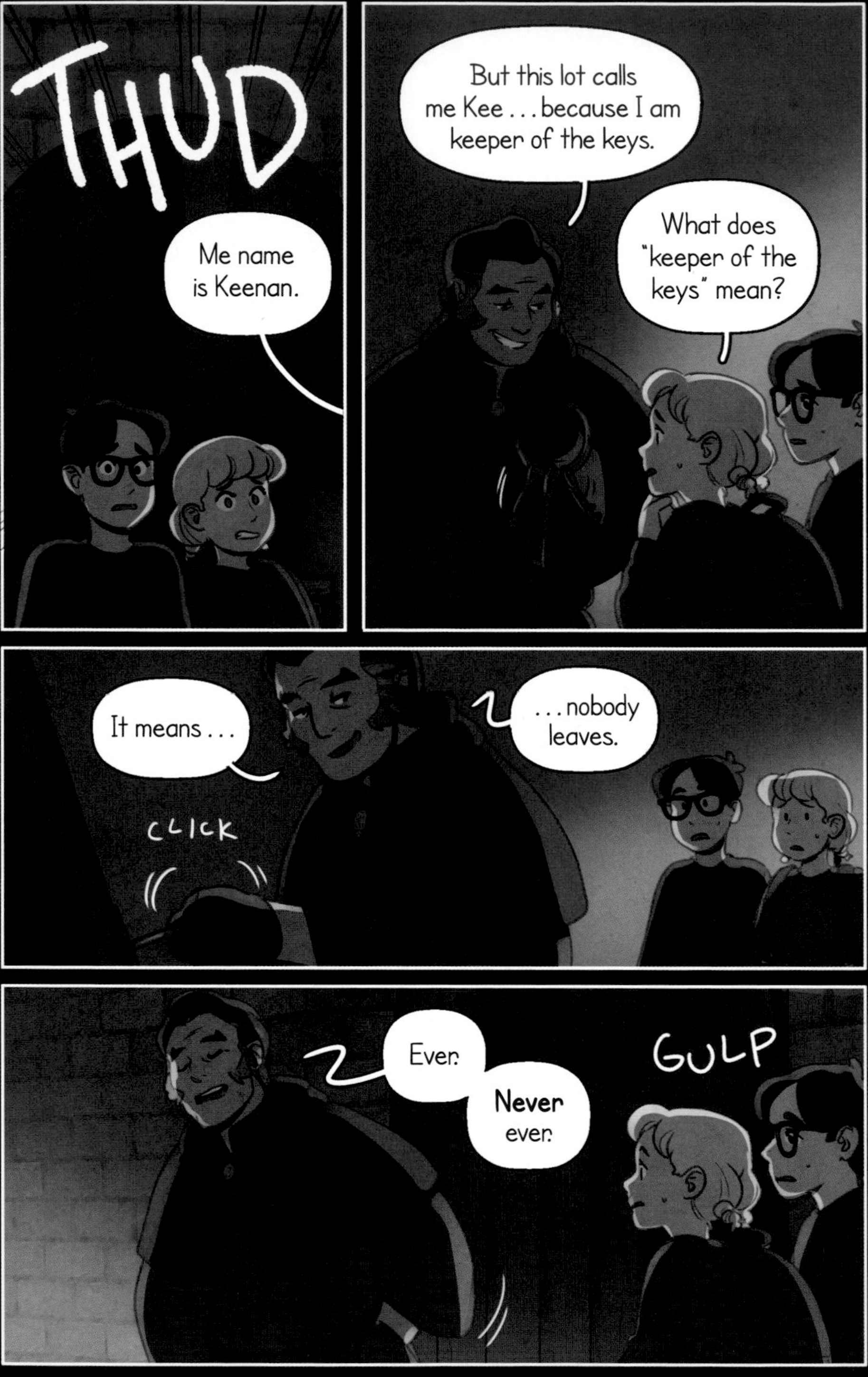
THUD
Me name is Keenan.
But this lot calls me Kee . . . because I am keeper of the keys.
What does "keeper of the keys" mean?
It means . . .
CLICK
. . . nobody leaves.
Ever.
Never ever.
GULP

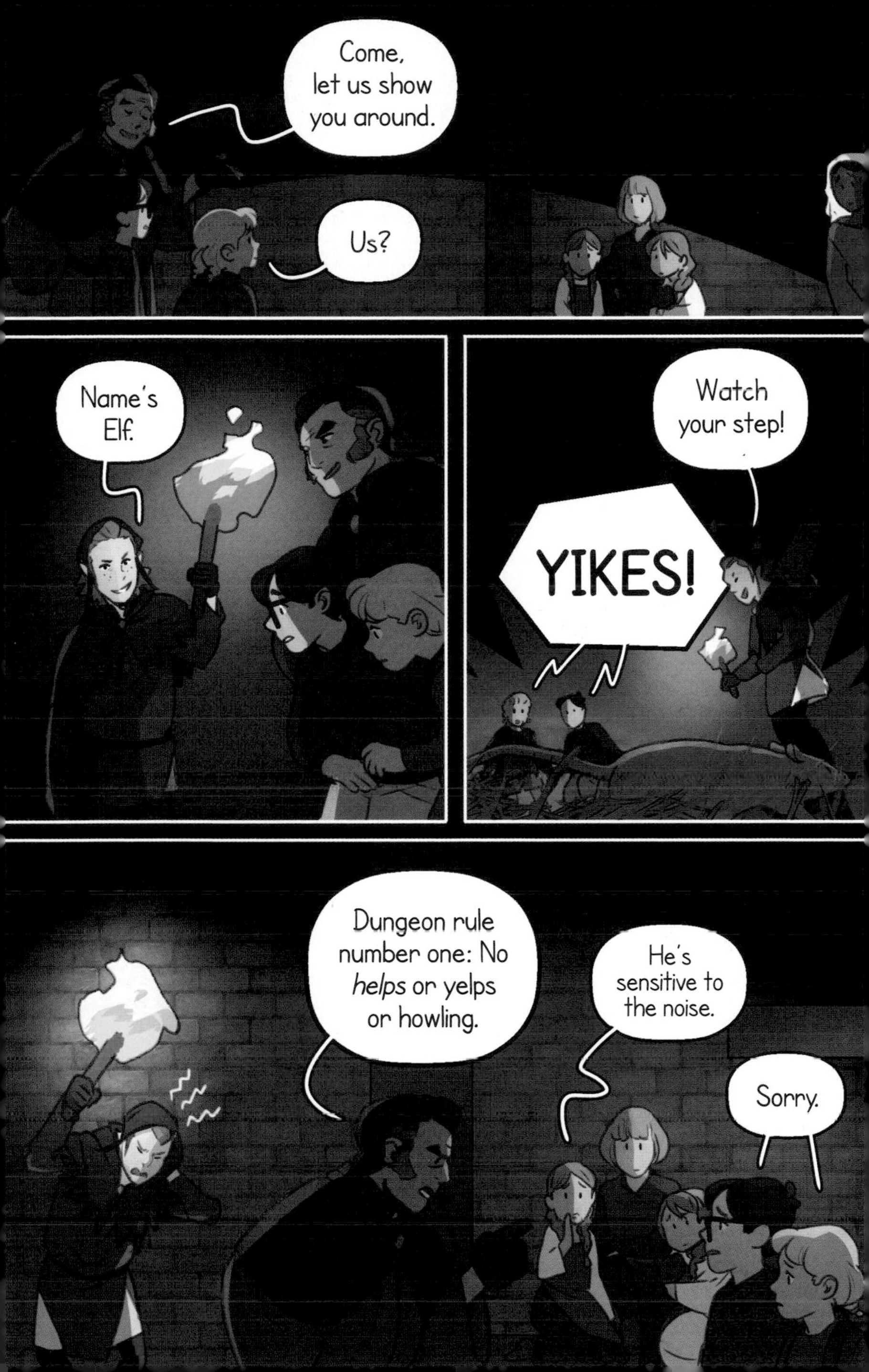
Come, let us show you around.
Us?
Name's Elf.
Watch your step!
YIKES!
Dungeon rule number one: No *helps* or yelps or howling.
He's sensitive to the noise.
Sorry.

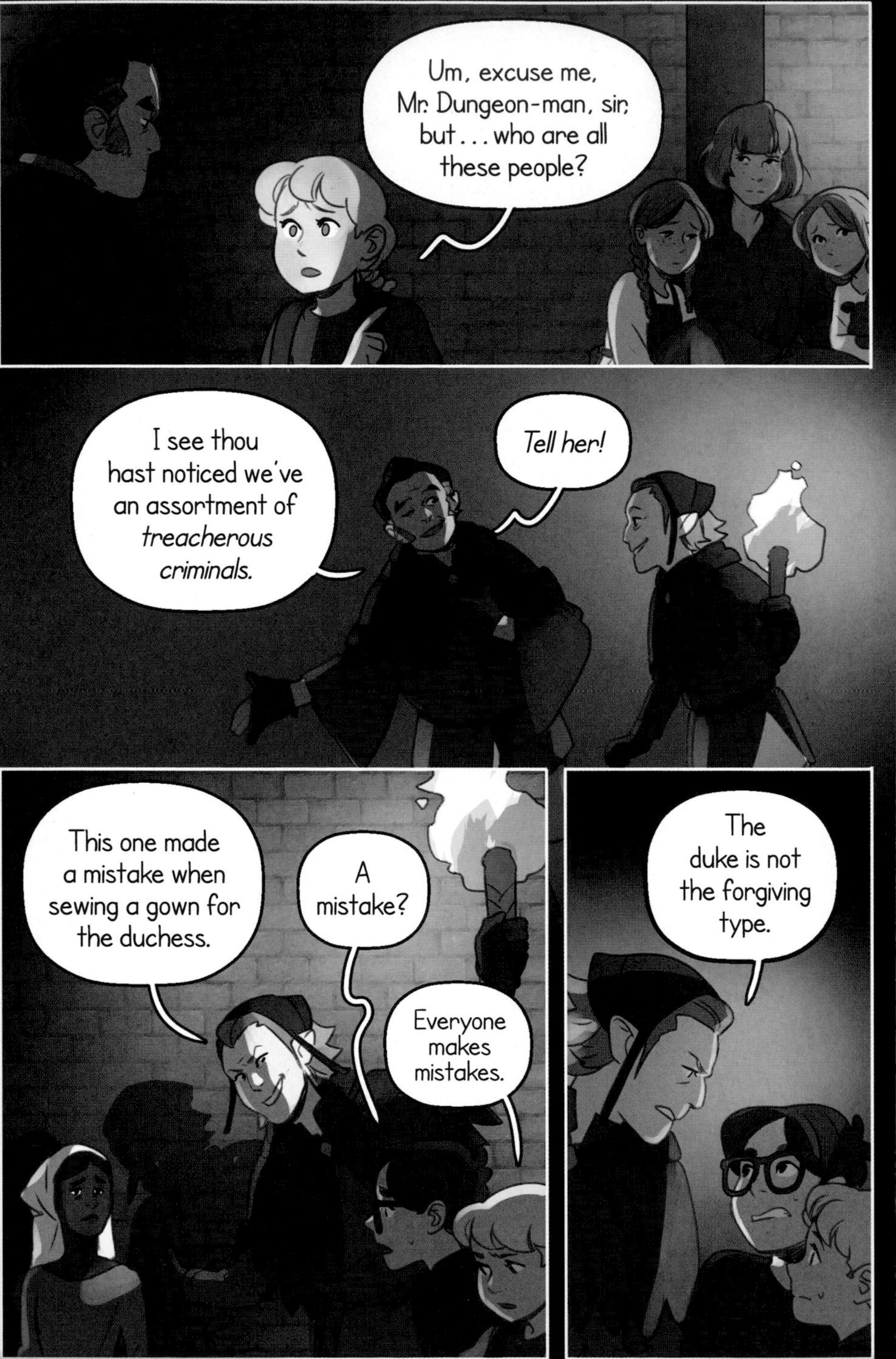
Um, excuse me, Mr. Dungeon-man, sir, but . . . who are all these people?
I see thou hast noticed we've an assortment of *treacherous criminals.*
Tell her!
This one made a mistake when sewing a gown for the duchess.
A mistake?
Everyone makes mistakes.
The duke is not the forgiving type.

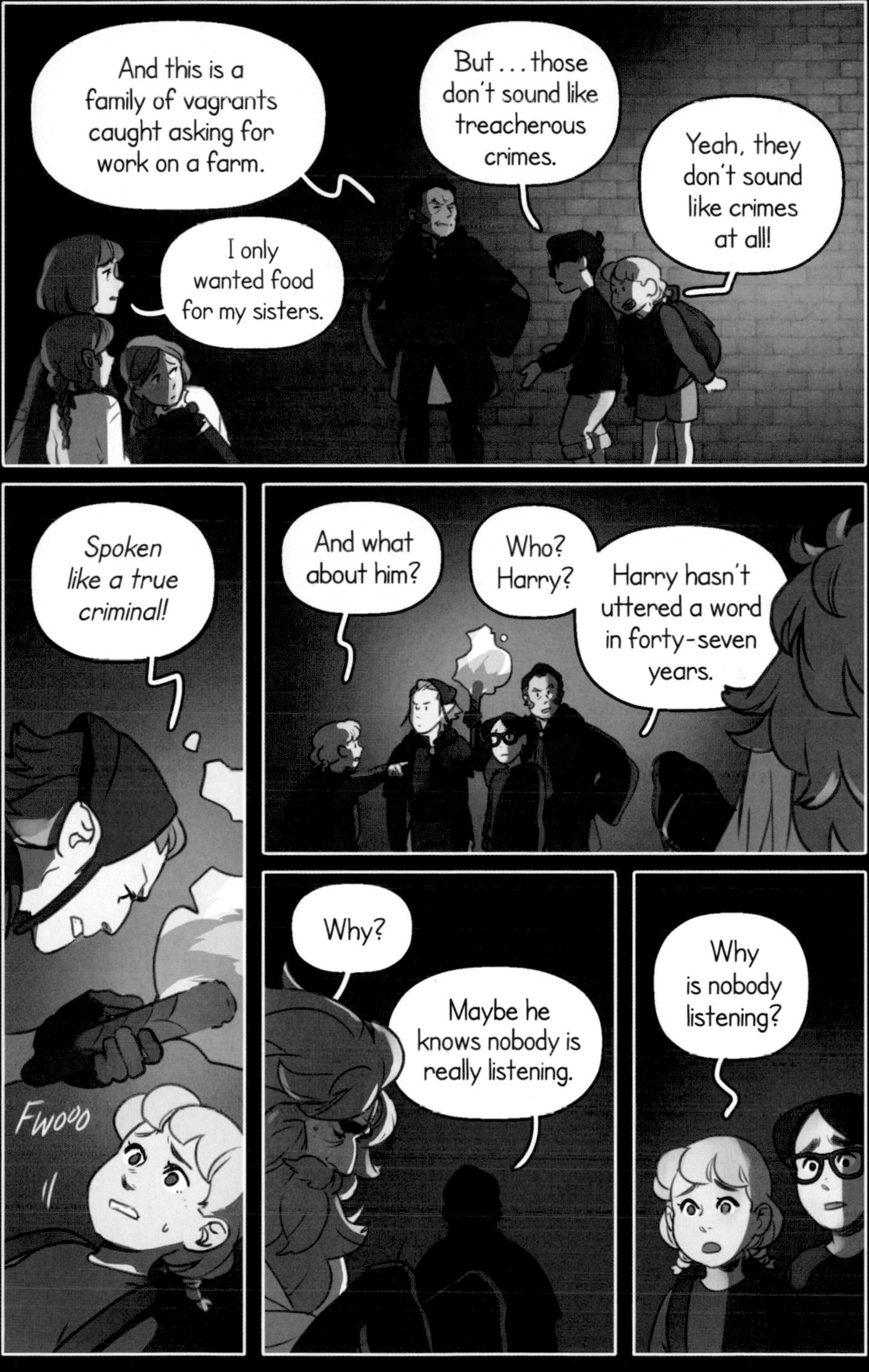
And this is a family of vagrants caught asking for work on a farm.
I only wanted food for my sisters.
But . . . those don't sound like treacherous crimes.
Yeah, they don't sound like crimes at all!
Spoken like a true criminal!
FWOOO
And what about him?
Who? Harry?
Harry hasn't uttered a word in forty-seven years.
Why?
Maybe he knows nobody is really listening.
Why is nobody listening?

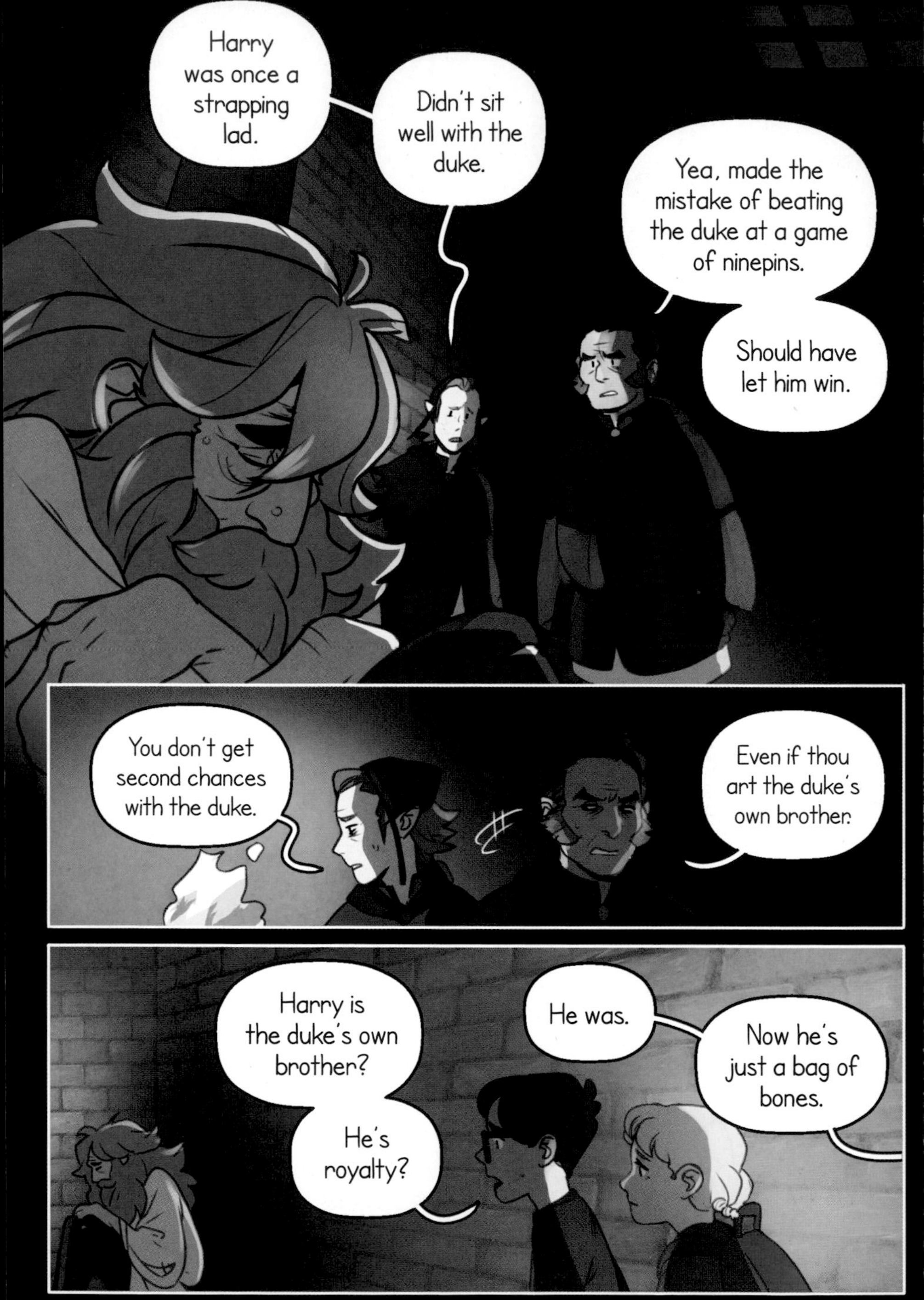
Harry was once a strapping lad.
Didn't sit well with the duke.
Yea, made the mistake of beating the duke at a game of ninepins.
Should have let him win.
You don't get second chances with the duke.
Even if thou art the duke's own brother.
Harry is the duke's own brother?
He's royalty?
He was.
Now he's just a bag of bones.

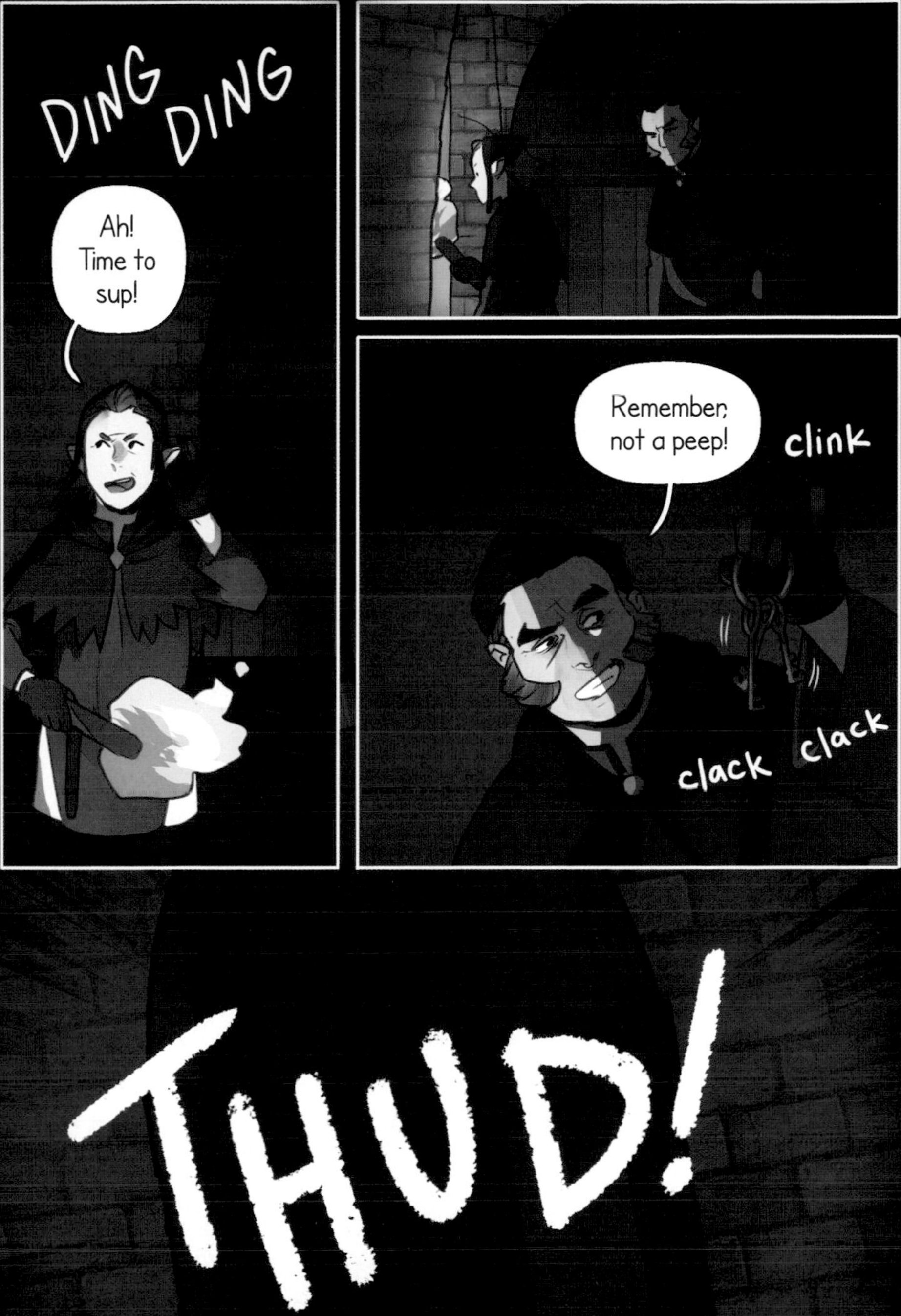
DING DING
Ah! Time to sup!
Remember, not a peep!
clink
clack clack
THUD!

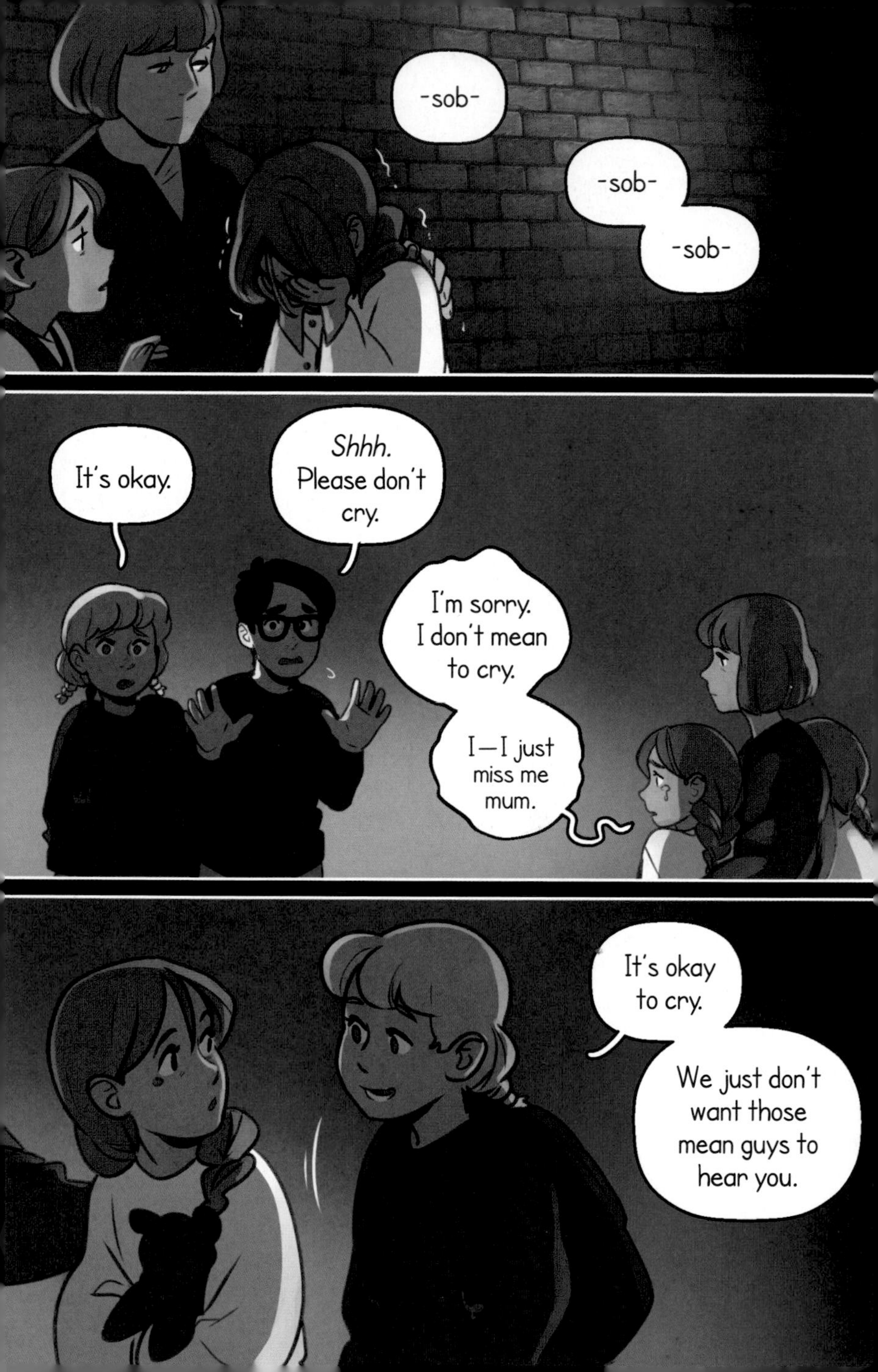
-sob-
-sob-
-sob-
It's okay.
Shhh. Please don't cry.
I'm sorry. I don't mean to cry.
I—I just miss me mum.
It's okay to cry.
We just don't want those mean guys to hear you.

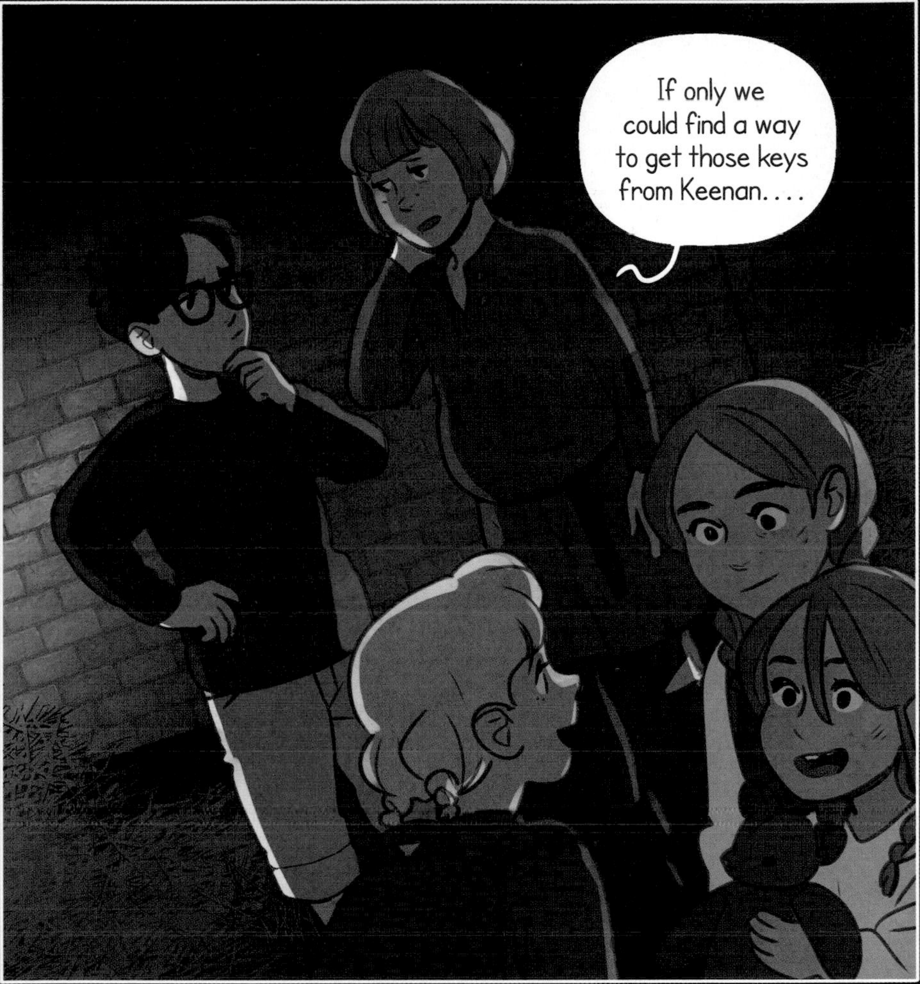
If only we could find a way to get those keys from Keenan. . . .

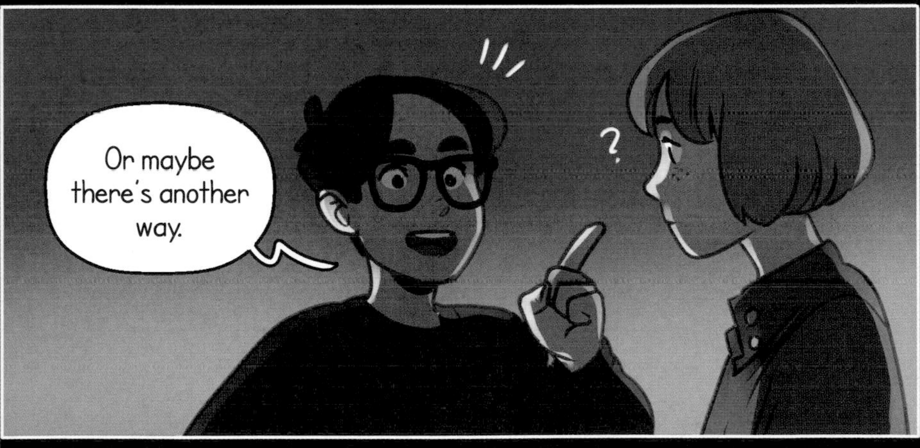
Or maybe there's another way.

CHAPTER SEVEN
A Secret Passage

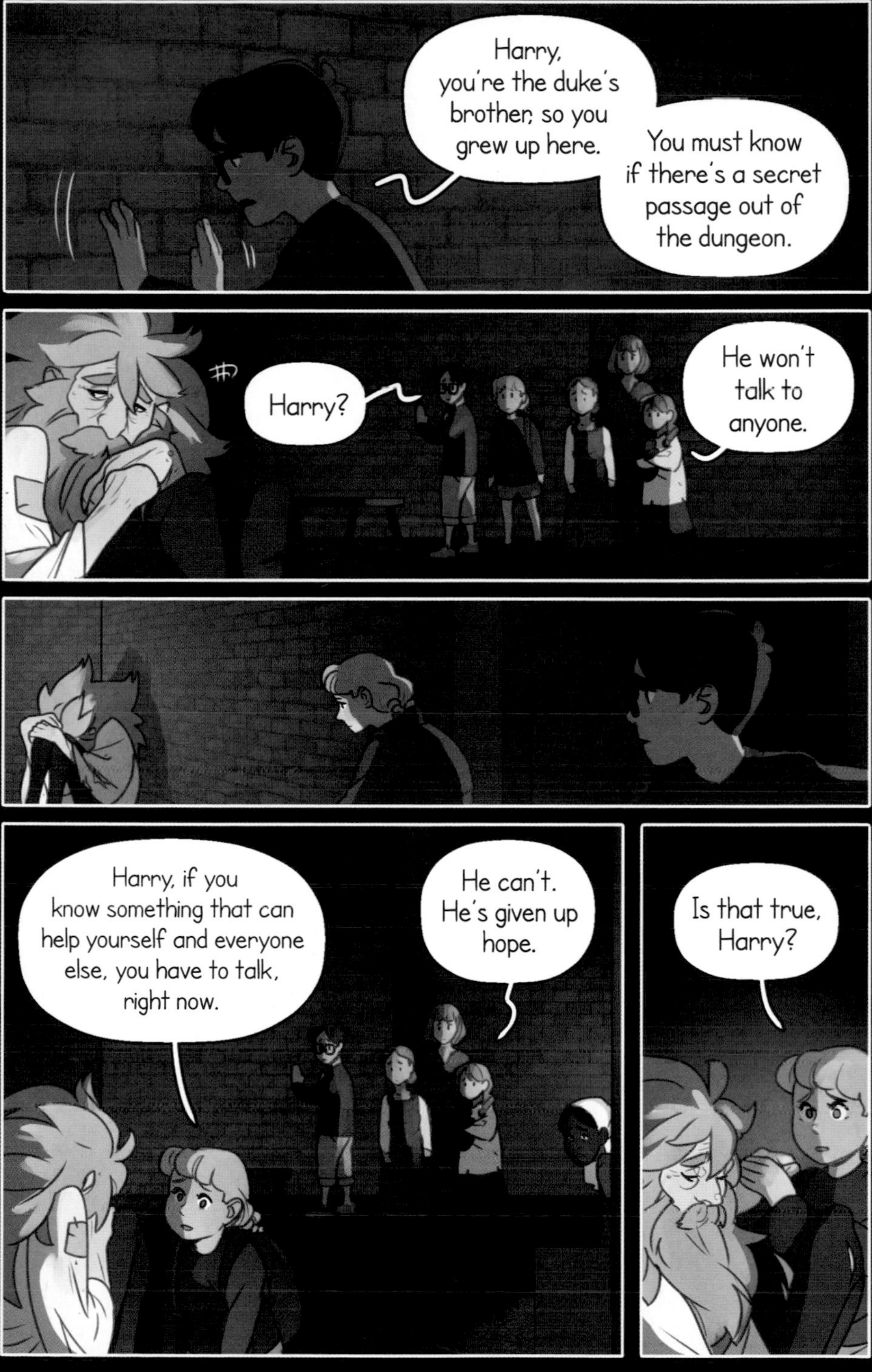
Harry, you're the duke's brother, so you grew up here.
You must know if there's a secret passage out of the dungeon.
Harry?
He won't talk to anyone.
Harry, if you know something that can help yourself and everyone else, you have to talk, right now.
He can't. He's given up hope.
Is that true, Harry?

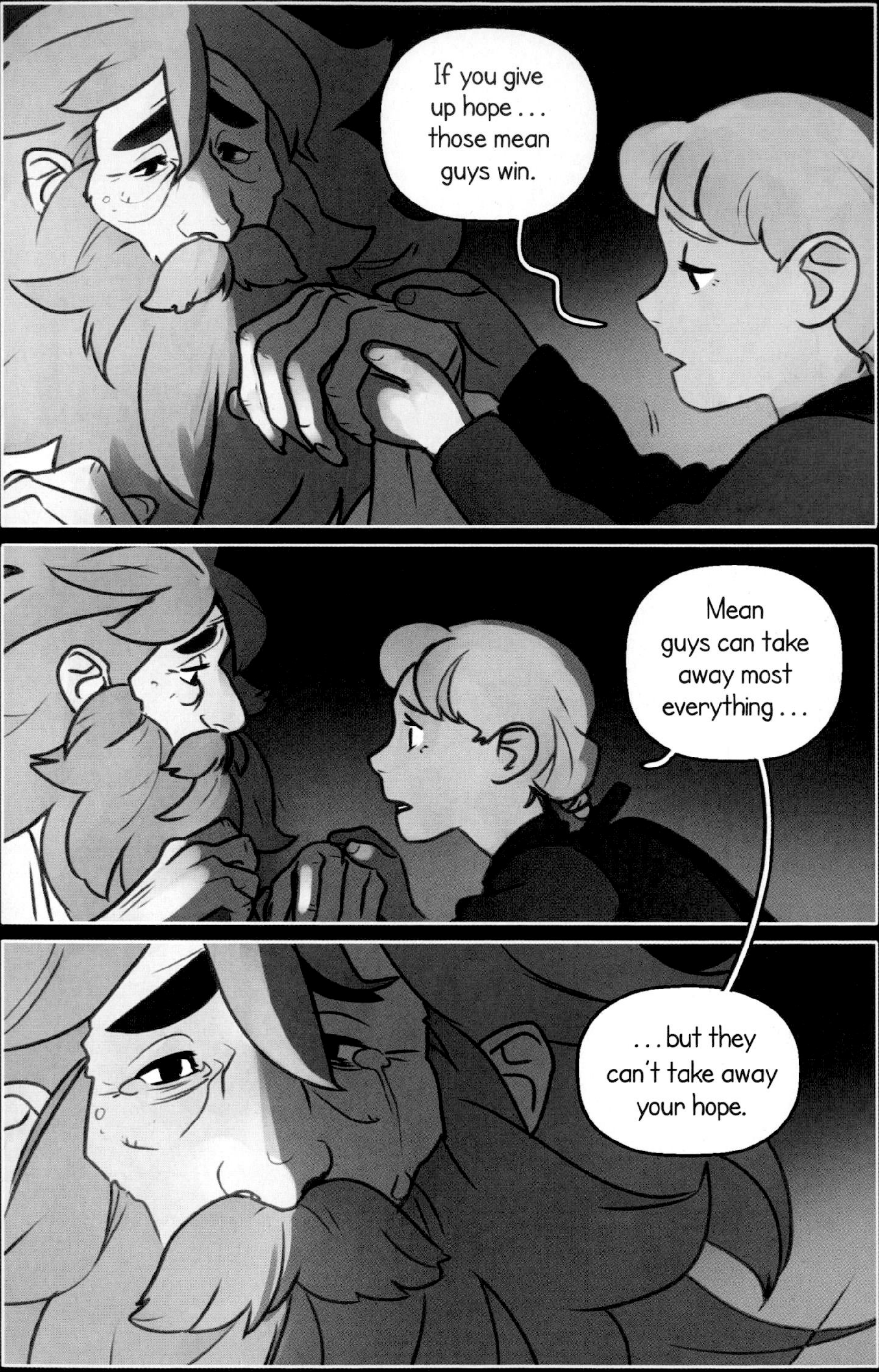
If you give up hope . . . those mean guys win.
Mean guys can take away most everything . . .
. . . but they can't take away your hope.

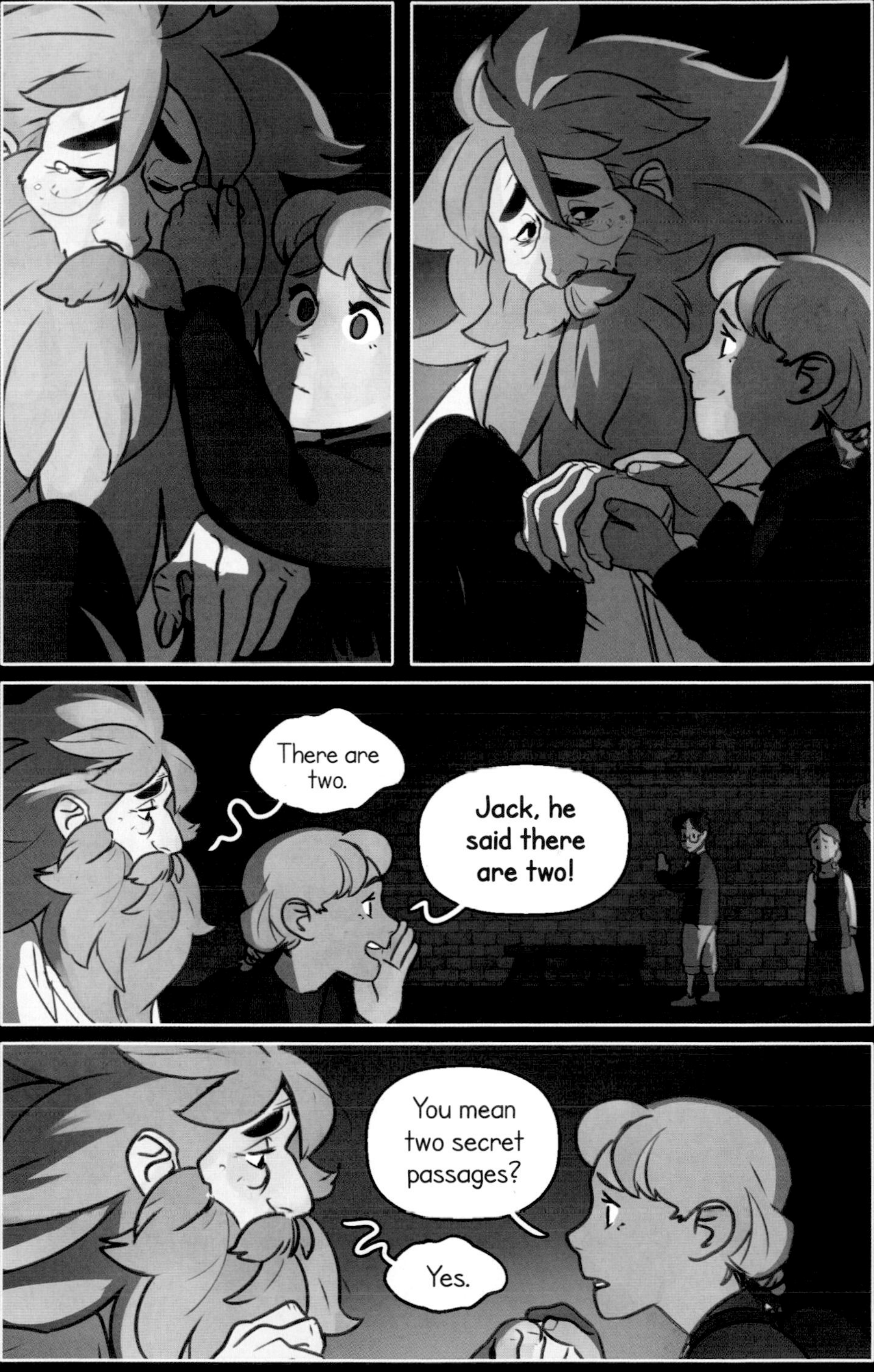
There are two.
Jack, he said there are two!
You mean two secret passages?
Yes.

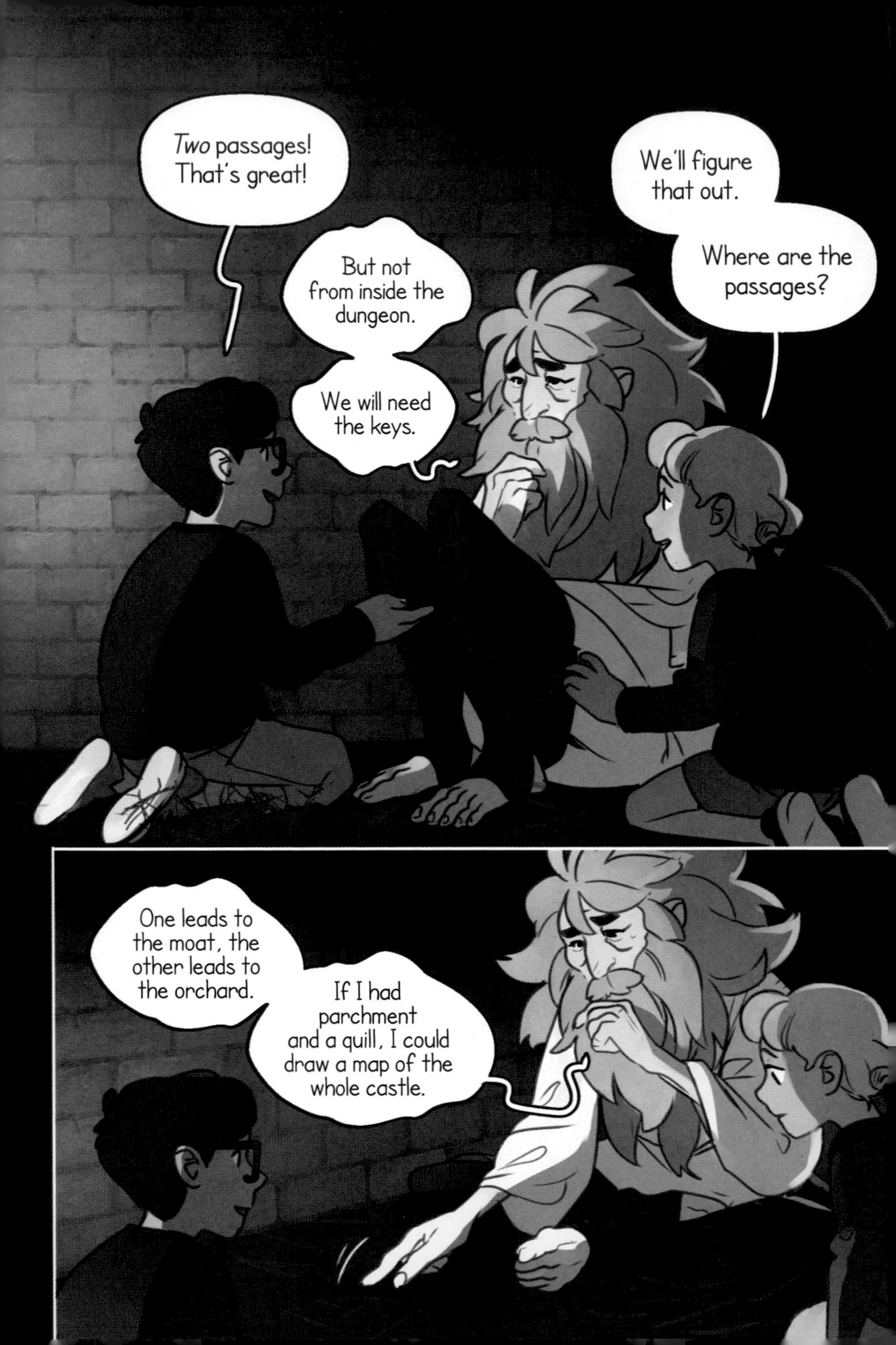
Two passages! That's great!
But not from inside the dungeon.
We will need the keys.
We'll figure that out.
Where are the passages?
One leads to the moat, the other leads to the orchard.
If I had parchment and a quill, I could draw a map of the whole castle.

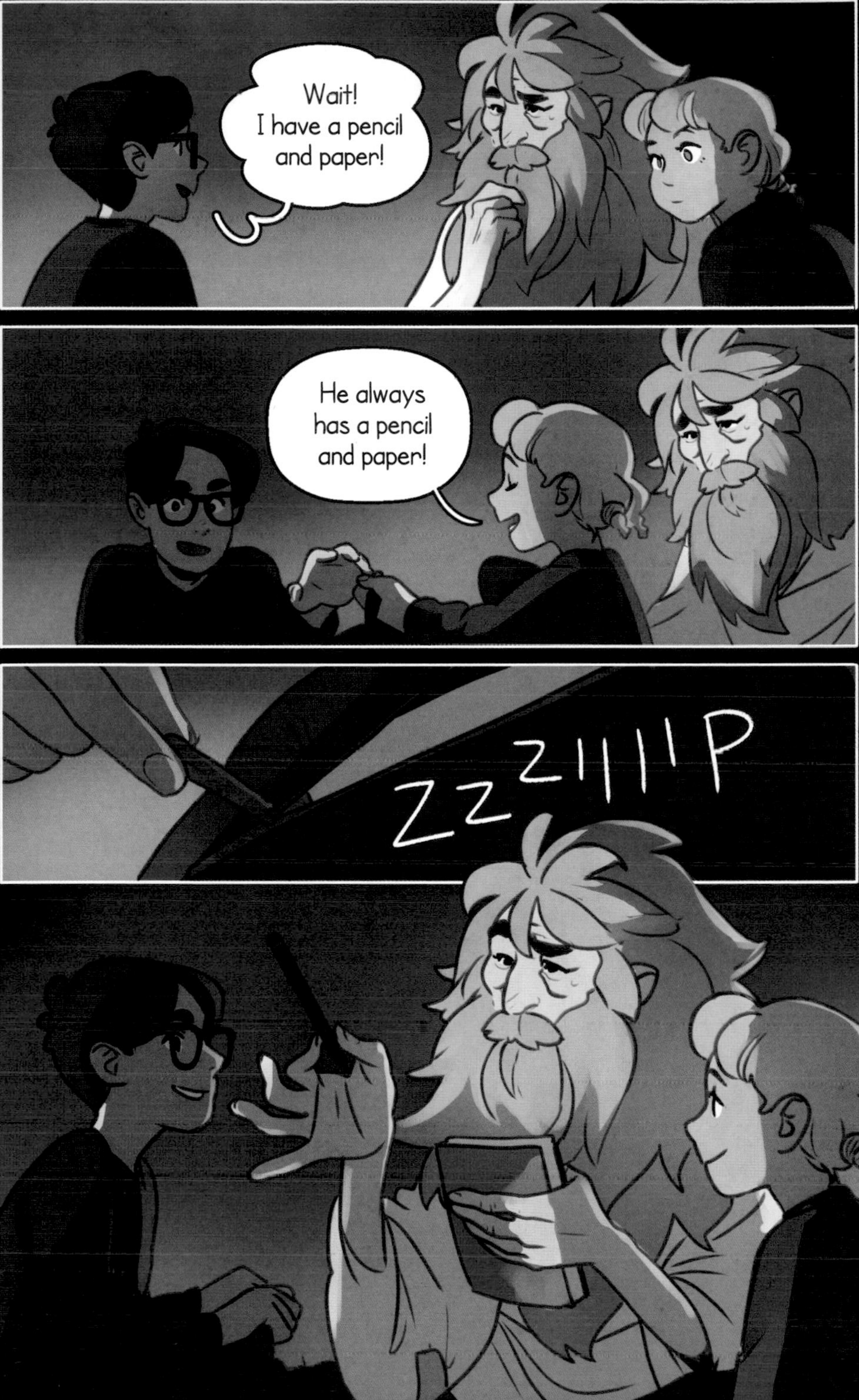
Wait!
I have a pencil
and paper!
He always
has a pencil
and paper!
ZZZIIIIP

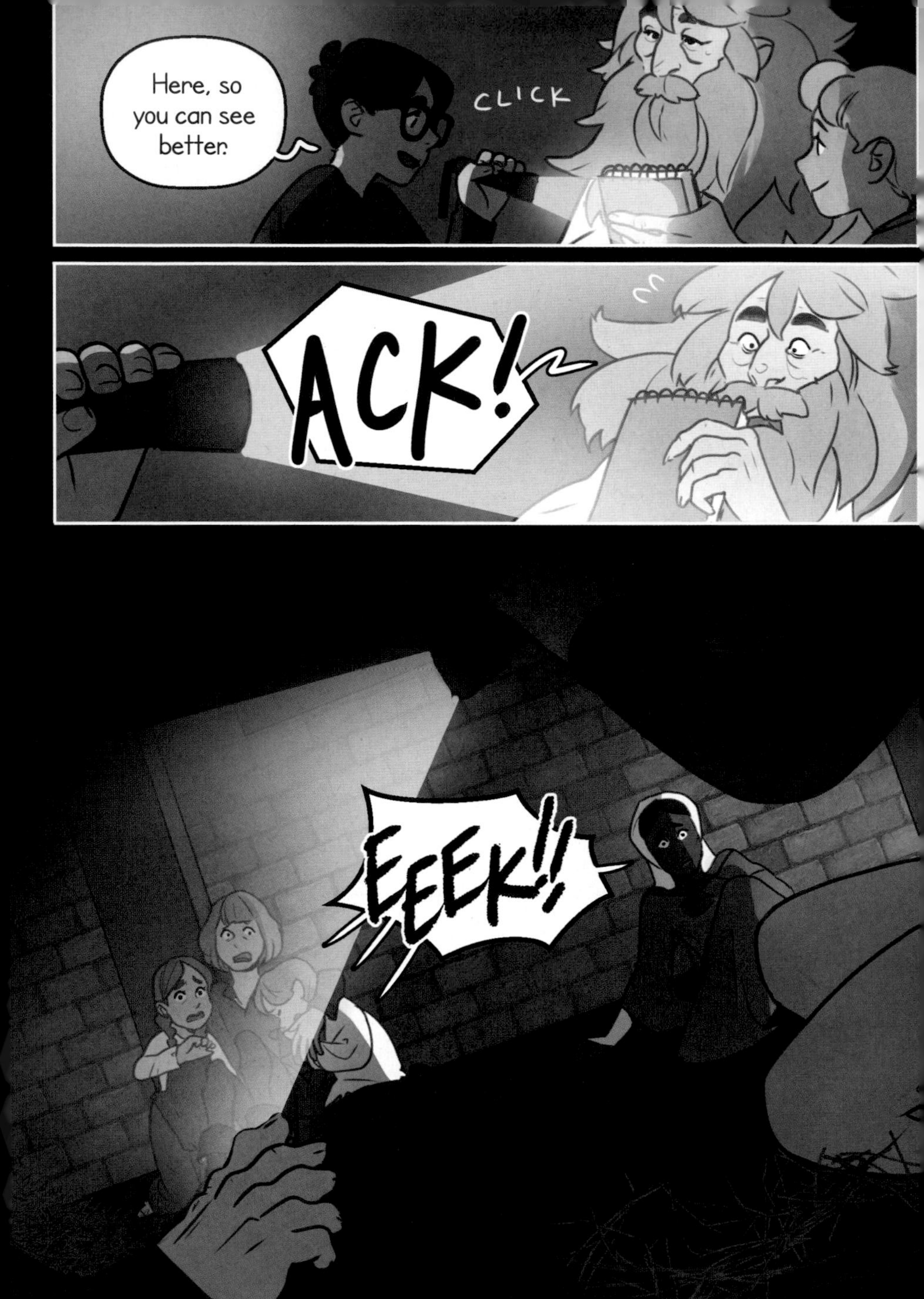
Here, so you can see better.
CLICK
ACK!
EEEK!!

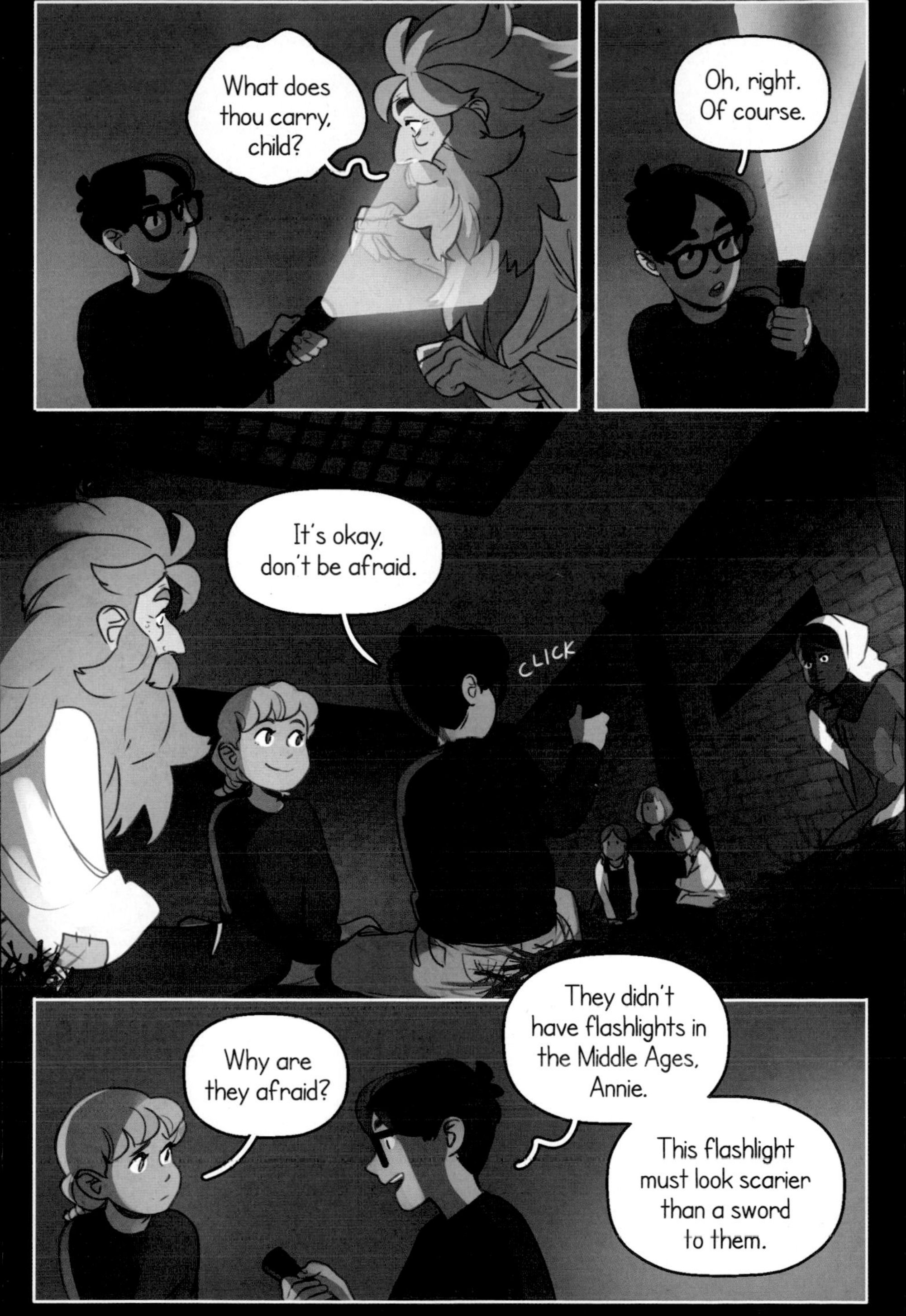
What does thou carry, child?
Oh, right. Of course.
It's okay, don't be afraid.
CLICK
Why are they afraid?
They didn't have flashlights in the Middle Ages, Annie.
This flashlight must look scarier than a sword to them.

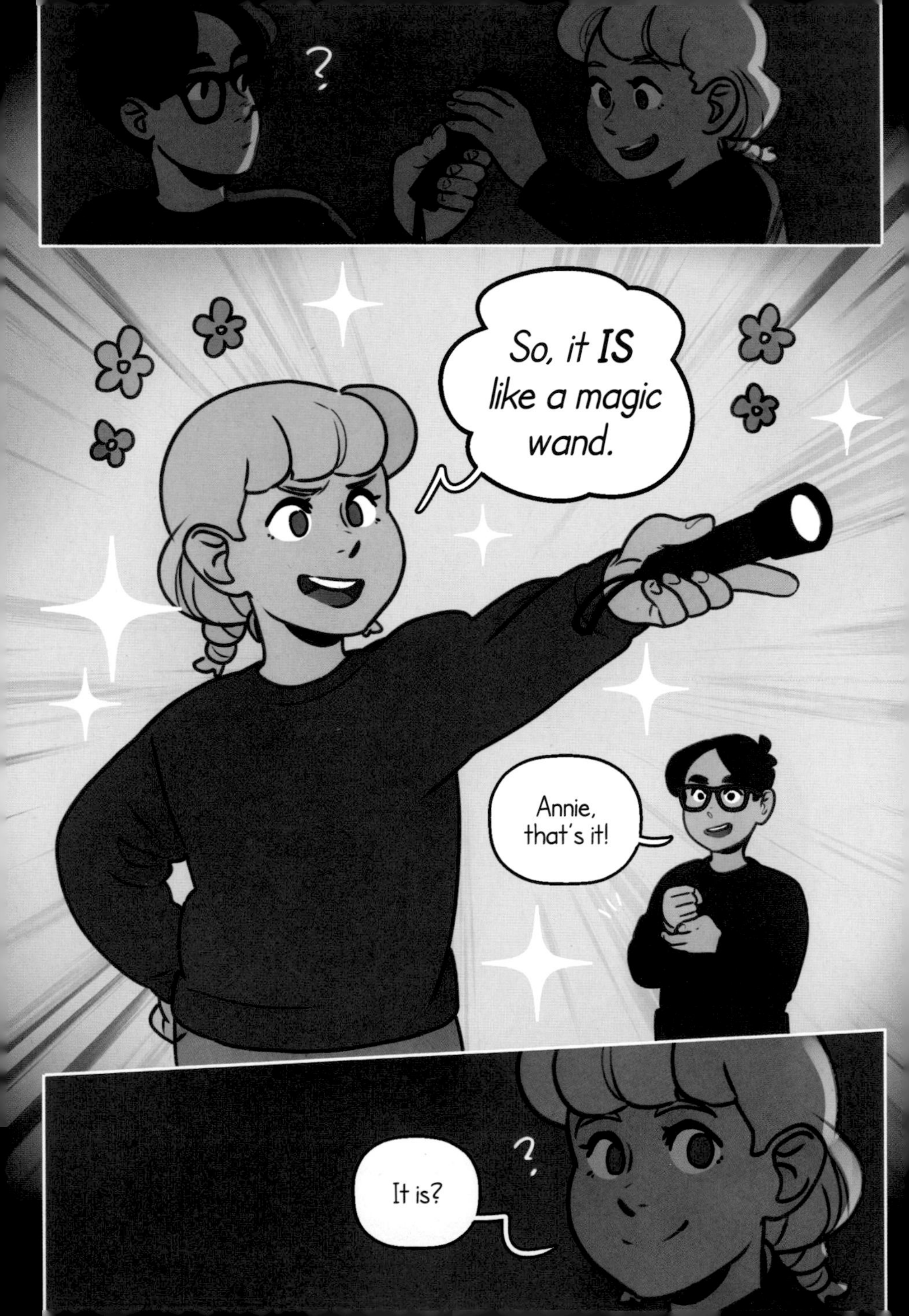

?
So, it IS like a magic wand.
Annie, that's it!
?
It is?

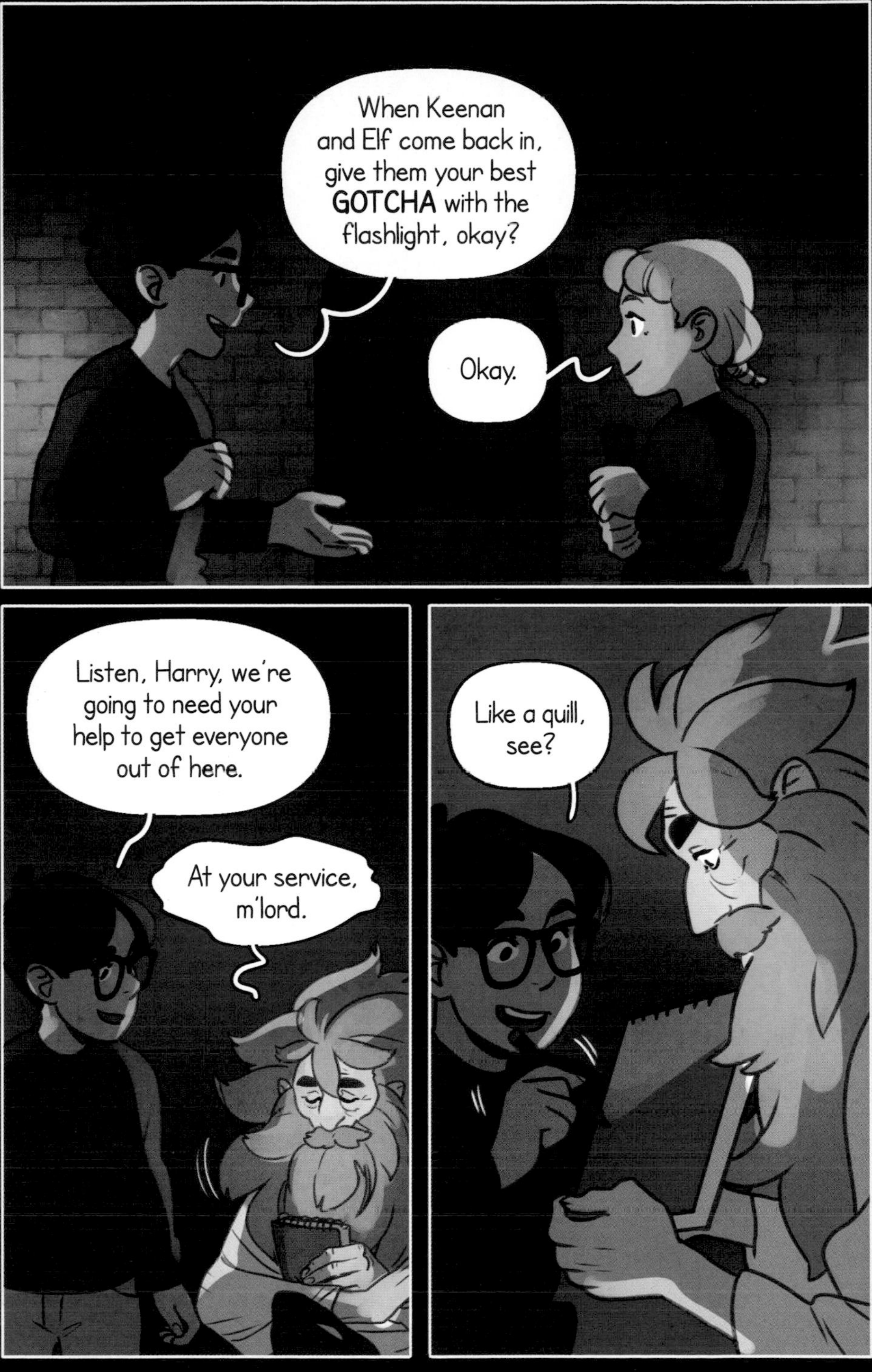
When Keenan and Elf come back in, give them your best GOTCHA with the flashlight, okay?
Okay.
Listen, Harry, we're going to need your help to get everyone out of here.
At your service, m'lord.
Like a quill, see?

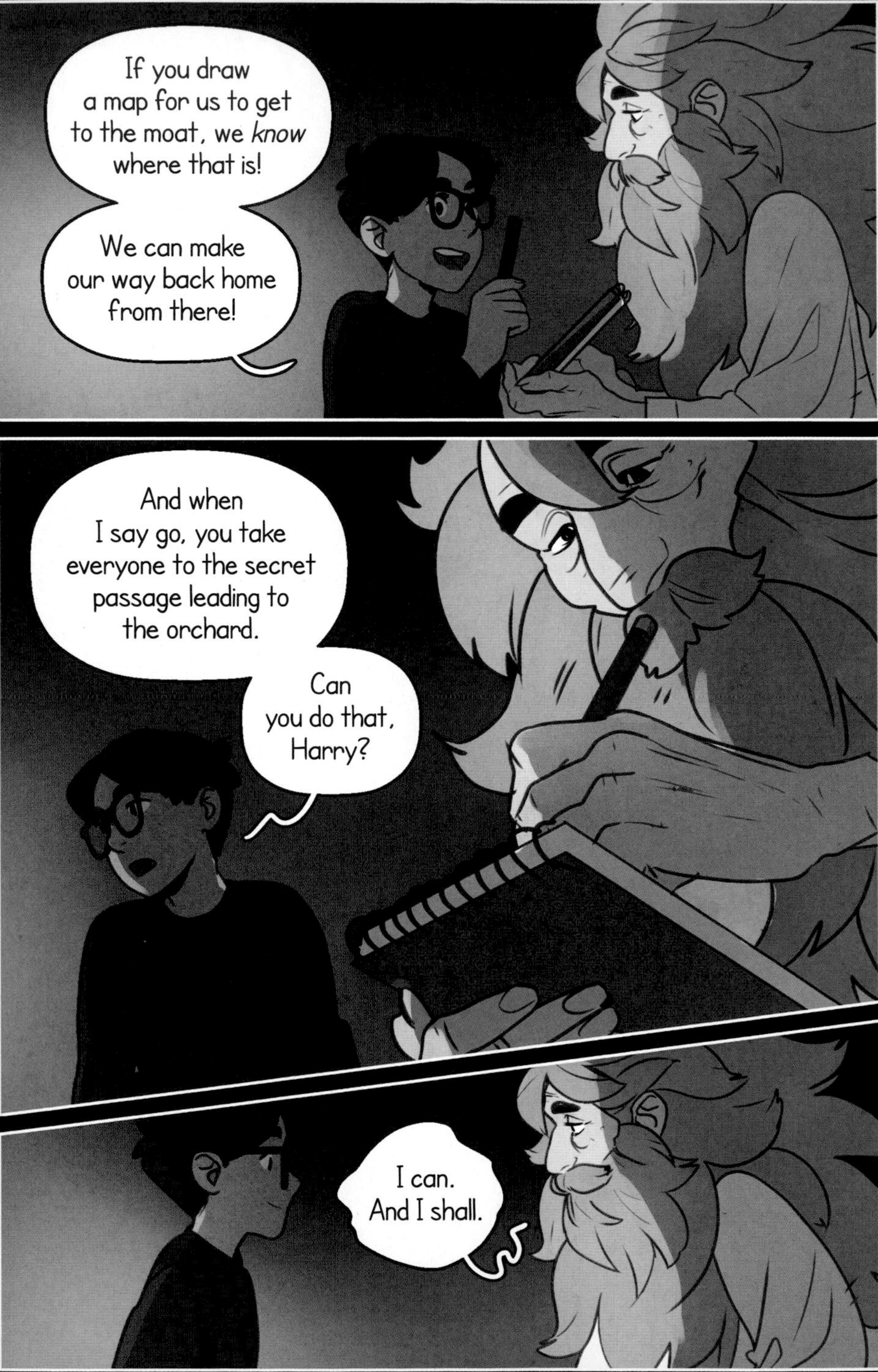
If you draw a map for us to get to the moat, we *know* where that is!
We can make our way back home from there!
And when I say go, you take everyone to the secret passage leading to the orchard.
Can you do that, Harry?
I can. And I shall.

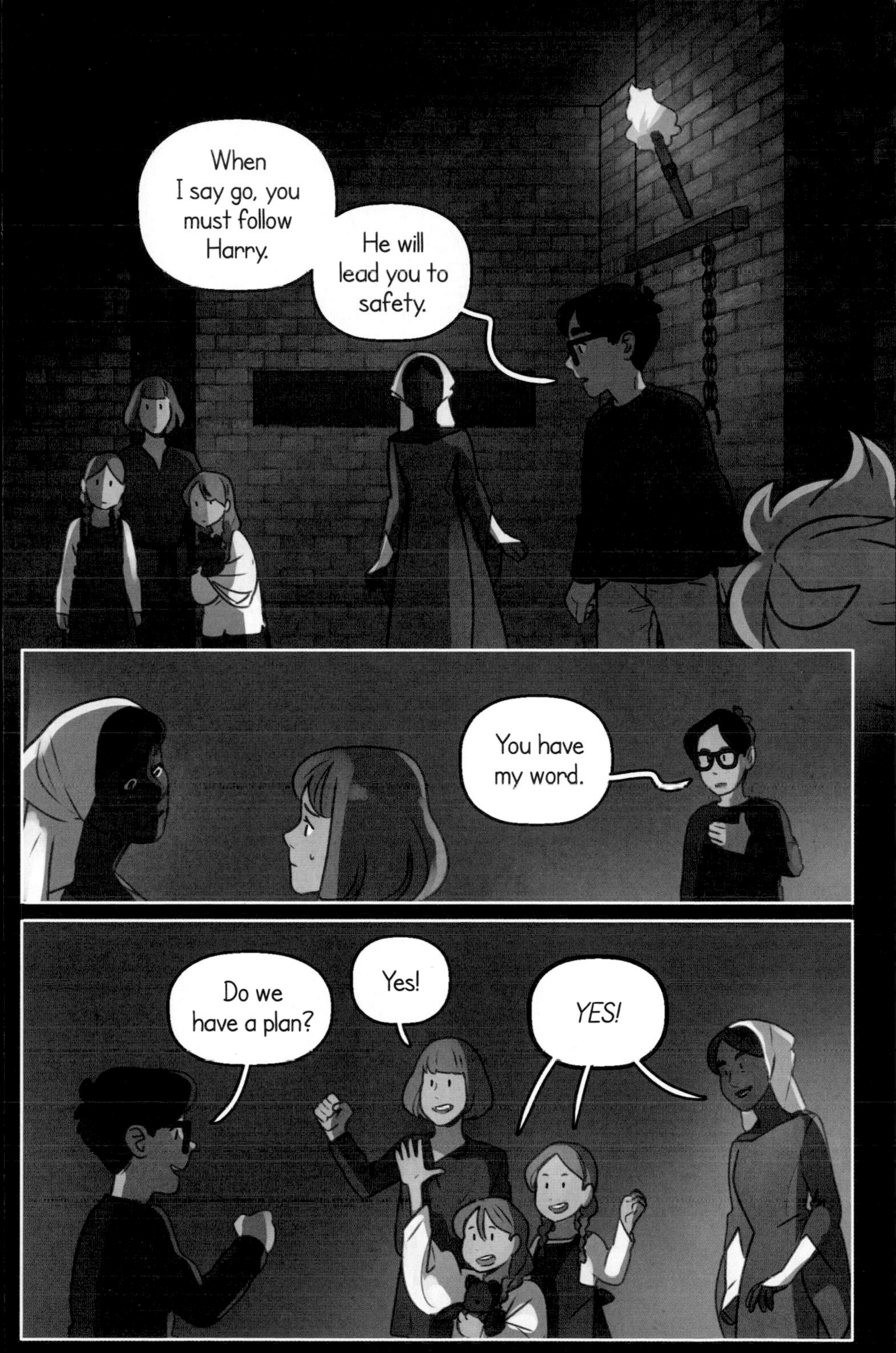
When I say go, you must follow Harry.
He will lead you to safety.
You have my word.
Do we have a plan?
Yes!
YES!

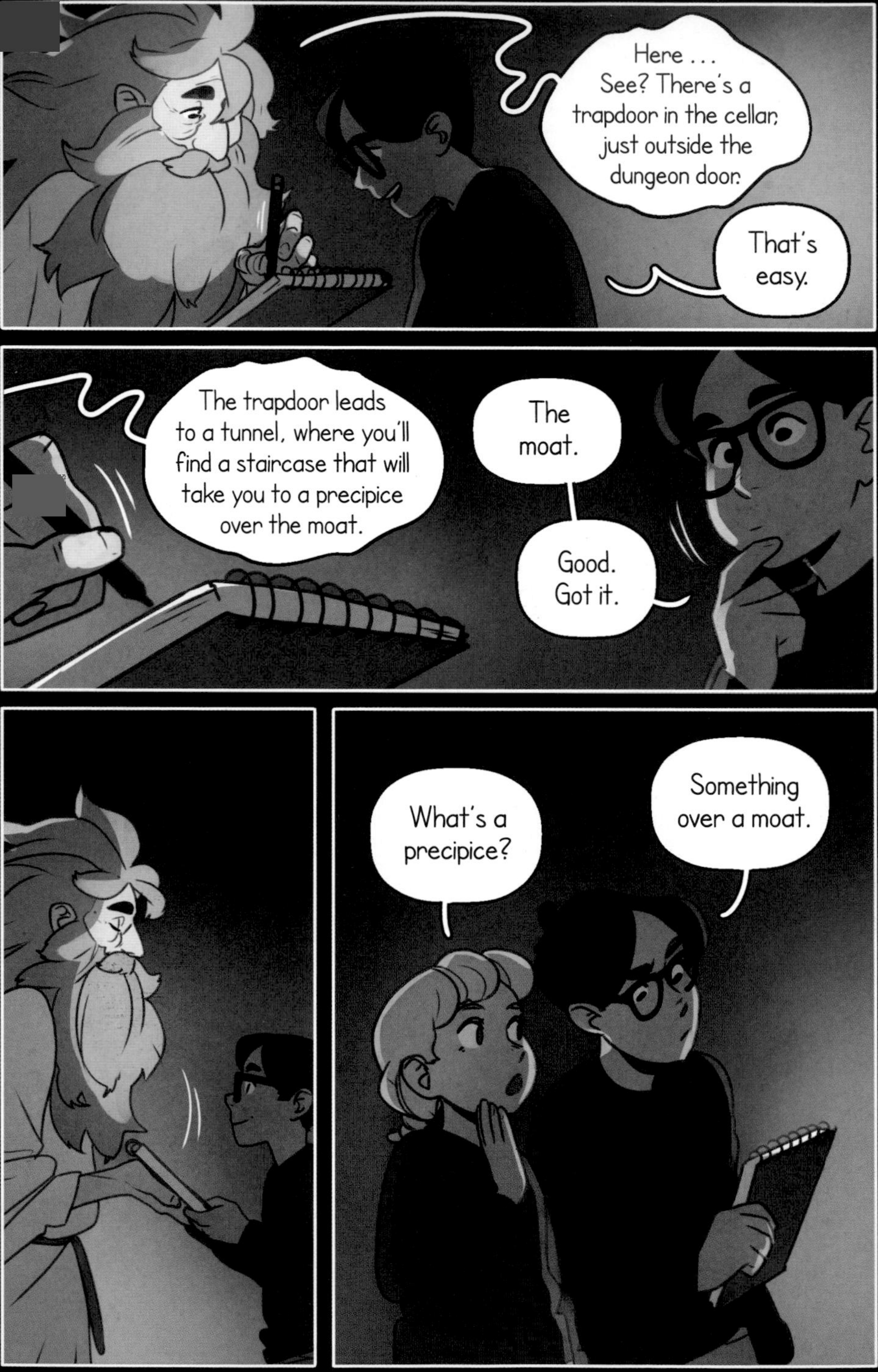
Here . . .
See? There's a trapdoor in the cellar, just outside the dungeon door.
That's easy.
The trapdoor leads to a tunnel, where you'll find a staircase that will take you to a precipice over the moat.
The moat.
Good. Got it.
What's a precipice?
Something over a moat.

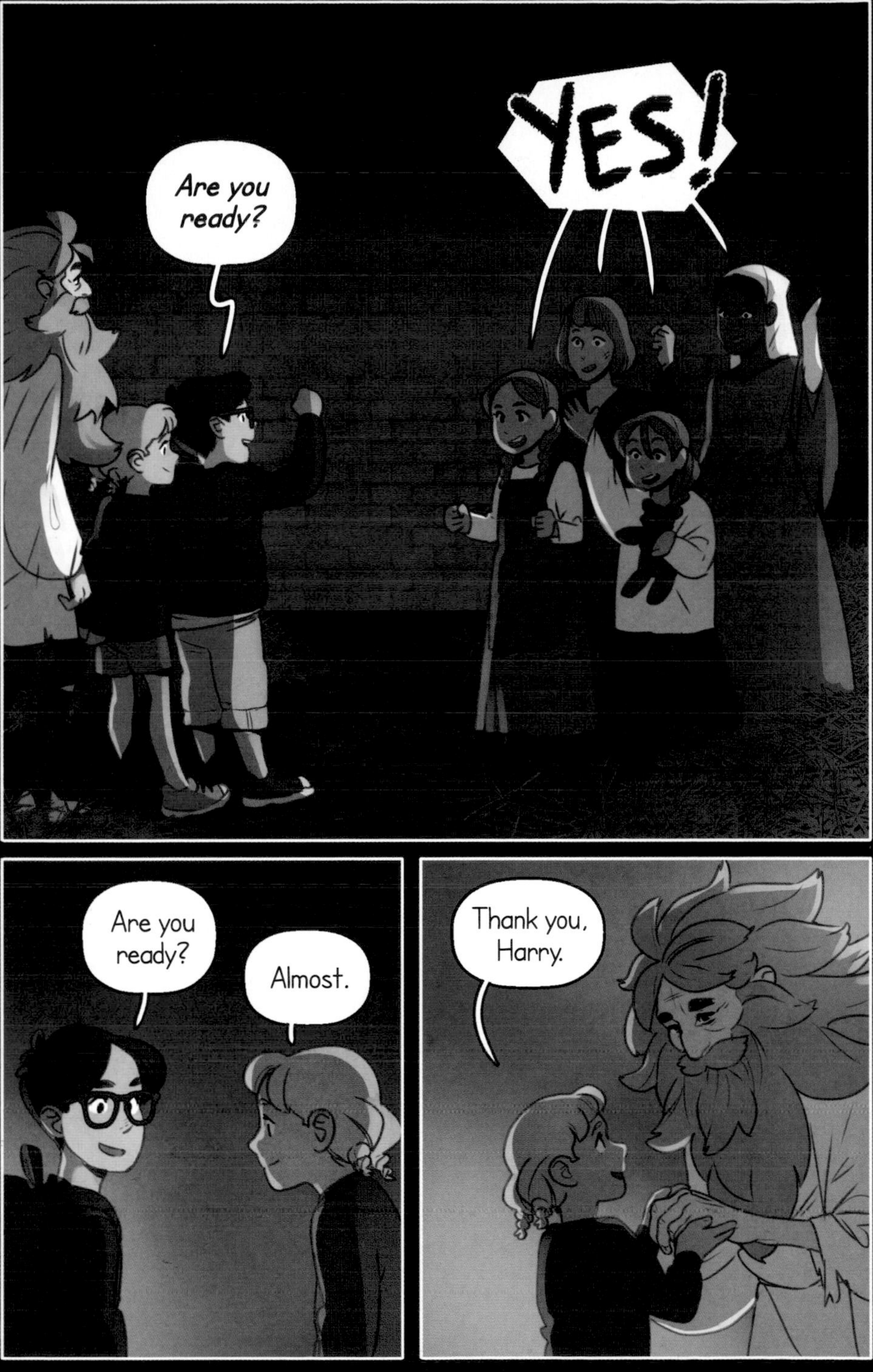
Are you ready?
YES!
Are you ready?
Almost.
Thank you, Harry.

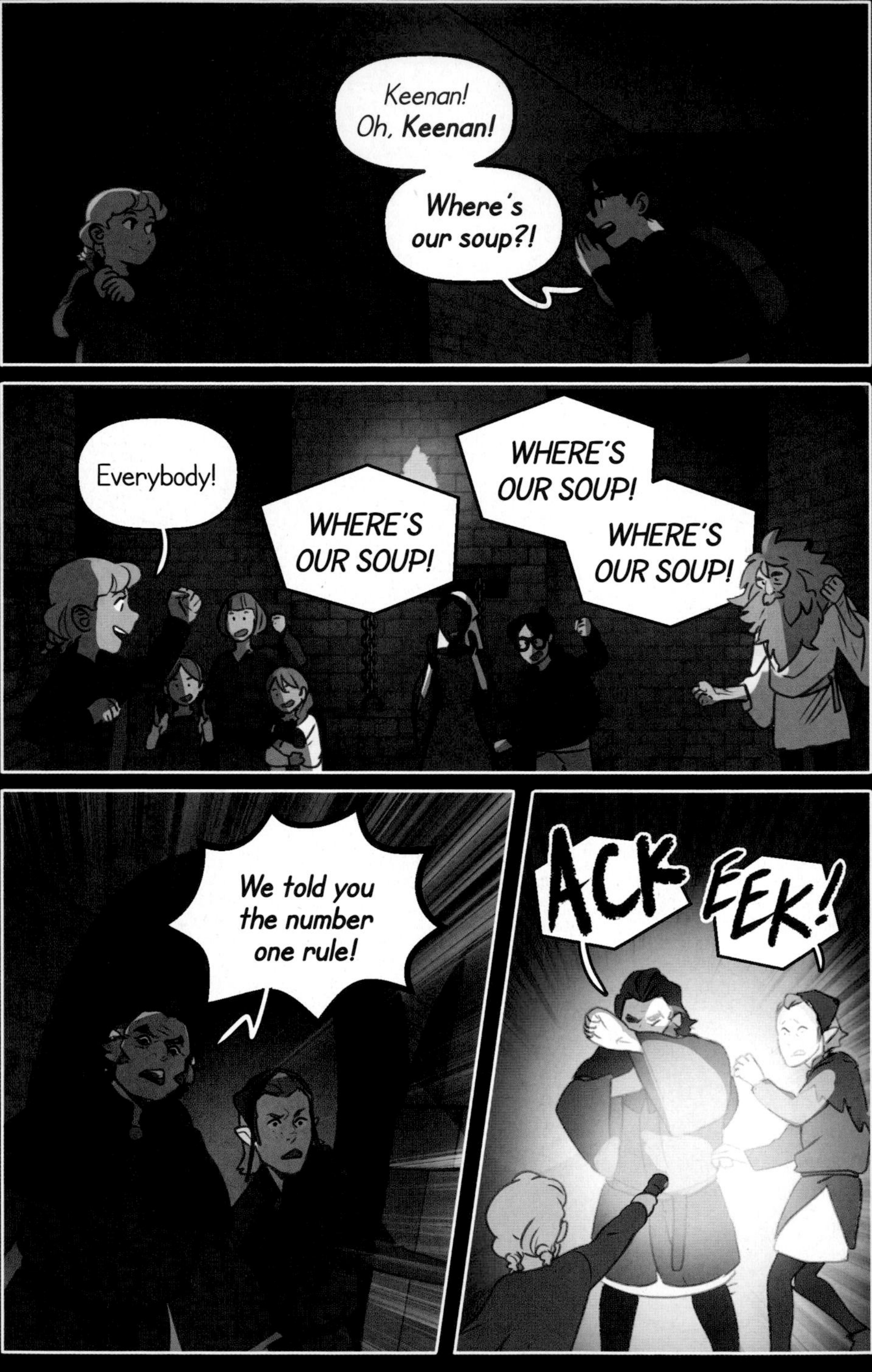

Keenan!
Oh, Keenan!
Where's our soup?!
Everybody!
WHERE'S OUR SOUP!
WHERE'S OUR SOUP!
WHERE'S OUR SOUP!
We told you the number one rule!
ACK
EEK!

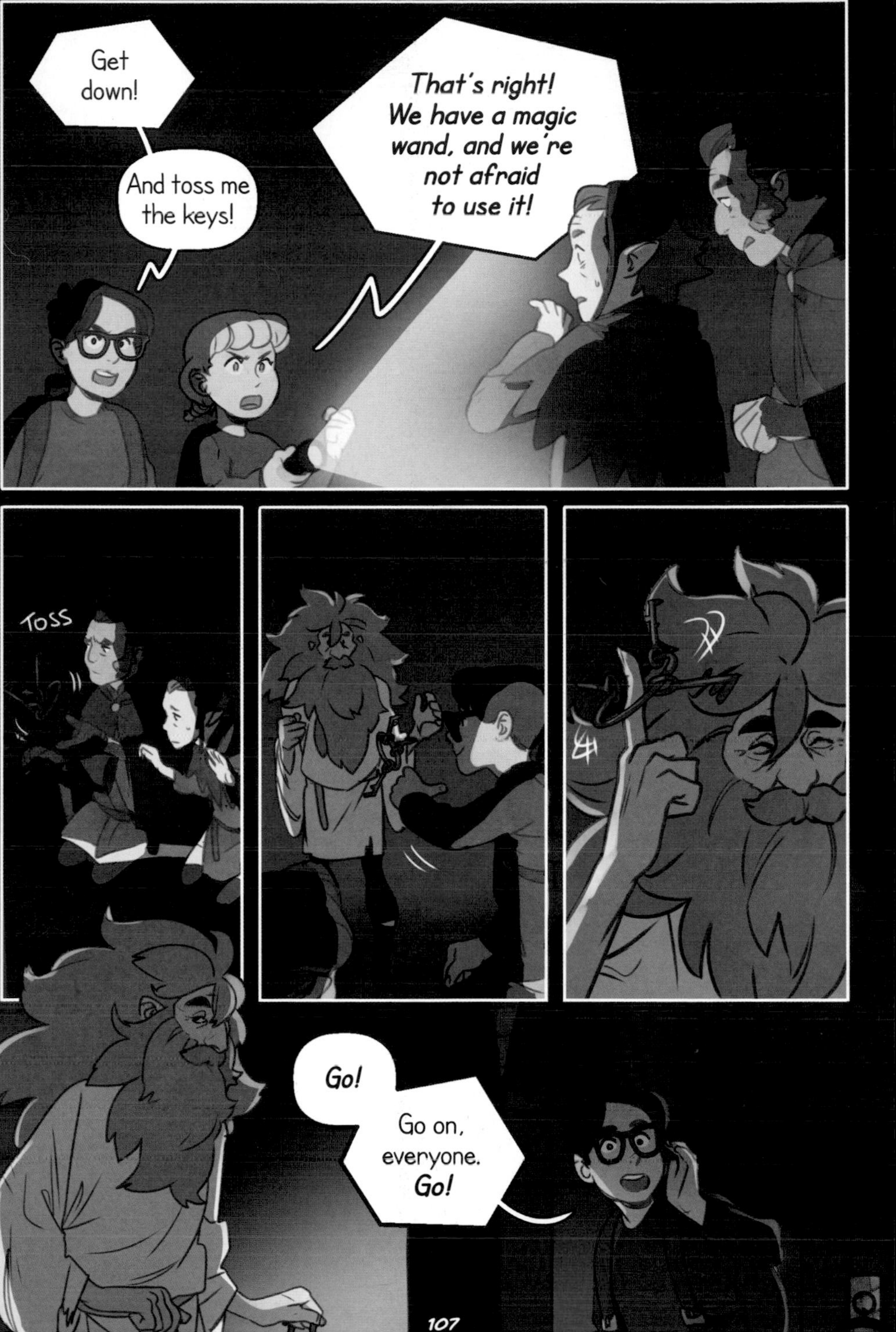
Get down!
And toss me the keys!
That's right! We have a magic wand, and we're not afraid to use it!
TOSS
Go!
Go on, everyone. Go!

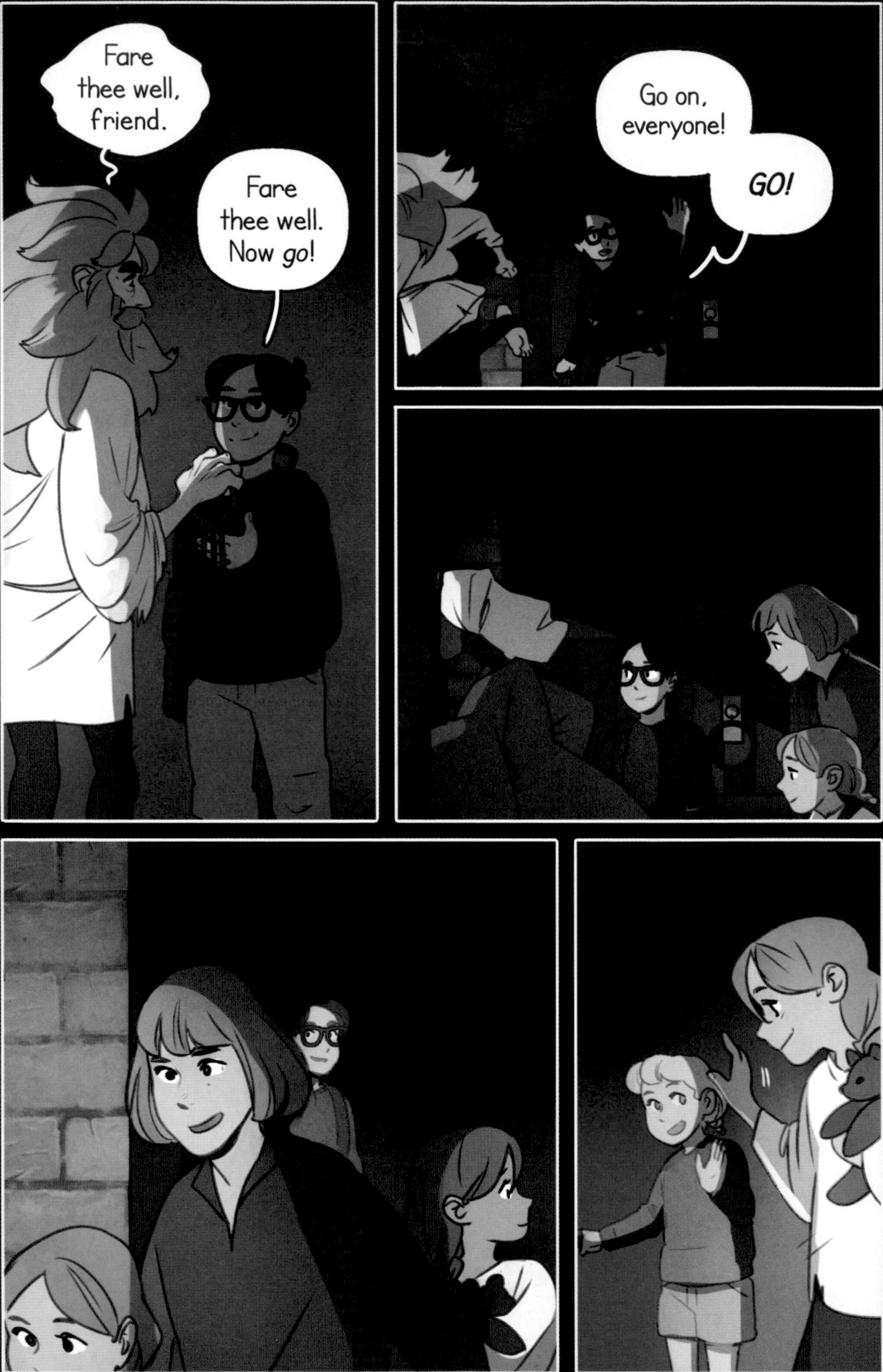
Fare thee well, friend.
Fare thee well. Now *go*!
Go on, everyone!
GO!

CHAPTER EIGHT
The Knight

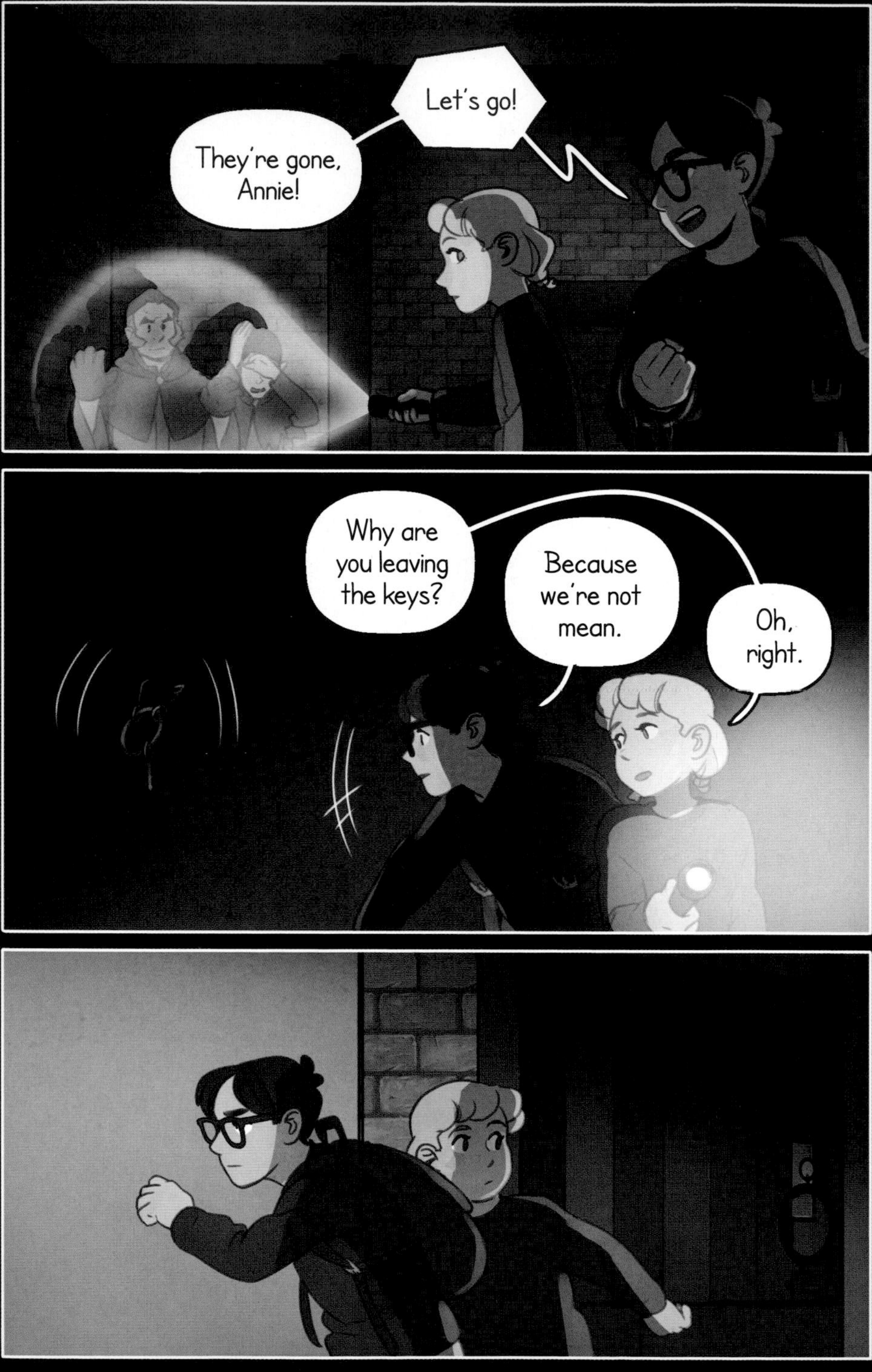
Let's go!
They're gone, Annie!
Why are you leaving the keys?
Because we're not mean.
Oh, right.

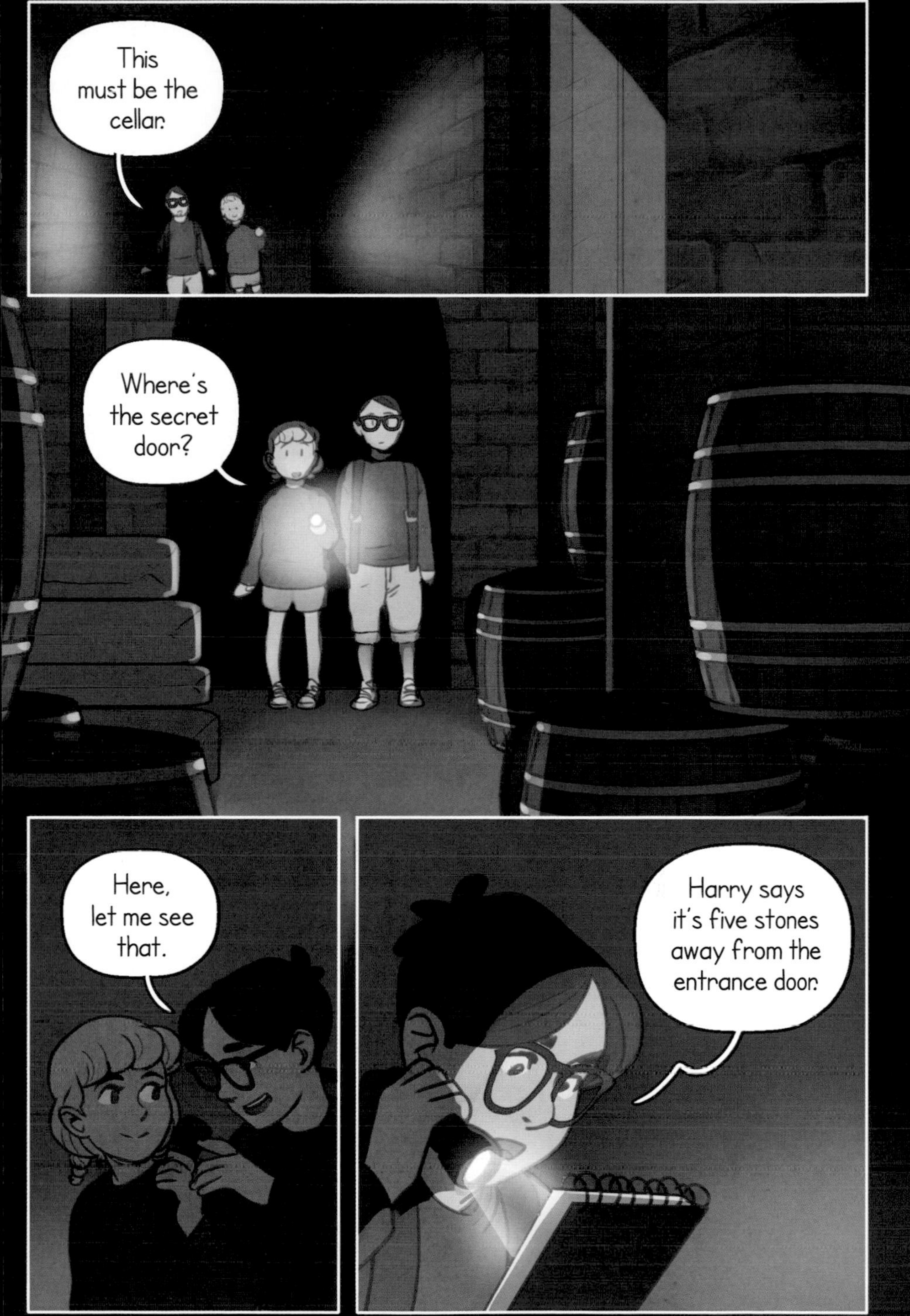
This must be the cellar.
Where's the secret door?
Here, let me see that.
Harry says it's five stones away from the entrance door.

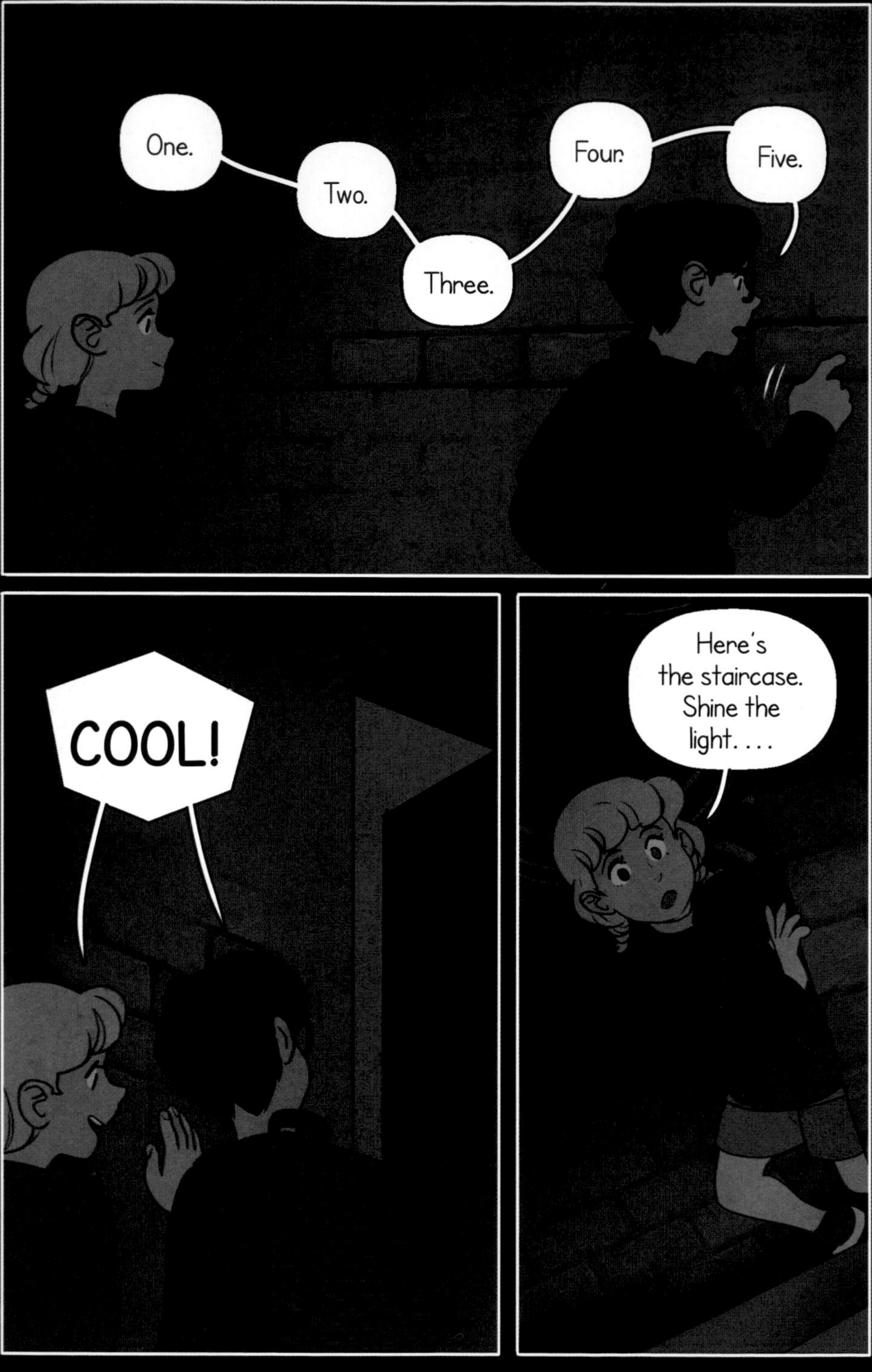
One.
Two.
Three.
Four.
Five.
COOL!
Here's the staircase. Shine the light. . . .

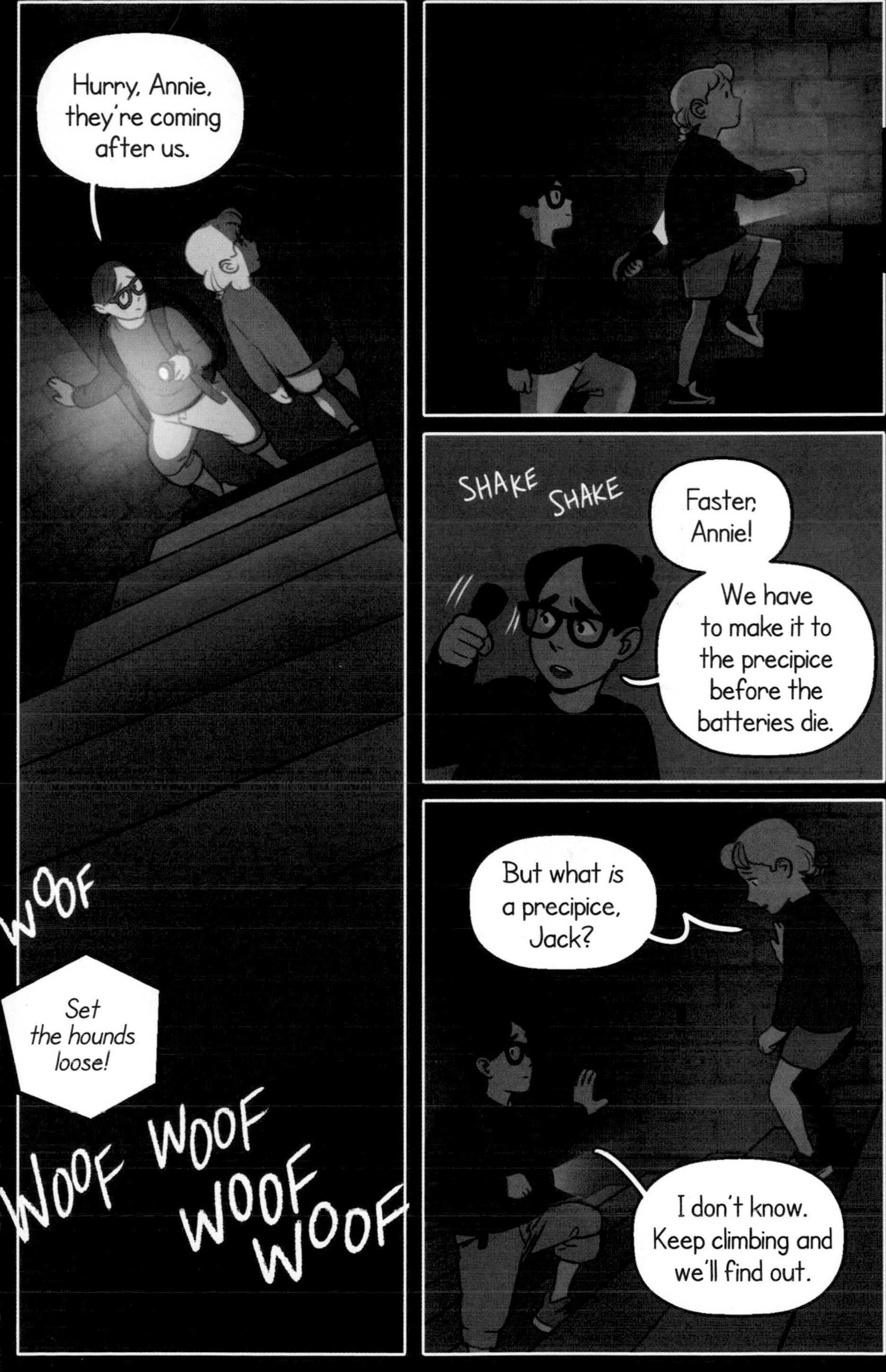
Hurry, Annie, they're coming after us.
WOOF
Set the hounds loose!
WOOF WOOF
WOOF
WOOF
SHAKE SHAKE
Faster, Annie!
We have to make it to the precipice before the batteries die.
But what *is* a precipice, Jack?
I don't know. Keep climbing and we'll find out.

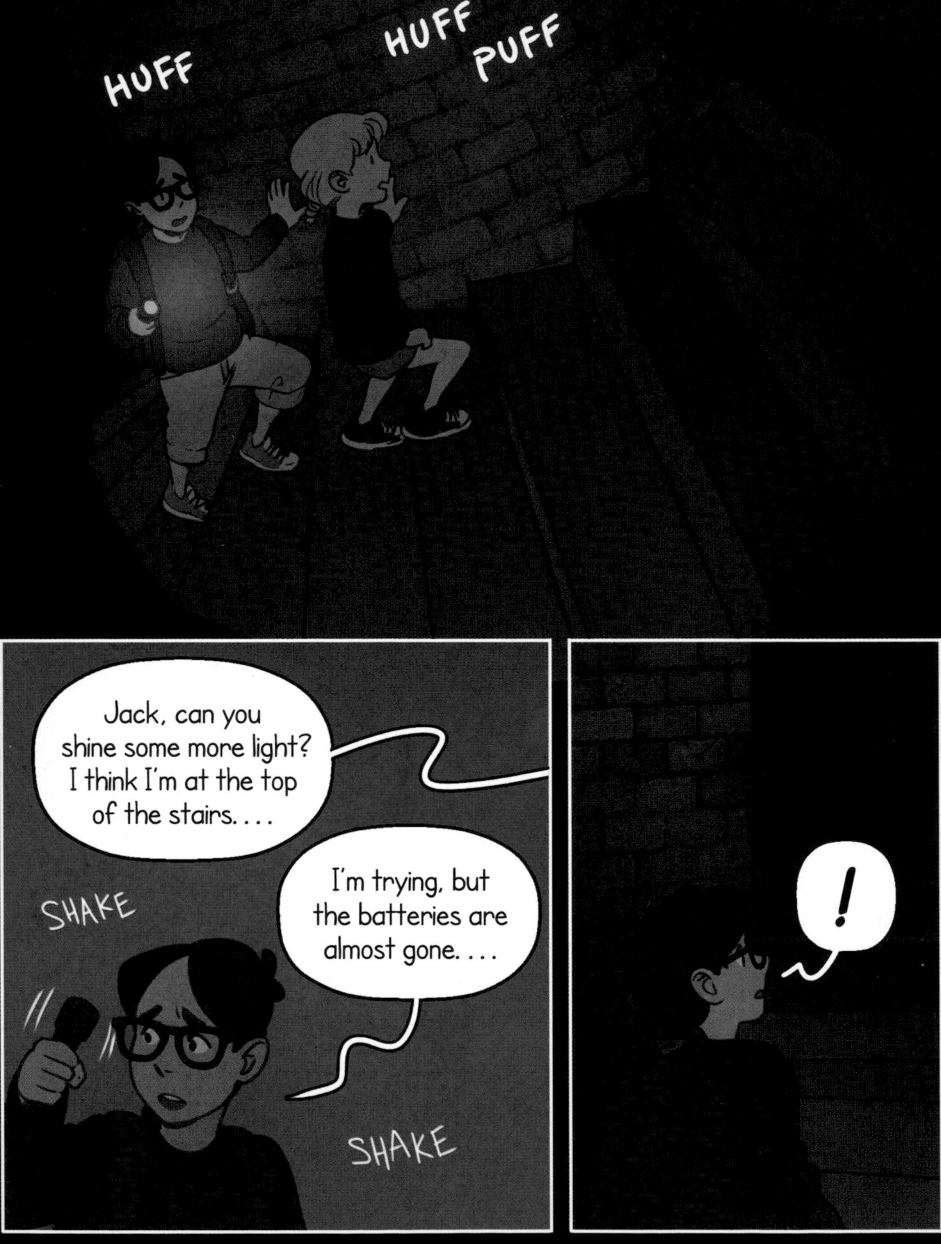
HUFF
HUFF
PUFF
Jack, can you shine some more light? I think I'm at the top of the stairs. . . .
SHAKE
I'm trying, but the batteries are almost gone. . . .
SHAKE
!

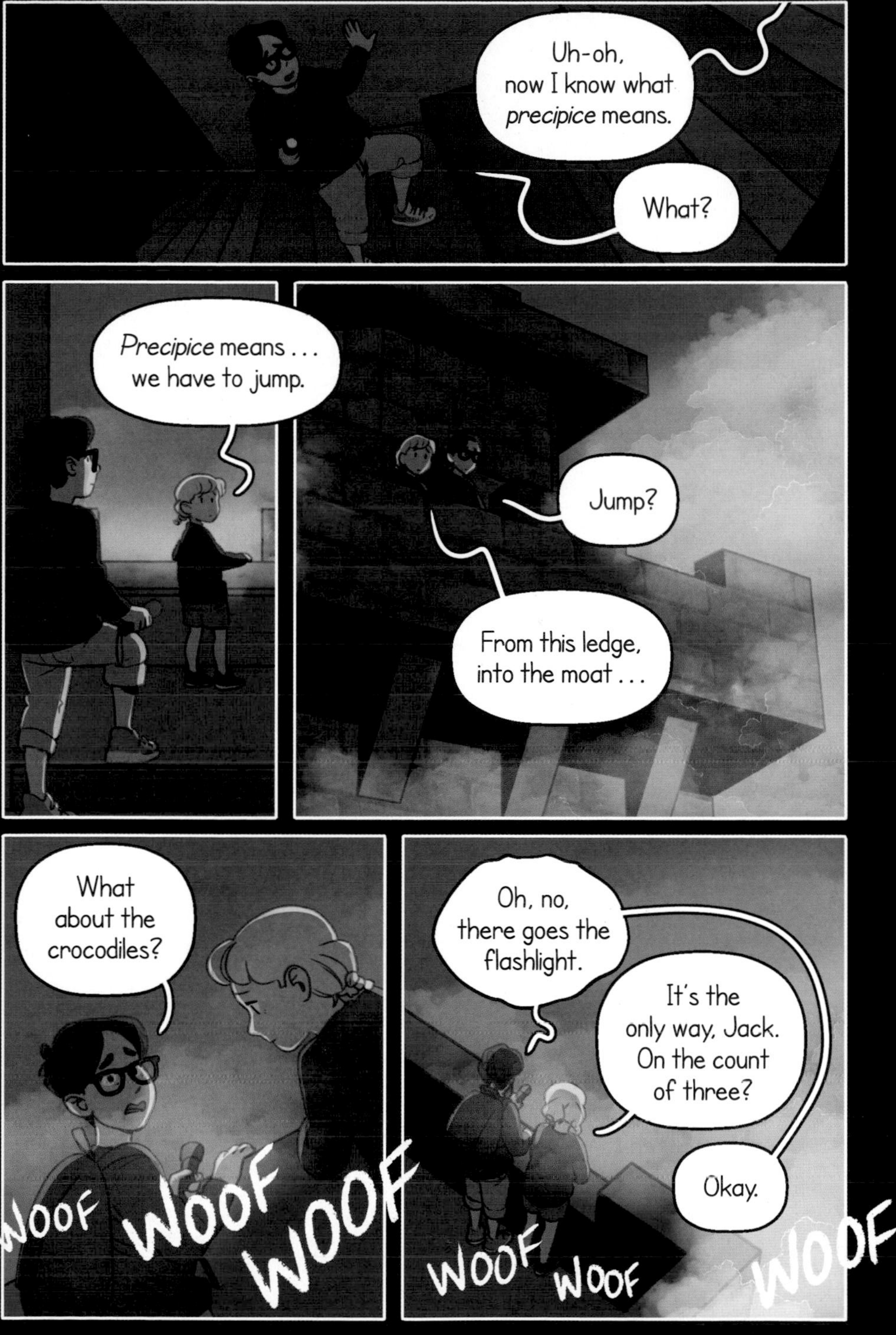
Uh-oh, now I know what *precipice* means.
What?
Precipice means . . . we have to jump.
Jump?
From this ledge, into the moat . . .
What about the crocodiles?
WOOF WOOF WOOF
Oh, no, there goes the flashlight.
It's the only way, Jack. On the count of three?
Okay.
WOOF WOOF WOOF

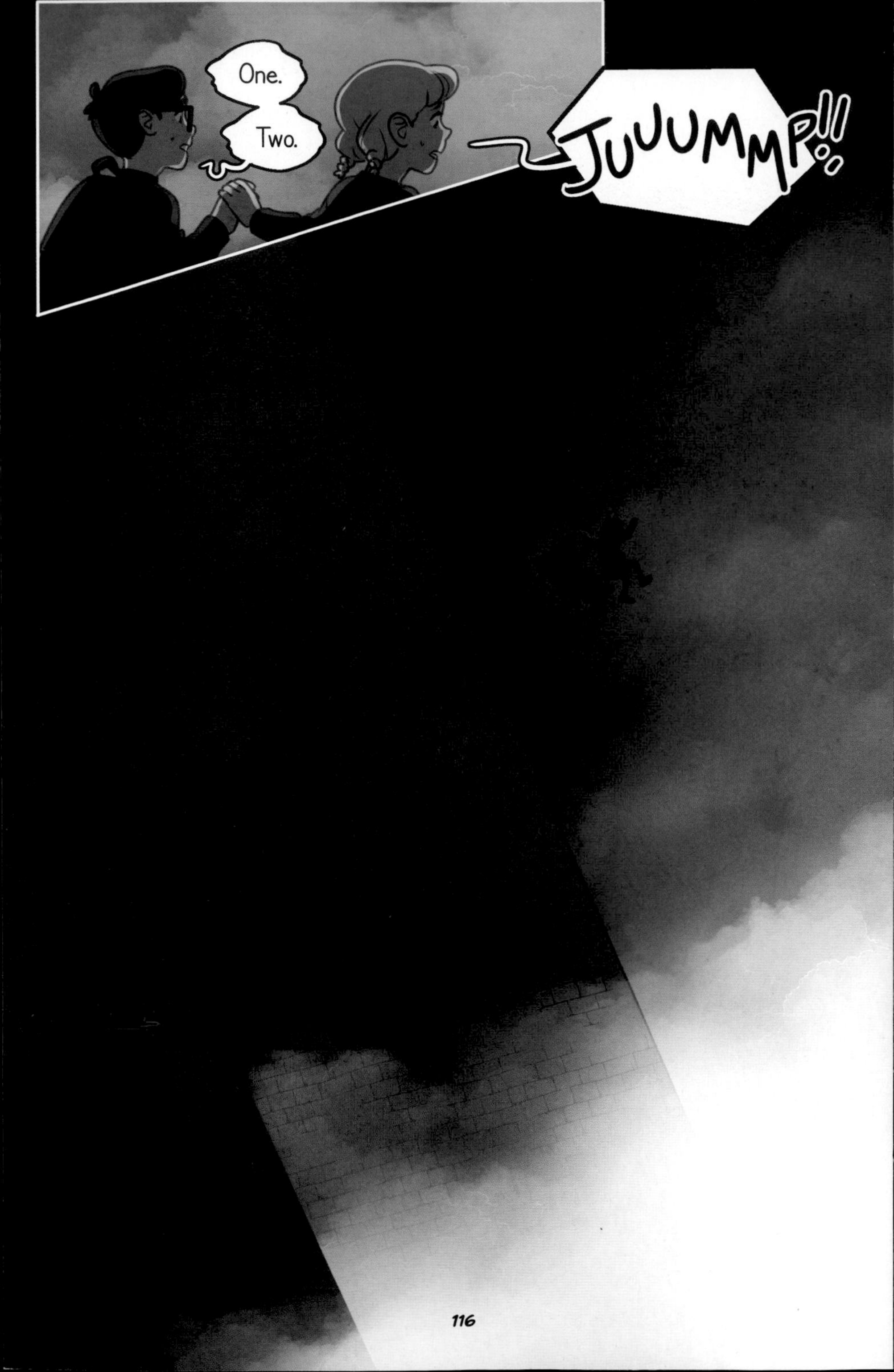
One.
Two.
JUUUMMP!!

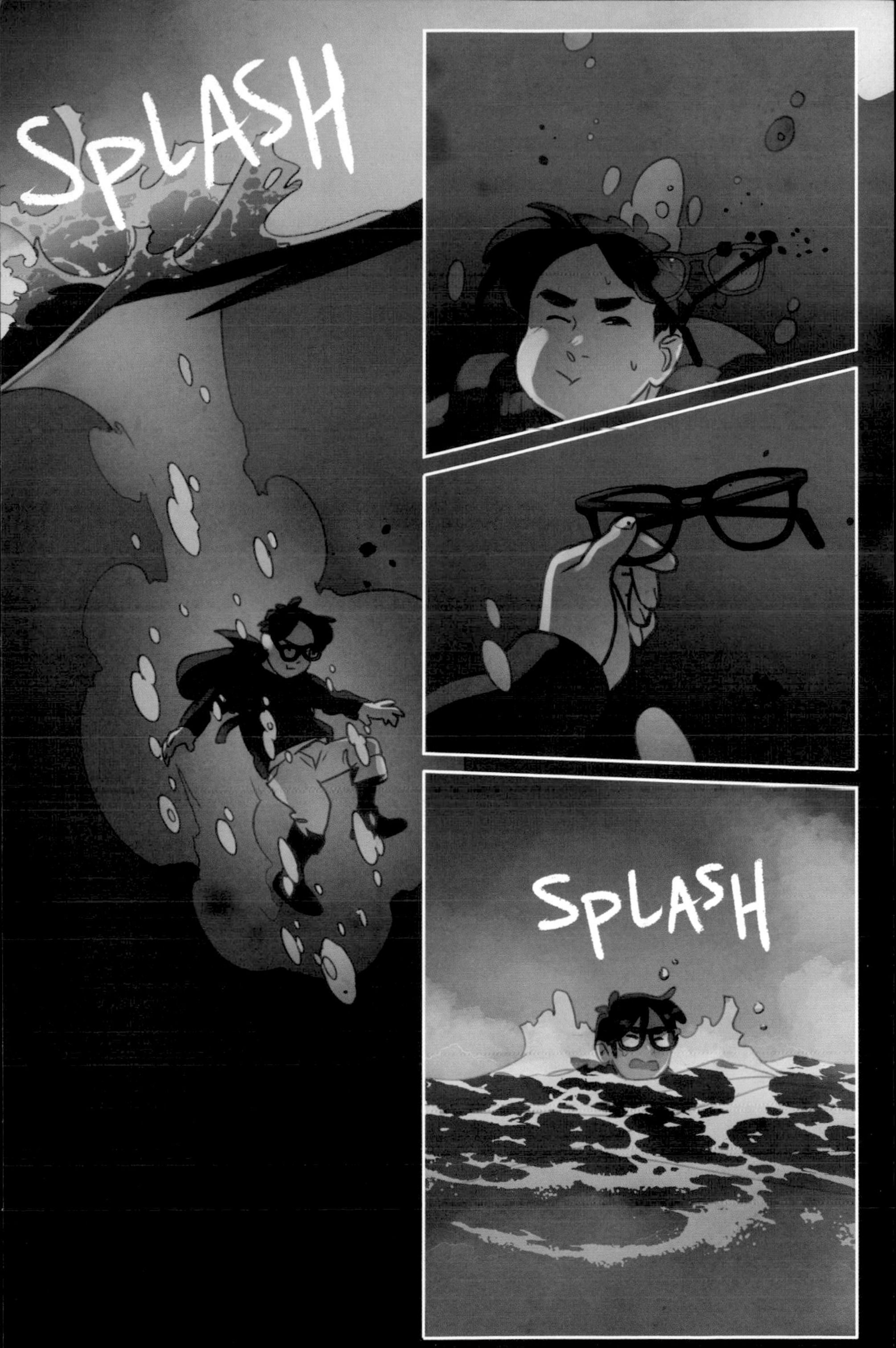
SPLASH
SPLASH

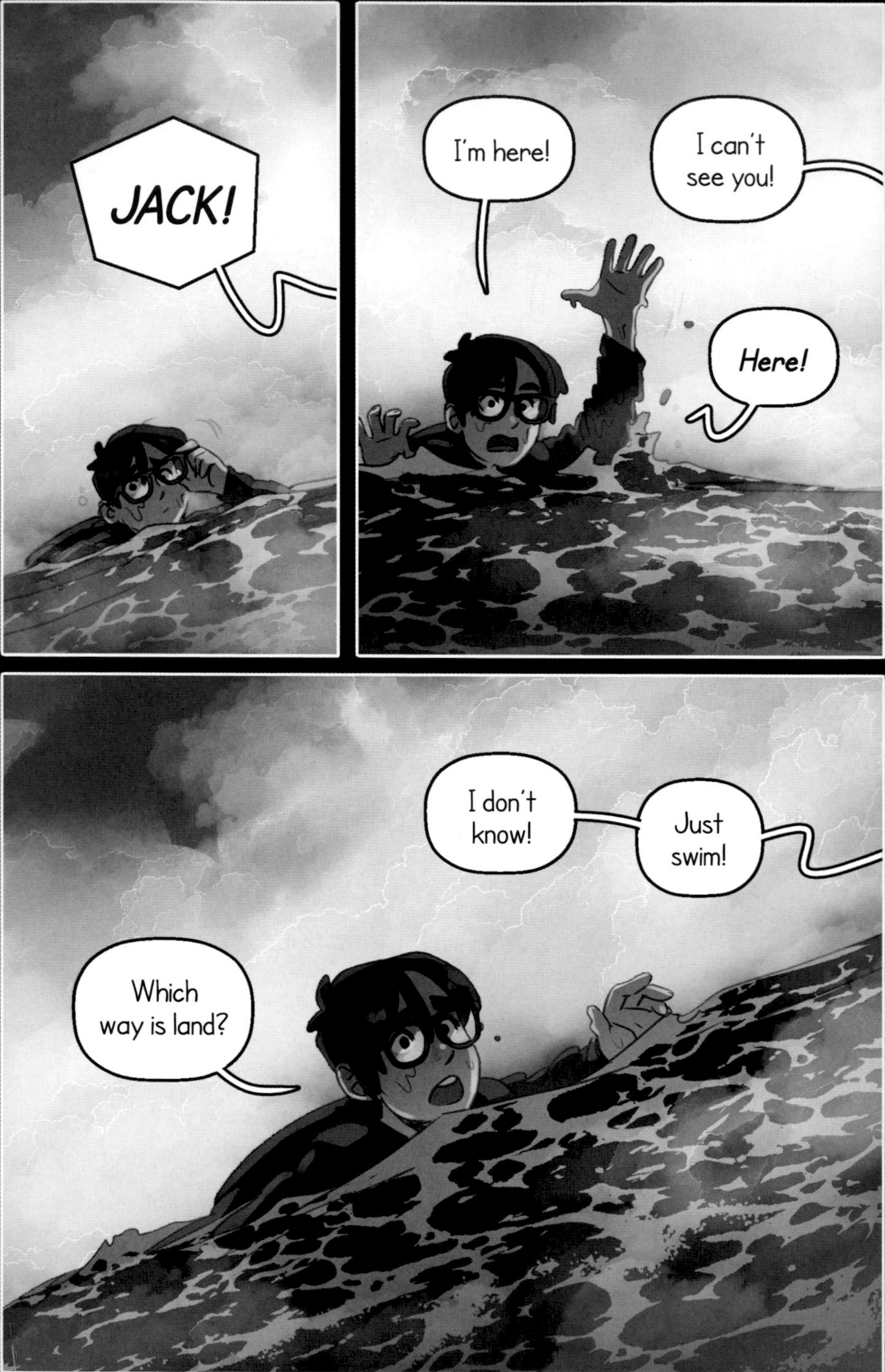
JACK!
I'm here!
I can't see you!
Here!
Which way is land?
I don't know!
Just swim!

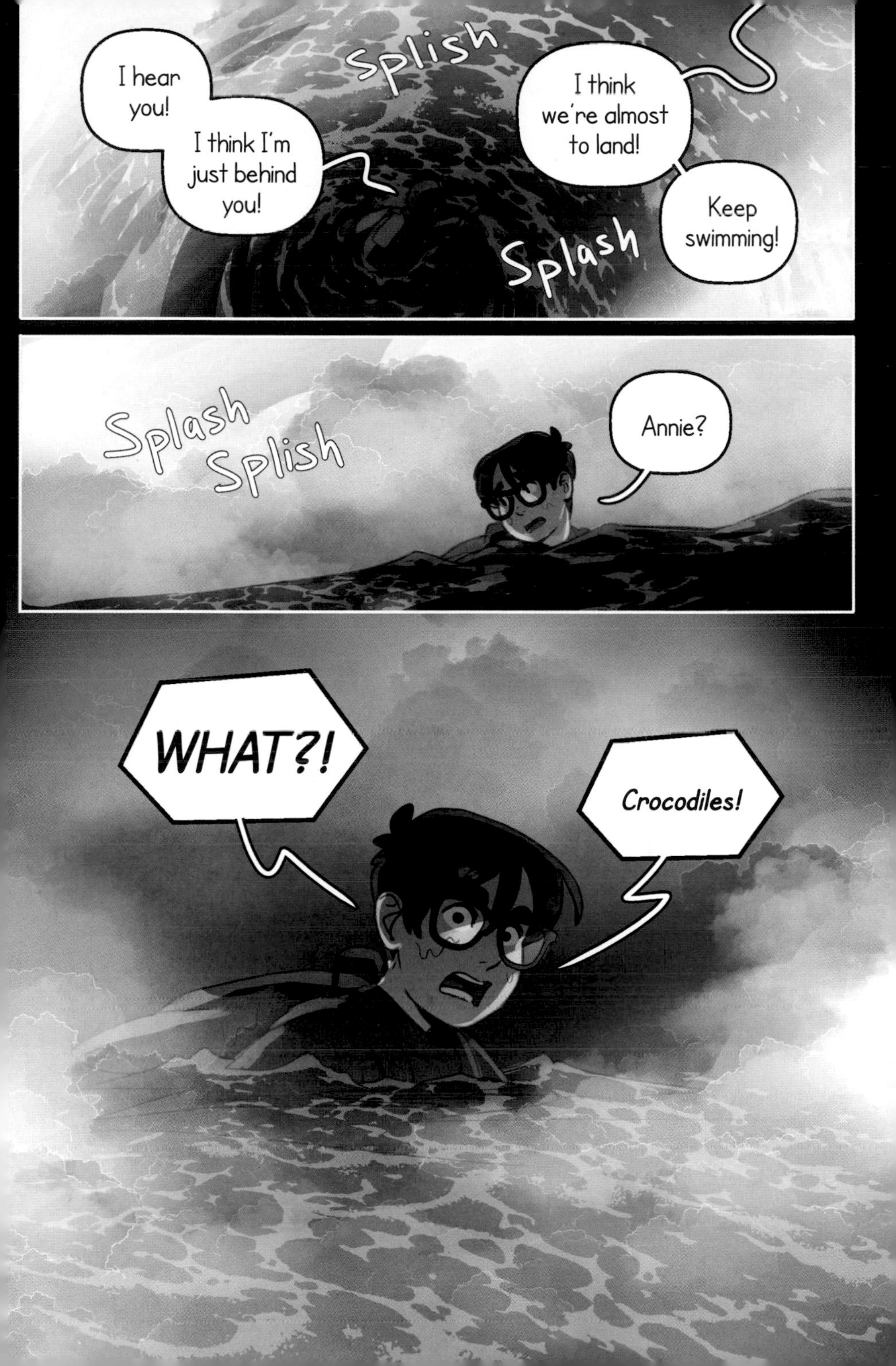
Splish
I hear you!
I think I'm just behind you!
I think we're almost to land!
Keep swimming!
Splash
Splash
Splish
Annie?
WHAT?!
Crocodiles!

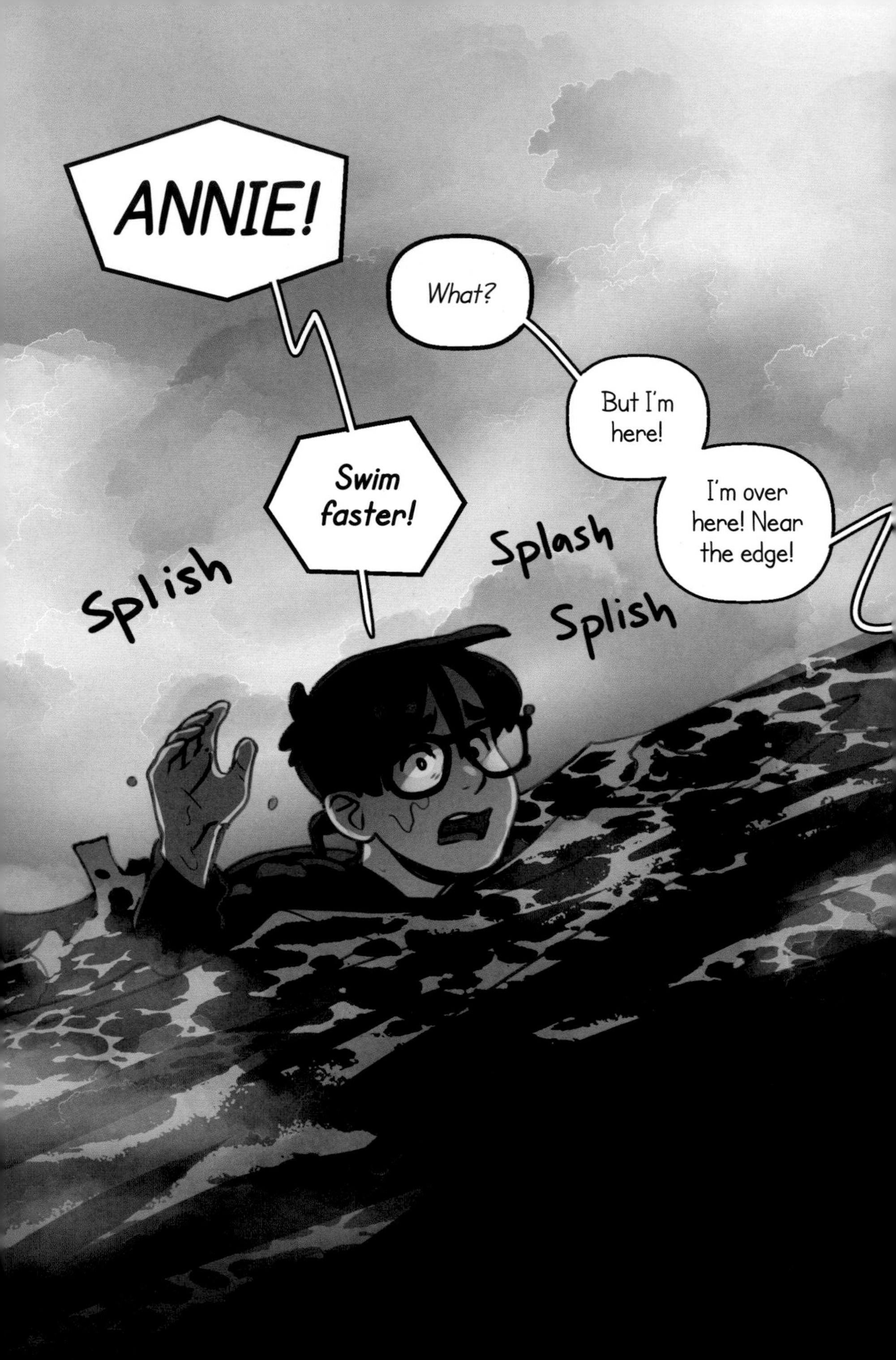
ANNIE!
Swim faster!
What?
But I'm here!
I'm over here! Near the edge!
Splish
Splash
Splish

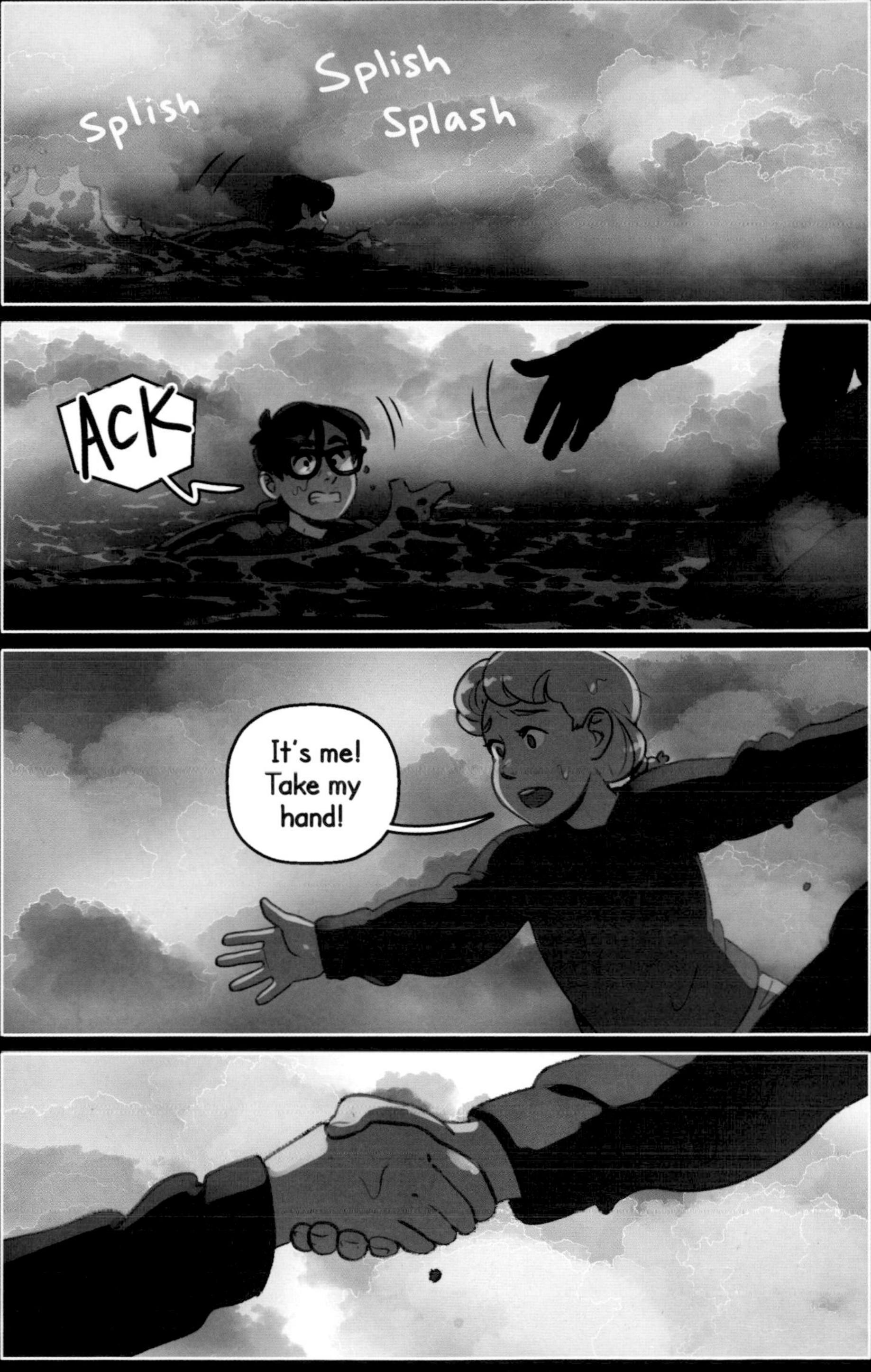
Splish
Splish
Splash
ACK
It's me! Take my hand!

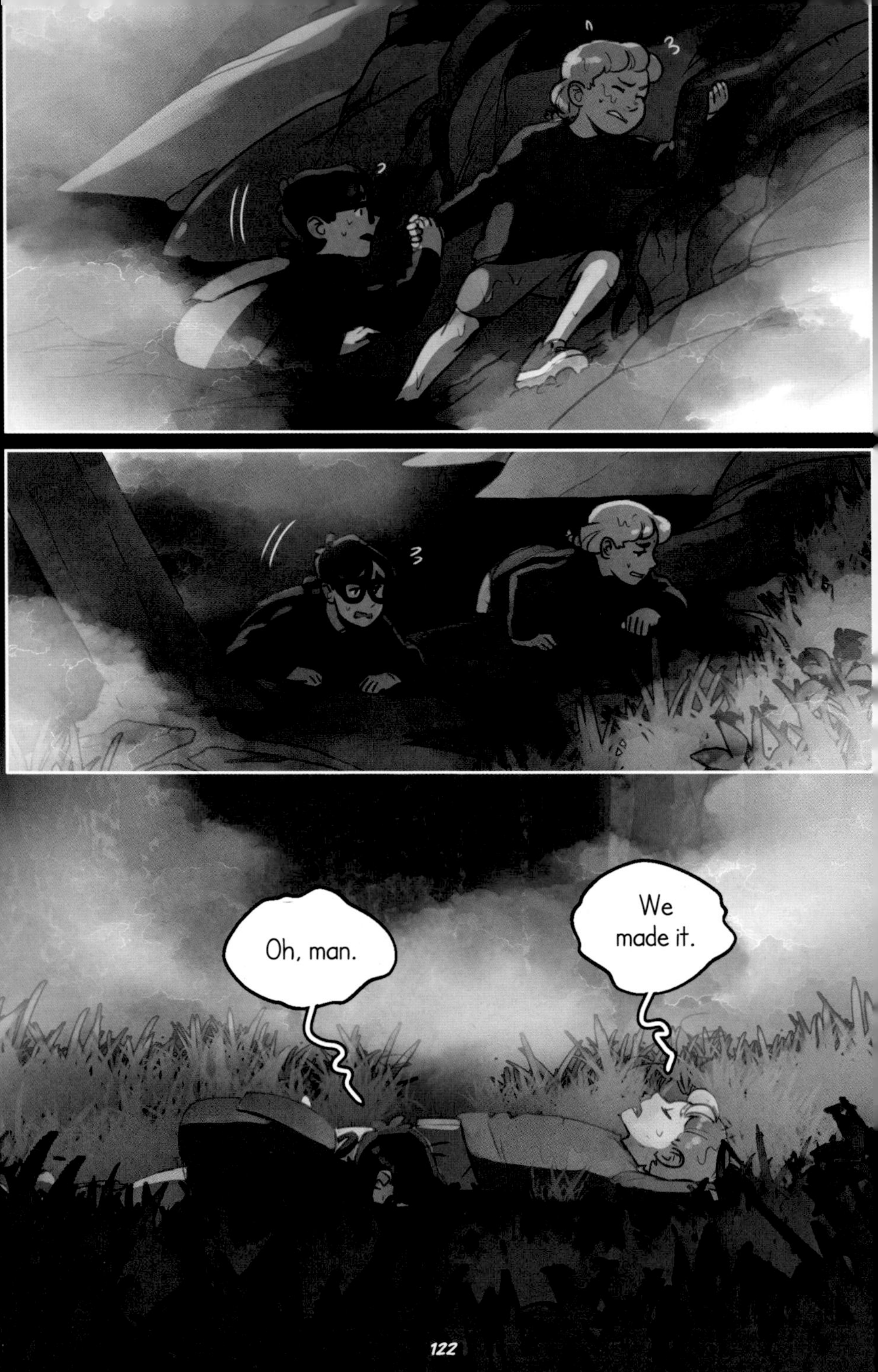
Oh, man.
We made it.

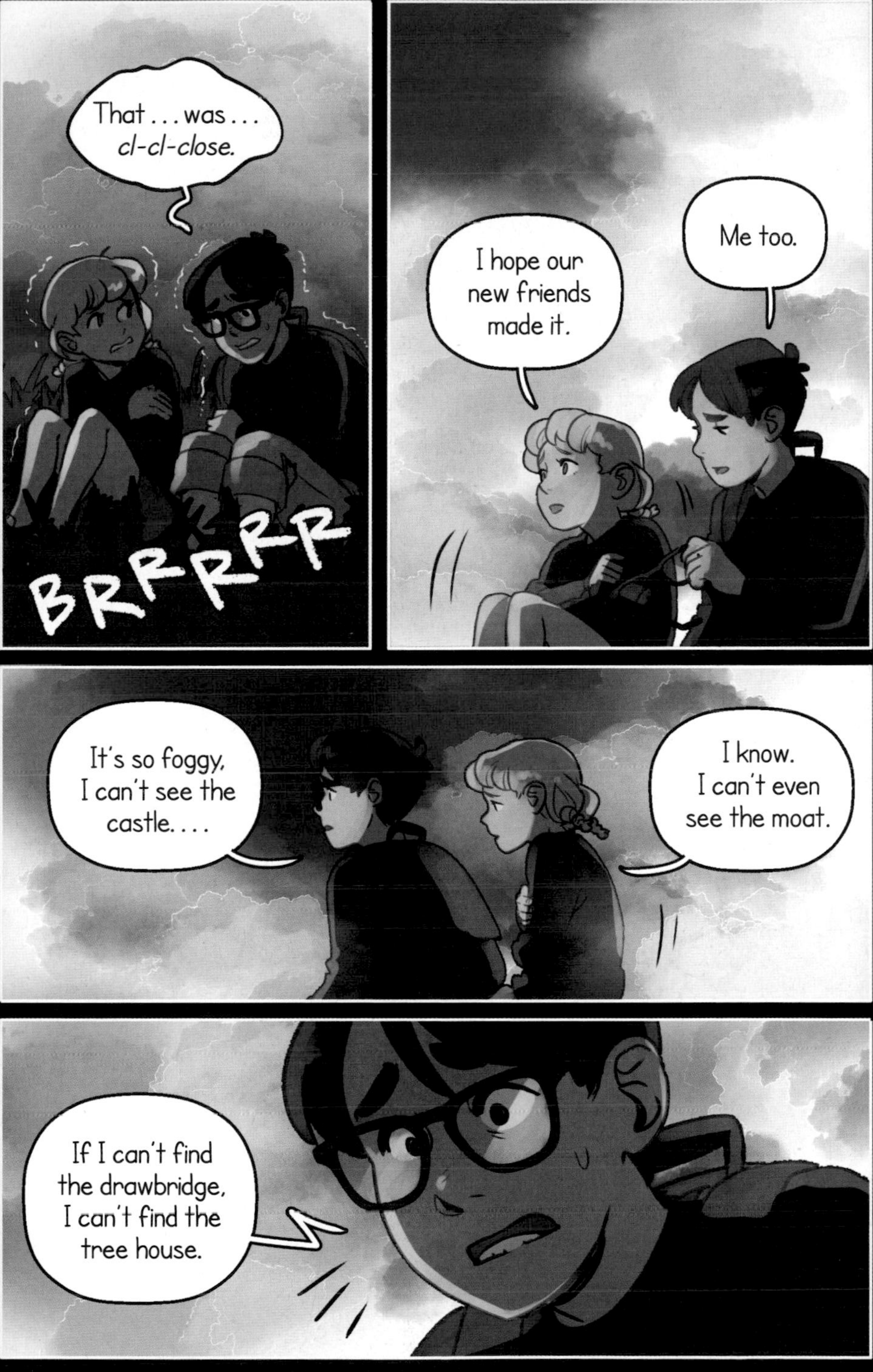

That . . . was . . . *cl-cl-close.*
BRRRRR
I hope our new friends made it.
Me too.
It's so foggy, I can't see the castle. . . .
I know. I can't even see the moat.
If I can't find the drawbridge, I can't find the tree house.

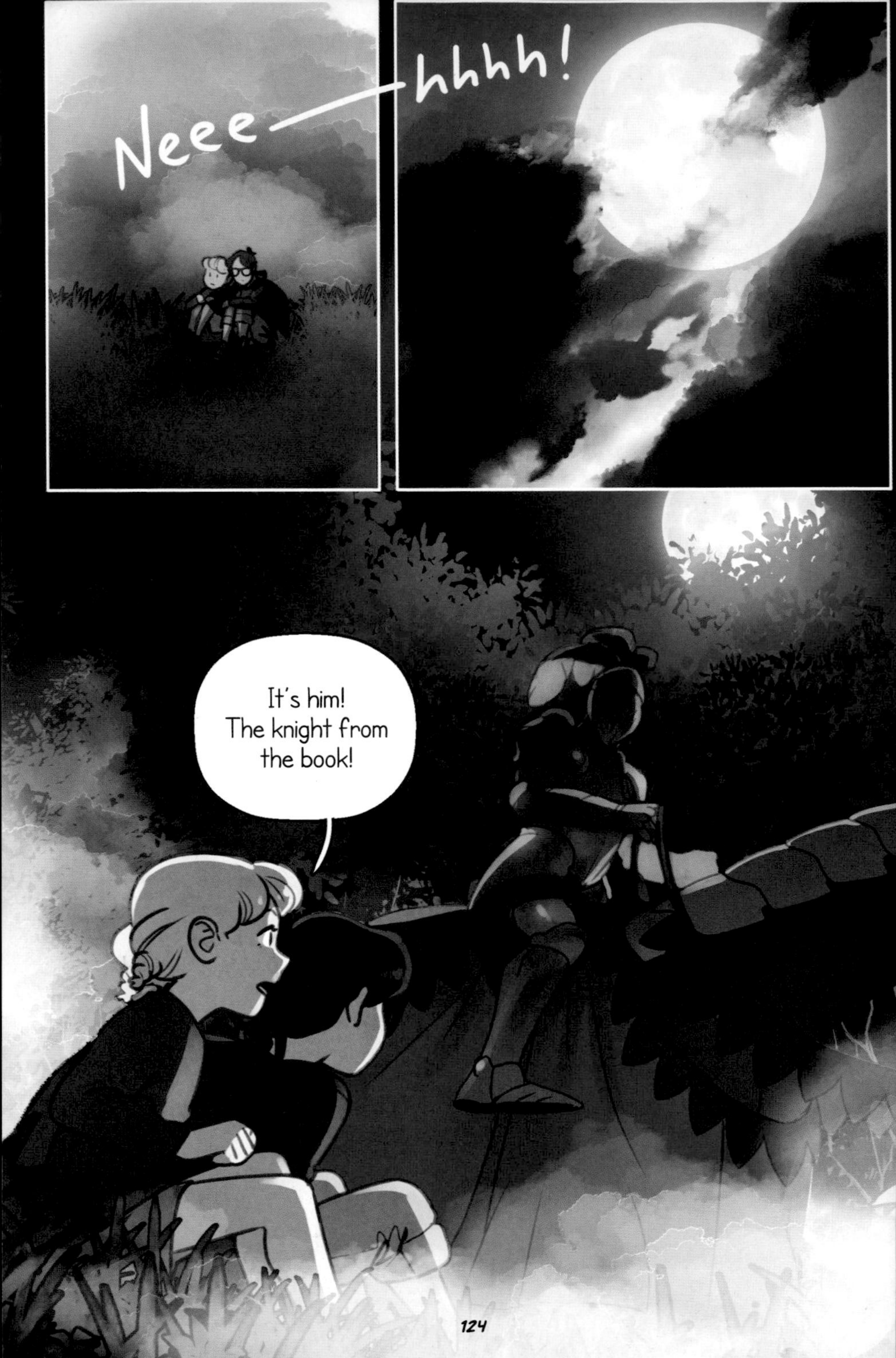
Neee—hhhh!
It's him! The knight from the book!

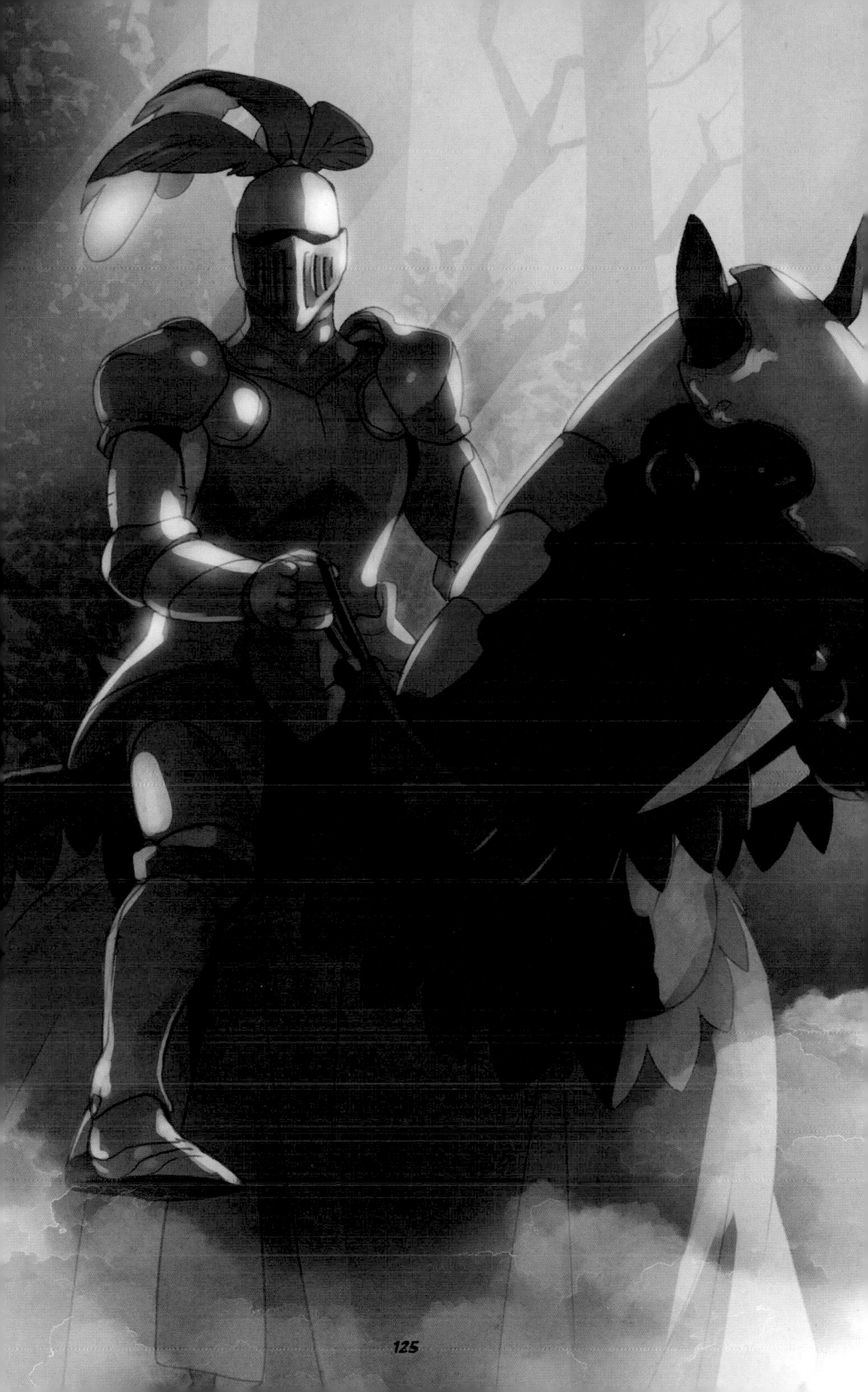

CHAPTER NINE
Under the Moon

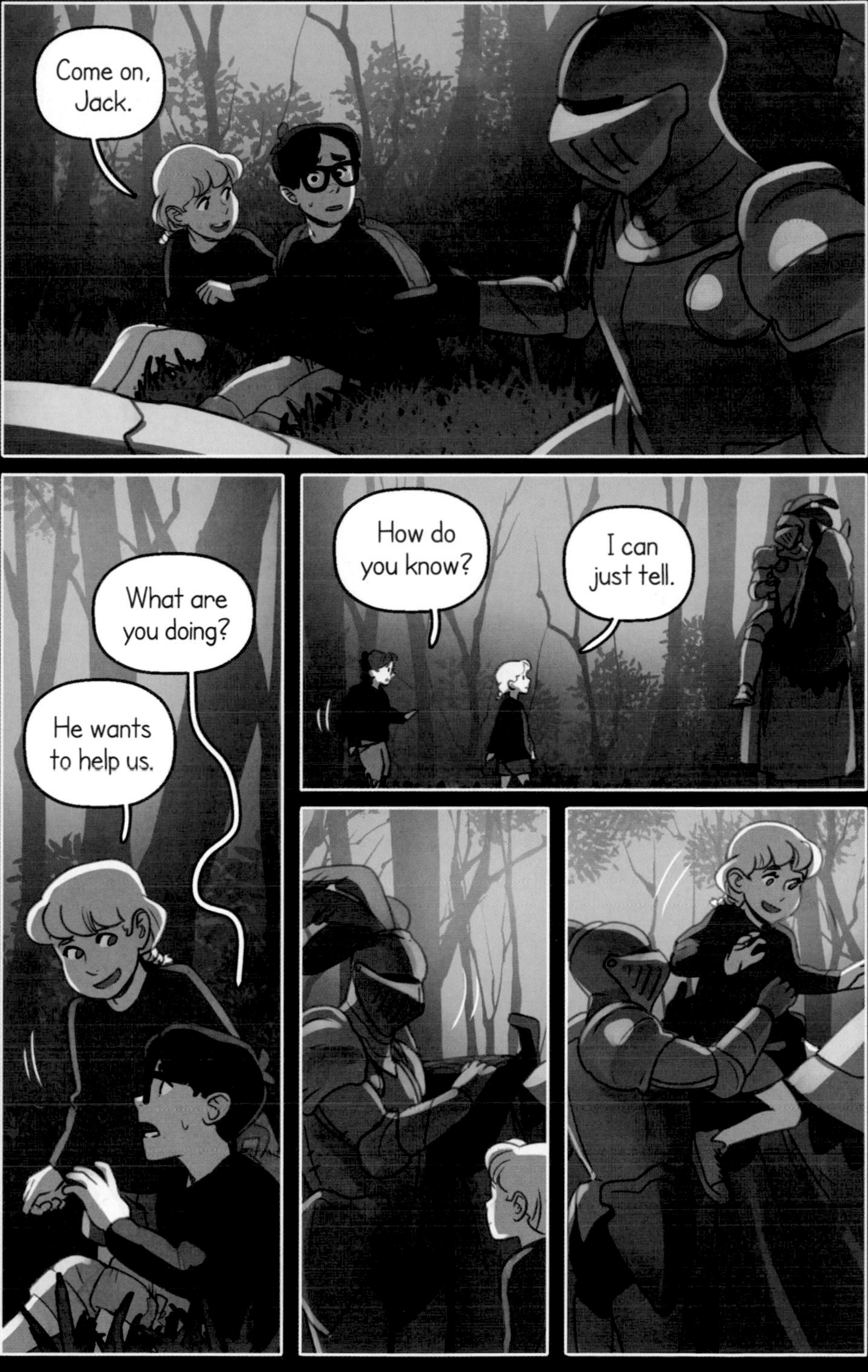
Come on, Jack.
What are you doing?
He wants to help us.
How do you know?
I can just tell.

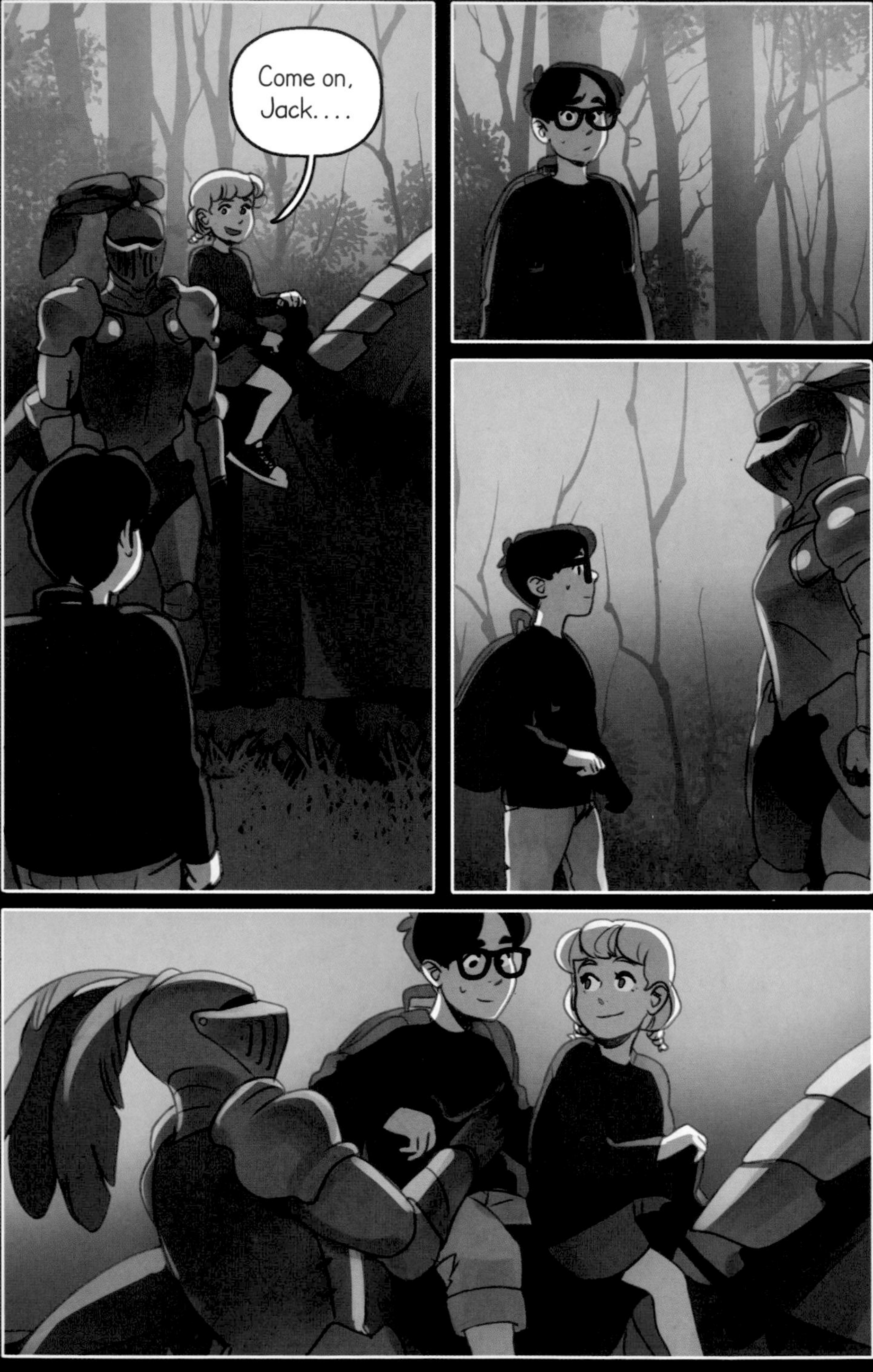
Come on, Jack. . . .

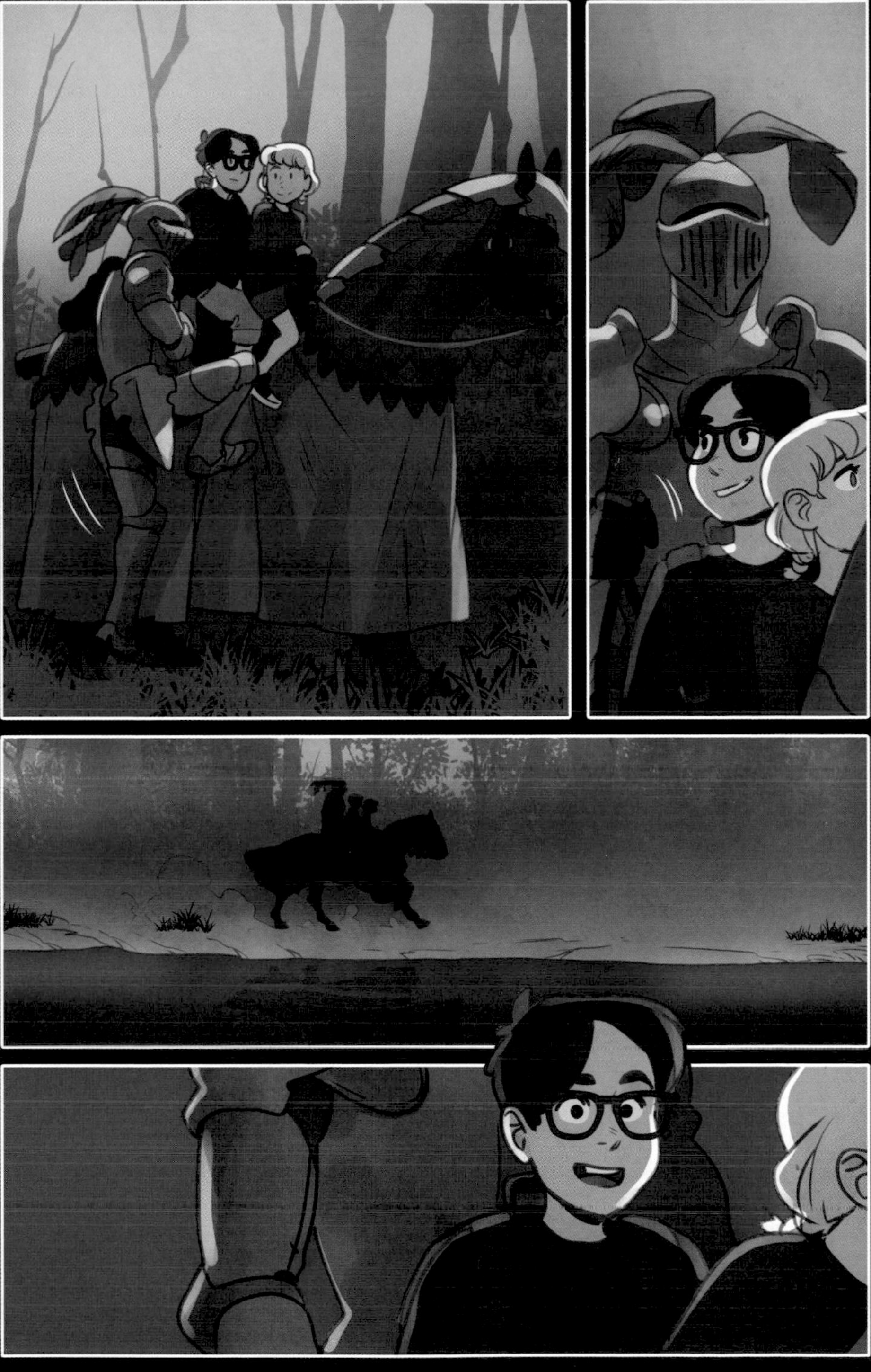

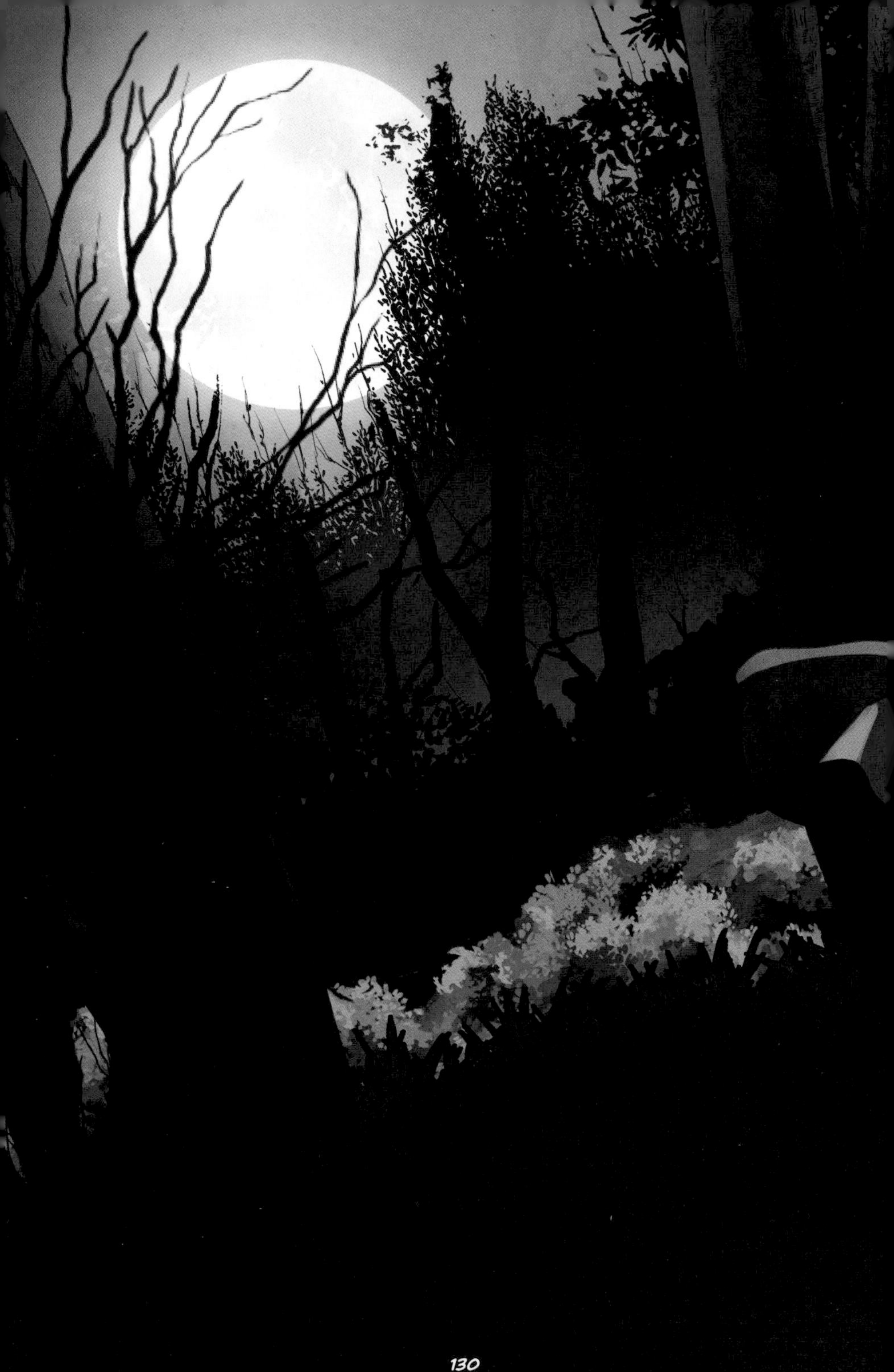

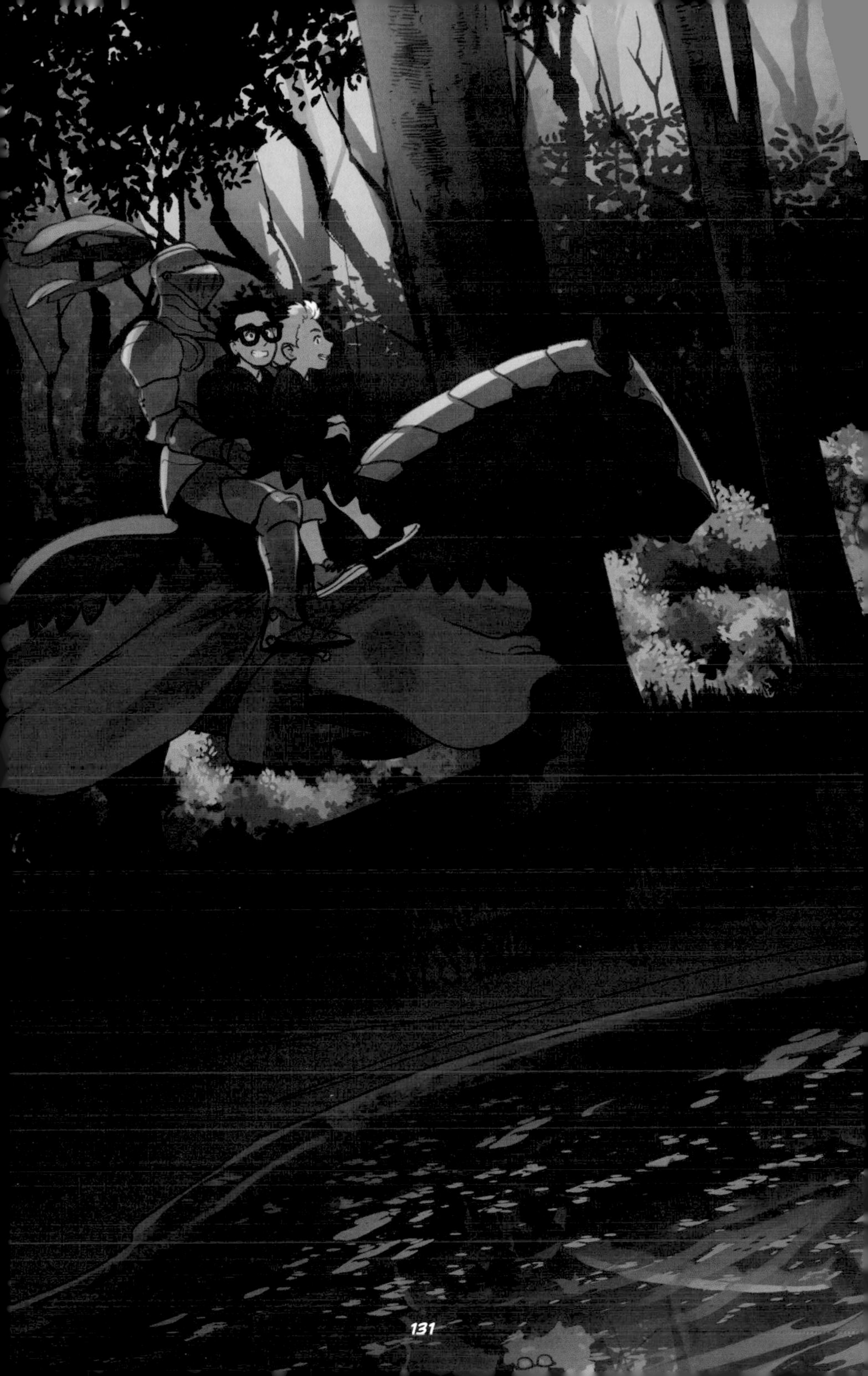

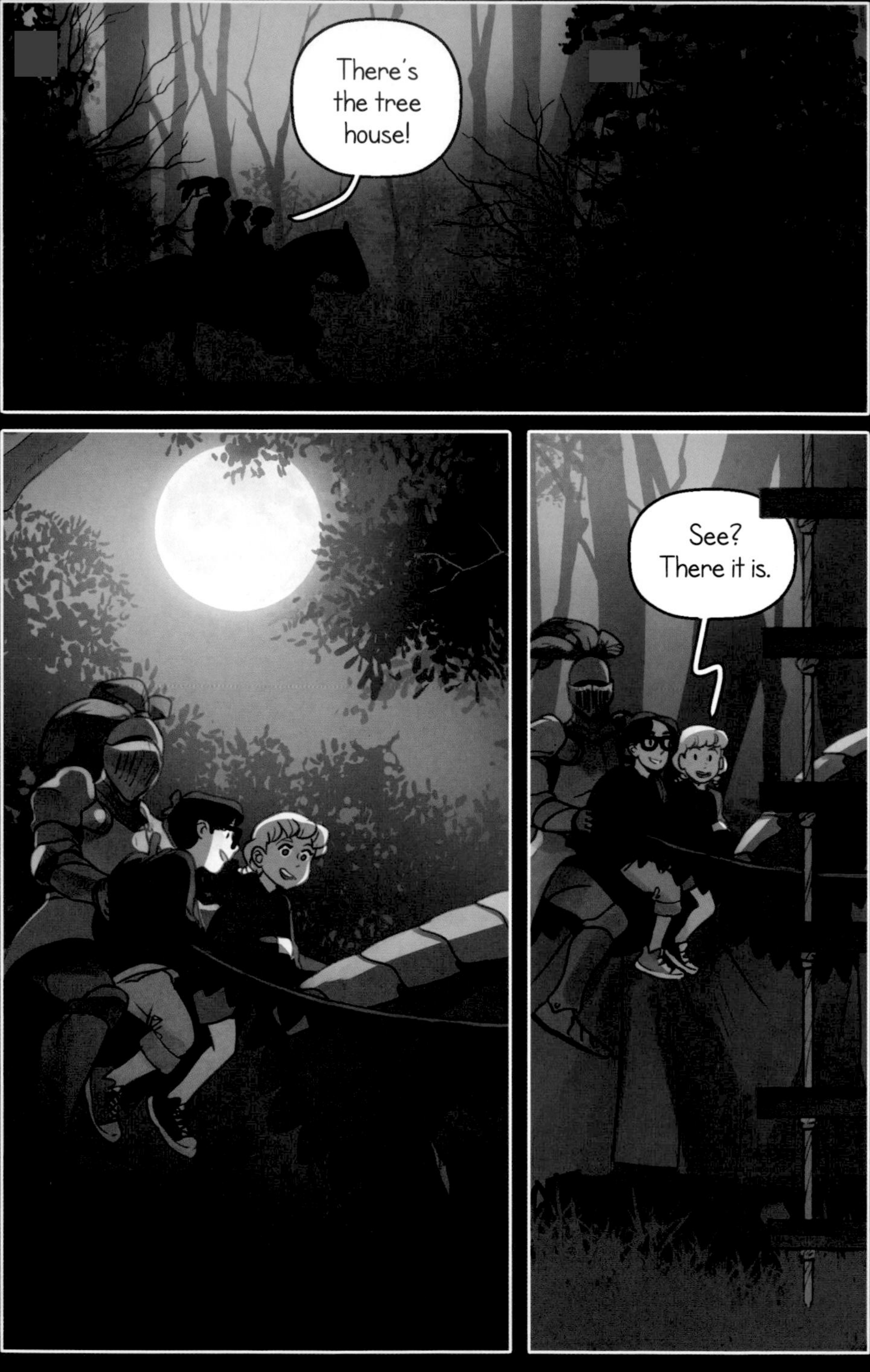
There's the tree house!
See? There it is.

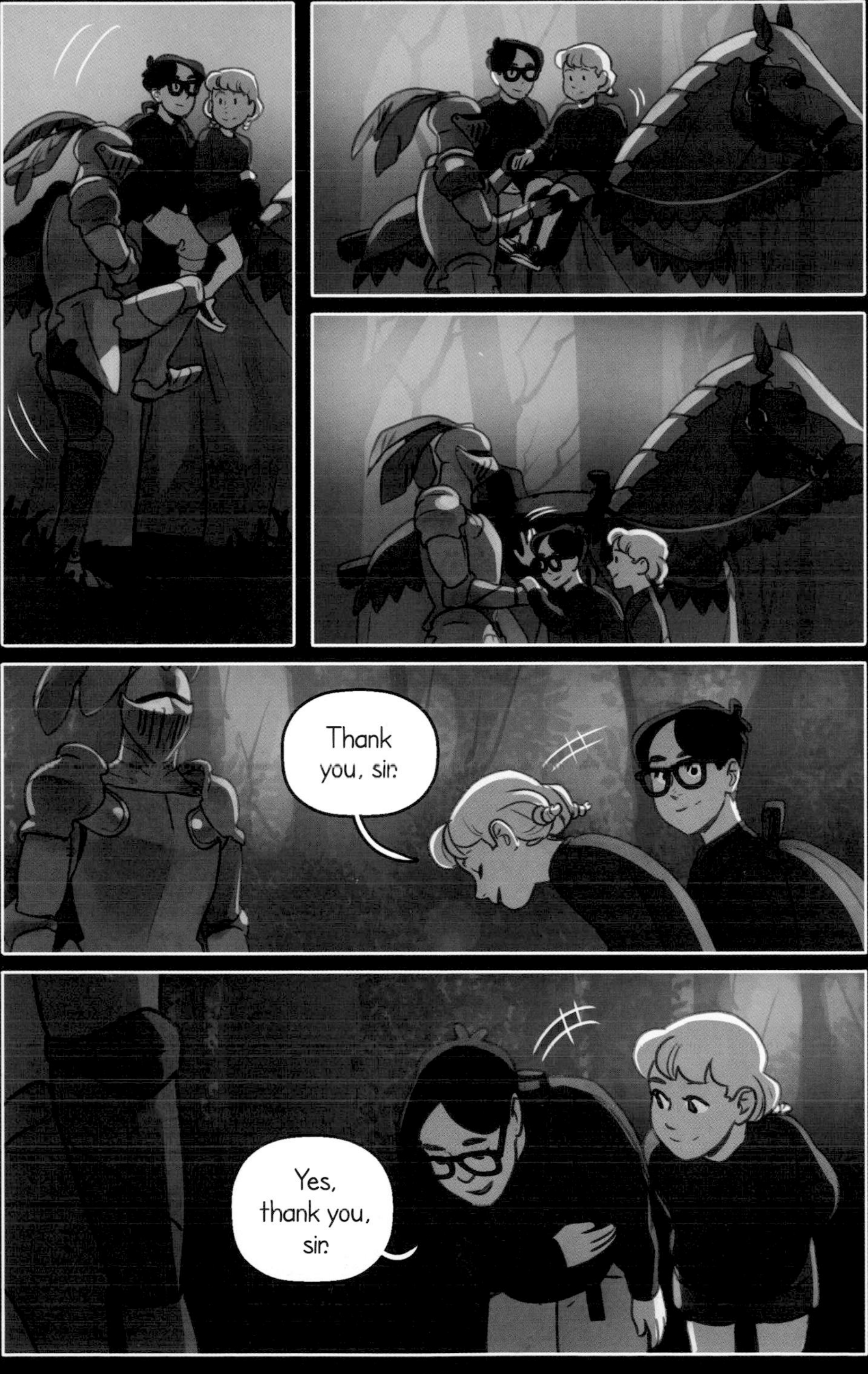
Thank you, sir.
Yes, thank you, sir.

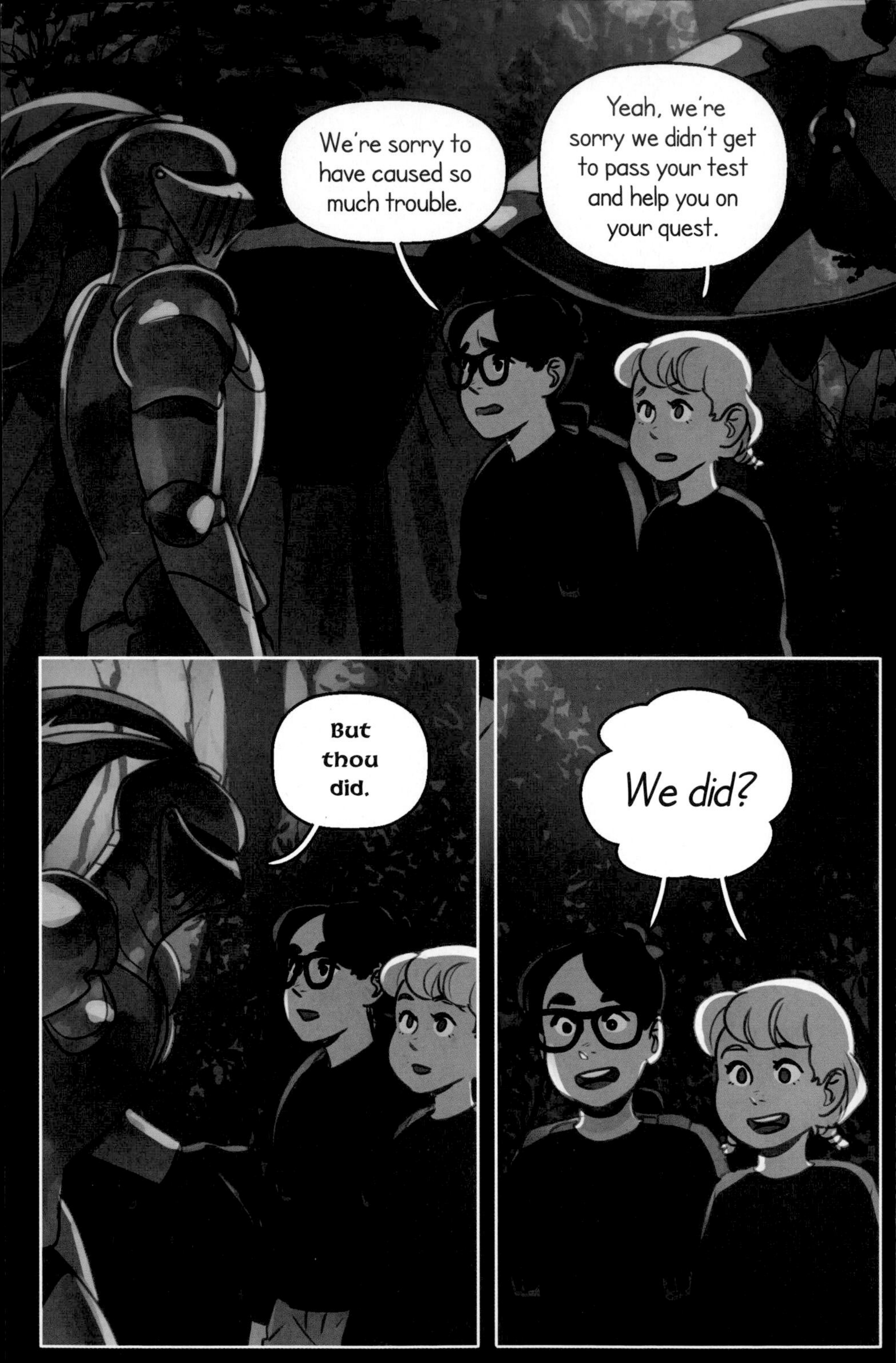
We're sorry to have caused so much trouble.
Yeah, we're sorry we didn't get to pass your test and help you on your quest.
But thou did.
We did?

Thou protected and freed the innocent.

And thou did it without sword or might.

We did use a flashlight.

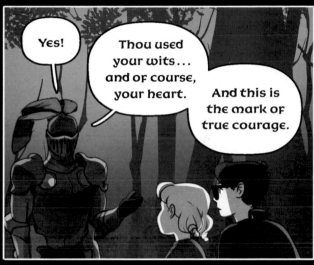

Yes!

Thou used your wits... and of course, your heart.

And this is the mark of true courage.

So that means our new friends escaped?

They can go home now?

Indeed.

Kneel, please.
Now bow your heads.
YOU DID NOT COUNT THE COST
BUT BRAVELY GAVE YOUR BEST
RESTORING HOPE WHERE IT WAS LOST
YOU HAVE PASSED MY TEST
YOU HAVE PASSED MY TEST

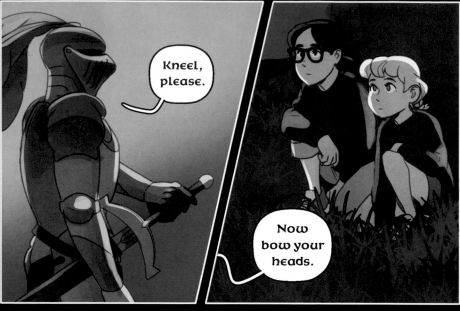

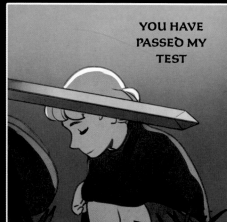

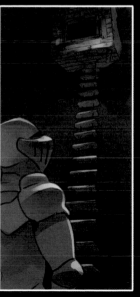

Good speed on your journey home.

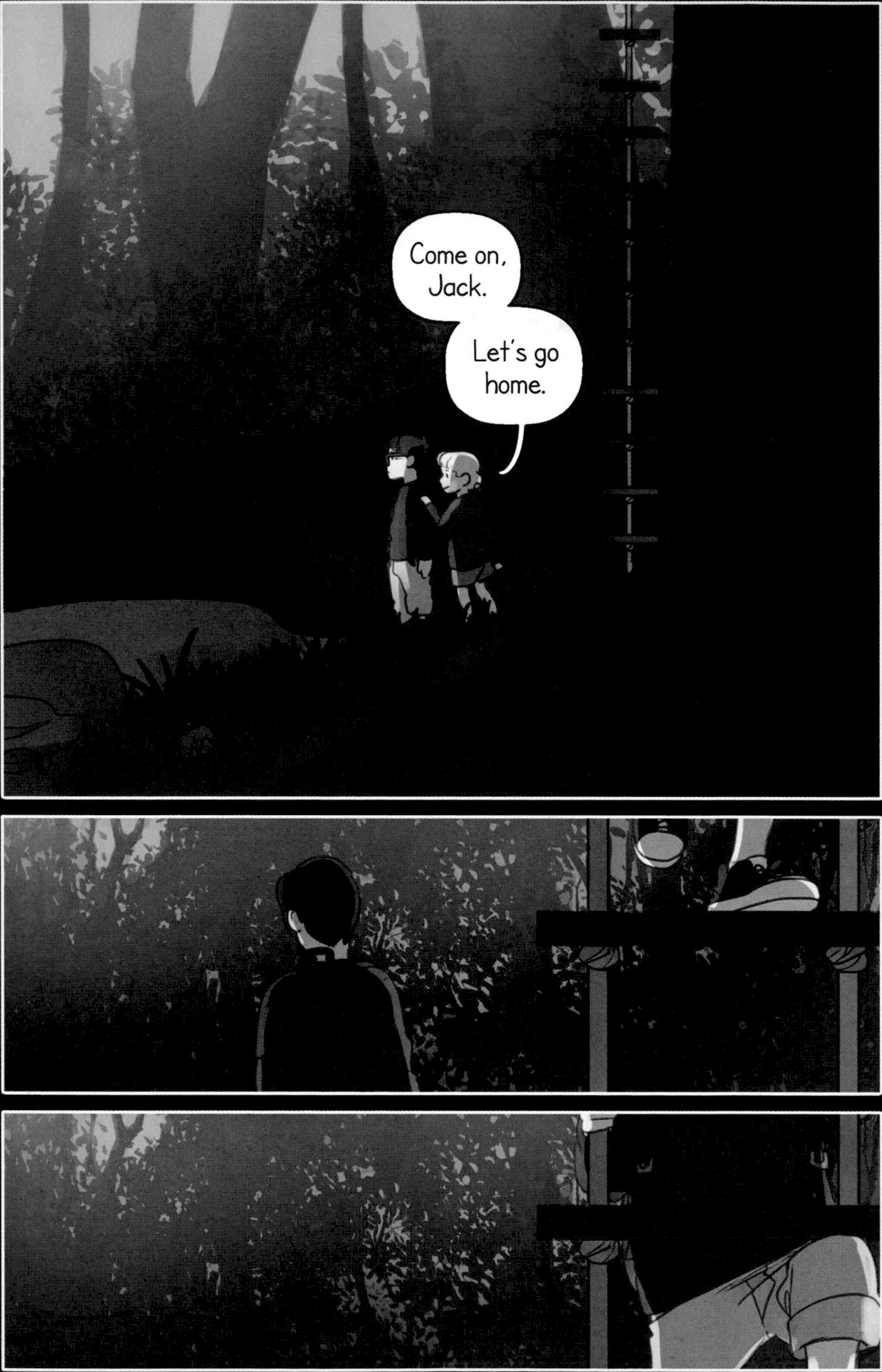
Come on, Jack.
Let's go home.

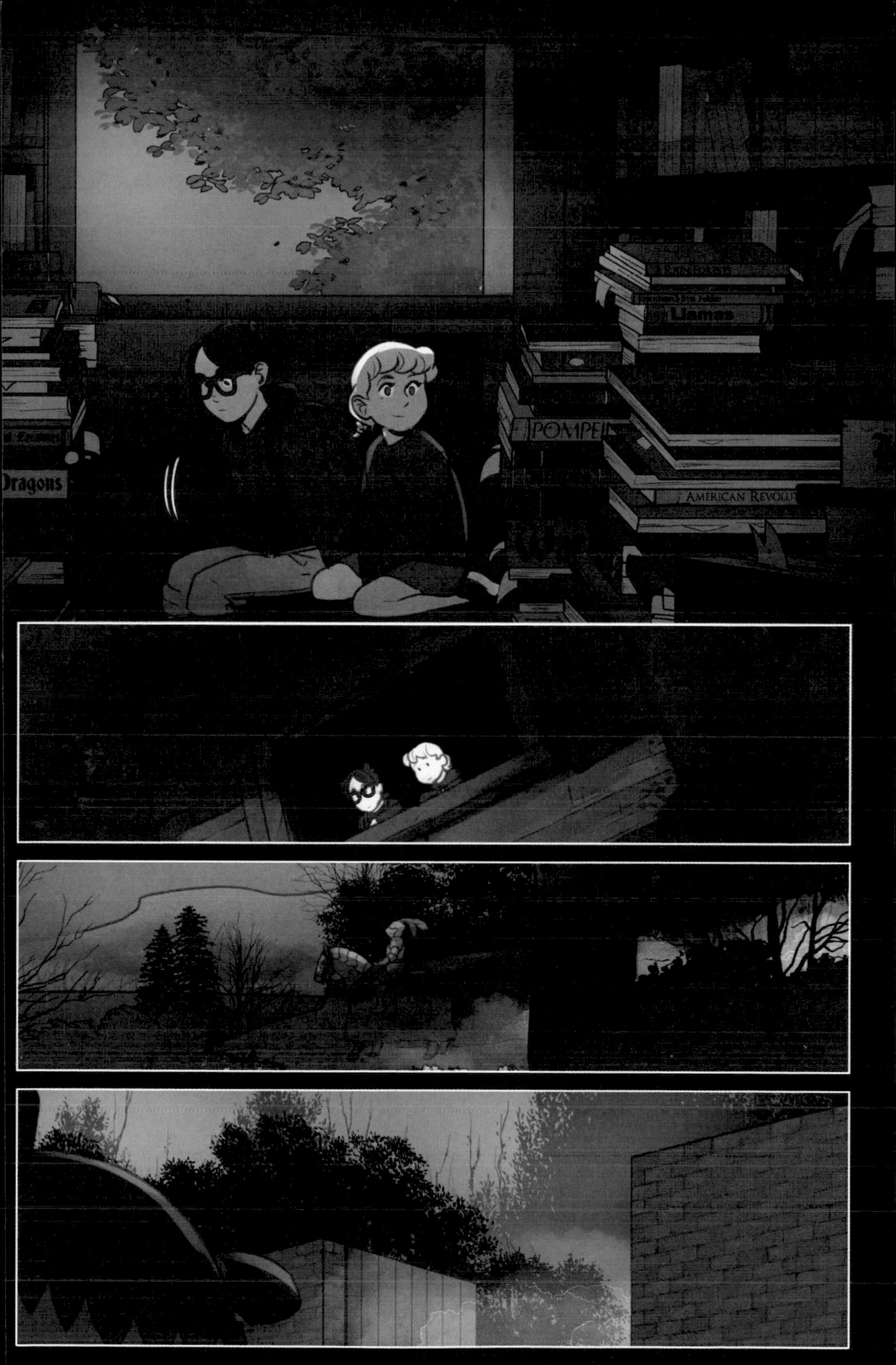
Dragons
Llamas

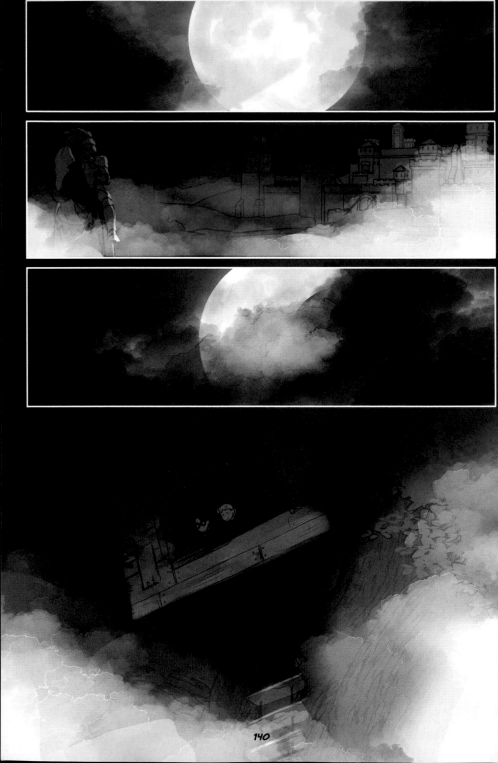

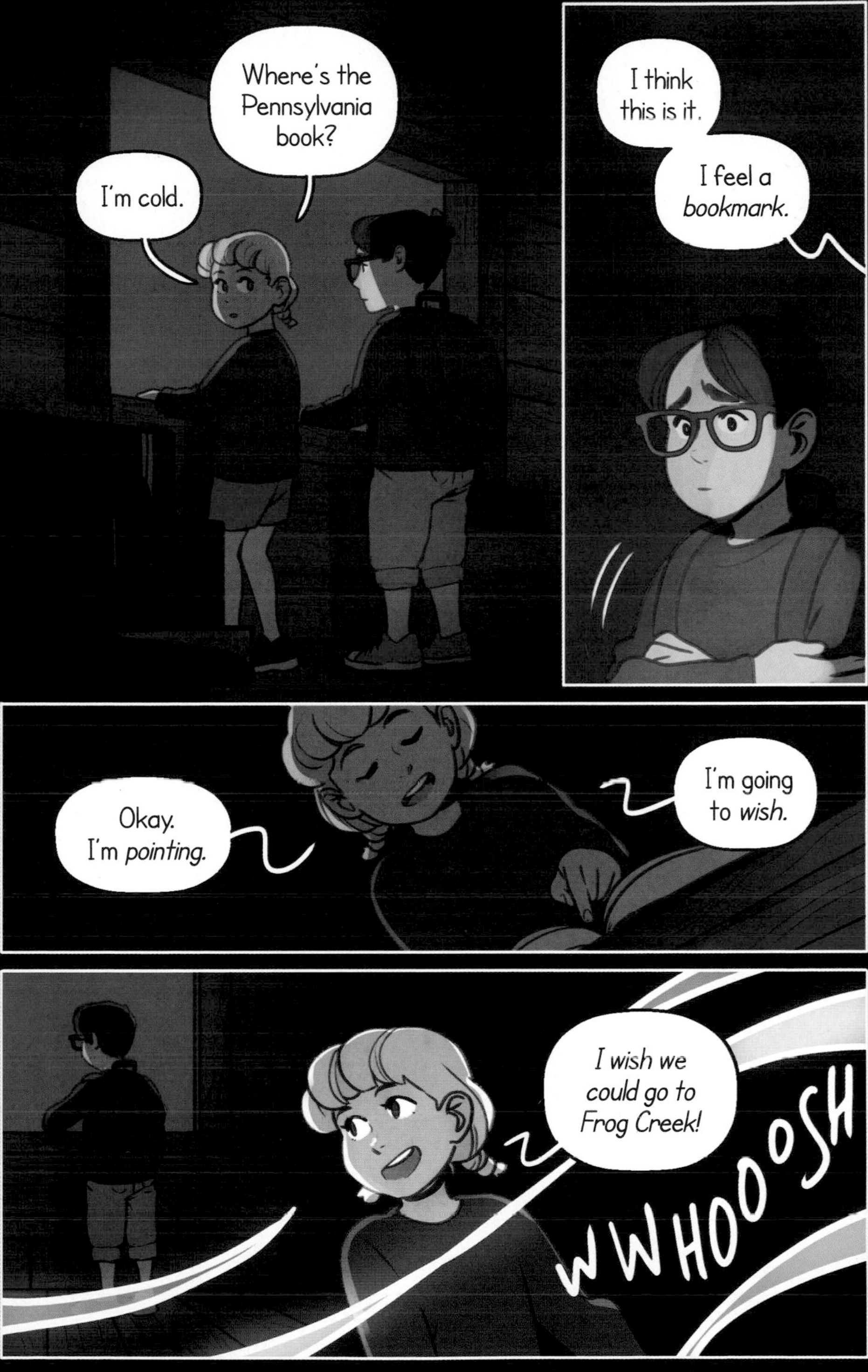

Where's the Pennsylvania book?
I'm cold.
I think this is it.
I feel a *bookmark*.
Okay. I'm *pointing*.
I'm going to *wish*.
I wish we could go to Frog Creek!
WWHOOOSH

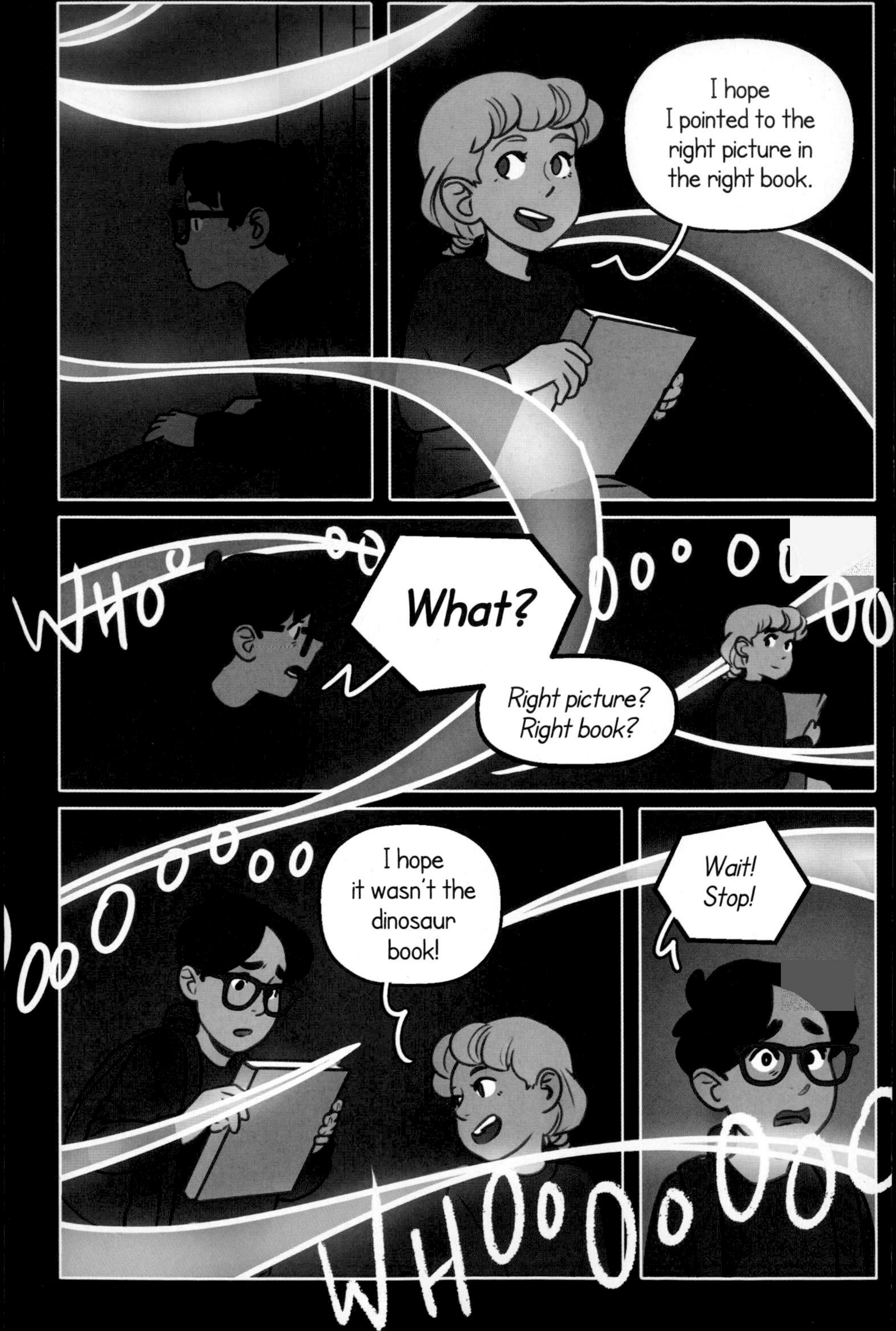
I hope I pointed to the right picture in the right book.
WHOOOOOOO
What?
Right picture? Right book?
OOOOOO
I hope it wasn't the dinosaur book!
Wait! Stop!
WHOOOOOOO

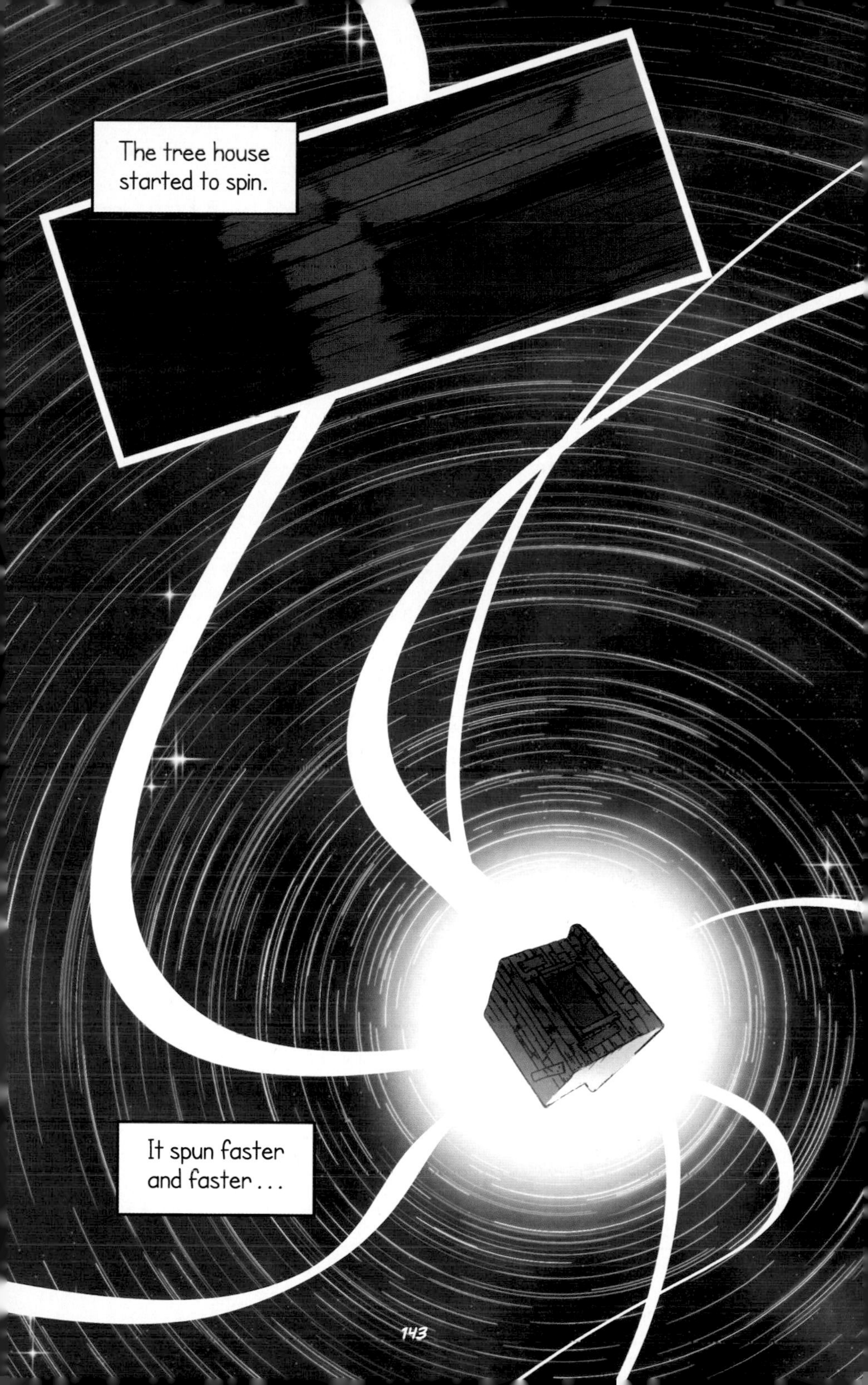
The tree house started to spin.
It spun faster and faster . . .

CHAPTER TEN

One Mystery Solved

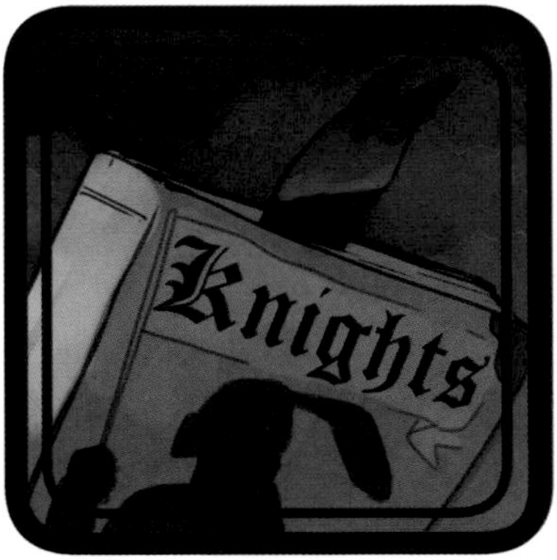
Knights

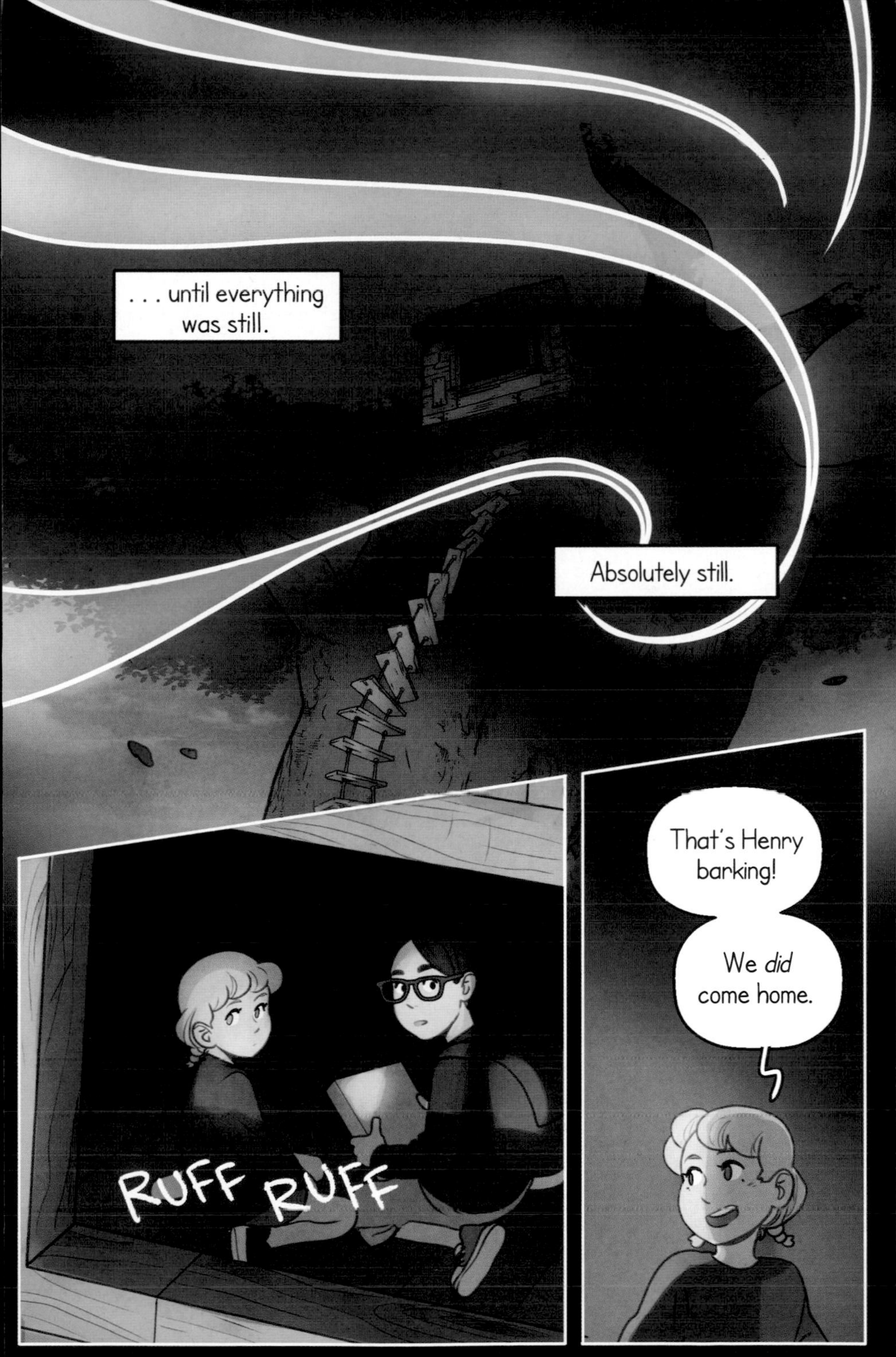
. . . until everything was still.
Absolutely still.
RUFF RUFF
That's Henry barking!
We *did* come home.

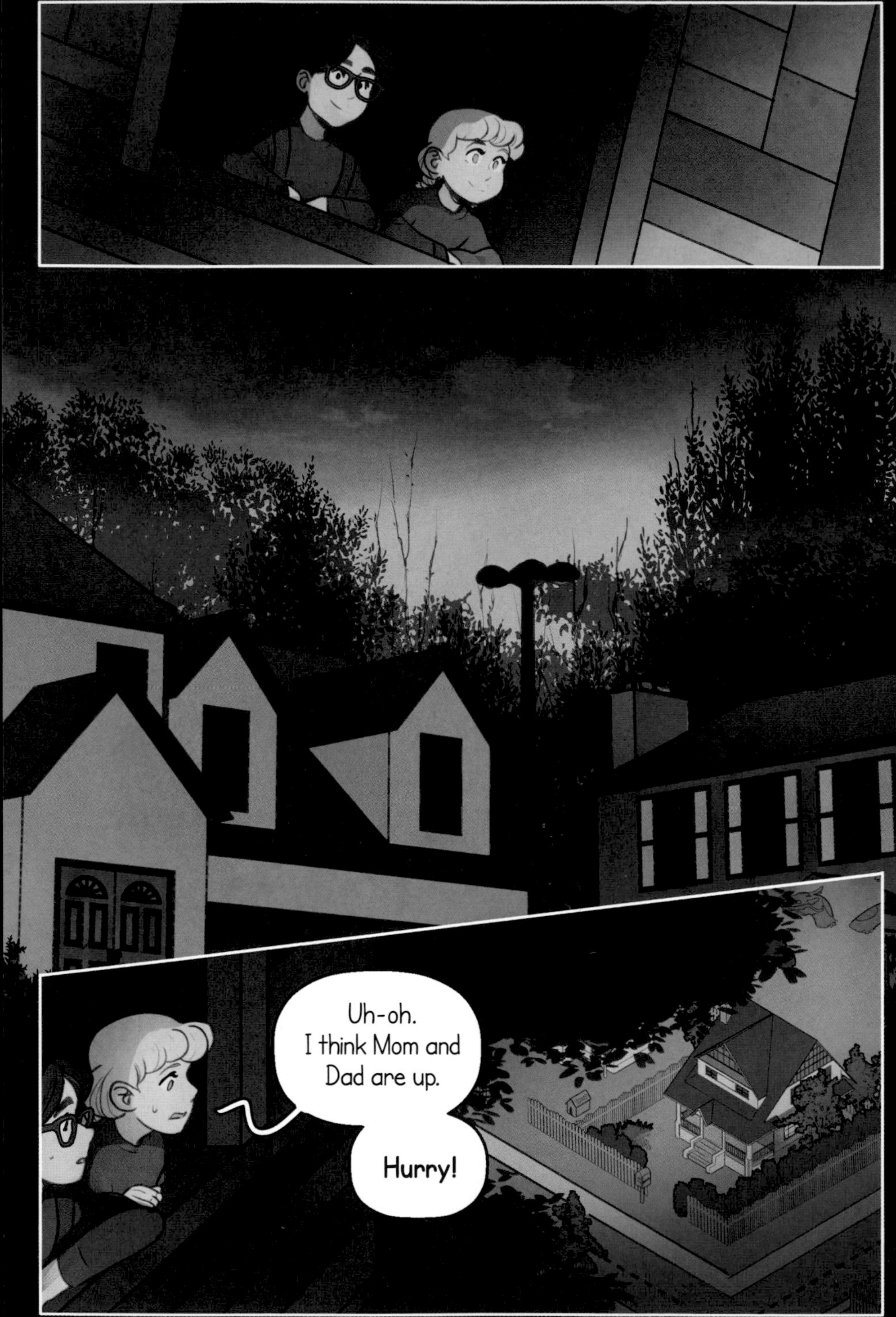
Uh-oh.
I think Mom and
Dad are up.
Hurry!

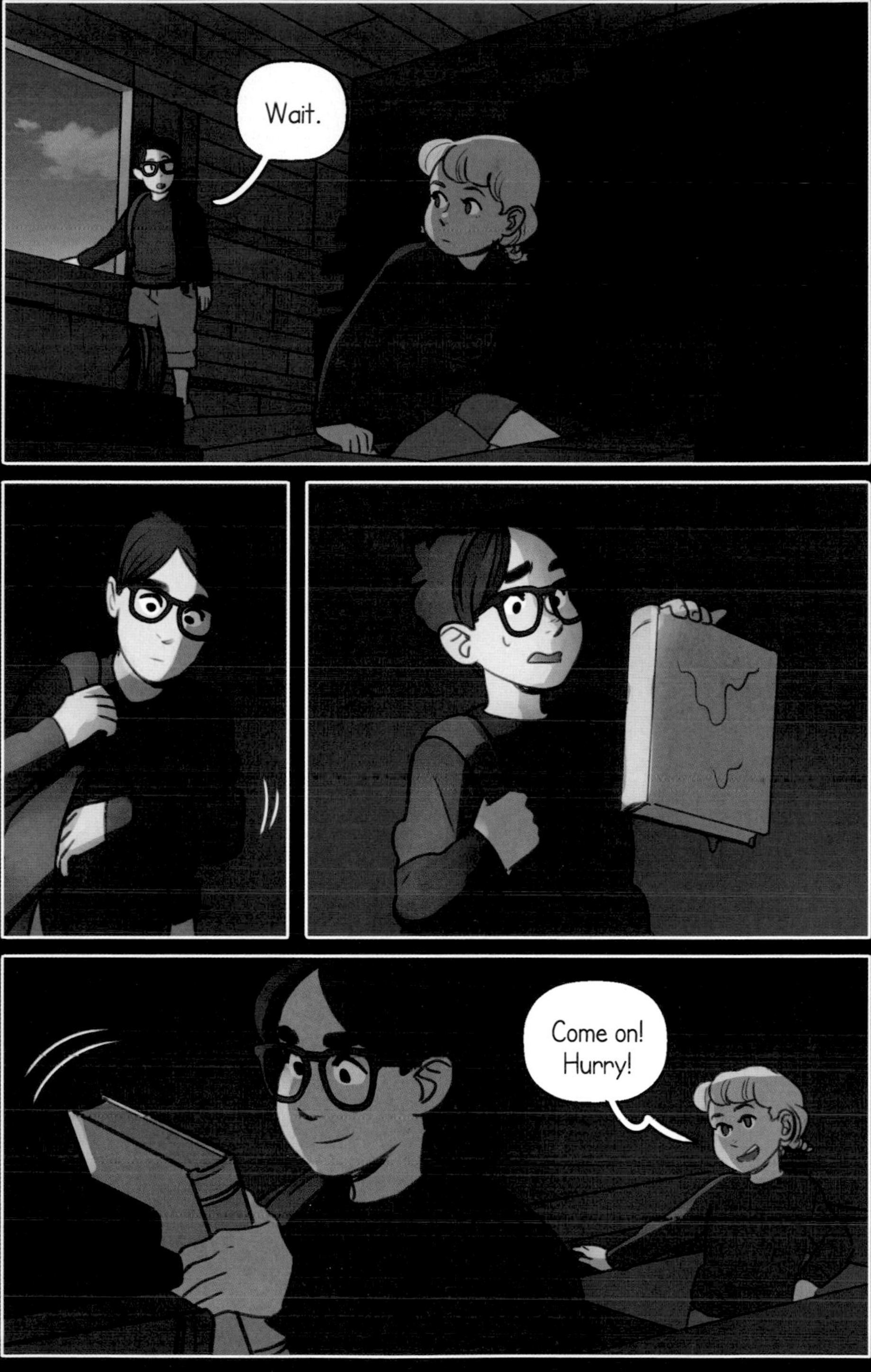
Wait.
Come on! Hurry!

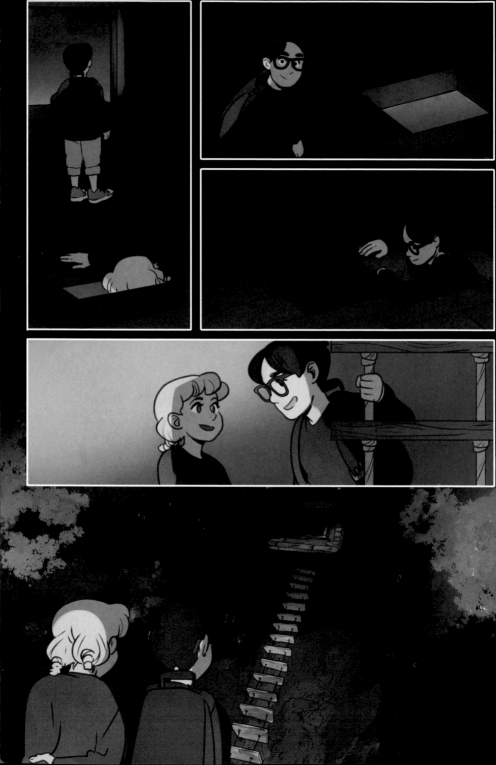

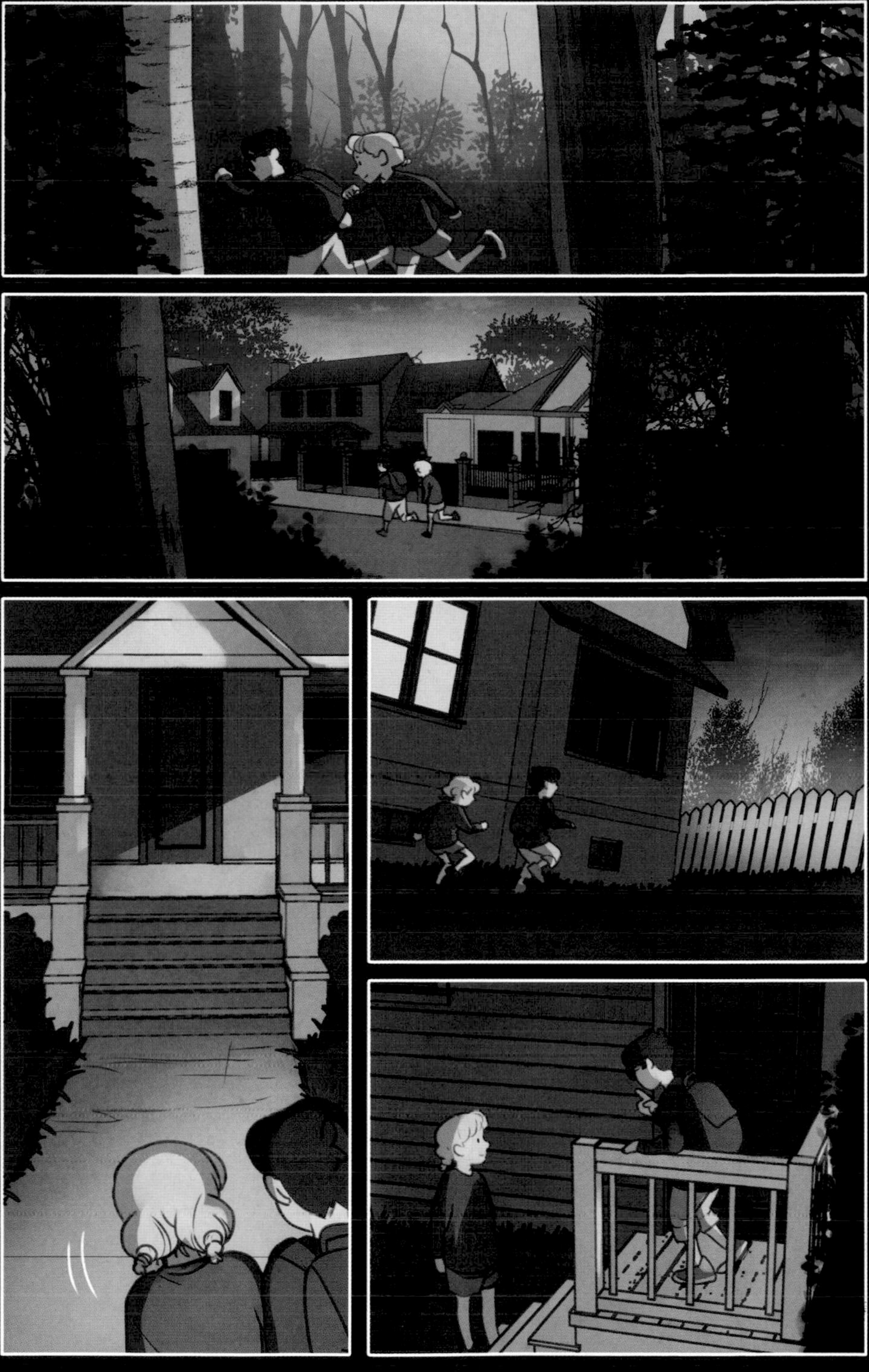

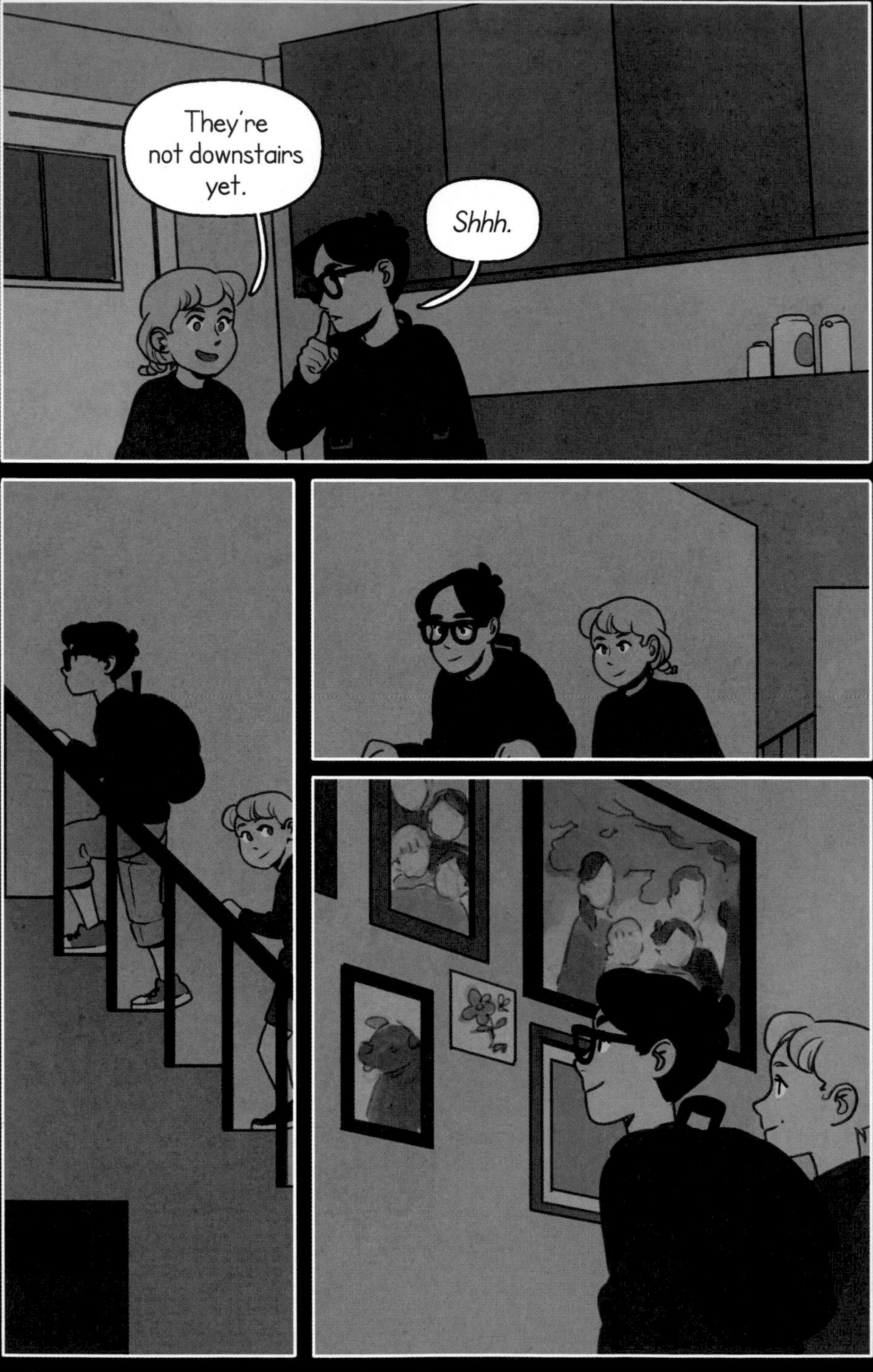
They're not downstairs yet.
Shhh.

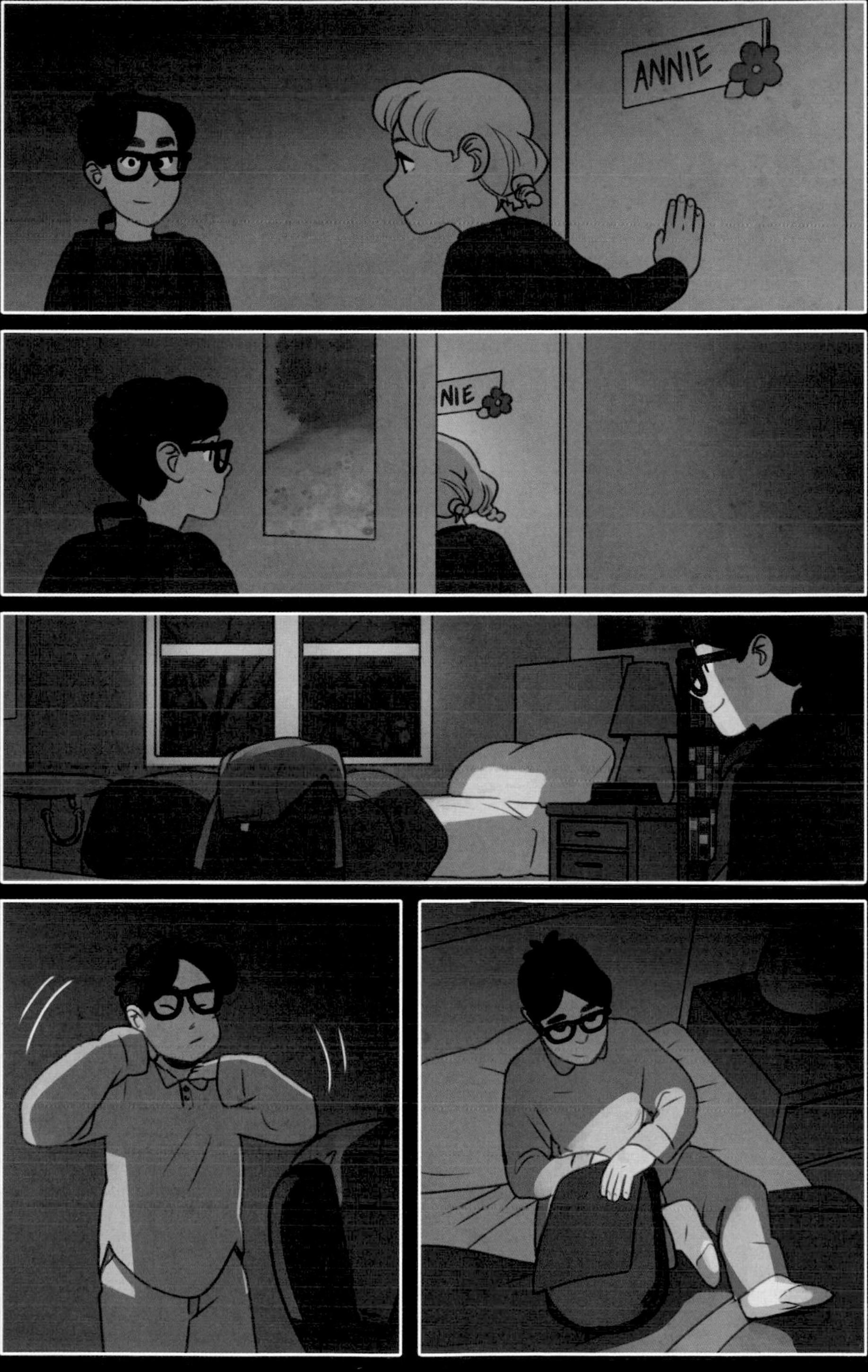
ANNIE
NIE

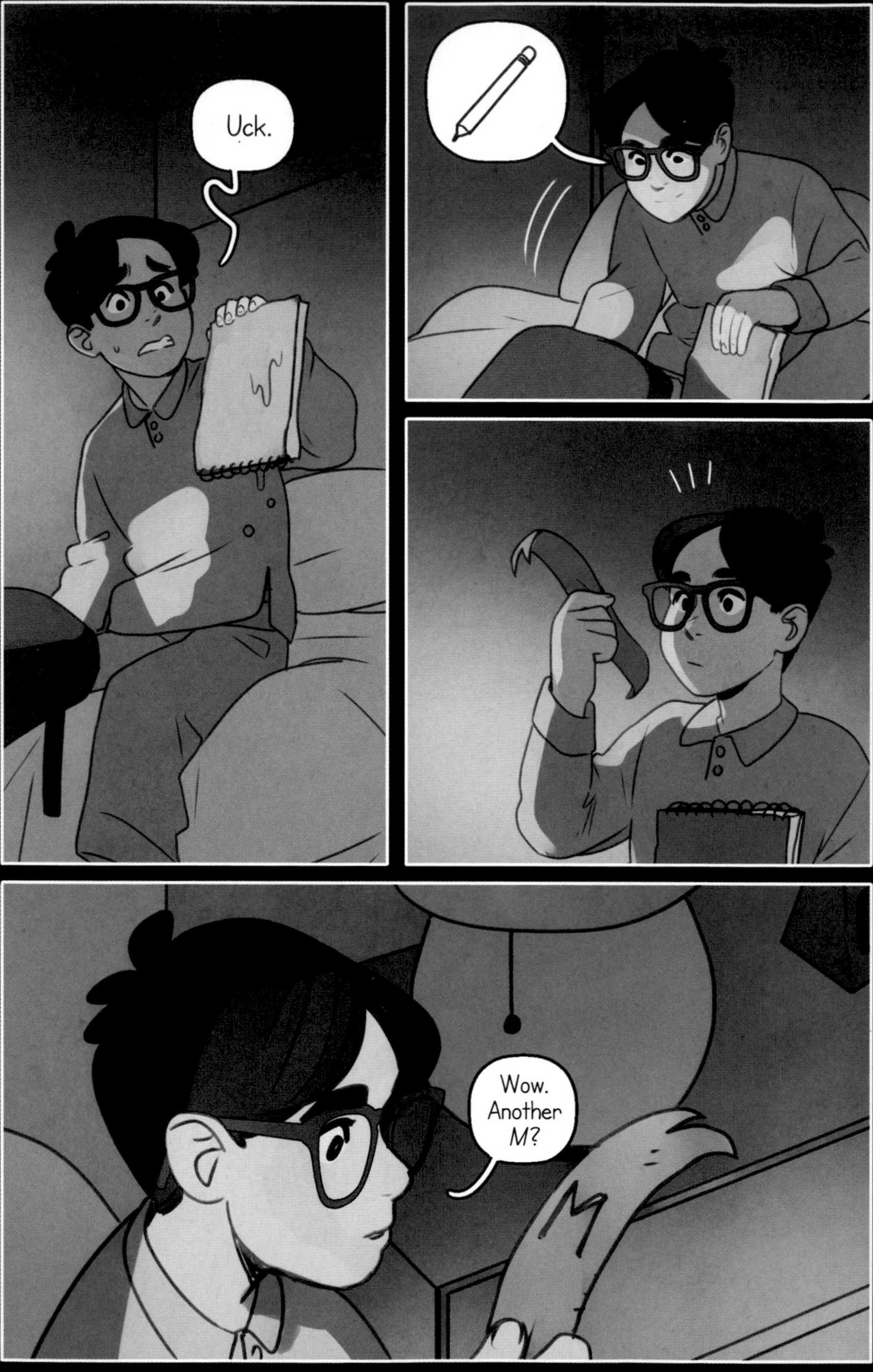
Uck.
Wow. Another M?

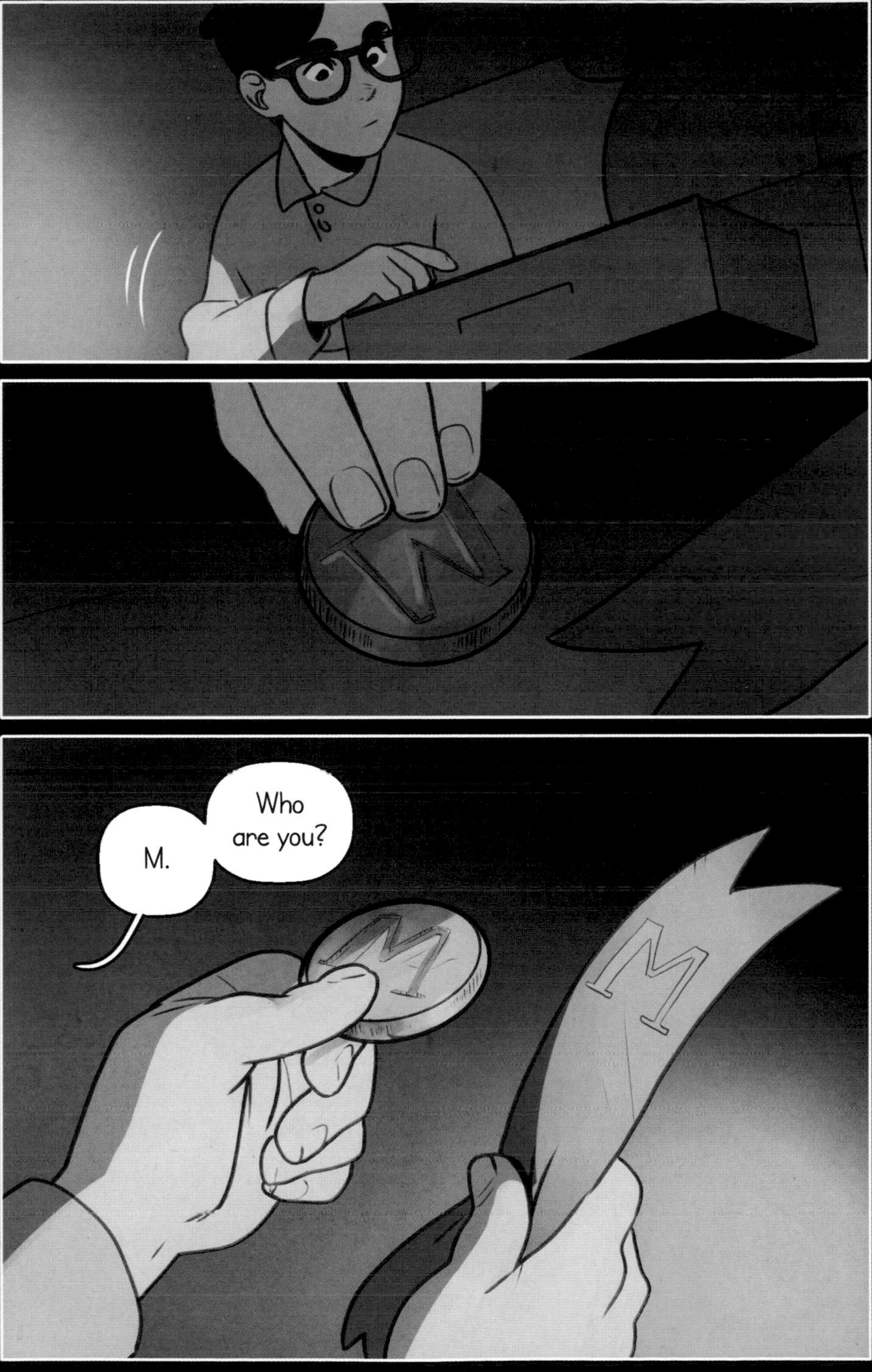
Who are you?
M.

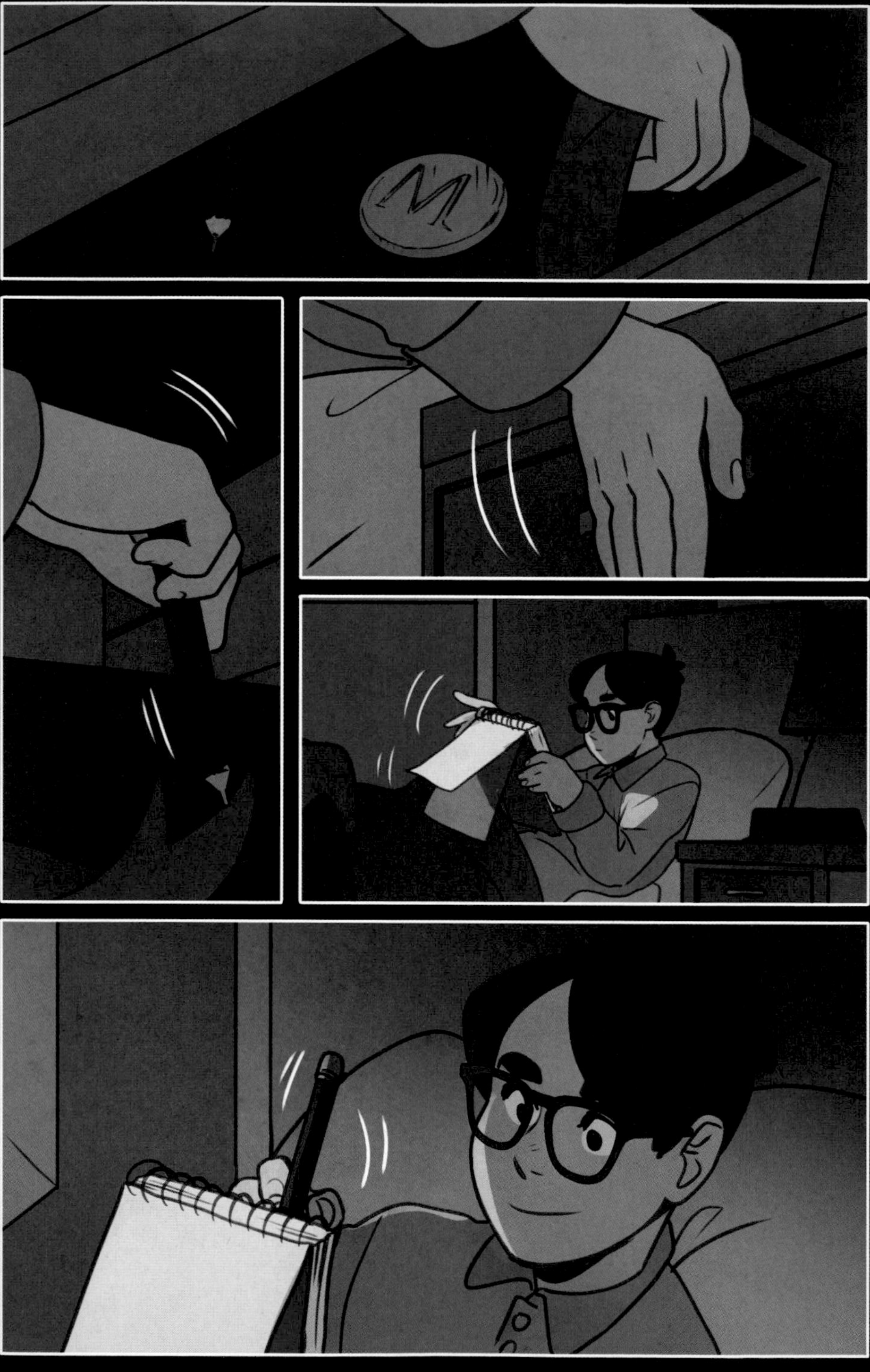

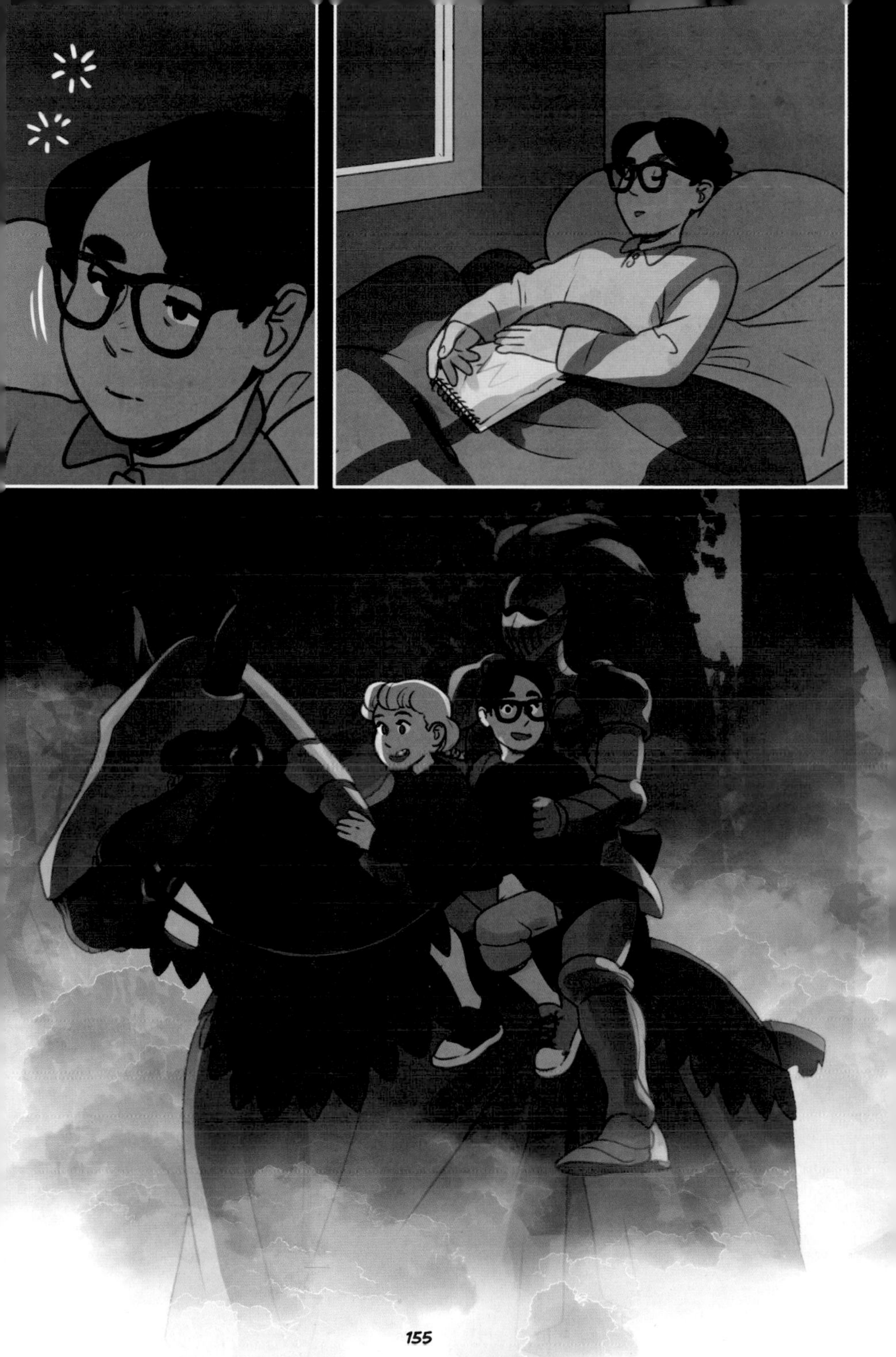

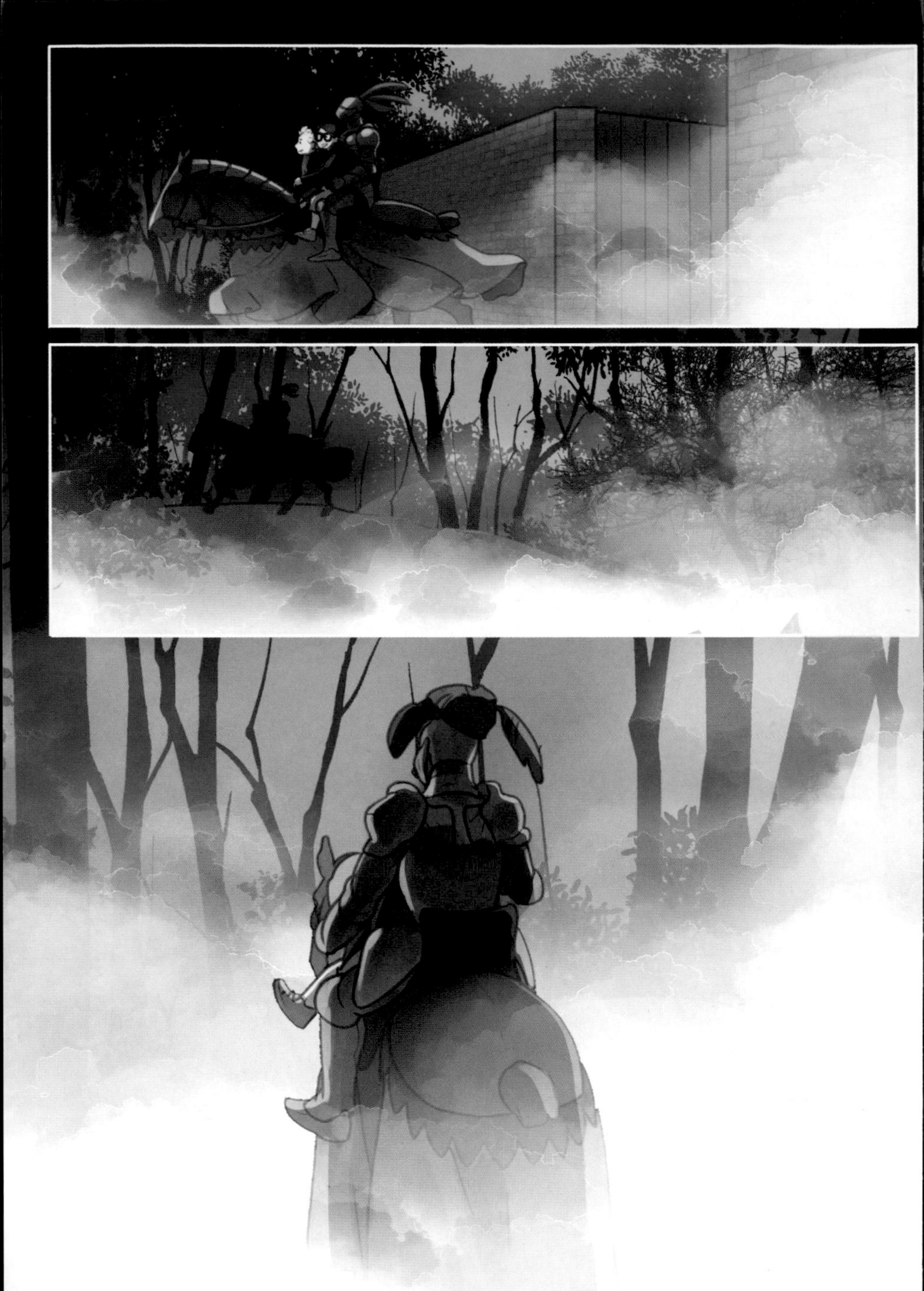

Missed the first adventure? Get whisked back to the time of dinosaurs with Jack and Annie in . . .

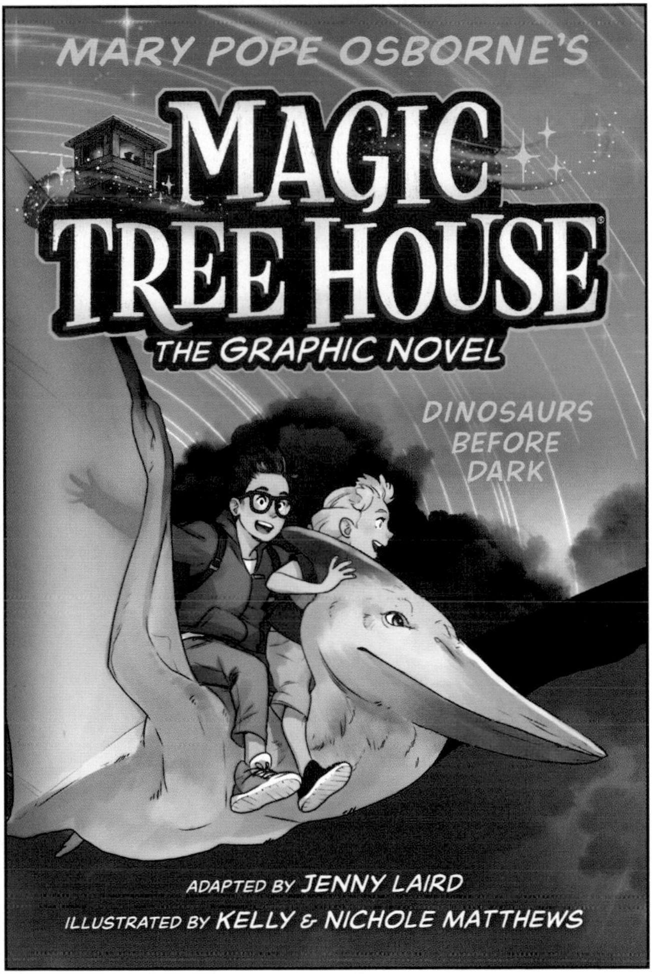
MARY POPE OSBORNE'S
MAGIC TREE HOUSE
THE GRAPHIC NOVEL
DINOSAURS BEFORE DARK
ADAPTED BY JENNY LAIRD
ILLUSTRATED BY KELLY & NICHOLE MATTHEWS

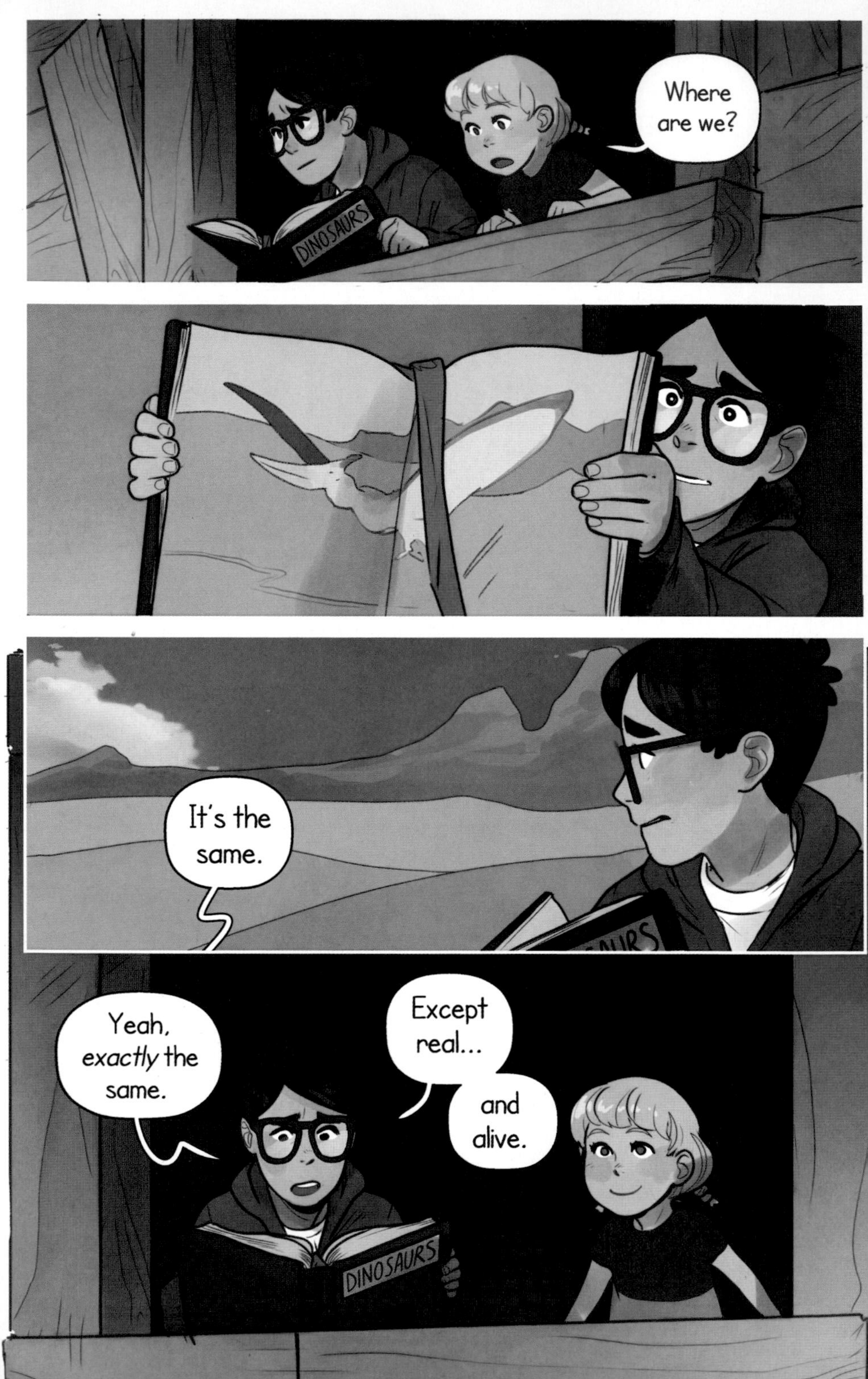
DINOSAURS
Where are we?
It's the same.
Yeah, *exactly* the same.
Except real...
and alive.
DINOSAURS

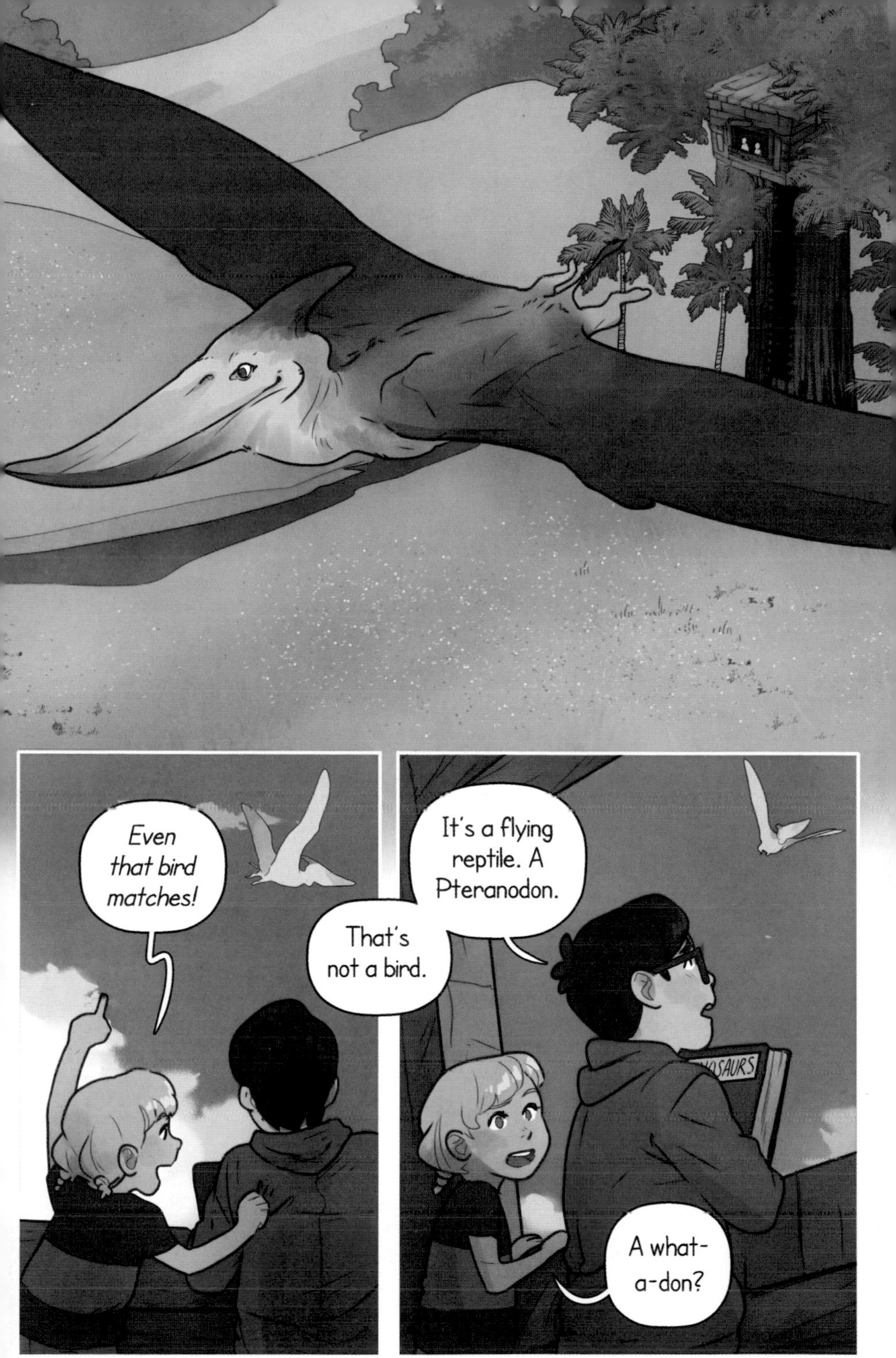
Even that bird matches!
That's not a bird.
It's a flying reptile. A Pteranodon.
A what-a-don?

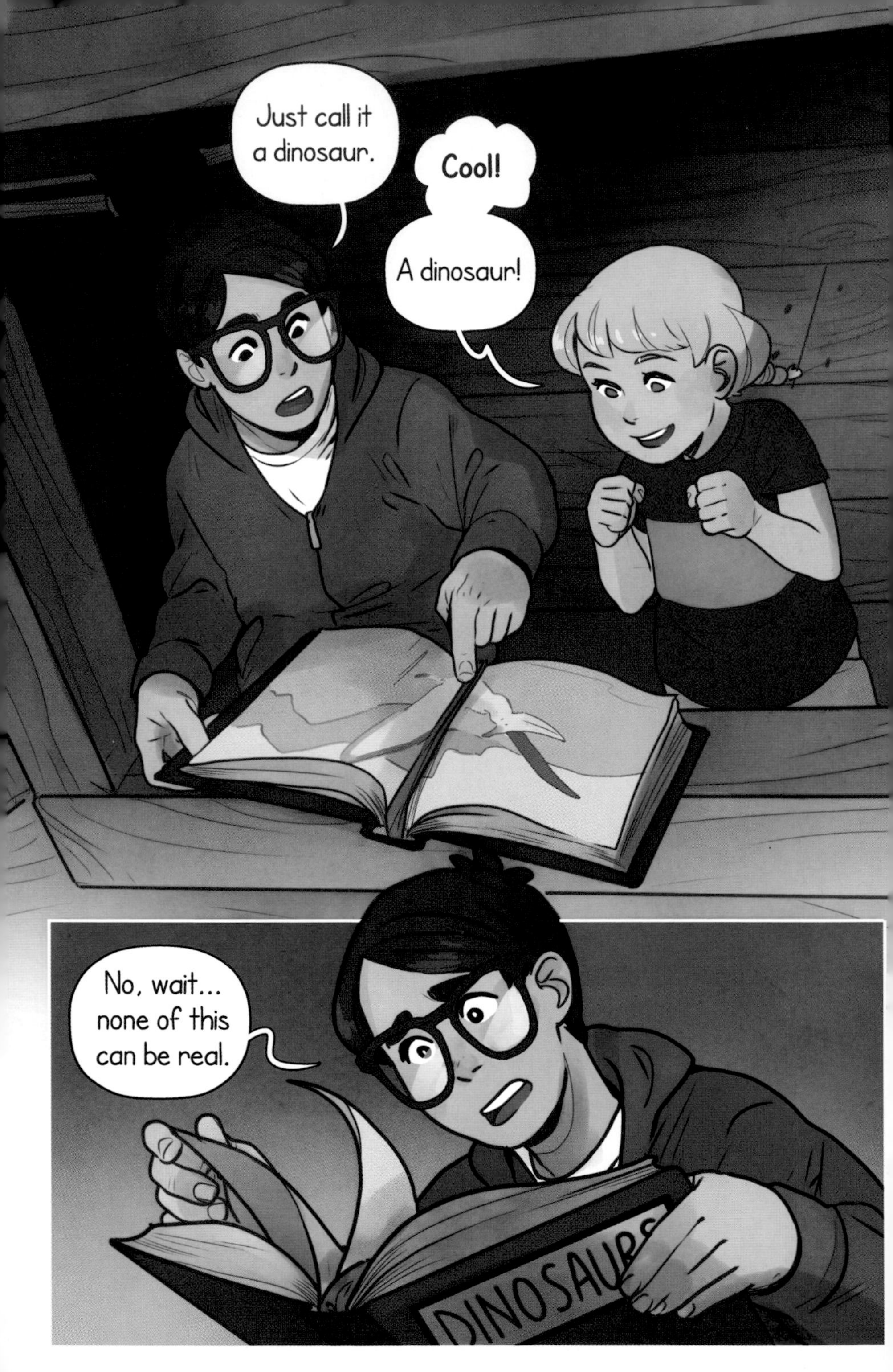
Just call it a dinosaur.
Cool!
A dinosaur!
No, wait... none of this can be real.
DINOSAURS

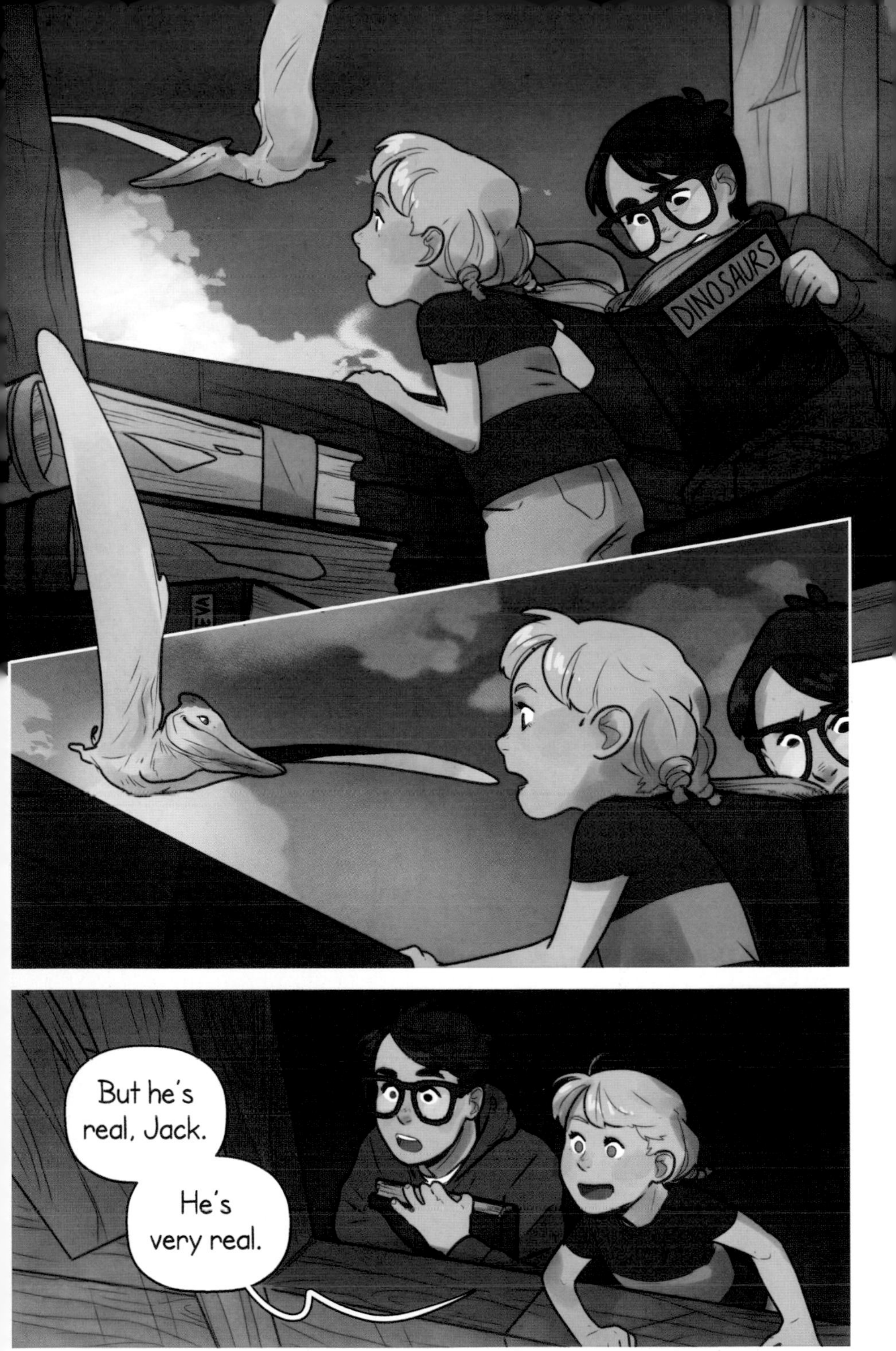
DINOSAURS
But he's real, Jack.
He's very real.

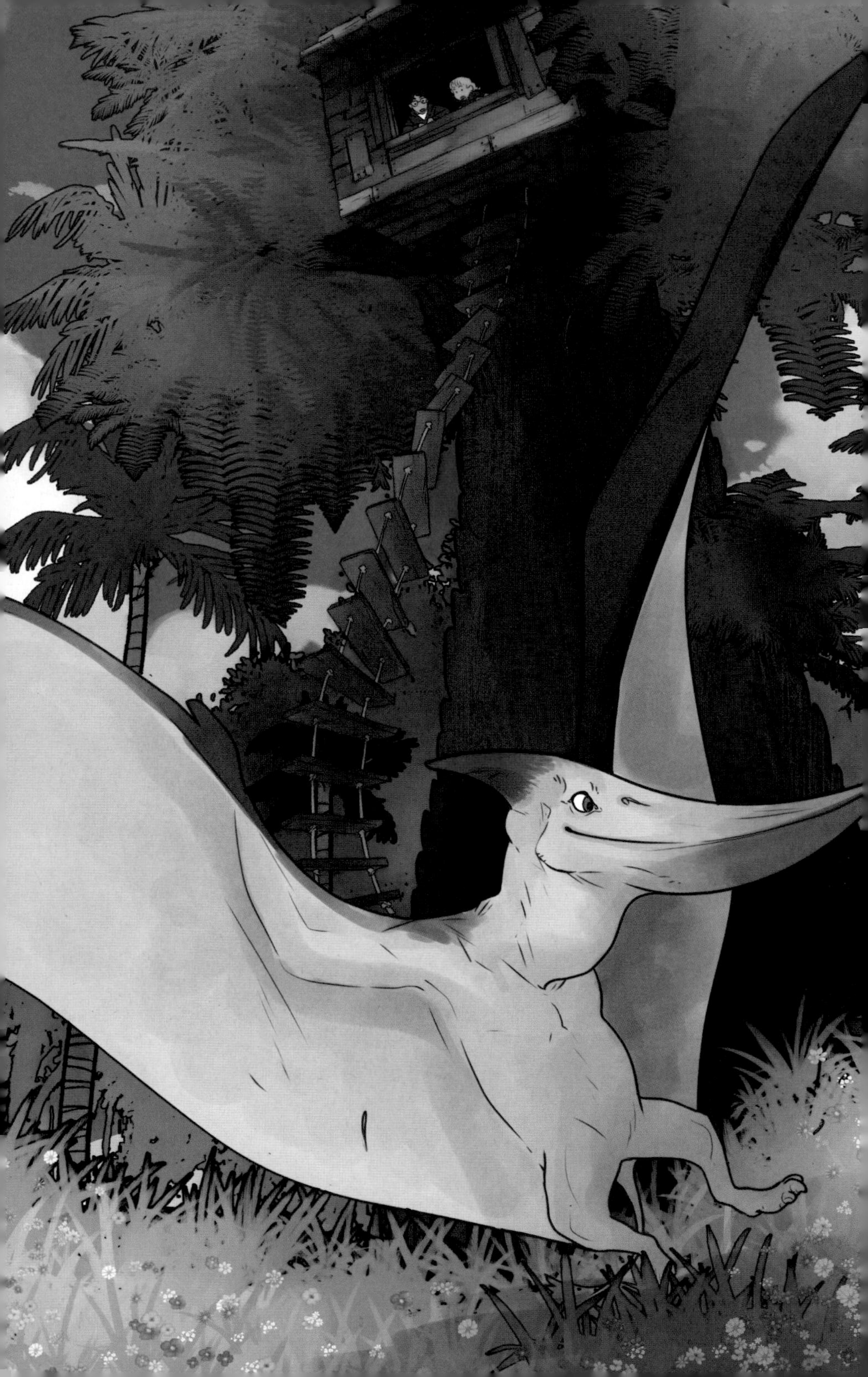

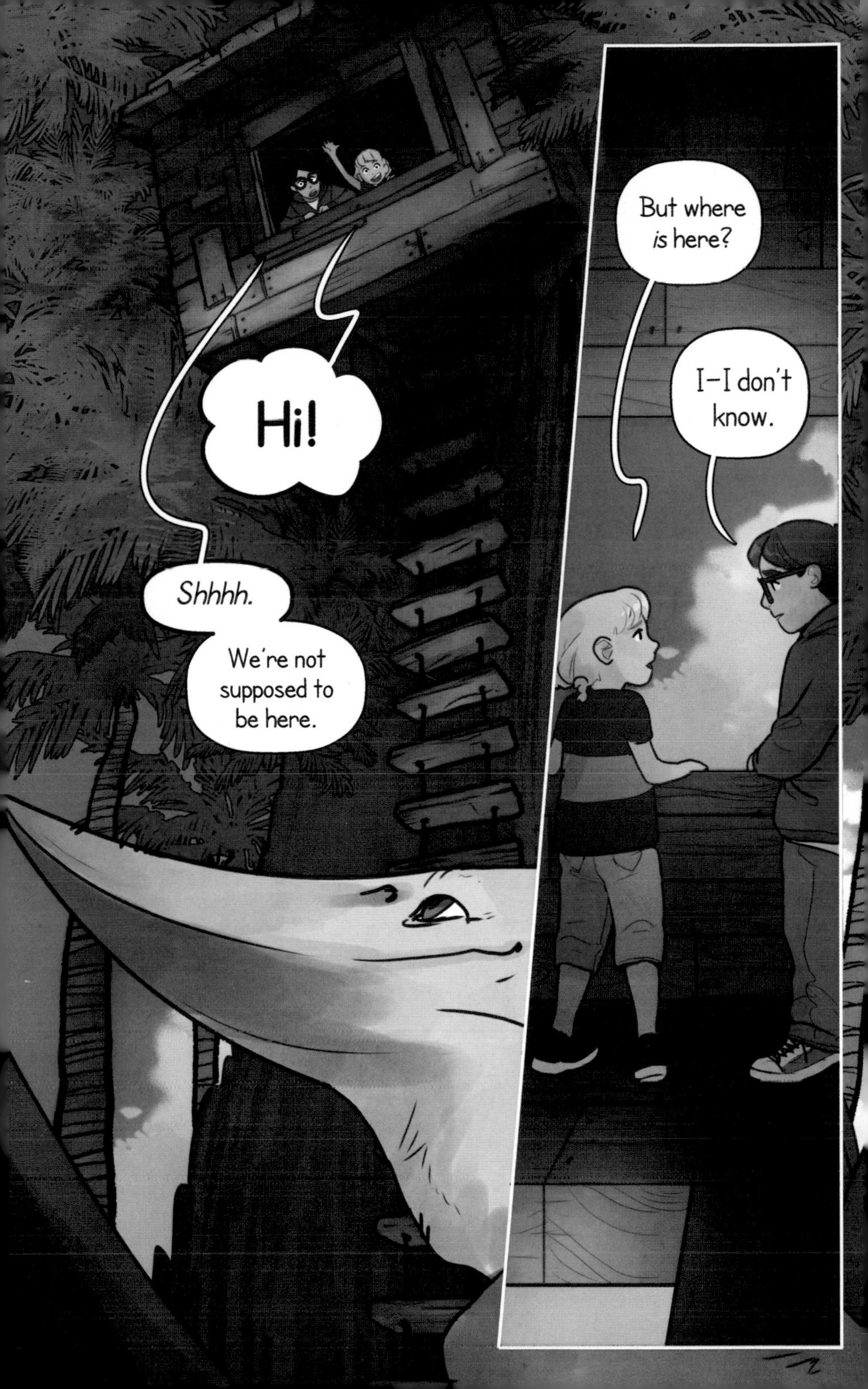
Hi!
Shhhh.
We're not supposed to be here.
But where *is* here?
I–I don't know.

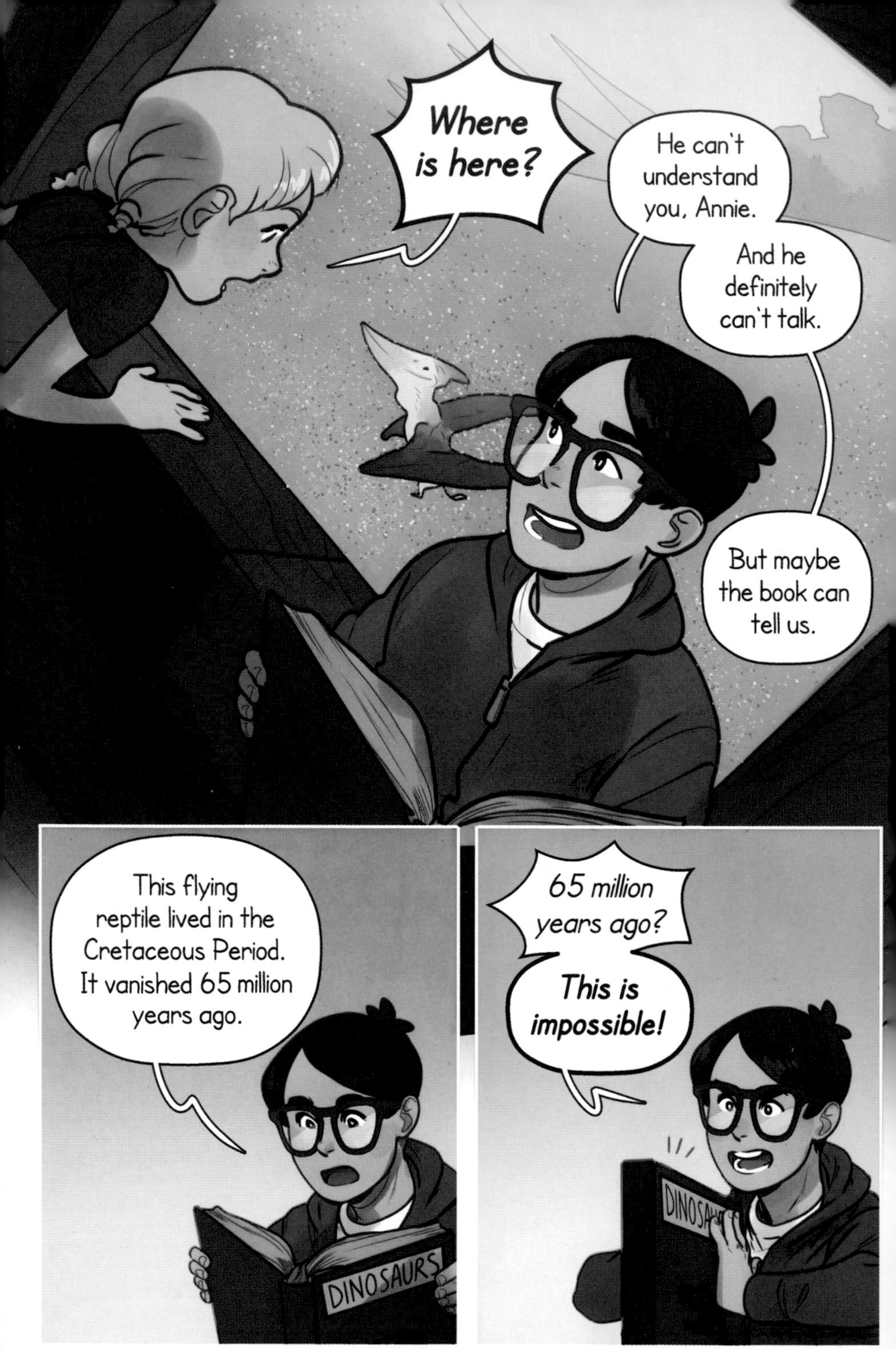
Where is here?
He can't understand you, Annie.
And he definitely can't talk.
But maybe the book can tell us.
This flying reptile lived in the Cretaceous Period. It vanished 65 million years ago.
DINOSAURS
65 million years ago?
This is impossible!

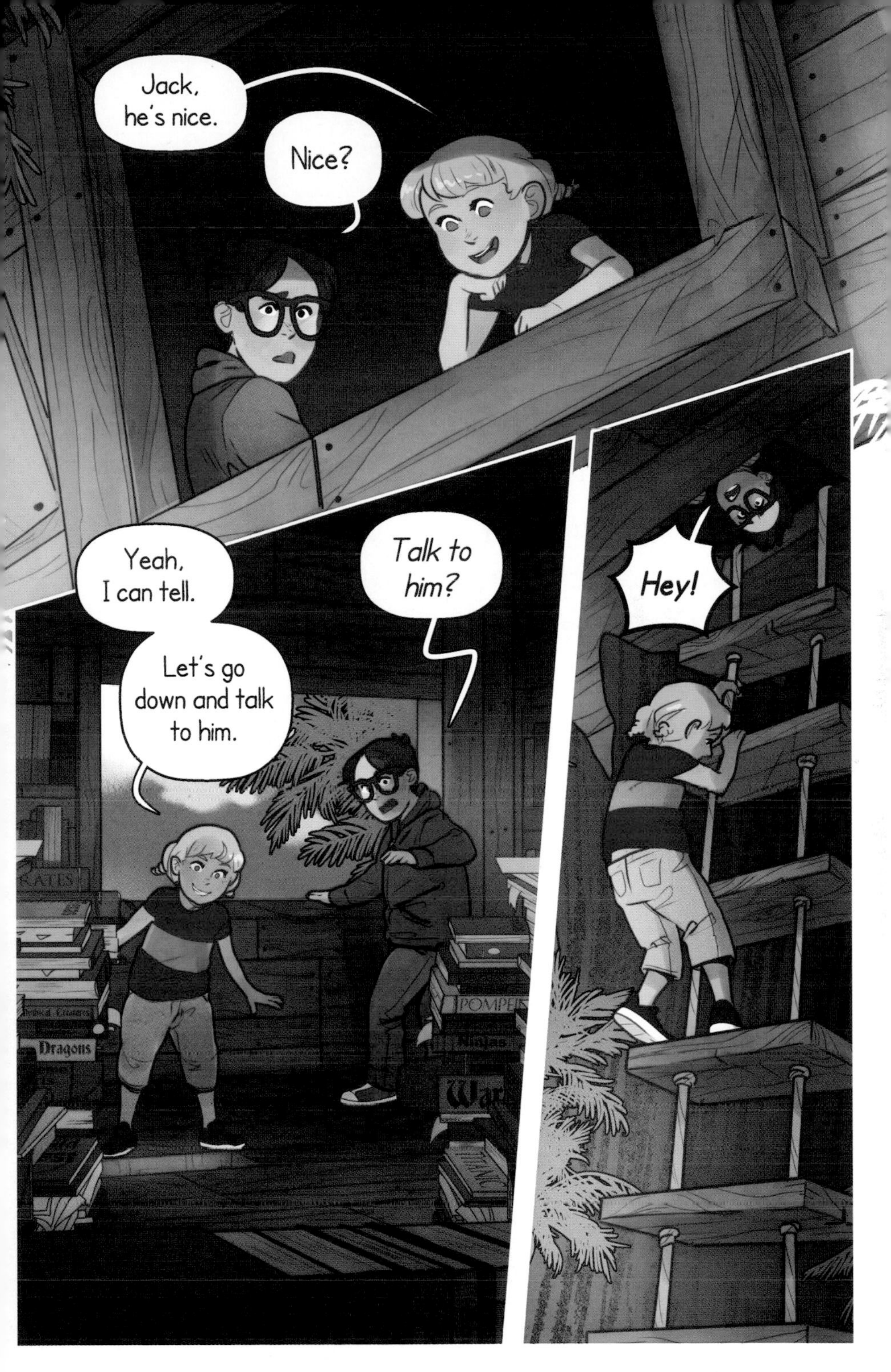
Jack, he's nice.
Nice?
Yeah, I can tell.
Let's go down and talk to him.
Talk to him?
Hey!

LET THE
MAGIC TREE HOUSE®
WHISK YOU AWAY!

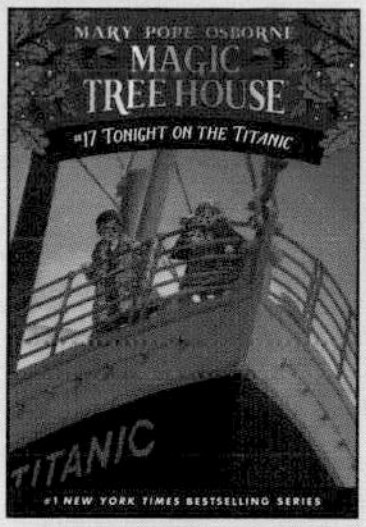
MARY POPE OSBORNE
MAGIC TREE HOUSE
#17 Tonight on the Titanic
TITANIC
#1 NEW YORK TIMES BESTSELLING SERIES
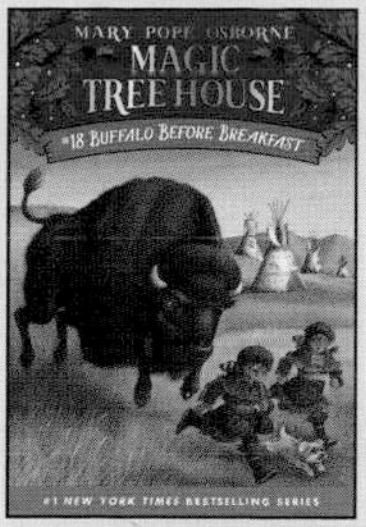
MARY POPE OSBORNE
MAGIC TREE HOUSE
#18 Buffalo Before Breakfast
#1 NEW YORK TIMES BESTSELLING SERIES
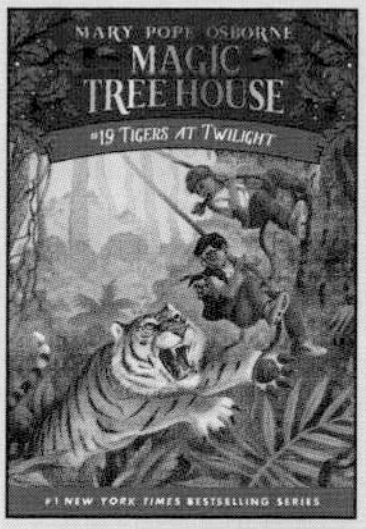
MARY POPE OSBORNE
MAGIC TREE HOUSE
#19 Tigers at Twilight
#1 NEW YORK TIMES BESTSELLING SERIES
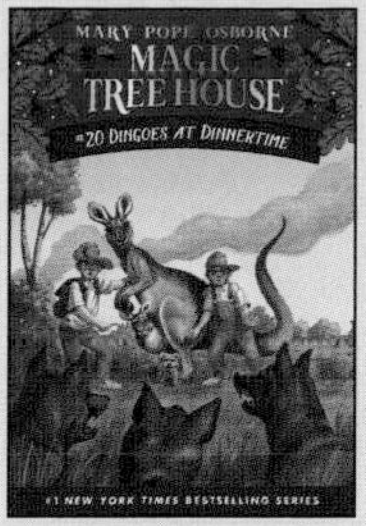
MARY POPE OSBORNE
MAGIC TREE HOUSE
#20 Dingoes at Dinnertime
#1 NEW YORK TIMES BESTSELLING SERIES
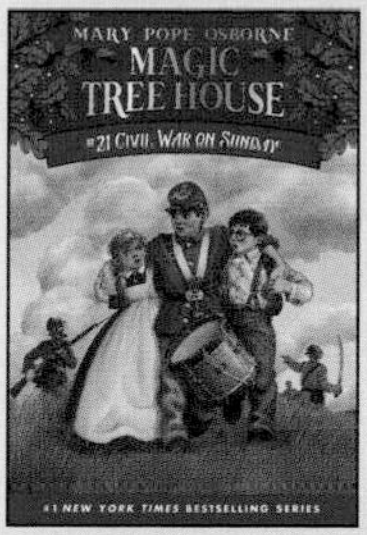
MARY POPE OSBORNE
MAGIC TREE HOUSE
#21 Civil War on Sunday
#1 NEW YORK TIMES BESTSELLING SERIES
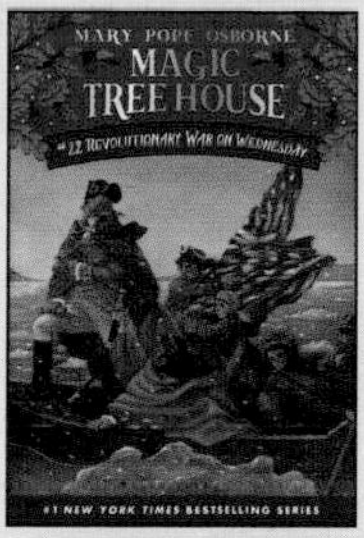
MARY POPE OSBORNE
MAGIC TREE HOUSE
#22 Revolutionary War on Wednesday
#1 NEW YORK TIMES BESTSELLING SERIES
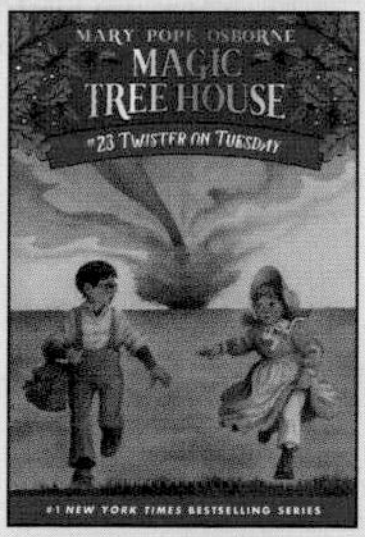
MARY POPE OSBORNE
MAGIC TREE HOUSE
#23 Twister on Tuesday
#1 NEW YORK TIMES BESTSELLING SERIES
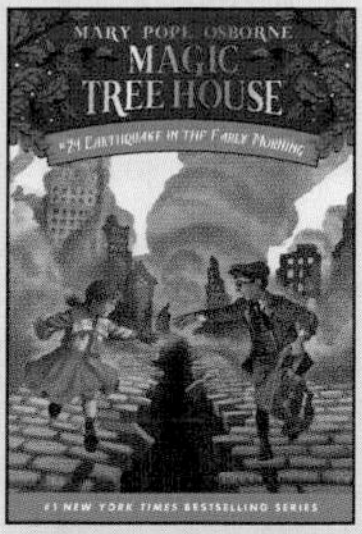
MARY POPE OSBORNE
MAGIC TREE HOUSE
#24 Earthquake in the Early Morning
#1 NEW YORK TIMES BESTSELLING SERIES
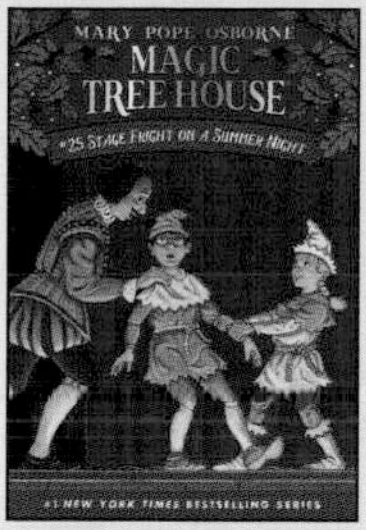
MARY POPE OSBORNE
MAGIC TREE HOUSE
#25 Stage Fright on a Summer Night
#1 NEW YORK TIMES BESTSELLING SERIES
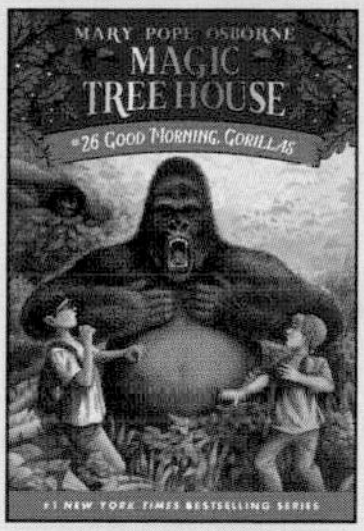
MARY POPE OSBORNE
MAGIC TREE HOUSE
#26 Good Morning, Gorillas
#1 NEW YORK TIMES BESTSELLING SERIES
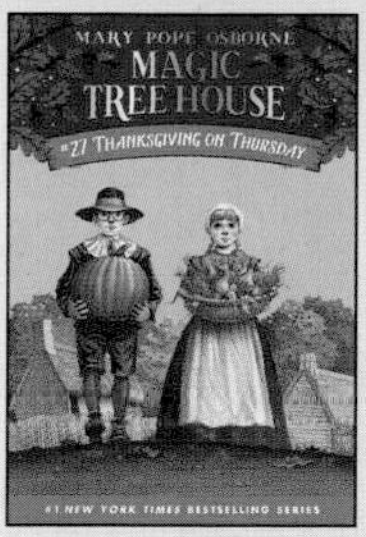
MARY POPE OSBORNE
MAGIC TREE HOUSE
#27 Thanksgiving on Thursday
#1 NEW YORK TIMES BESTSELLING SERIES
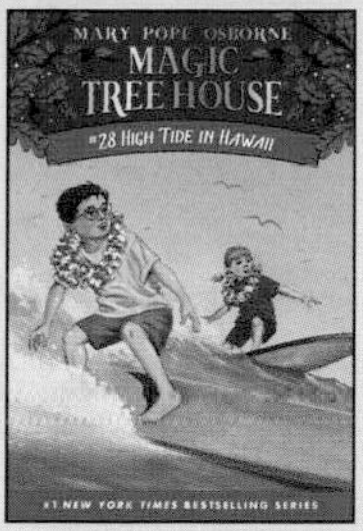
MARY POPE OSBORNE
MAGIC TREE HOUSE
#28 High Tide in Hawaii
#1 NEW YORK TIMES BESTSELLING SERIES
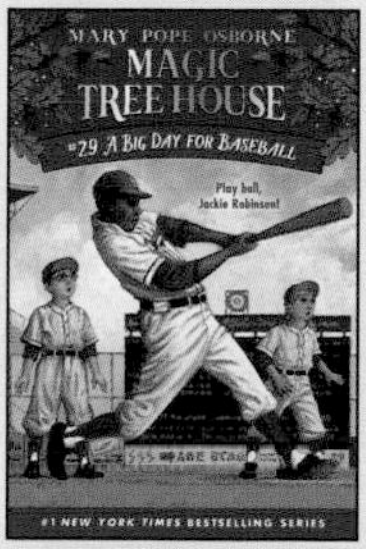
MARY POPE OSBORNE
MAGIC TREE HOUSE
#29 A Big Day for Baseball
Play ball, Jackie Robinson!
#1 NEW YORK TIMES BESTSELLING SERIES
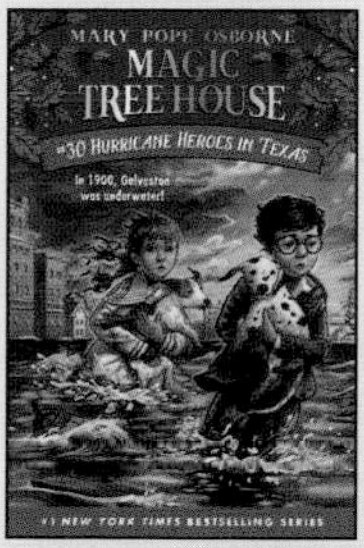
MARY POPE OSBORNE
MAGIC TREE HOUSE
#30 Hurricane Heroes in Texas
In 1900, Galveston was underwater!
#1 NEW YORK TIMES BESTSELLING SERIES
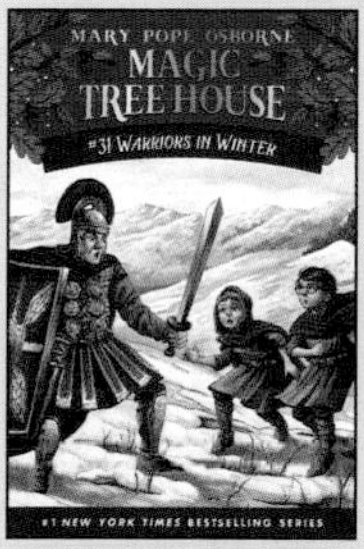
MARY POPE OSBORNE
MAGIC TREE HOUSE
#31 Warriors in Winter
#1 NEW YORK TIMES BESTSELLING SERIES
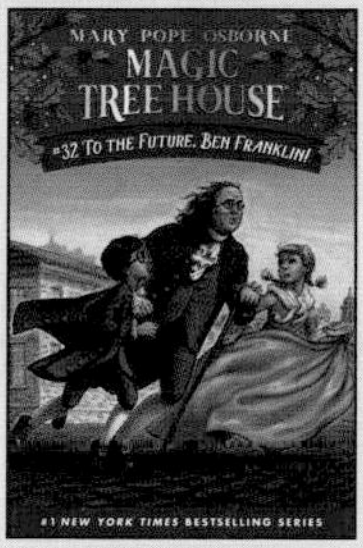
MARY POPE OSBORNE
MAGIC TREE HOUSE
#32 To the Future, Ben Franklin!
#1 NEW YORK TIMES BESTSELLING SERIES
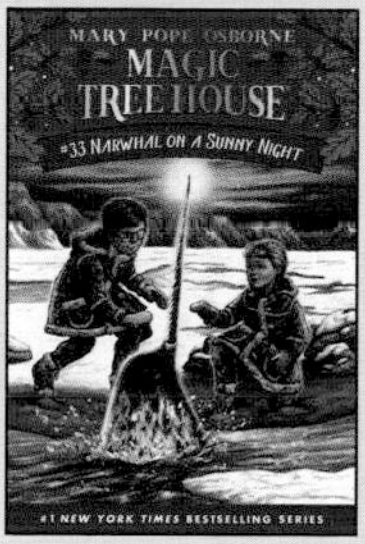
MARY POPE OSBORNE
MAGIC TREE HOUSE
#33 Narwhal on a Sunny Night
#1 NEW YORK TIMES BESTSELLING SERIES
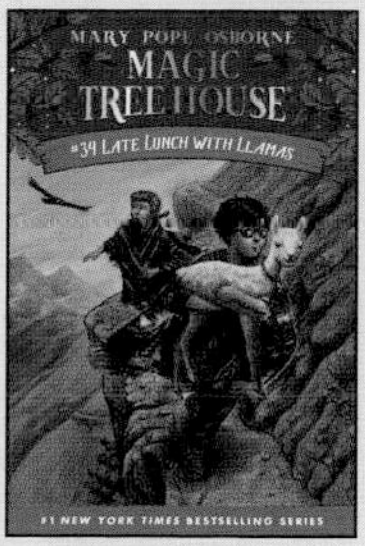
MARY POPE OSBORNE
MAGIC TREE HOUSE
#34 Late Lunch with Llamas
#1 NEW YORK TIMES BESTSELLING SERIES
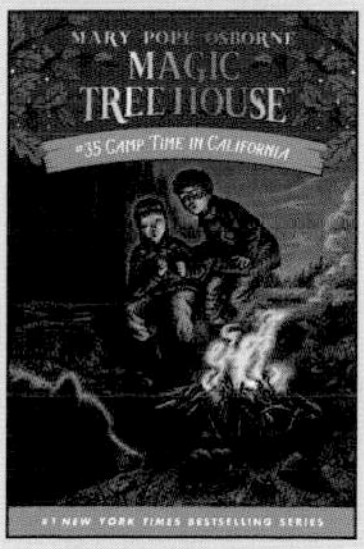
MARY POPE OSBORNE
MAGIC TREE HOUSE
#35 Camp Time in California
#1 NEW YORK TIMES BESTSELLING SERIES

TRACK THE FACTS WITH JACK & ANNIE!

MAGIC TREE HOUSE FACT TRACKER
Dinosaurs
A COMPANION COMPANION TO MAGIC TREE HOUSE #1: Dinosaurs Before Dark
Will Osborne and Mary Pope Osborne

MAGIC TREE HOUSE FACT TRACKER
Knights and Castles
A NONFICTION COMPANION TO MAGIC TREE HOUSE #2: The Knight at Dawn
Will Osborne and Mary Pope Osborne

MAGIC TREE HOUSE FACT TRACKER
Mummies and Pyramids
Will Osborne and Mary Pope Osborne

MAGIC TREE HOUSE FACT TRACKER
Pirates
Will Osborne and Mary Pope Osborne

MAGIC TREE HOUSE FACT TRACKER
Rain Forests
Afternoon on the Amazon
Will Osborne and Mary Pope Osborne

MAGIC TREE HOUSE FACT TRACKER
Space
Midnight on the Moon
Will Osborne and Mary Pope Osborne

MAGIC TREE HOUSE FACT TRACKER
Titanic
Tonight on the Titanic
Will Osborne and Mary Pope Osborne

MAGIC TREE HOUSE FACT TRACKER
Twisters and Other Terrible Storms
Twister on Tuesday
Will Osborne and Mary Pope Osborne

MAGIC TREE HOUSE FACT TRACKER
Dolphins and Sharks
Dolphins at Daybreak
Mary Pope Osborne and Natalie Pope Boyce

MAGIC TREE HOUSE FACT TRACKER
Ancient Greece and the Olympics
Hour of the Olympics
Mary Pope Osborne and Natalie Pope Boyce

MAGIC TREE HOUSE FACT TRACKER
American Revolution
Revolutionary War on Wednesday
Mary Pope Osborne and Natalie Pope Boyce

MAGIC TREE HOUSE FACT TRACKER
Sabertooths and the Ice Age
Sunset of the Sabertooth
Mary Pope Osborne and Natalie Pope Boyce

MAGIC TREE HOUSE FACT TRACKER
Pilgrims
Thanksgiving on Thursday
Mary Pope Osborne and Natalie Pope Boyce

MAGIC TREE HOUSE FACT TRACKER
Ancient Rome and Pompeii
Vacation Under the Volcano
Mary Pope Osborne and Natalie Pope Boyce

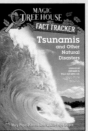

MAGIC TREE HOUSE FACT TRACKER
Tsunamis and Other Natural Disasters
Mary Pope Osborne and Natalie Pope Boyce

MAGIC TREE HOUSE FACT TRACKER
Polar Bears and the Arctic
Polar Bears Past Bedtime
Mary Pope Osborne and Natalie Pope Boyce

MAGIC TREE HOUSE FACT TRACKER
Sea Monsters
Dark Day in the Deep Sea
Mary Pope Osborne and Natalie Pope Boyce

MAGIC TREE HOUSE FACT TRACKER
Penguins and **Antarctica**
Mary Pope Osborne and Natalie Pope Boyce

MAGIC TREE HOUSE FACT TRACKER
Leonardo da Vinci
A NONFICTION COMPANION TO MAGIC TREE HOUSE #38: Monday with a Mad Genius
Mary Pope Osborne and Natalie Pope Boyce

MAGIC TREE HOUSE FACT TRACKER
Ghosts
A NONFICTION COMPANION TO MAGIC TREE HOUSE #42: A Good Night for Ghosts
Mary Pope Osborne and Natalie Pope Boyce

MAGIC TREE HOUSE FACT TRACKER
Leprechauns and **Irish Folklore**
A NONFICTION COMPANION TO MAGIC TREE HOUSE #43: Leprechaun in Late Winter
Mary Pope Osborne and Natalie Pope Boyce

MAGIC TREE HOUSE FACT TRACKER
Rags and **Riches**
Kids in the Time of Charles Dickens
A NONFICTION COMPANION TO MAGIC TREE HOUSE #44
Mary Pope Osborne and Natalie Pope Boyce

MAGIC TREE HOUSE FACT TRACKER
Snakes and Other **Reptiles**
A NONFICTION COMPANION TO MAGIC TREE HOUSE #45: A Crazy Day with Cobras
Mary Pope Osborne and Natalie Pope Boyce

MAGIC TREE HOUSE FACT TRACKER
Dog Heroes
A NONFICTION COMPANION TO MAGIC TREE HOUSE #46: Dogs in the Dead of Night
Mary Pope Osborne and Natalie Pope Boyce

MAGIC TREE HOUSE FACT TRACKER
Abraham Lincoln
A NONFICTION COMPANION TO MAGIC TREE HOUSE #47: Abe Lincoln at Last
Mary Pope Osborne and Natalie Pope Boyce

MAGIC TREE HOUSE FACT TRACKER
Pandas and Other **Endangered Species**
A NONFICTION COMPANION TO MAGIC TREE HOUSE #48: A Perfect Time for Pandas
Mary Pope Osborne and Natalie Pope Boyce

MAGIC TREE HOUSE FACT TRACKER
Horse Heroes
A NONFICTION COMPANION TO MAGIC TREE HOUSE #49: Stallion by Starlight
Mary Pope Osborne and Natalie Pope Boyce

MAGIC TREE HOUSE FACT TRACKER
Heroes for All Times
A NONFICTION COMPANION TO MAGIC TREE HOUSE #51: High Time for Heroes
Mary Pope Osborne and Natalie Pope Boyce

MAGIC TREE HOUSE FACT TRACKER
Soccer
A NONFICTION COMPANION TO MAGIC TREE HOUSE #52: Soccer on Sunday
Mary Pope Osborne and Natalie Pope Boyce

MAGIC TREE HOUSE FACT TRACKER
Ninjas and **Samurai**
A NONFICTION COMPANION TO MAGIC TREE HOUSE #5: Night of the Ninjas
Mary Pope Osborne and Natalie Pope Boyce

MAGIC TREE HOUSE FACT TRACKER
China
Land of the Emperor's Great Wall
A NONFICTION COMPANION TO MAGIC TREE HOUSE #14: Day of the Dragon King
Mary Pope Osborne and Natalie Pope Boyce

MAGIC TREE HOUSE FACT TRACKER
Sharks and Other **Predators**
A NONFICTION COMPANION TO MAGIC TREE HOUSE #53: Shadow of the Shark
Mary Pope Osborne and Natalie Pope Boyce

MAGIC TREE HOUSE FACT TRACKER
Vikings
A NONFICTION COMPANION TO MAGIC TREE HOUSE #15: Viking Ships at Sunrise
Mary Pope Osborne and Natalie Pope Boyce

MAGIC TREE HOUSE FACT TRACKER
Dogsledding and Extreme Sports
A NONFICTION COMPANION TO MAGIC TREE HOUSE #54: Balto of the Blue Dawn
Mary Pope Osborne and Natalie Pope Boyce

MAGIC TREE HOUSE FACT TRACKER
Dragons and Mythical Creatures
A NONFICTION COMPANION TO MAGIC TREE HOUSE #55: Night of the Ninth Dragon
Mary Pope Osborne and Natalie Pope Boyce

MAGIC TREE HOUSE FACT TRACKER
World War II
A NONFICTION COMPANION TO MAGIC TREE HOUSE #28: World at War, 1944
Mary Pope Osborne and Natalie Pope Boyce

MAGIC TREE HOUSE FACT TRACKER
Baseball
A NONFICTION COMPANION TO MAGIC TREE HOUSE #29: A Big Day for Baseball
Mary Pope Osborne and Natalie Pope Boyce

MAGIC TREE HOUSE FACT TRACKER
Wild West
A NONFICTION COMPANION TO MAGIC TREE HOUSE #10: Ghost Town at Sundown
Mary Pope Osborne and Natalie Pope Boyce

MAGIC TREE HOUSE FACT TRACKER
Texas
A NONFICTION COMPANION TO MAGIC TREE HOUSE #30: Hurricane Heroes in Texas
Mary Pope Osborne and Natalie Pope Boyce

MAGIC TREE HOUSE FACT TRACKER
Warriors
A NONFICTION COMPANION TO MAGIC TREE HOUSE #31: Warriors in Winter
Mary Pope Osborne and Natalie Pope Boyce

MAGIC TREE HOUSE FACT TRACKER
Benjamin Franklin
A NONFICTION COMPANION TO MAGIC TREE HOUSE #32: To the Future, Ben Franklin!
Mary Pope Osborne and Natalie Pope Boyce

MAGIC TREE HOUSE FACT TRACKER
Narwhals and Other **Whales**
A NONFICTION COMPANION TO MAGIC TREE HOUSE #33: Narwhal on a Sunny Night
Mary Pope Osborne and Natalie Pope Boyce

MARY POPE OSBORNE is the author of many novels, picture books, story collections, and nonfiction books. Her #1 *New York Times* bestselling Magic Tree House® series has been translated into numerous languages around the world. Highly recommended by parents and educators everywhere, the series introduces young readers to different cultures and times, as well as to the world's legacy of ancient myth and storytelling.

JENNY LAIRD is an award-winning playwright. She collaborates with Will Osborne and Randy Courts on creating musical theater adaptations of the Magic Tree House® series for both national and international audiences. Their work also includes shows for young performers, available through Music Theatre International's Broadway Junior® Collection. Currently the team is working on a Magic Tree House® animated television series.

KELLY & NICHOLE MATTHEWS are twin sisters and a comic-art team. They get to do their dream job every day, drawing comics for a living. They've worked with Boom Studios!, Archaia, the Jim Henson Company, Hiveworks, and now Random House!

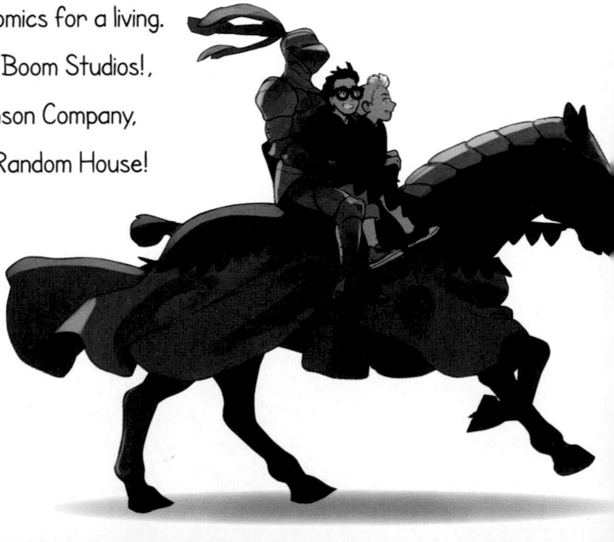